THE SECOND STORY WINDOW

MARGIE WOOD

Published by TeaTime Press

Copyright © Margie Wood, 2019

ISBN: 978-1-7331802-1-4

Ebook ISBN: 978-1-7331802-0-7

This is a work of fiction. The events and characters described herein are imaginary and are not intended to refer to specific places or living persons. The author has represented and warranted full ownership and/or legal right to publish all the materials in this book.

Cover designed by Anna Coleman and Gordon Saunders

Edited by Nancy Rue

Production coordinated by Gordon Saunders

Dedicated to my precious Daddy,
Charles Rineley Wood (1930-2018)

I loved sharing our fascination for Victorian houses.
Miss you every day!

CHAPTER 1

$\mathcal{M}$atthew Chandler strode off the elevator, leather business bag over one shoulder and covered coffee cup in hand. He stopped at the end of the thirty foot glass wall to study the gold embossed door sign. Canon Financial. Some day his name would be there. He'd make sure of that. The double doors opened when he brushed past the electronic eye.

Matthew nodded his greeting to Carla, the company receptionist, already talking into her headset with a client. He continued into the atrium where co-workers assembled every morning. The company rumor mill that he avoided like the plague. Bits of conversation reached Matthew's ears.

"The market is down again."

"Dreading the calls from my clients yelling about losing their money."

"Will it stabilize any time soon?"

The bad news about the stock drop had hit Matthew's Wednesday morning market alert earlier. This fluctuation was a stirring up of an overreaction to a normal market swing – which this crowd should know. What the heck. He'd seen it happen at least a dozen times since joining Canon Financial a decade ago. He had no doubt there'd be a significant growth of his personal portfolio this quarter.

"Morning, Stan." Matthew greeted the older man that had taught him the good, the bad and the ugly of the financial world.

Stan lifted his Starbucks coffee cup in a saluted response and continued his conversation with a young intern sipping from a Dunkin' Donuts cup.

How did they drink that stuff? He'd much rather have a gourmet cup from For Five Coffee Roasters on the bottom floor of their building. Their deco art cup and sleeve even set them apart from the rest.

Matthew pushed through the second set of glass doors into the office hallway. His assistant, Stacy, looked up from her computer, a smile covering her face. "Good morning, Mr. Chandler." She leaned across the desk to hand him a thick FedEx package.

"How's it going today, Stacy?"

Matthew smiled at the petite redhead who'd recently joined the Canon team to assist him and his business partner, Logan Montgomery. What a difference to see a genuine smiling person greet him. The stone face of the last assistant had gotten on his nerves. Turned out she'd been a hopeless case of losing files on her messy desk and screwing up his calendar. He hated to see anyone lose their job but . . .

Stacy's confidence and organization had won him over her first week of work. Matter of fact, she had an uncanny way of knowing what he was going to ask for almost before he did.

"The Grant file is on your desk," she said.

Case in point.

"Great, thanks." He set the coffee on the edge of her desk so he could tuck the Fed Ex package under his arm. Two sips worth sloshed out onto the wood. He should have put the cover back on.

"Hey, sorry about that."

"No harm done." Stacy whisked open the bottom drawer of her desk and swiped the spill with a paper towel.

Matthew headed down the hall to the first office, covered coffee back in hand. She was definitely a keeper.

Logan Montgomery stuck his head out of his open office door, located next to Matthew's. Dressed in slacks and a polo shirt, he'd always been the more casually dressed of the two of them. As far as he was concerned, suits were for weddings, funerals and business meetings that had the potential to earn six figures.

Logan's deep voice echoed in the empty hall. "You're in early today." He flashed his usual goofy grin. "What, did you read your clock wrong? Or did you ever go to bed?"

"Yeah, yeah." Matthew waved him off. "Really wanted to finish the Grant proposal this morning. We can't take the chance of losing this one."

"No kidding. This could be our big break." Logan took two steps into the hallway. "Maybe we'll retire to the Bahamas."

"Not a chance. We've worked hard and we're playing with the big boys now." Matthew stopped at his door and unlocked it. "Let's meet in thirty minutes to finalize the proposal."

"Sure thing." Logan grinned again and retreated to his office.

As Matthew slipped into his and closed the door behind him, bright sunlight flooded through the picture window. The glass architecture of the sleek new World Trade buildings glimmered in the distance. To many they symbolized hope for a bright financial future after such horrific, unthinkable destruction.

Matthew tossed the FedEx package on a chair. He wasn't expecting anything; he'd deal with it later.

He lowered his lanky six foot frame into the leather desk chair, flipped open his laptop and finished the black coffee. The only way to drink it as far as he was concerned. The proposal he'd worked on late into the night appeared on the screen. He'd need plenty of caffeine to keep him awake today. He reached for the phone to instruct Stacy to set up the crucial meeting.

On second thought, better to wait until after he talked through the final details with Logan. Charles Grant was an influential, powerful man in New York City and rich. Very rich. This could be the deal of a lifetime. They needed to be on their A game.

Logan rapped on the door and stepped in before Matthew could respond. "You stay up late last night working on this deal?"

"Bingo, my brilliant friend. That's why we make such a great team." Matthew rubbed his bloodshot eyes.

Friends since elementary school, they knew each other so well. It was almost spooky the way they could finish each other's sentences, and a great boost for scoring business accounts when they could have whole conversations in boardrooms without saying a word.

"What's this?" Logan pointed at the package. "Got another deal going on you haven't told me about?"

He wadded a scrap of paper and threw it at the wastebasket beside the desk. It bounced off the rim and landed by Matthew's foot.

"You play better racquetball than you do basketball." Matthew leaned down and picked up the trash, eyes still on the computer screen. "No idea what's in the package. I'll look at it later. Let's do one more review on the proposal. I think we're about ready to land this deal."

After lunch Matthew stepped out into the hall with his empty coffee mug, headed to Stacy's area for a refill. He needed the white space after concentrating on figures all morning. Eva Pearce chose that moment to slip out of her office too. No doubt she'd planned it that way.

Dressed in a navy pinstriped suit, matching heels and perfectly coiffed hair, she looked like something out of the

American Express magazine – the one that catered to a lifestyle he would someday be able to afford. How she was buying expensive suits on a Canon salary was a mystery to him.

"Matthew." She batted her false eyelashes at him. " Want to get together tonight?" She took a step closer.

"No, sorry. I'm working late."

He resisted the urge to roll his eyes. He did NOT need her trying to snuggle up to him right now. Besides, the thought didn't do anything for him – a message he had yet to get across to her.

"Come on. You can't work 24/7." Eva tapped the toe of the shoe that probably cost more than his assistant's entire wardrobe. She stepped even closer, her flowery perfume overpowering his personal space. "Let's have our own private meeting in your office and lock the door."

Matthew stepped back and checked the corridor, both ways. They were alone. Thank goodness. Nothing ruined his day more than office gossip. Especially about him. And no way was she coming into his office. The last time she was in there, he thought he'd have to call Security to remove her.

"Look, Eva. This is not the place to discuss our private business."

Eva straightened the pinstriped suit coat and squared her shoulders. "All right. Meet me for a drink. I promise, you won't be sorry."

Maybe it was worth one more shot to get her to lay off. "I'll have to check my calendar."

Matthew gulped the fresh air and headed down the hallway. Things had gone way too far with this woman. He really needed coffee now.

Mental note to self: listen to Logan more often. He'd been spot on with his advice to keep work and personal life separate. Too bad he hadn't listened.

After a restless night of figures dancing through his dreams, Matthew arrived at the office an hour early on Thursday morning. He'd sent Stacy a text to hold his calls. And to keep the coffee coming.

Landing the Grant account was his number one goal right now. How cool would it be to manage the largest portfolio in the firm? His and Logan's careers would soar to a new level. No doubt they would prove to Canon's CEO they were an unstoppable team.

His stomach rumbled. How had he forgotten to eat breakfast? That wasn't like him. He never missed a meal.

The numbers on his laptop screen blurred. He took a sip of coffee to clear his head. The leather chair creaked as he leaned back.

Logan's proposal was outstanding. The best Matthew had ever seen his partner create. Sure, Mr. Grant had hundreds of advisors to choose from but he and Logan had earned a reputation for maximizing a client's portfolio by maintaining a balance between risk-taking and security. With their track record, they had this in the bag. The meeting next week couldn't come soon enough.

Matthew caught a glimpse of himself in the window and grimaced. His old man's face stared back at him. Matthew let the chair come forward. There was no reconciling the wrestling match between wanting to succeed like John Chandler and wanting to be absolutely nothing like him. He gave a soft sniff. He could hear his father now.

"So you aced your way through Wharton. Lucky break to get in with Canon so quickly."

Matthew stood up and grabbed his coffee mug. More caffeine and less remembering.

The stomach grumbling continued throughout the morning,

making Stacy raise her eyebrows when she delivered his sixth cup of java. There was nothing more he could do on the Grant account now, anyway, so Matthew took himself out to the deli down the street, carefully avoiding Eva, who wouldn't darken the door of a sandwich place. He'd never seen her eat anything besides lettuce.

When he returned to the office, his still restless eyes landed on the unopened package where he'd tossed it the day before. He'd been so preoccupied he hadn't even noticed it still lying there.

He took a sip of steaming coffee from the mug Stacy had handed him when he passed her desk. She deserved a raise.

Matthew ripped open the plastic envelope and dumped the contents on his desk. He picked up the letter attached to the stack of documents.

Dear Mr. Chandler. I'm James Ross from Smith, Harris and Ross in Denver, Colorado. As the executor for the estate of Jacob Chandler, I'm writing to inform you of an inheritance.

Matthew blinked and read the paragraph again.

Why would that old coot leave him anything? Matthew hadn't seen his Uncle Jacob in years. He examined the letterhead stationery. Looked authentic. One could never be too careful in a world of scammers and forgery.

He Googled the lawyer's address. The results verified the address in Denver. James Ross was listed among the attorneys.

Hmmm ... okay, I'll bite. What did you leave me, Uncle Jacob?

You are the new owner of the Rose Haven estate in Chandler Springs, Colorado.

Matthew scratched his jaw.

What? That old house? Memories tried to nudge at him, but he shoved them aside. The place was at least a hundred years old and must be falling down by now. He scanned the letter again. Yeah, this had to be a mistake.

A knock on the door jerked Matthew out of his thoughts. He rolled his shoulders, not realizing they were so tight. "Come in."

Logan poked his head in the open door. "Hey."

Matthew motioned toward the documents scattered on his desk. "You'll never believe this. My deceased uncle left me an inheritance."

"For real? Which uncle?" Logan plopped down in the opposite chair and put his feet on the desk.

"Believe it or not, my dad's older brother." Matthew pointed to the paperwork. "I'm the proud owner of a 110-year old Victorian home in the mountains of Colorado." He rolled his eyes.

Logan pulled his feet to the floor and leaned forward in his chair. "That's actually cool."

"Depends on your definition of 'cool', Matthew said.

Logan gave him a half grin. "So, what'll you do with this old house?"

"No doubt sell it. I haven't been in touch with anyone on that side of the family since my parents' divorce years ago."

"So you're talking your dad's side."

Matthew felt himself bristle. "My father's."

Logan put up a hand. "Sorry. Sore subject."

Matthew leaned forward in his chair. "Remember when we were kids and I made up the story that he'd died in a car accident and we'd all gone to his funeral and then cried over his grave?"

"Yeah, I do. Didn't your mom ground you for a month for lying?"

"She did. But it was worth it. I told the story so many times that I believed it." Matthew grimaced. "As far as I'm concerned John Chandler is dead."

A semi-awkward pause fell, but Matthew didn't try to fill it. The subject of the absent father: not going there either.

In true form, Logan broke the silence. "Old houses usually

need lots of repairs. Too many horror stories about old homes becoming money pits."

"Yeah, tell me about it." Matthew sat straighter in his chair. "Well, I'm not going to be saddled with a monstrosity. I'd much rather dump it. I could handle a vacation home in the tropics."

Logan made a high-five motion. "Cool plan. Make sure I get an invite." His cell vibrated. He stood and moved toward the door. "Are we on for racquetball tomorrow? I reserved a court for noon."

"Sure. I'd love to beat you again."

Logan raised a thumbs-up. "In your dreams, buddy." He stepped into the hall, closing the door behind him.

Matthew stacked the attorney's documents into a pile and laid them on the edge of his desk. It all seemed to be on the up and up. There was one way to find out for sure. He picked up the receiver and dialed the familiar number. His mother had probably already been up for hours, attending yoga class with her friends or having her nails done. She answered on the second ring.

"Hi, Mom. Hope I'm not calling too early." He glanced at the clock. It was two hours earlier in Denver.

"Matthew. It's great to hear from you. How are you?" Her voice reminded him of melting honey.

Matthew leaned back in his chair and slipped into an easy conversation with Nora Chandler Bennett. Her voice had always calmed him and made him think of first grade when Jeb Johnson put the snake in his desk and scared the heck out of him. Totally embarrassing for a six-year old. Over fresh baked cookies and cold milk, his mom had told him to take back the power to be himself. And put on his game face when he saw the other kids again. As usual his dad was no help at all. Probably at a high level corporate meeting or something.

"Doing well, Mom. How are you and Pete?"

"Busy as always. Finishing a dozen crocheted blankets for the preemie babies in the NICU."

Matthew could hear glass clanging, like she was unloading the dishwasher.

"My little way of giving back after the nurses took such good care of you so many years ago."

"That's really cool, Mom." Of course he didn't remember it, but Matthew had heard the story of being born a month early. More than a few times.

Nora continued. "Pete constantly reminds me to slow down since we're retired. That word's not in my DNA."

"I hear ya, Mom. I must have gotten it from you." Those two words ... slow down ... had never been a part of his vocabulary either. He frowned at the mental image of his stepfather. Something about the guy rubbed him wrong. But if his Mom was happy . . .

"Documents arrived yesterday from Uncle Jacob's lawyer. Did you know I was inheriting the old house?"

Matthew raised his cup to his lips and grimaced. He'd have to get Stacy to bring a fresh cup.

"Oh yes, I heard your Uncle Jacob inherited the house when your grandparents, Austin and Evelyn passed away." Nora paused. "You remember Jacob, don't you? He was the loud, stocky one."

Matthew thought about the strange little man who had come for a Sunday dinner at Rose Haven during his summer visit there so long ago. He'd never seen anyone arrive at the dinner table with uncombed hair and slurred words. A few days later, Matthew had been hiding on the backstairs, out of sight, when he heard the adults whispering about Uncle Jacob, the black sheep of the family, and his "thirst problem". Years later Matthew realized his uncle had struggled with an alcohol addiction.

"Yeah, Mom. How could I forget him? He used to call me squirt."

"Jacob always had a pet name for everyone. He called me Sunshine."

"That's fitting." Matthew had to agree she reminded him of a ray of light. Bright and cheerful. Made it harder to understand how his dad could leave her. Nora's voice jolted him back to the present.

"Pete and I actually saw Jacob a few months ago. A number of years ago Rose Haven got too big for him, and he moved to a health care facility in South Denver."

"For real? Did he remember you?"

"Amazingly, he did. It's been years since I've seen him, but his mind was still sharp. He told me he'd had a falling out with your dad years ago and he intended to leave the house to you."

"Uh, Mom, and you didn't think to tell me this?"

"I wanted to, son. Jacob swore me to secrecy. Maybe he knew how'd you react." Nora sighed.

"You got that right. The old place always creeped me out. The creaky floors especially. I'd peek over my shoulder to see if anyone was following me." Matthew chuckled. Even now spending a night in the old place didn't seem very appealing.

"Austin and Evelyn were probably in their 60's back then, but they seemed ancient in my ten-year old mind."

Nora's laugh sounded like a tinkling bell. "You've always had a good imagination."

"Yeah, I guess so. I can't imagine owning the old place, though." Matthew frowned. "And if it's been empty for years, who knows what kind of shape it's in now?"

"What will you do with it?"

Matthew reined in the memories of the creepy floors. "I don't know, Mom. Why would I want an old house in Colorado? Probably sell it."

"I think you should at least see the property before you

totally dismiss it. Can you take time off and come out for a visit? I'd love to see you."

"Logan and I are finalizing a huge account. If we can nail it . . ."

Matthew heard his mother's loud sigh on the other end of the line.

"I'll check my calendar and let you know soon," he said.

"Thank you. You've made your mother's heart happy. It's been too long, you know."

"Yeah, I know. I'll be in touch.

"Bye, son. Love you."

"Love you too." Matthew hung up the phone.

A ski trip to Breckenridge to celebrate the Grant account didn't sound like a bad idea. A little reward for the hard work he'd put in over the past weeks. Flying down the slopes. Sipping a hot toddy in the lodge. Yeah, he could get into that.

Charles Grant hadn't signed on the dotted line yet. But he had a gut feeling about this one.

CHAPTER 2

*I*n the weekly staff meeting on Friday morning, Stacy delivered the good news to Matthew and Logan that the Grant meeting had been confirmed for the following Wednesday at 10 a.m. She'd reserved the most elegant Canon conference room, facing the Hudson River, and ordered specialty coffee and pastries. Anything else she could do for them?

Matthew wanted to round his desk and kiss the pretty red head. Her meticulous attention to detail took a load off him. But it would be incredibly bad form. He restrained himself.

Later, during their lunch game, Matthew swung at the ball. The racket whooshed and hit nothing but air. Dang, what the heck was wrong with him today?

Logan dried his face with a sweat towel and slung it over his shoulder. "Ready for a break?"

Without a word, Matthew headed toward the edge of the court.

"You okay? You're only about halfway here right now."

"Yeah. A lot on my mind." Matthew grabbed a towel from his bag to wipe down the racket.

Logan fist bumped his arm. "The house?"

"Yeah, among other things."

Logan's mouth eased into a loose grin. "What'd you decide to do?"

Matthew swiped his face with a sweat towel. He might as well tell him. "I'm going to Chandler Springs next week."

Logan's normal grin moved into a frown. "Seriously? This is the worst time for you to be away."

"Yeah, I know. I'm not leaving until after the Grant meeting."

"You sure it can't wait until next month? We'll have the deal wrapped up by then." Logan's jaw clenched. "That house has been there forever, Matt. It's not going anywhere. We need to be on our toes if we want to snag this account."

This conversation was getting too intense. Matthew could count on one hand the times he'd seen Logan react like this. "Sorry, bud. I can't explain it, but I've got to do this now. I'm always accessible by e-mail, text, phone. Send up a smoke signal."

Logan facial muscles relaxed. "Gotta trust your judgement, I guess. We've known each other for way too long."

"Right back at ya, man." Matthew grabbed his gym bag. "I'm as invested in this deal as you are. You know how this business goes . . . Our pitch will be perfect, and we still may not get an answer right away. I'll be gone less than a week." Matthew pushed the locker room door open. "I'm hitting the showers."

Logan started in after him. "Hey, mind if I ask about Eva? I heard you two in the hallway yesterday."

The hairs bristled on the back of Matthew's neck. "Were we that loud?"

"Nah, I was coming around the corner and saw you. From her body language, looked like a serious conversation."

"Yeah, not the best decision to get involved with her." Matthew rubbed his jaw. "Back in the crazy busy days around Canon, spending time with her relieved some of the stress."

"Until she got too clingy?"

"Yep, exactly. Showing up at my door with an overnight bag without an invitation wasn't cool. And I let her know it."

Logan grimaced."What now?"

"I hope she's gotten it through her head we are not a couple. And will never be."

"Didn't I tell you she was bad news?"

"Yeah, you did." Matthew pressed his lips together.

"And did you listen?"

Matthew opened his mouth to respond. But he knew his friend was right. As usual.

The racquetball game and talking to Logan about his house plans had relaxed Matthew more than he realized. A few office details to wrap up and he was ready to start his weekend.

At 3:30 Eva's name appeared on his desk phone screen. Logan's voice played in his head. Eva was bad news. He should ignore the call. But no doubt she'd march down the hall and plant herself in his office. The phone seemed a better option. He picked up the receiver on the fourth ring.

"Hey, Eva. What's up?"

"Checking to see if we can meet later."

Irritation prickled at him. He had to put a stop to this now. "Let's meet at Woody's after work today."

"Isn't that place a little public? I was thinking Chaz. It's much more . . ."

"I'm good with Woody's." Clearly 'intimate' was the word she was going for, and he wanted to avoid that like the flu.

The sun was already setting on the city when Matthew held the door open at Woody's and let Eva pass through. He'd shed the suit coat and tie before he'd left the office. But of course, Eva was dressed like she was going to a Broadway show. How did she walk in those stilettos? Or, for that matter, such a tight skirt? He took a deep breath. This evening could not end soon enough. He nodded in agreement at the well-lit table the manager offered. Eva would have opted for a dark corner, which he did NOT need for this conversation.

"I'm so glad we're doing this. Finally." Eva's sexy voice floated across the table, and she rested her warm hand on top of his.

Matthew stifled a grunt. She'd be singing a different song once he said what he was about to say. He'd seen her attitude turn on a dime before. The server stopped at their table. Perfect timing. He ordered himself a scotch on the rocks and a strawberry daiquiri for Eva. He hadn't even asked what she wanted. Maybe he did know her too well.

When the server stepped away, Matthew took another deep breath. He seemed to be doing that a lot tonight. If he wasn't careful, he was going to hyperventilate.

"Look, Eva. I have to be honest with you. We've had some fun times together. The ski trip to Connecticut was a blast."

Eva gave him a sly grin. He didn't mention they'd slept together there for the first time. At this point it was probably better not to go there.

Matthew continued on. "You inspire me with your enthusiasm to hit life hard and be the best. I appreciate that."

Eva's smile turned to a pout. "I sense a "but" coming."

"I don't think we're right for each other. And I don't want to be tied down to a serious relationship."

Eva blinked twice. Matthew was waiting for crocodile tears. He'd seen it often enough lately when she didn't get her way.

She swiped at her face with her napkin. "But, honey, we are right for each other. And with our business track record, we'll be the power couple of New York City. Partners in business and partners in life."

Yeah, right. You mean my power. Matthew shook his head. "I'm sorry things went this far. I never meant to hurt you."

His voice softened. He nodded his thanks as the server placed the Scotch in front of him. Thank goodness he'd ordered a double.

Eva's lip pushed out farther. "Just give us a little more time."

Her perfume had started assaulting his nose. He was all for a nice smelling woman, but why did she think she needed to bathe in the stuff?

Matthew picked up his glass and gulped half the contents. "I'm sorry, Eva. There's nothing more to say." He stood up and drained his glass. "I have an early morning meeting."

Before she could remind him tomorrow was Saturday, Matthew pulled out his wallet, slapped a twenty on the table and made his way through the crowd to the door. If she called after him, he didn't hear it for the noise. Which was just the way he planned it.

Matthew tried to focus over the weekend on the Grant meeting. He also dodged several text messages from Eva. "We need to discuss this further." And later ... "We're not done yet, Matthew. Call me." He didn't respond to any of them. He'd made himself clear. There was nothing more to say.

Sunday night he stared at the ceiling until after midnight. Fitful sleep finally came but he felt like a flounder flopping on the ground after swallowing a fisherman's hook. What was stealing his sleep? Anxiety over the Grant account? Not at all. No doubt he and Logan were ready.

It was this house thing. Why was it bugging him so much? He rubbed his head. The thought of anything connected with his father always stressed him out.

Matthew arrived at the office on Monday morning bleary eyed and distracted. It was almost amusing to see the surprised look on Stacy's face when he refused her offer for coffee. That was a first. The gnawing in the pit of his stomach had taken away the appeal today.

Matthew entered his office and closed the door. He was tempted to lock it for privacy but trusted Stacy to steer away any visitors. He opened his calendar and worked mentally through each day. The Grant meeting was scheduled for Wednesday, and then he could catch a flight to Denver on Friday. He typed a note on his phone to find a realtor in Chandler Springs before he left New York to speed up the process of listing the house. Sign the papers, spend a day or two skiing in Breckenridge, visit his Mom and Pete and fly home.

Yeah, that would work. He'd be gone less than a week. He pulled his credit card from his wallet and booked the Friday morning flight. Then he put his feet up on the desk and stretched back. He and Logan were on the verge of landing the biggest account of their careers. Eva was out of his life for good. The sale of the family house already feeling like a thorn in his side would be completed. Then he could ski and visit family.

That feeling didn't last long. Matthew was packing up for the day when his phone vibrated. Eva. He was tempted to ignore the text. Moments later a second message appeared on his phone screen. This woman was persistent. She said she had good news. Maybe she was moving to Alaska. He could only hope. He punched in her number.

"Hi, Matthew. Wanted to share my good news." Her shrill voice grated on his nerves like a dentist drill.

"Shoot." And please make it fast. I'm busy.

"Liberty Financial offered me a position."

Matthew froze, brief case half open. "Seriously?" He had to give it to the woman. She was definitely a go-getter. And great news for him. He wouldn't have to figure out a way to dodge her every day at the office.

"You're the first to know. I start next Monday."

Matthew could imagine the look on Eva's face. Like she'd

scored the sale of the year at Nordstrom's. "Congrats. I wish you well."

"It was a hard decision. I like Canon, but I couldn't pass up this opportunity."

"Mind if I ask how this came about?" Matthew was curious in spite of himself.

"Oh, I met Rob Hartman the CEO of Liberty at a party not long ago. When he found out I worked at Canon, he mentioned a position coming open at his firm. As they say, the rest is history."

Yeah, I'm sure you turned on the charm. "Well, you were in the right place at the right time." If Logan was here, they'd being doing high fives. He was totally rid of this woman.

"If I don't see you before I leave Canon, I wanted to say thanks. I appreciate what you taught me about the business." Her voice was soft and sexy.

For a moment he remembered the good times they'd shared. Cuddling in the ski chalet after an exhilarating day on the slopes. Though he hadn't planned for them to share a bed it seemed right at the time. The smart, romantic, energetic woman was a charmer for sure. The memories shifted. Her recent angry outbursts and clinginess were more than he could handle. For being so confident in business matters, she was way too needy in relationships.

"You're welcome. Have you told Logan? Or anyone else?"

"No, haven't had a chance. Could you pass the message on to them for me?"

"Of course." Possibly over a bottle of champagne. "Best wishes Eva."

He couldn't believe the lightness he felt when he disconnected the call. He was free.

∼

On Tuesday, Matthew opened his office door and stepped into the hall, empty coffee mug in hand. He stopped at Stacy's desk and was about to ask for a refill when she smiled from earring to earring.

"You're a welcome sight after the person who was standing here a moment ago demanding my time."

Matthew frowned. "Must have been Eva."

"Oh yeah." Stacy held up a full page "to do" list. "The nerve of that woman. Since when am I her personal assistant?"

"Well, one consolation is the list means she's leaving Canon. Did she tell you that?"

Matthew had never seen such a huge grin on Stacy's face.

"Oh, my gosh. Really? Of course she didn't. We're not on speaking terms since her position is so much more important than mine." Stacy flung her hand out for emphasis.

Matthew laughed. "I'm glad you don't believe that rubbish. We couldn't survive without you."

"Thanks. I love working with you. And Logan."

Matthew nodded and put out his hand. "Can I see the list?"

"Sure." Stacy handed the paper to him.

Matthew gave a loud sniff. "Pick up her dry cleaning? You've got to be kidding."

"She's such a diva."

"I'll tell you what." Matthew pulled a pen from his pocket. "If you can complete the three started items, the rest of this list can go back to her. If she gives you any grief, let me know. I'll deal with her."

"Thank you. You're the best." Stacy turned to the Keurig, inserted a k cup and waited for Matthew's ceramic Wharton mug to fill.

He nodded and accepted it back. If it wasn't so full, he'd be tempted to skip down the hall back to his office.

CHAPTER 3

*M*atthew guided the rented Lexus around the circular drive. He cut the engine, released his seat belt and opened the door. Amazing. The old girl was still standing. He'd half expected to see a caved-in roof and overgrown yard.

The imposing three story house looked much as he'd remembered. Multi-level bay windows, gabled roof, full turret, gingerbread trimmed wrap around porch. The wicker rockers were even there.

The sun glinted on the second story window. Memories hit him full force. This house. How fitting. The room that had changed his life forever.

Good grief. One look at the place and he was ten years old again, spending time here with his grandparents. Austin and Evelyn had been nice but lived in this creepy house built by his great-grandparents. He could remember hiding under the covers at night so he wouldn't see any ghosts.

Full of ghosts – both the ones he'd imagined as a young boy and the real ones that had haunted him ever since.

His phone vibrated in his pocket and shook him back to

reality. He better get this over with before he said forget it and headed to the airport.

He pulled out his phone. Logan maybe? Eva's name showed on the screen. The chick was like a pit bull. He didn't get her at all. He'd made it more than clear he wasn't interested.

He turned the phone off and dropped it back into his pocket. He could afford to miss a call or two. This wasn't going to take long.

As he approached the wide porch, the old oak front door opened and a slender blonde woman dressed in jeans, knee length boots and a tan duster coat stepped out. If this was the realtor, she wasn't what Matthew had expected. Totally the opposite of the professional women he knew in New York. He had to admit he was lovin' her mountain look.

"You must be Matthew Chandler," the blonde said.

Her voice reminded him of a latte, although for the life of him, he didn't know why. He always drank his coffee black.

"Right," Mathew said. "And you are ... ?"

As he stepped up onto the wide veranda, he couldn't help noticing her eyes. Blue. Striking. Like a pair of sapphires.

Lattes. Sapphires. Wow, was the high altitude affecting his brain that much? He steadied his focus. This was business.

"Amelia Richardson, owner of Richardson Realty." She offered her hand, which was as slender as the rest of her. And minus the pricey manicure Eva always had going on.

Matthew accepted her handshake. Warm. Like – all right, he had to stop.

"We've managed this property for several years," she was saying. "We're glad you're here."

Something in her expression said otherwise. He let it slide. The house wouldn't be his for long anyway.

"Please come in," she said and moved to the side.

He stepped into the vestibule. The creak of the wood floor greeted him. And a memory slammed him in the face. Floors that creaked when he walked down the hall. Turning around to see if someone was following him. Probably a ghost. Sheer terror those first few nights.

"Mr. Chandler?"

He looked up to see – what did she say her name was? – the realtor staring at him curiously.

"Place hasn't changed much," Matthew mumbled. "The floors still creak." He toed a loose corner baseboard as he pulled his mind-files back into place. "Seems I'm the last heir of the Chandler family. Lucky me."

He forced a wide grin. She didn't smile back.

"Let me take you on a tour," she said. The latte voice had lost some of its foam.

Amelia moved through the hallway toward the ornate staircase. "Do you know the history of this house?"

Matthew did, sort of, but he decided to let her talk while he looked around at everything that was falling apart. The ca-ching of a cash register echoed in his head.

"Your great-grandparents, Evan and Emma Chandler, built this house in the early 1900's."

Matthew touched the golden oak carved balustrade. He'd slid down that bannister a few times until Grandfather Austin caught him. Another memory he tossed into the circular file. The first spindle was loose. More dollar signs.

Amelia turned through an arched doorway. "This was Evan and Emma's parlor." Despite the ornate fireplace, the focal point of the room, with its elaborate cherrywood mantelpiece supported by a pair of double columns, Matthew noticed the crumbling hearth. The cash register sounds were adding up quickly.

Amelia stared at him again, like she was waiting for him to say something. Anything. Matthew pointed to a faded portrait above the fireplace, featuring dour-looking faces.

"So that's my family, huh?" he said. "Happy bunch."

"Yes, that's right. Evan and Emma with their children. Evan founded Chandler Springs after discovering gold on this property." Amelia's voice warmed. She was clearly getting to what she considered the good part. "He eventually became mayor and built several prominent buildings in town. He was quite the big shot in his day."

So maybe the apple didn't fall far from the tree.

Matthew glanced at a shabby horsehair sofa and two wing-back chairs flanking triple bay windows. The bright Colorado sunshine filled the room despite the cold January day. In Manhattan, he was used to gloomy and depressing winter mornings. This could be a good selling point. But he'd have to get rid of this furniture, which no amount of sunshine could make up for. Who kept stuff like this?

Matthew turned at the sound of Amelia sliding pocket doors open behind him. The warped wood scraped the insides of the hidden channels. Ca-ching.

Matthew followed her into the dining room. A strip of peeling wallpaper curled at eye level. "How long did you say the house has been empty?"

"Only a little more than five years," Amelia said.

Nice spin.

"After your grandparents passed away, your uncle Jacob lived here for a short time," she went on.

"Did he leave anything in the wine cabinet, or did he take it all with him?"

Amelia stopped in front of a hand-carved hutch filled with china and crystal. Those blue eyes narrowed, but he could see her making the decision not to go where he was trying to take her. Note to self: this realtor has no sense of humor.

"Not much has changed," she said. "Most of these antiques belonged to your great-grandparents, Evan and Emma, and were well preserved through the years by your grandparents."

Matthew stood before the display, hands on hips. "Can you

recommend an estate auctioneer in this area? This stuff should be worth several thousand dollars at least."

Amelia's face stiffened. So did her voice. "Mr. Chandler, you're not serious. You're not selling this house."

"Actually, I am," Matthew said. "You're a realtor. Why do you think I called you?"

Amelia cleared her throat. "We've managed the property since Jacob Chandler moved to assisted living in Denver. I thought you were here to see your family inheritance."

Matthew thought the woman was going to cry. What was it to her? You'd think she owned the place herself. "Look, I know it's the family home and all that, but I'm not exactly the sentimental type. I don't need it."

"So – no honoring your ancestors –"

Matthew put up his hand. "Look, Miss ... Richardson, was it? Believe me, I have no interest in this house or my family history. So, either you get it on the market for me or I find another realtor."

She didn't bristle the way most people – well, women – did when he pulled out the corporate exec voice. She just stared at him with those sapphire eyes. Finally, she nodded.

"Fine," she said, all traces of the smooth, rich latte gone. "I'll draw up the paperwork."

She walked past him to the door, floor boards creaking under her step. Matthew looked back to see if any ghosts were following.

CHAPTER 4

*I*n the safety of her car, Amelia dug a tissue from the bottom of her purse. Hot, angry tears flowed down her cheeks. Checking the side mirror, she pulled through the circular drive of the Chandler property and headed toward her office.

Figures raced through her mind. If she pulled money from her retirement, if she lived on rice and beans and ramen soup for years. If she could snag a few big commissions in the next few months. If her mother would give her a loan. Could she make it work?

Maybe, just maybe. Then reality hit her square in the face. Banks didn't approve home loans on the "what if's". The realization twisted in her gut. The house alone was beyond her means, not to mention the repairs the place desperately needed.

It was just that the way Matthew Chandler had waltzed into the house and announced he was selling it brought her blood to a rolling boil. What a jerk. How could he let that beautiful property go without a second thought? What she wouldn't give to own Rose Haven. And he had no idea how important it had been to his grandparents to keep the house in the family.

Amelia pulled into her assigned parking spot. In spite of the battle going on in her head, a sense of pride washed over her. Ten years ago, she'd never have believed she'd own Richardson Realty. Austin Chandler had been so kind to leave her the brick building in his will. Built by Evan Chandler in the 1920's, it faced busy Main Street and was perfect for her real estate business. If this could happen, why not another miracle, right?

Inside the office, Amelia greeted her receptionist, Tiffany. The young girl had desperately needed a job and showed promise. Amelia had decided to groom her for the real estate business.

"Please take messages for me," Amelia said to her. "I'm not available the rest of the day, unless it's an emergency."

"Sure, Amelia." Tiffany twirled a stray piece of red hair. "Anything I can do for you?"

"No. But thanks for asking."

Amelia made her way down the hall. Thankfully the workday was almost over. She closed her office door and sighed. Dealing with the pompous Mr. Chandler had given her a headache. She pulled an aspirin bottle from her top desk drawer. It was nothing new to be upset by clients. Especially the ones that looked at 50 houses and still couldn't find one they liked. So what was it about this guy?

Amelia sat down on the couch facing the picture window. She'd never tire of the majestic mountain view. Austin and Evelyn Chandler. Good friends and such sweet people. Wouldn't they be shocked to know the plans their grandson had for the lovely home they hoped to keep in the family for generations?

Amelia opened her laptop. If Matthew Chandler didn't want the house, owning it would be her dream come true. The current quarterly sales spreadsheet showed the figures she needed. She accessed the National Bank of Colorado's website to fill out the loan application. Then made a note on her calendar to follow up with Nick Houston, the loan manager in a few days. They'd known each other for years, and she knew he'd help her any way he could. It was a long shot, but she wasn't giving up without a fight.

With some effort, Matthew pushed open the sliding pocket doors to Evan's study and stepped inside. The room smelled of dust and leather. One wall, from floor to ceiling, overflowed with volumes of books, most rather old looking. A memory of his grandfather, updating figures in the household account books, puffing on his pipe, flashed through Matthew's mind. For a minute, he thought he could even smell the tobacco Austin always smoked. If his grandparents had raised him, how would his life have been different?

Matthew sighed. What was it about this house? He'd never had these kinds of thoughts before. He mentally slid them into a metal drawer and slammed it shut.

Matthew lowered his lanky frame into the leather chair. Cool. Great spot to set up his laptop while he was here. He leaned back and propped his feet on the corner of the dusty desk. For its age, the chair felt surprisingly comfortable. Almost like the one in his New York office? Nah, had to be a coincidence.

He scrolled through the missed calls on his cell phone. He looked forward to talking with Logan later. His nerves grated when he heard Eva's frantic voice on the last message, obviously perturbed because he hadn't returned her texts. That would be a return call for another time. A long, long time.

Matthew hit the auto dial button and connected with his assistant. "Stacy, how's it going?" Why did talking with Stacy make him think of coffee? He could use a good cup right about now. "I'm still in Colorado."

"Mr. Chandler, good to hear from you. How are things going in ski country?"

"Can't wait to hit the slopes." Matthew paused. "This house deal is a pain, though. It's taking longer than I thought. Plan to wrap everything up in a few days and then on to Breckenridge. Please clear my schedule for next week."

"Absolutely. I'll take care of it."

Matthew leaned forward in his chair. "Any news on the Grant account?"

"I was hoping Logan had told you. Mr. Grant's assistant called this morning and said he will need more time to make a decision."

Matthew ran his hand through his hair. The presentation had come off without a hitch, and he felt confident they had the account. So sure, in fact, he'd booked the flight out here. Logan was right; it was a bad time to be away from the office. But he knew Logan. Trusted him with his life. Besides, he was only a phone call away.

"Thanks. I'll catch up later with Logan. Call if you need anything." Matthew disconnected.

His stomach growled, and he realized he'd missed lunch. He locked the front door and headed to his car. With any luck he wouldn't run into Realtor Lady out there.

Victorian homes lined the downtown streets of Chandler Springs, reminding Matthew of the one he was selling. He hoped the realtor, what was her name again? – would call him today to sign the paperwork. Funny, he knew the color of her eyes, but not her name. The way she'd acted at their first meeting, she must love all these old houses too. Not him. He couldn't wait to get back to his high-rise condo.

Matthew sat at a stop sign and watched people maneuver

their way in and out of the antique shops on Main Street. He had to admit there was a slower pace here than the crowded streets of Manhattan. Cameras hung from some of the shoppers' necks, so obviously this was a tourist town. Colorado t-shirts must have been the dress code of the day, no doubt purchased from a local vendor.

Matthew turned onto Main Street and spotted The BlueBird Cafe. Red checked curtains filled the windows, window decals advertising home cooked meals. Yeah, this place would work. His stomach growled again, and he pulled into an empty space in front. Nice. No problem with parking in this little one-horse town. He'd never find a spot so easy at home.

He exited his car and glanced in the front window. Not packed like so many places he was used to. A bell jingled when he opened the front door and stepped in. Seating himself at an empty table, covered with a red checked cloth to match the curtains, he scanned the menu. Rocky Mountain Oysters. No thanks, he'd pass.

Hunger gnawed at his stomach, but questions gnawed harder at his mind. From the moment he'd found out about Rose Haven, there'd never been a question of selling it. He had no use for it, and it was a bitter reminder of his absentee father and the family he'd never really known. He pushed the thoughts into the mind circular file. Again. Wow, that thing must be full by now.

A burly woman with a Harley motorcycle tattooed on her forearm and hair wrapped in a red bandana interrupted his thoughts. "What can I get for you, doll?" She smacked her chewing gum, looking at him.

Matthew stared at the menu to regain his composure. Must be a Colorado thing. He was used to dealing with fine dressed women like Stacy and Eva. He forced himself to look up at the waitress. "I'll have a burger, well done, fries and black coffee."

"Sure thing." She scribbled his order on a yellow pad. "You new in town? Haven't seen you around before." The gum thing again.

Matthew cringed. Another pet peeve of his. People who smacked gum while they talked. "Yeah, I'm just here for a few days."

"Where you stayin'?"

Wow, was this lady nosey. "At Rose Haven." Normally a friendly guy, he wasn't ready to engage in conversation.

"Ah... you must be the Chandlers' grandson."

"That's right." He really didn't feel like revealing his personal life to her. And the two men at the counter were staring at him as well.

"Welcome to Chandler Springs. I'm Wanda." She scribbled another note on her pad. "We all loved Austin and Evelyn. Heard you inherited their house. When you movin' in?"

News sure spread fast around this town. Another reason he didn't want to live here. "Actually, I'm not. I'm selling the place."

"Selling? You're kidding, right? Don't you know the house was built by the original Chandlers and has been in the family for over a hundred years?" Her voice boomed across the restaurant.

Matthew stared at her. "I live in New York City. I don't need a house here." Not like he owed her an explanation.

"Yeah, it's your decision. But I think it's sad the house won't stay in the family. That was one of Austin and Evelyn's biggest wishes, you know." Smack. Smack. "Your food will be out in a few." She turned and made her way through the swinging doors into the kitchen.

Matthew had a sudden urge to have someone test his food before he ate it. He picked up his phone and scrolled through the stock reports. From the corner of his eye, he watched the two men at the counter. One pointed at him, then pulled his hand down when Matthew looked over at them. He knew he was fodder for the locals. And he certainly wouldn't be winning any prizes for popularity in town when the townsfolk heard about his plans to sell the house. For once maybe gossip would work to his advantage. He'd suck it up if it meant a sale.

Matthew finished his meal and drove back to the house. He stood beside the car and studied the exterior. The question of the day was: sell as is or make a few repairs before the house went on the market? The rockers on the wraparound porch held no appeal. Maybe in about 30 years. He could almost hear Logan pulling out the geezer jokes. Smiling, he walked around to the south side of the house. A quick inventory of the grounds wouldn't hurt.

A black wrought iron fence surrounded a small rose garden. The heavy gate hinges groaned when Matthew flipped the latch and slipped in. Someone had been here recently, because the moist ground was freshly mulched. Matthew walked on the winding pebbled path through the flowers.

A sign in front of two dormant rose bushes caught his attention. "LaReine Victoria" and "Ferdinand Pichard". Sounded very old fashioned and European. He pulled out his cell phone to take pictures. The rose garden could be a great selling feature to list on the MLS.

He felt something squish under his foot. Great, someone didn't clean up after their dog. He stepped out of the gated area, into the grass to wipe the dog poo off his Italian leather shoes. He hoped this wasn't an omen of his time here. Now he'd have to find someone to clean them. He could find a shoe shine on about every corner in New York City. Did Chandler Springs even have one?

"Hello." He turned around to find the real estate agent staring at him.

"Someone forgot to clean up after their dog." Matthew

continued rubbing the shoe in the velvety green grass, his face reddening.

"Oh." Amelia winced. "I'm so sorry. My dog was over here the other day. The gate to the flower garden must have been open..."

"One reason I've never liked dogs," Matthew muttered under his breath.

He noticed the unwelcome substance had somehow smeared onto the cuff of his dress slacks. Lost in thought of the dog he'd like to shoot right now, he didn't notice the woman leave until he saw her making her way down the block.

Back in the house, Matthew removed his shoes at the door and slipped into the study where he'd left his suitcase. His New York life called for dress clothes most of the time but thank goodness he'd thought to pack casual clothes. He slipped on jeans, t-shirt and tennis shoes and hung the soiled dress slacks over the back of a chair. No dry cleaner pick-up service here. He should send Miss Real Estate agent the bill.

The day was slipping away; he'd better figure out where to sleep. He tugged his suitcase up the first set of steps of the grand staircase and stopped on the landing at the rose designed stained glass window. Light poured through the colored glass, creating patterns on the worn carpet at his stocking feet. Cha-ching. More money for repairs.

He pulled out his cell and wrote a note. At this rate, he was going to need a multi-page notebook. And win the lottery.

At the top of the stairs, Matthew glanced down the long hall. Many of the bedroom doors stood open. The old wooden floor creaked as he peeked into the first room, feeling like an intruder. This was his house... for now. . . but it was a place he didn't belong.

He started toward a bedroom door on the other side of the stairs when a memory hit him full force.

He sucked in a breath.

This was the room when it had all begun. He stopped in the doorway and could see himself watching out the window onto the driveway.

Matthew shook himself back to reality. Painful memories he'd buried so long ago flooded out before he could stop them. He put his hand on his chest and felt his heart beating wildly.

He was ten years old again. Sleeping in this room while his parents took a vacation. He could remember hiding under the covers at night when the old house creaked.

He had been so excited when Grandpa Austin told him his parents were picking him up after what seemed like forever. He'd looked forward to getting home and enjoying the rest of the summer playing with his friends.

But it made no sense when his Mom had come in the house alone. Was his dad parking the car? He wanted to ask but one look at his mom's face told him to stay silent. With tears in her eyes, she told him that they were staying at Rose Haven and Dad was going back to their house in Denver to pack his belongings.

He'd be gone before they got home.

"Gone?" Matthew's thoughts climbed over each other.

"I'm sorry, Matthew. Your dad wants a divorce. He's moving to another city."

Matthew's young heart couldn't take it. He'd rushed up two flights of stairs and stared out this exact bedroom window. His dad's car was at the end of the driveway, turning onto the street. How could he leave like that? He didn't even say goodbye. Didn't his dad love him? Matthew had used a shirt sleeve to swipe at the tears running down his face.

Floorboards creaked, and he'd turned around to see Grandpa Austin standing at the bedroom door watching him, tears in his own fading eyes. He'd opened his big arms wide. Matthew had run to him, burying his face in the old man's chest. He'd felt the pain of rejection and abandonment from John Chandler ever since.

A dog barking in the next yard brought Matthew back to the present. Well, one thing for sure, he wasn't ever sleeping in this room again. Or feeling this kind of pain. His father was dead to him. That was the only way he'd been able to survive.

Matthew closed the door. He'd actually like to padlock it to keep the memories from tumbling out again.

He started farther down the hall. In the next room a four-poster bed sat in front of floor-to-ceiling windows. An antique dresser and double armoire filled the opposite wall. A braided rug covered the middle of the hardwood floor. Not exactly his style.

And the clothes he now sported weren't his style either. His reflection in the full length oak mirror made him think of Logan.

Matthew noticed a pattern as he looked in each room. Large bed, matching dresser and armoire. Not a whole lot of imagination if you asked him. But, then, nobody had. At the end of the hall, he passed the attic stairs, debating if he should explore up there or wait for another day. Might find all kinds of valuable antiques to sell at the estate auction.

He decided to wait and pulled his suitcase into the first bedroom. It was the largest and if he remembered right, had belonged to Austin and Evelyn. And probably Evan and Emma before them.

Back downstairs, seated in Evan's worn brown leather chair in the study, Matthew rubbed the cracked wooden arms. He leaned back and studied the gigantic mahogany desk. What kinds of deals had Evan proposed and completed in this room, from this desk? Had his own strong work ethic come from Evan? He'd never thought much about his great-grandfather.

When the sun lowered behind the mountains, dimmed light cast shadows across the wooden floor. The huge, empty house was no comparison to Matthew's comfortable condo. He could always stay in a hotel. Then he thought of his lunch experience. Staying here beat scrutinization by the townies. Besides, he was tired and had had enough memories for one day. Yeah, the sooner he got rid of this place, the better.

Amelia rose early and pattered into the kitchen. Reaching for the carafe, she stopped. No, she'd keep her vow to drink less coffee and enjoy a healthy morning smoothie instead. She pulled almond milk, spinach, flax, chia seeds and fruit from the fridge. As the machine whirled away, she mentally reviewed the day's schedule. Her stomach twisted at the thought of the 10 a.m. meeting with Mr. Chandler.

Carrying the fruity concoction to her home office, she booted up her laptop. No e-mails from the pompous fool. Disappointing. She hoped he'd had a midnight revelation about the importance of keeping his family home.

Amelia grabbed a tissue and swiped at the moisture on her cheeks. Austin and Evelyn Chandler had been such kind souls. How she missed them. Some of her favorite childhood memories had happened in their home. Brian came to her mind. She missed him even more. If they had married, she probably could have talked him into buying the Chandler's house. Her dream home.

She reached down and petted Harley. The Golden Retriever lay stretched out under the desk, his head resting on her foot. She was secretly glad he had left a deposit for Matthew in the rose garden. Served him right.

Amelia finalized the paperwork for the Chandler listing and hit the print button. It hurt her soul to think the beautiful house would be sold to strangers. It would be a long shot if her own loan application was approved. More like a miracle.

She pulled the papers from the top loader and made a final proof. A smile touched her lips. What she wouldn't give to burn them. Her professional side took over. She would assist Mr. Chandler with this sale. But nothing could stop her from praying he came to his senses before they received an offer.

CHAPTER 5

*T*he water sputtered and then shot out with a force when Matthew turned the shower knob. He let the rust colored stream run while he grabbed clean clothes and his shaving kit. When it ran clear, he stepped in. Funny how the knock in the bathroom pipes was still there. It would cost a fortune to update the plumbing in this old house. He couldn't imagine the bottom line to renovate this entire monstrosity. Ca-ching.

Thirty minutes later, ready to face the new day head on, Matthew booted up his laptop to scan e-mails. He plopped in the chair. An e-mail from Logan.

Matthew took a long sip of coffee that, in truth, wasn't as good as Stacy's and clicked on Logan's note. His eyes scanned the e-mail, and with each line he felt his face sag. What the heck was going on? He had to agree with what Logan said in his last line:

"The more time passes, the better chance we have of losing this guy."

No kidding. Matthew shot a quick reply back that he'd call

later. They had to come up with a strategy. He wasn't giving up without a fight.

Matthew's stomach grumbled. A good cup of coffee and hot breakfast would help get the energy flowing and the wheels turning. He hadn't noticed any other eating places in town, so the Bluebird Cafe it was. And with any luck, the gum smacking waitress wouldn't be working today.

When he walked through the door, the same two grisly-faced men from the day before eyed him over forks full of fried potatoes. He found a table far from their stares. He wasn't in a mood to be sized up today.

Matthew spotted Wanda at another table. Same bandana, same tattoo. And probably the same gum.

She smiled his way. "Hello there, sugar. Didn't know if we'd see you again."

There certainly wouldn't be any red carpets rolling out for him. "You have good coffee." Not as good as his special brew at home, but it would do for now. He stared at the stained plastic menu.

Wanda peered down at him. "Had a change of heart about the house?" Smack, smack.

"No, I haven't." As if it's any of your business. "It's going on the market today."

"That's a shame." Wanda frowned and pulled her yellow pad from her apron pocket. "What'll it be this morning?"

"I'll have the breakfast special, eggs over easy and crispy bacon. Biscuits and gravy. And keep the black coffee coming."

He was a lot hungrier than he'd realized, probably because he'd only eaten one meal yesterday. And he was going to need the 4,000 calories for the day he had ahead. And later a run.

"Coming right up." Wanda headed toward the kitchen. She stopped and looked back at him.

Matthew shivered. If looks could kill ....

Matthew's text notification pulled him back to reality. The

two old guys at the counter renewed their stares like they'd never seen a cell phone before. You'd have thought he'd pulled a time machine out of his pocket. Matthew wanted to pick it up and introduce them to the 21st century. One look at their dour faces told him he'd better mind his own business.

He nodded his thanks when Wanda appeared with a brown ceramic mug of steaming black coffee and looked at the cell phone screen. Maybe the text was from Logan? He rolled his eyes. Eva. He ignored it. He didn't want indigestion before he'd even eaten a bite.

Wanda appeared with two plates of food, clouds of heat curling up from them. He could only hope she hadn't spit in any of it. He nodded his thanks again and she left. Good, he really didn't want to have to defend his decisions. Especially with her.

Pouring the thick sausage gravy over the split biscuits, he thought about Logan. How to convince Mr. Charles Grant they were the right company for him? Yeah, he needed to get this house thing settled quickly so he could get back to the office, where he belonged.

Matthew finished his meal. Wanda wasn't around so he laid a twenty on the table and exited the building. Maybe the nice tip would soften her a bit. He doubted it, though. He made his way to the real estate office up the street.

Amelia stood in the reception area talking with Tiffany when the door jingled and Matthew stepped in.

"Good morning, Mr. Chandler." She wondered if he could see through her fake smile. With the slim pickin's of single men in Chandler Springs, it didn't seem fair such a good looking man was such a cad.

Matthew interrupted her thoughts with a curt nod. Must be

New York for "nice to see you too." What a jerk. She'd love to give him a piece of her mind.

"We'll be in the conference room, Tiffany," she said.

Tiffany nodded and pushed her red hair behind her ears. Amelia mentally prepared herself for the barrage of questions that would come later. Always seemed to happen when a good looking man was around. A quirk Amelia chose to overlook in light of Tiffany's reliability and fun personality. Dealing with the past receptionist had been a nightmare Amelia would rather not relive. Tiffany was definitely a keeper.

Amelia picked up a folder of documents from the desk. Normally it was a thrill for her to list a house. Not this one. She'd had heartburn and a sleepless night. She led Matthew to the small conference room at the end of the hall, imagining Mr. New York City would turn up his nose at her homey mountain decor.

"Please have a seat in here." Amelia intentionally kept her voice monotone. It was the only way to keep her true emotions from lashing out at him.

Matthew chose the chair closest to the door and sat down. He fiddled with the pen in front of him.

Amelia wanted to hit him over the head with the folder. Maybe it would knock some sense into his stubborn brain. The thought made her smile. She'd have to resign herself to the fact that the beloved house would be sold.

Without a sound, save the scratch of pen on paper, Matthew signed each document and pushed them all toward her.

"Are you okay with a lock box on the front door?" Amelia asked.

Matthew shrugged. "Yeah, not a problem."

"Do you want to be notified about showings?"

"Yes. You can call my cell. Leave a message if you need to."

Her questions felt so forced. Not like her normal small talk with clients. "How long will you be in town?"

"Just a few days." Matthew headed toward the door. "I'm hoping for a quick sale. I trust you will make that happen."

Amelia nodded. The lump in her throat almost choked her.

Matthew walked the brick-lined street, his mind running 100 miles an hour. The Grant proposal, the house, the real estate agent. Good grief. He'd come up against some cold business-women before. Why was this Amelia chick getting under his skin? He'd better get a grip.

What he wouldn't give for a lively game of racquetball with Logan right about now to help burn off those breakfast calories and clear the cobwebs from his brain. He found himself back at his car, got in and drove to the house. He punched the familiar number into his cell phone.

"Hey Matt, it's good to hear from you."

"Right back at ya." Matthew balanced his cell phone under his chin, unlocked the front door and headed to Evan's study. Seemed to be his safe place in this ginormous house.

"Stacy sent us both a calendar appointment for a week from Friday."

"Yeah, for what? A racquetball game?"

"Even better. Charles Grant has requested a meeting with us."

Matthew sucked in his breath and pumped his fist in the air. "Yes!" He caught the phone with the other hand before it could drop to the floor. "Best news I've heard all day. My gut tells me this is it. He's signing with us."

"I sure hope you're right."

"Always the pessimist." Matthew plopped into Evan's leather chair.

"More like realist."

"Have a drink, buddy, and calm your nerves. Oh, and I

signed the paperwork to put the house on the market. My flight is this Friday. Keep your calendar open this weekend. We've got work to do."

Matthew leaned back in Evan's chair. Could this day get any better?

"Hey, Eva e-mailed me asking about you. Wants to make sure you're doing okay."

The hairs bristled on Matthew's neck. The woman was like a ball and chain. "What did you tell her?"

"Nada. I think she still has the hots for you." Logan paused. "I've never trusted her."

Matthew grinned. "You're suspicious of everyone."

"It's my nature. I don't trust too quickly."

"Don't I know it. Took ten years before you trusted me with a key to your place." Thought he'd have to sign a sworn affidavit, if he remembered right. "I'll deal with her when I get home. Talk soon."

Matthew disconnected the call. The excellent news about Grant was too good to let that woman ruin his afternoon.

Later in the day, Matthew stood in the entry hall with the repairman he'd called to inspect the house. "Well, what's the verdict?"

The coverall dressed man pointed to a full screen list on his I-pad.

"You've definitely got problems. The roof is shot, and the plumbing needs to be updated."

No big surprise. He had eyes and had seen the obvious. But the cost of these repairs. That was the real question. "How much will this set me back?"

"Give me a second and I can give you an estimate." The man started tapping again on his I-pad.

Matthew nodded.

"Hello?"

Matthew turned and saw Amelia Richardson standing in the vestibule, looking as icy as she had earlier.

"I knocked..."

Matthew motioned toward the repairman.

"Ah. So you decided to get an estimate after all."

"The cost of repairs will determine if I can accept counteroffers, Miss Richardson."

Matthew pressed his lips together. The sour look on her face said it all. Before he could elaborate, he heard the repairman clear his throat.

"I have a number for you, Mr. Chandler. Would you prefer to hear it in private?" He looked at Amelia.

Yeah, let her hear it. It might eliminate the romanticism she had going on about this house. "Nope, go ahead. It's no big secret."

The man held up his I-pad for Matthew to see the final figure.

"What? You've got to be kidding me? Seventy-five thousand dollars to fix this old place? That's highway robbery." Matthew shook his head.

The man's face reddened. "I'm sorry, Mr. Chandler. At the bottom you'll notice the nice discount I gave because of the business I've done in the past with your grandparents."

"Well, I have to think about it." Matthew started toward the vestibule, this meeting obviously over. "I'll call you if I'm interested." He opened the door.

The man followed him and stepped out onto the front porch. "We'd be happy to do business with you, sir."

I bet you would. "Thank you." Matthew stepped back in the house and closed the door. He'd forgotten the Richardson woman was still there. "Something I can do for you?"

Stone faced and lips pursed, she finally found her voice. "I've scheduled a showing for tomorrow afternoon."

"Excellent." He widened his eyes at her. When she didn't respond – was the woman made of stone? he said, "Anything else?"

"No. I'll let myself out." Amelia slid out the front door as quickly as possible.

For the next two days, Amelia teetered back and forth between near rage at the arrogant Mr. Chandler and desperate hope from Nick Houston about the loan. She staged monologues in her head about how she'd used Garrett Burke's repair services in the past and didn't appreciate seeing him treated like dirt. Her opinion of Matthew Chandler had just fallen another notch. On the bank loan end, she tried to imagine herself doing the happy dance when she got the phone call, telling her she could buy the house.

It was more like a funeral march on Wednesday morning when she opened the e-mail from Nick at the bank. She leaned back in her office chair and read his words several times, her eyes blearing.

"Dear Amelia, I regret to inform you the loan application has been denied. I'm sorry. Your business track record speaks for itself. I brainstormed every loan possibility and even contacted two lending agencies myself. With the real estate market crash a few years ago, banking regulations have been tightened. I'd love to approve the loan, but my hands are tied. Nick."

Amelia chewed her lower lip. Not totally unexpected. But not the miracle she'd hoped for either. A raw pain twisted deep in the pit of her stomach. This felt like the death of a long, cherished friend. Could she ever forgive Matthew Chandler for selling his beautiful family estate?

CHAPTER 6

*M*atthew drained the last drop of hot toddy and set the mug on the edge of the rock fireplace. The business in Chandler Springs was behind him. Thank goodness. He leaned back on the leather couch, legs stretched out, arms crossed behind his head. The fire behind him crackled.

Man, this was the life. Someday when he retired... His eyes closed for a moment and then he sat straight up. He'd rest later. Right now the Breckenridge slopes were calling his name.

Outside, Matthew tightened his boots to the skis and pushed his way through the deep snow toward the lift. Yes! Short lines. Wednesdays were usually less busy. The only thing missing was Logan. He made a mental note to plan a ski trip back out here soon with his friend. Logan on skis. What a hoot that would be.

The bright Colorado sunshine reflected off packed snow on Peak Number 8. Matthew pulled his goggles over his eyes and enjoyed the ride to the top, wind whipping against his face. The ski lift made him feel like he was floating in the sky, legs dangling as the ground moved farther and farther away. A memory hit him ... his 9 year old attitude, hands on hips, telling his dad the bunny slope was for babies. He wanted to ride straight to the top and ski down like the big boys.

Thankfully his dad had talked him into starting on the beginner slope, and even that gentle slope twisted his stomach as he stood at the top looking down. But there was nothing like the thrill when he made it to the bottom, and skiing had been in his blood ever since. The faster, the harder the slopes, the more challenge.

After the stress at work and getting the house up for sale, he was ready to fly down this mountain. Once off the lift, the need for speed spurred him forward to the edge.

Matthew glanced to his left. A young girl dressed in a multi-colored parka, body stiff, timidly slid her skis a few inches at a time. Happened all the time, novices looking for the bunny slope, riding the ski lift too long and ending up on the higher, more dangerous courses. Then they had no idea how to get back down.

He looked over at the girl again. She must have worked up her courage to try it. He wanted to tell her to go for it. Hopefully she'd get the same kind of rush he always did.

Matthew maneuvered toward the edge of the mountain and pushed off with his poles. The sound of his skis skimming the snow, adrenalin singing through his veins as he gained momentum ... ah, he could do this all day.

The next thing he knew a multicolored flash was flying in front of him. He tried to yell a warning and push his skis in the opposite direction. But it was too late. He plowed into her, the two tumbling together a few yards before crashing into a packed snowbank. Sharp pain shot through Matthew's right hip and leg.

What the heck had just happened? It felt like someone was driving a posthole digger into his bone. He opened his mouth to ask the girl if she was okay. Barely a squeak came out. He must

have had the wind knocked out of him. He tried to take a deep
breath but the pain in his leg intensified.

A rescue crew from the ski patrol arrived minutes later. A
woman in a pink parka skied down to aid the girl. A young
bearded man, snow on his whiskers, bent over Matthew.

The man pulled Matthew's goggles off. "You okay, buddy?"

Still dazed, Matthew looked up at him and grabbed his right
leg. "Hurts," he mumbled.

The paramedic radioed to the top for a carrier. "He'll need
immediate attention at the bottom of the hill."

Two skiers were beside him within moments, pulling an
orange carrier piled with blankets. Pain ripped from his ankle
to his thigh when the medics attached a splint to his leg. The
two rescuers picked him up gently and placed him on the
carrier. That was the last thing he remembered.

Matthew opened his eyes and slowly blinked a few times. A
shadowy figure approached the bed and touched his hand. He
wished his head would stop spinning.

"How are you feeling, honey?"

He felt the warmth on his hand and immediately recognized
his mother's voice. What was she doing here?

"Like I've been hit by a Mac truck. Where am I?"

"You took a pretty nasty fall on a ski slope in Breckenridge
this morning." His mom's hand shook when she brushed a stray
silver hair from her face. Nora Chandler Bennett didn't shake.
He must be in worse shape than he thought. "The rescuers told
me you were trying to avoid a collision with another skier."

Matthew closed his eyes. A faint memory of the ball of color
that had come flying at him. He knew she wasn't ready for the
difficult slopes.

"And my leg?" He motioned to his casted right leg, propped on two fluffy pillows.

"The surgeon rejoined the fractures with pins. You'll be here a few days."

Matthew grimaced and tried to reposition himself in the hospital bed. Pain shot through his head and his leg. He'd planned to return to New York the day after tomorrow to prepare for the big meeting next week with Charles Grant.

"The doctor should be around soon. Maybe you should ask for more pain meds."

Matthew shook his head. "I'll get through it."

He hated feeling this groggy. He reached for the plastic straw cup on his bedside table but couldn't move for the weight of the cast. Nora handed it to him. Nothing he hated more than feeling helpless.

"How long have I been here?" He had no idea what day it was.

Nora brushed the hair from his eyes. "Since about noon. You went to Breckenridge Medical Center first and then they transferred you here to Swedish by ambulance. Thank the Lord you had ID on you. I arrived while you were in surgery."

"My rental car is still parked up there."

Nora rolled her eyes. "Leave it to you to be worried about that. Pete said he'd take care of it for you. You won't be able to drive for a while anyway. Should he return the car to the rental company?"

"Yes."

At least that's what he thought he said before his eyelids slammed shut again, in spite of every effort to keep them open.

Two days later Matthew balanced on the edge of the hospital

bed. He'd made it to 35 without a broken bone. And now his first one was a doozy.

He'd have no problem saying adios to this place. No nurses to wake him during the night. Didn't they realize how long it took to get comfortable with this behemoth thing on his leg? He'd wanted to bite their heads off.

Couldn't wait to sleep in his own bed. Good grief. He must have hit his head in the collision. He was in Denver, not New York. And stuck here for a while. What lousy luck.

He'd planned to be back at work at Canon by now, not cooped up in a hospital with awful food that couldn't contribute to anybody's healing. Thankfully Logan and Stacy were handling business in New York. But he couldn't wait to get back. He needed to be there.

A burly male nurse, with more hair on his arms than his head, pushed a wheelchair into Matthew's room. He set the brakes and pulled out the foot rests.

"Your chariot, sir." He flashed Matthew a perfect smile. A little too perfect. The guy probably had never suffered a broken leg.

Matthew frowned. No thanks. He could walk. Yeah, right. The crutches in the corner looked like a torture contraption. How would he ever get down to the car on those things?

"I can do it myself," Matthew tried to mumble when the nurse grabbled him under the arm to help him into the wheelchair.

"Go for it." The medical assistant let go and moved back, arms crossed, watching.

Matthew tried to lift his casted leg off the bed. The weight threw him backwards onto the rumpled sheets. Feeling helpless was not his style.

The assistant stepped forward again and effortlessly lifted him under each arm. The guy must be a body builder.

Nora waltzed into the room dressed like she was ready for a yoga class. "All ready?"

Matthew sighed. A lively game of racquetball with Logan sounded good right about now. He looked down at the cast. Yeah, wasn't happenin' anytime soon.

Nora balanced the crutches in one arm, her purse over the other shoulder. "Pete is pulling the car around and will meet us at the front entrance." Nora stopped at the door. "Oh, don't forget your get well plant from your co-workers." She picked it up. "Can you hold it on your lap?"

Matthew nodded. Nice gesture from the office but he couldn't look at it every day. He'd just be reminded he should be back at work and not stuck in Colorado. He'd dump the thing when he got back to the house.

Or maybe give it to the real estate lady. He'd be seeing lots more of her since his doctor had already told him not to even think about flying home to New York for a minimum of four weeks. Something about the severity of the injury and the danger of blood clots. Yada yada. He was good at tuning out doctor lingo. Especially advice he didn't want to hear. He was young and strong and would recover in a week or two.

Pete and Nora had invited him to stay with them in Denver. But their place was small. And he couldn't stand the thought of his mother constantly fretting over him. Rose Haven would have to do. He could work from Evan's library until he found a way to get back to New York.

～

"Hey Matt. How you doin'?" Logan sighed. "Couldn't believe it when your Mom called me with the news. Dude, you're a mad dog on the slopes. No way this happened to you."

Matthew frowned. "Bad break." He looked at the cast from

thigh to toes. "In more ways than one. You ought to see this monster of a cast."

"Do you remember talking to me a couple of days ago?"

"Barely. I was really in and out from the pain meds. Hope you didn't tell me anything important." Matthew repositioned the pillow under his leg.

"Not really. Basic office stuff." Logan paused. "Eva's been asking about you."

"Yeah, she texted when I was in the hospital. Probably irritated her that I didn't answer."

"Man, that doesn't even begin to describe it. She wanted to know why she wasn't notified immediately. What is wrong with her? Anyway, I told her you were home now and recovering."

"Not exactly. Recovering, yes. Home, no. I won't be home until I'm back in New York." Matthew hadn't felt this edgy in a long time.

Logan ignored that. "Hate to bring this up now. But Grant cancelled the meeting for next week. Stacy said something about he was called out of the country on business."

A pain shot through Matthew's leg, and he grimaced. "Guess it doesn't matter at this point. I'm stuck here for a while."

"Yeah, I was afraid of that. I do have good news though."

"Great... I need some right about now."

"I've booked a flight and arrive in Denver tomorrow night."

"No way. For real?" Matthew smiled, probably the first time in days. He hated to admit it, but he hadn't felt totally sane without Logan giving him grief every ten minutes. Of course, he wasn't going to tell him that. "I'll have a marker ready for you to sign my cast."

"Will do. And we'll have plenty of time to brainstorm the Grant account. But the main reason I'm coming is to help you out."

"Of course." Matthew looked down at his cast. "Right now, I need all the help I can get."

CHAPTER 7

*A*melia dialed Matthew's number. Again. After three rings it went to voice mail. She couldn't believe she was leaving another message. For someone in such a hurry to sell their house, he wasn't making this easy.

Adrenaline coursing through her veins at her pious client, she pushed the disconnect button. She slowed her pace and took a few deep, slow breaths. No client, or man, for that matter, was worth the stress.

The brisk north wind caught her hair, and she rearranged it in the ponytail holder. She stopped to watch two squirrels fighting over a nut. One grabbed it and chased the other one up a tree. Birds chirped their sweet songs on this bright, sunny day. Amelia made a conscious decision to push away the anger and enjoy the remaining two block walk to the Bluebird Cafe. A nice lunch with her mother always calmed her nerves.

Ruth Richardson met her daughter on the sidewalk outside the front door. Amelia leaned down to kiss her cheek. She could only hope in the coming years she would age as gracefully as her mother.

"Thanks for meeting me for lunch, Mom." She held the door open for her mother to enter first.

"I appreciate the invitation." Ruth hurried through the door and stood inside, brushing her windblown hair from her face. "You doing okay? You look a little stressed." She stopped at the coat tree and hung her wrap and scarf.

Amelia hung her own coat and followed her mother to a table, flowing green maxi skirt flapping at her black ankle boots. She propped her pink shades on top of her head and smoothed her hands over her tunic blouse. The stress was draining out already.

"I'm all right."

Amelia pretended to study the menu. She knew better than to try to pull anything over on her mother. She looked up into Ruth's blue eyes, a darker shade than her own and beautiful. "I'll admit it. I'm still upset about the Rose Haven estate sale."

Ruth reached across the table and touched her daughter's hand. "I'm sorry Mr. Chandler doesn't feel the way we do about the house."

"Yeah, me too." Amelia studied the menu again.

Wanda appeared at their table. "Hey ladies. What can I get for you today?"

"Hi Wanda."

Amelia averted her eyes from the newest tattoo of a red rose on the waitress's neck. Amelia loved flowers but how anyone could do that to their body was beyond her. She shrugged to no one in particular. Wanda's great personality and love for people helped her overlook the oddities.

"Are you ready to order, Mom?"

Ruth closed her menu. "I'll have the soup and salad with unsweetened tea."

"Same for me." Amelia handed her menu to Wanda.

Wanda peered down at Amelia, revealing a wad of gum as she talked. "Too bad about Rose Haven. You handling the sale?"

Amelia nearly choked on a sip of water. "Yes I am."

"That Matthew Chandler is a fine looking man. Not my type, but..."

Amelia brushed her arm across the table as she reached for her water. Her keys clattered to the floor. Good distraction. She didn't need the town knowing how she really felt about this fiasco.

Never one to give up, Wanda continued. "Have you seen him lately?"

"No, not for a few days. I understand he went to Breckenridge."

"Boy, did he. Had a skiing accident and came home with a cast from here to here." Wanda motioned to her thigh and then ankle. "He was in here last night with a friend visiting from New York."

Amelia grabbed for her water glass and took another sip. "Oh no. I'm sorry to hear that." She didn't like the man, but she didn't want to see him hurt either. At least . . . not badly.

"That's nice of you. Especially since he's selling the house we all love. Your food will be out in a few." Wanda turned and headed to the kitchen.

"Well, I guess that explains why he hasn't answered my calls." Amelia watched her mother playing on her new I-phone. "Mom, are you listening to me?"

"Sure, honey. Heard every word you said. Just trying to figure out how to set up voicemail."

Amelia put her hand out. "I can do it for you."

"No, I need to learn." Ruth shook her head. "Sorry. I'm being rude. I'll figure it out later." She pushed the off button and slid the thing into her purse.

Amelia smiled at the numerous times her mother had told her she didn't need or want to use modern technology. This new phone had opened up a whole new world to her. "Let me know if I can help."

Wanda appeared with two salads and two cups of steaming soup on a tray. "If you need anything else, just holler."

Amelia watched her saunter away from the table. No bandana today, just bright red hair spiked in all directions. She was a hoot and one of the best sources of gossip in town. Amelia tried to be on her best behavior around Wanda, or the whole town would know her business.

Amelia took a bite of her salad.

"Did I tell you Sally from church thinks I should start a bakery?" Ruth laughed. "What a crazy idea."

Amelia looked at her mother. "No, it's not really. You're probably the best baker I know."

"Thanks, Honey. But you're my daughter, and you're supposed to say nice things."

"I only tell the truth." Amelia forked another bite of salad. "What if you start small from our kitchen?"

Ruth beamed. "I'll think about it. Maybe the ladies from church could get me some orders to start out."

"No doubt." Amelia sipped her ice tea. "Do you have any cookies? I'd buy several dozen from you today."

"Really, Amelia, you don't have to patronize me. I know you don't care much for sweets."

"Not for me. I'm closing on a house this afternoon and fresh baked cookies would be a nice housewarming gift."

Ruth tried to hide her smile. But failed. "I baked several batches this morning."

Amelia knocked on the heavy oak door. She could hear voices inside. A dark haired man in a baseball cap answered.

"Yes, can I help you?"

Amelia shifted her weight and held out her hand. "I'm

Amelia Richardson from Richardson Realty. I stopped by to talk to Mr. Chandler about a showing."

"I'm Logan Montgomery. Come in if you want. Matt's in the study."

Nice, friendly guy. Seemed like an oddball friendship with the cold Mr. Chandler. Amelia followed him down the hall.

"Hey, Matt. You have company."

Matthew looked up from his laptop, his right leg propped on a fluffy pillow. "Miss Richardson."

Amelia stepped closer and unbuttoned her coat. She wasn't staying long. And this house was freezing. "Sorry to hear about your accident."

"Yeah, tell me about it. Looks like I'm stuck here longer than I'd planned." Matthew rolled his eyes.

Amelia noticed his pale face. He'd obviously been through some trauma the past few days. Normally a sympathetic soul, she wanted to feel sorry for him but couldn't quite get there.

"Anything I can do for you?"

Matthew shook his head. "Not at the moment."

"Will this change anything with the house listing?" Amelia motioned toward his cast. She could only hope.

Matthew frowned. "Not in the least." He looked at his friend, still standing at the doorway of the study. "Logan will be helping me out until I can get around." He hesitated. "Oh, we'll need a minimum of 24 hours' notice to show the house."

Amelia noticed a slight quiver in Matthew's speech as he spoke. Must be the meds. Or had the all powerful Matthew Chandler finally found his own vulnerability?

"Yep, I'm the cook, the chauffeur and the maid." Logan showed a mouth full of teeth.

Amelia returned the sentiment. It was nice to have one happy person in the room. She turned back to Matthew. "I'd left several voicemail messages about a showing yesterday. I assume you received them."

Matthew nodded.

Not sure of his reaction, she continued on. "Our agreement was to notify you before a showing. I did call. Several times, in fact. I had no idea you'd had an accident. The prospective clients were visiting from Denver and needed to see the house yesterday during a visit here."

Matthew opened his mouth to reply. From the look on his face, it wasn't positive. Logan shot him a look, and he stopped.

"Understandable. How'd it go?"

"Never easy to tell. The couple really loved the house but I'm not sure they can get financing." Amelia had felt the sting first hand, but she wasn't about to tell him. "I won't keep you." She inched toward the door. "I'll be in touch."

Logan stepped aside to allow her to exit the study. In the hall with Amelia, he lowered his voice. "This has been a rough few days. I've never seen him like this." Logan pulled a business card from his shirt pocket. "Here's my number if you need to schedule a showing and can't reach Matt."

Amelia pulled her cell from her purse and punched the number into her contacts.

"Thanks. I appreciate that."

Amelia buttoned her coat and stepped onto the porch. A thin layer of ice covered the sidewalk, the grass. And her heart.

Amelia arrived home to Harley's licks and wild tail. She loved how her sweet boy could love so unconditionally. Filling his water bowl, she thought of Mr. Chandler. This whole situation was so infuriating. He was impossible. His arrogant attitude irritated her to no end.

She ran her hand across Harley's head and rubbed his ears. Somehow touching his soft fur had always calmed her. She'd better resign herself to the fact Mr. Chandler wasn't keeping the house. And sadly, now she knew it was out of her reach too. No matter what she said or didn't say, she'd never make him see the value of the property. Her dear friends Austin and Evelyn had done their best to carry on the family legacy Evan and Emma Chandler had started. If Matthew Chandler didn't care about ending that family connection, what could she do?

CHAPTER 8

$\mathcal{L}$ ogan rejoined Matthew in the study and grinned. "Man, your agent is a looker."

"Yeah, I guess." Matthew shrugged and stared at the computer screen. "She does have nice eyes."

"I noticed that." Logan plopped back on the couch.

"Okay, so she's nice looking. So what?" Matthew had had his fill of Miss Real Estate Agent. He was tired of feeling like a schoolboy being scolded for talking in class. She would never forgive him for selling the house.

Not that he really cared.

Logan held up both hands in surrender. "You okay? Not like you to be so edgy."

"Sorry, my man." Matthew stared at his computer again. "That woman just gets under my skin." He paused. "Let's talk about the Grant account."

"Shoot." Logan took the last gulp of his soda and threw the can toward the corner trash. "Good shot."

Matthew ignored him. "Too much competition out there. We've got to find a way to stay on his radar." Matthew pulled another pain pill from the middle desk drawer and downed it with water. He'd prefer a beer right now, but these meds were running his life. "He's out of town right now but I think there's more to it. What do you think is the hold up?"

"Grant is researching other companies?"

Matthew reeled his attention back in. Sometimes his head could still be loopy ... "Could be. But he seemed very interested in us. " Matthew scribbled that on a yellow legal pad anyway.

"Yeah, he did."

"Other ideas?"

"He's still shopping around?"

"Maybe. But Stacy told me yesterday that Grant's assistant told her he's about ready to make his choice." Matthew scribbled another note.

Logan sat still. "Could someone be influencing him to not sign with us?"

"Like who? The guy would have to be crazy. No one services their accounts like you and I do."

"Someone in our office? You have to admit it's a sweet deal. Who do we know who would steal it right out from under our noses?"

"Tom has never been too friendly." Matthew scribbled a reminder to ask Stacy."He does that sullen thing every time we score a new client."

"Maybe. But I don't see him putting the work into a proposal like we did. And he has his own top paying clients."

"Yeah, true." Matthew's phone dinged. He picked it up and looked at the screen. "Hey, for once it's not Eva. In fact, now that I think about it, I haven't heard from her in a few days."

"It's about time. Maybe she's finally gotten the message that you're not interested."

"I can only hope." Matthew powered off his phone. "I'll send Stacy an e-mail tomorrow about Grant. She hates office gossip as much as we do, but somehow she usually knows the scuttlebutt."

"And is there a Plan B if Stacy can't help?"

"I'll ask a couple of the guys in the office that we trust to keep their eyes and ears open. There's usually enough rumor mill going on around there to find out what's going on."

Matthew twirled the pen in his hand. He was so sick of this. He and Logan needed to be in the office. And now Logan was stuck here being his nursemaid. He'd had enough – he reached for his wallet on the desk corner and pulled out his credit card.

Logan's eyes went wide. "What are you doing?"

"Booking a flight home. I can't stand this anymore."

Logan stood and walked to the edge of the desk. "You know that's a bad idea, buddy."

"But it's what I need to do. We can't lose this account." He pulled up the airline website.

"What you need is a good night's sleep." Logan put his hand on Matthew's shoulder. "We'll talk to Stacy in the morning and come up with a plan."

Matthew sagged. "I hate it when you're right. I'm just going crazy here." He adjusted the pillow under his knee. Would the aching ever go away?

"No doubt. But I'm here to help you follow the doctor's orders. And to get better." Logan motioned to put the credit card back in the wallet. "Easy for me to say, but time and patience, my friend."

Matthew slid the card back in his wallet and slammed it on the desk. "Yeah, yeah. It's getting late. I'm going to bed."

Matthew couldn't believe how hard it was to get around in this bulky cast. By his third night home, he was fed up with sleeping on the couch. He needed good sleep in a firm bed. He stood at the bottom step and stared up at the fourteen narrow stairs. Why were they taunting him? He could do this.

He grabbed the railing and raised his casted leg up on the first step. Thank goodness Logan had tightened the spindles. He balanced and then raised his left foot. One down, thirteen to go.

Logan came around the corner from the hallway. "Here, let me help you."

"Nah, I'm gonna try this on my own." Matthew made it to the second step and then the third.

Logan stood at the bottom."Making great progress."

"I don't need a cheerleader." On the fifth step now.

"I'll be in the study." Logan backed away and moved down the hall. "Call me if I need to come pick you up."

"Yeah, I'm sure you'll know if I fall."

Tenth step. He was sweating like he'd just finished a lively game of racquetball. Crazy that a few steps could do that to him. Eleven. Twelve. Thirteen.

Finally he was at the top. Except for a dire emergency, he wouldn't be going back down before morning. He heard the doorbell ring and the creaking floor as Logan went to answer the door. No idea who that could be. He'd ask later.

Matthew hobbled down the hallway and stopped at the first doorway, to the room he'd been sleeping in since arriving the week before. His dress clothes from a meeting last week were still strewn over a chair. He'd deal with that tomorrow. He sat on the bed and maneuvered his leg up on the mattress. Right now he needed a good sleep.

Amelia knocked on the heavy wooden door. How had Keri convinced her to do this? She already knew the answer. Keri had been talking her into things since they were teenagers, and most of them had to do with men. She started to knock again when Logan opened the door.

Amelia handed him a square pan covered in foil. Keri stood on the porch beside her, grinning. "We wanted to drop this off.

"Thanks." Logan raised one eyebrow in question.

"Oh, it's a lasagna. Just made it today," Keri told him. She shook her red hair back over her shoulders. "And my name is Keri."

"I'm Logan. Nice to meet you." Logan stepped back into the hallway. "Want to come in? Matt just went up to bed."

Amelia eyed the stairs. "He made it all the way up by himself?"

"Yep. Took him a while. Not being able to get around is making him nuts. But he made it." Logan led them to the parlor.

"I just love this old house." Keri sighed. "They don't make 'em like this anymore."

"No, they sure don't." Amelia didn't want to go there. The tears were still too close.

"So, you're visiting?" Keri asked.

"Yep. I work with Matt in New York and we're racquetball partners. I keep him straight." Logan shot the girls a toothy grin.

"Have any pull with him regarding the sale of this house?" Amelia said.

"None. He's dead set on selling." Logan paused. "I have to admit, though, after being here for a few days, this house has a certain draw."

"You seem very intuitive. Maybe you can convince him not to sell," Keri said.

"I highly doubt it. When Matt makes his mind up to do something..."

Amelia heard a deep voice from the upstairs hallway.

Logan stepped into the hallway. "Coming." He turned toward Amelia and Keri. "Guess I better wrap this up, ladies. Nice meeting you. And thanks for tomorrow's dinner."

As Amelia and Keri headed toward the front door, Amelia looked back at the stairs. Matthew stood on the top landing, hair standing on end and dressed in pajama bottoms with the right pant leg cut out. The heavy cast replaced it.

Amelia hesitated. Should she acknowledge him? The scowl on his face made the decision for her. "Good night." She continued out the door, Keri following.

Logan closed the heavy door after the ladies exited and looked up the staircase at Matthew. "Need something?"

"Thought I heard voices."

"Amelia and her friend Keri dropped off a pan of lasagna."

"Oh."

"That's it? Just oh? I guess I'm a more gracious host." Logan started up the stairs.

"Nice of them. Wonder what they wanted?"

"Now you sound like me. Too suspicious."

"Yeah, I guess I do." Matthew turned and hobbled back to the bedroom.

Amelia kept in step with Keri. The weather had warmed enough to walk to Rose Haven. They were within a block of returning to Keri's.

"I'm surprised you talked me into going over there."

Keri winked. "Well, neither one of them bite."

"No, they don't." Amelia pulled her wrap tighter when a cold gust of wind came up. Maybe her suggestion to walk hadn't been such a great idea.

"What if it's not him personally, but his plans to sell the house. The place that you've loved most of your life."

"Yeah, that's true. Maybe." Amelia held the screen door open while Keri unlocked the front door. "I just can't let that house go without a fight."

"Yeah, I know. Remember when we were ten and you always wanted to play dress-up in the attic?"

"I haven't thought about that in years." She followed Keri into the house. "I loved that old bridal gown and veil that we found up there. I always wanted to walk down the grand staircase of Rose Haven and into the arms of my prince charming."

"Life sure didn't turn out the way we imagined back then." Keri flipped on the kitchen light. "Up for a cup of tea?"

"Sure." Amelia slid into a dining chair. "I thought it was going to turn out that way with Brian."

Keri glanced up from poking buttons on the microwave, eyes drooping.

"He really was the love of your life, wasn't he? I don't know how you survived when he died."

Amelia shrugged. She wasn't sure she had. Keri touched her hand.

"Sad, sad times. I'm so glad you made it." She pulled two ceramic mugs of hot water from the microwave when it dinged.

"If it hadn't been for you and my mom...." Amelia dunked a tea bag into the boiling water. "And God. He really got me through the worst nights."

"Yeah, He's like that."

"So will you ever marry?" Amelia pulled the tea bag from her cup and sipped it.

"I don't know." Keri leaned back in her chair. "Will you?"

"Guess it depends if I meet the right guy." Amelia bit into a cookie from the plate Keri set on the table.

"Yeah, me too. I'm pretty happy right now. The catering business is booming. Have a great church. And great friends. What more could I ask for?"

"I saw how you looked at Logan tonight." Amelia wiped the crumbs from her face with a napkin and drained her teacup.

Keri rolled her eyes. "You've got to be kidding."

"You have to admit he's a nice looking guy. And probably around your age." Amelia raised an eyebrow.

"I'll give you that. But what about the fact that he lives in New York? That's not exactly commuting distance." Keri took a sip of her tea. "Besides, I don't even know him."

"True." Amelia stood to put her empty cup in the sink.

"What about Matthew Chandler? I notice you don't even call him by his first name."

Amelia turned to look at her friend. "Nope. Better to keep it all business."

"He's nice looking too."

"Really? I hadn't noticed. Probably cause I'm usually steaming every time I leave an encounter with him."

She couldn't shake off the negative feelings for Mr. Chandler. It wasn't like her to get worked up about not liking someone but that man really got under her skin.

CHAPTER 9

$\mathcal{M}$atthew disconnected the call. He knew his mom meant well but she lived just a little too close right now. New York had always been a nice, safe distance away. She'd called to announce that she and Pete would be arriving tomorrow to spend a few days. Great. Just what he needed. He could deal with his mom's great cooking. And could ignore her constant chatter.

But Pete was another story. Loud and obnoxious barely described the man. Thank goodness Logan ran interference for him in that relationship. And was good at it.

Matthew popped another pain pill and washed it down with cold coffee. This huge house was closing in on him. He was counting the days until he returned to New York. The time couldn't pass quick enough.

"Well, which is it?"

Matthew looked up to see Logan standing in the study door dressed in jeans, a tee shirt and ball cap, staring at him.

He tried to focus despite the throbbing in his leg. "Huh? Sorry, you talking to me?"

"You do that a lot lately."

"Blame it on the pain meds. What were you asking?"

"Want to have lunch here or in town?"

Matthew considered the options. Crutches and finding a place to prop up his leg were a chore. But he was suffocating in this place ...

"Let's go out."

"You got it. I'll be ready in five minutes."

Matthew hobbled to the corner and balanced on his crutches. He was finally getting the hang of these contraptions. But he couldn't wait to drive again. He followed Logan out the door.

"Good thing you rented an SUV with leg room." He looked down at the plaster thing on his leg. "I'd never fit in a car with this monstrosity."

Logan started the vehicle and pulled through the circular drive. "You okay with the Bluebird?"

"Yeah, that's fine. It's become our regular hang out." Matthew adjusted his sunglasses. "My mom and Pete are coming tomorrow to stay for a few days."

"Oh." Logan turned onto Main Street. "Maybe it's time for me to leave."

"Not a chance. I love my mom, but she can drive me batty. And you know how it is with Pete."

Logan nodded. "Well, I'm here until Friday then." He stopped in front of the cafe. "Can you manage from here?"

Matthew scanned the parking options. The first empty space was halfway down the block. "Yeah." He hated feeling so helpless. He opened the door and swung his right leg out on to the curb.

Logan appeared with the crutches from the back seat. "Here you go."

"Thanks, man. Don't know what I'd do without you." Matthew got his balance and started toward the door.

Logan patted his shoulder. "Always got your back. I'll go park the car."

Matthew stood outside in the sunshine and watched tourists stroll by. What he wouldn't give to do that himself. He breathed in the fresh, cold mountain air. Actually a pretty nice day for the end of January. They'd made a good choice to get out of that gloomy house.

Logan jogged from up the street and held the restaurant door open. "Ready?"

"Yep." Matthew swung his gimp leg through the door.

Logan pointed to the first empty space by the window. "Let's get that table."

No looking for seating in the back of the restaurant these days. Everything was calculated by the fewest steps possible. Matthew followed on his crutches. He sat down and propped his leg on the opposite chair.

Wanda stood at the counter, talking to a local. "Be right with you boys." Long sleeves covered both arms. No tattoos visible today.

Matthew grimaced. He'd hoped it was her day off. He didn't feel like being grilled. Especially about the house.

"Hi guys." She laid menus in front of them. "Can I start you with some drinks?"

"Black coffee." Matthew couldn't believe how much he missed coffee.

"I'll have a Coke." Logan opened his menu.

"Sure thing. Be right back." Wanda headed for the kitchen.

Matthew smiled. "No gum today."

"Noticed that. Maybe she was asked to tone it down."

"Could be." Matthew stared at the plastic menu. At least this one had been wiped clean recently.

Wanda returned with their drinks. "Two good looking guys having lunch on this beautiful sunny day. Sounds like a recipe for trouble to me." Smack, smack. So she'd found some gum after all.

"What'll it be, boys?" She stood poised with pen and paper, ready to write.

Matthew cleared his throat, trying to muffle a laugh. She had to be the most comical waitress he'd ever encountered. If she just didn't try to get into his business.

"I'm paying, so order anything you want," Logan said.

"Too bad they don't have filet mignon." He grinned. "But I'll have the Rainbow Trout with baked potato and salad."

He hadn't eaten trout since fishing with his grandfather Austin in a stream close to town so many years ago.

"Make that two."

"Got it. Your food will be out shortly." Wanda blew a bubble and headed to the kitchen.

"Guess we were wrong about the gum."

"Yep. She must have a stash in the back." Logan laughed. "Question for you." He played with the end of the straw peeking out from the top of his drink.

Matthew looked at him. "Shoot."

"Would it be so bad to keep the house? You could probably rent it out."

"Who would want to live in such a huge place?" Matthew lifted the ceramic mug of steaming black coffee to his lips.

"I can think of a blonde real estate agent who loves that place."

Matthew looked over the rim of his cup. "She's got you drinking the historical house Kool-aid too."

"Nope. I just see value in that big ole place. With some repairs it could be a beauty."

"For some other family, yes. But not for me."

Before Logan could respond, Matthew held up his hand. "End of discussion. I'm not keeping the house. Let's not even go there."

Logan shrugged. "Okay, you're the boss."

Wanda returned and plopped a plate of food in front of each of them. "Anything else I can get you?"

"The boys" both nodded their thanks. The smell of the trout had already sucked them in.

Matthew's cell phone buzzed. He wasn't expecting a call. Eva's name appeared on the screen. He sighed. One of these days he'd answer. But this wasn't the day. He ignored the vibrating. "Eva. Wonder if she'll leave a message this time."

Logan looked at him. "She's calling again?"

"Yep, every few days. The last voice mail about sent me over the edge. She seems to think we're getting back together when I return to New York."

"I keep telling you, she still has the hots for you."

Matthew shook his head. "No way. That woman is looney tunes."

"Well, you've got a little time to figure it out. Have you bought your ticket home yet?"

Matthew grinned again. "Soon. Doctor appointment in a couple of weeks. I'm counting on clearance to travel."

"Maybe I should stay until then." Logan forked another bite of fish.

"Nah. Not necessary. My mom and Pete will help me get to the doctor appointment in Denver and then to the airport when I fly out."

"And that'll be it? Wash your hands of the house?"

"Yep, pretty much. When the property sells, the realty company can work with me online and by fax."

"I've kind of started liking this little town." Logan forked a bite of fish and devoured it. "And really good fishing by the taste of this." He finished the last bite and wiped his mouth.

"Seriously?" Matthew rolled his eyes. "You've got to be kidding."

Logan sat back in chair, arms folded. "Would make a great place to retire."

"Yeah, in about 30 years. We've got deals to seal, things to do, money to make. Don't start talking retirement on me."

"Just getting a little tired of the big city grind is all." Logan smiled. "I could get used to this slower pace."

Matthew took the last bite of his food and threw his napkin in the empty plate. "We'll finish this conversation some other time. I've got to get my leg in a more comfortable position."

Wanda appeared from the kitchen. She'd added some bright red lipstick to go with her red bandana. Reminded Matthew of a clown at the circus. She laid the ticket in front of Logan. "Anything else I can get you?"

"We're good, thanks." Logan pulled two bills from his wallet and handed them to her. "Keep the change."

Wanda nodded. "Always good to see you two. And by the way, you boys know anything about gold in the old Chandler mine?"

Matthew looked at Logan, eyebrows raised. "Nope. Hasn't been mentioned by the real estate agent. Figured it probably played out years ago."

"Well, I had a conversation last week with a surveyor that believes there's still gold in the hills around here. Made me think of your place.'

My place. In Matthew's mind those words didn't compute. It had always just been his grandparents' house. And gold? Wouldn't that be a kick in the pants? Inheriting a gold mine.

"Know how to contact this surveyor? I may give him a call this week." He managed to keep a straight face. Best to keep his emotions neutral for now.

Wanda dug in her apron pocket and pulled out a business card. "He said to call him any time."

"Thanks, I just may do that." Matthew stood and hobbled to the door, Logan following. This just might be his lucky day.

CHAPTER 10

*N*ora and Pete knocked on the front door at 10:00 the next morning. Good thing Logan had called a cleaning service. Matthew didn't want his mom to see any messes. Two employees and a full day of cleaning had the place looking decent. Well, as decent as this old house could look.

Nora stepped into the foyer and grabbed Matthew in a bear hug, leaving a waft of her signature perfume. "I'm so happy to see you."

Matthew leaned into his crutches to regain his balance. That woman had some strength.

"Good to see you too, Mom."

Matthew noticed Pete had put on a few belly pounds, and was it his imagination or was the guy's hairline receding? Before he could greet him, Pete turned to Logan.

"Hey, Logan. Thanks for flying out to help."

Logan shook Pete's hand. "Anything for my good friend." He headed toward the front door. "Let me help you get the luggage."

"An extra hand would be appreciated."

Pete opened the front door, and Logan followed him out.

Matthew ignored the snub from Pete. Suited him just fine. He sure wouldn't lose any sleep over it.

He looked at his mom. "You're only staying a few days."

"Honey, you know how women are. We need lots of stuff."

Matthew shook his head. No kidding. He could get by with the bare essentials: his laptop, business bag and a backpack.

Pete and Logan stepped back into the foyer with flowered suitcases.

"Where should we put these?" Logan asked.

"Mom, do you want to go upstairs and pick a bedroom? We have several options."

He'd already guessed she would choose the turret room, complete with Emma's antique rocker positioned in the bay window to enjoy the mountains. Nora would describe it as a romantic room with a stunning view. He knew his mother too well.

"Sure, honey. I'll go up in a minute. How you doing on these stairs?" She pointed up the first flight.

Matthew shrugged. "No big deal. Got it figured out." Now if she'd asked a week ago...

Pete and Logan headed through the front door for another load.

"Wow, you really are moving in."

Matthew leaned on his crutches. He wished he could help with the luggage. Another reason for Pete to critique him.

"We brought some groceries. Didn't know if two single guys would do much cooking."

"Good idea. Happen to bring any coffee? I could use a good cup right now, and we ran out this morning."

Nora smiled. "I know you well, son. I brought my extra Keurig and your favorite blend." Nora motioned toward the box Pete was carrying toward the kitchen. "I'll make you a cup as soon as we get unpacked."

Matthew leaned toward her for a hug. "Thanks." That might make up for Pete being here in his space.

"I'm planning a nice meal for tonight. Any friends you want to invite over?"

He hadn't been here long enough to make friends.

"No, not anyone I can think of. Don't know many people in town." And he'd like to keep it that way.

"Well, if you think of anyone, let me know. It's never too late to add an extra plate or two."

The only other people he knew were the real estate agent and her red haired friend, and that wasn't happening.

"Thanks, Mom."

Nora kissed his cheek. "Anything for my son. I want to enjoy my time with you. No telling when you'll be back in Colorado again."

"You never know." Matthew winked at her.

Matthew actually enjoyed seeing his mom in her element. She spent the afternoon in a flurry of activity, unpacking and preparing lunch for three hungry men. And he knew she loved every minute. Pete on the other hand... What a piece of work.

After eating soup, a sandwich and fruit, Matthew excused himself to the sunporch to enjoy his second cup of coffee. He looked forward to afternoon naps in the reclining rocker. He'd better enjoy it while he could. It would all change when he returned home and went back to work. His office door had a lock and he could always catch a few ZZZ's on the couch. But afternoon naps had never been on his radar. With his high energy, he'd always gone from morning to evening, even on the busiest days. Sometimes he hated the way this leg injury and especially the pain meds had slowed him down, but it did have its perks.

Seemed like he'd only been asleep for a few minutes when Matthew's eyes shot open. A loud voice was booming from the kitchen. How happy he would be when the loud mouth went home. He hobbled inside, following the aroma of roast beef and garlic.

"Smells good in here."

Nora stood at the old wood burning cook stove mashing potatoes in a huge pot. "This thing reminds me of the one my grandmother had." She wiped the sweat from her forehead with a paper towel.

"I'm surprised it still works." Matthew balanced on his crutches and watched her.

Nora nodded. "The true test will be the pot roast." She pointed to the oven.

"Sorry I can't be much help."

Matthew eased into a chair at the kitchen table and propped his casted leg on the chair across from it.

"You could cut up the salad ingredients for me."

Nora waited for a response.

"Sure."

He'd never enjoyed working in the kitchen, but he had to do something to feel useful.

Nora pulled a glass bowl from the cabinet and a knife from the drawer.

"Good thing I remembered to bring this stuff. Wasn't sure what was left in this house."

"Logan and I didn't find much when we were looking around the other day."

Nora pulled lettuce, tomatoes and cucumbers from the refrigerator and set them on the table in front of Matthew. "Think of anyone you'd like to invite tonight?"

"Nope." Matthew opened the bag of greens and dumped the contents into a bowl. "But somehow I have the feeling that you did."

"I hope you don't mind. I called and invited them while you were resting."

"Them?"

"Ruth and Amelia Richardson."

"Really?"

Why would his mother invite the real estate agent? She'd probably want to attack him with the butcher knife he was using right now if she had the chance. And who was Ruth?

Matthew looked at his mother. "Care to explain?"

"Ruth is an old friend. And Amelia is her daughter. That's all."

Somehow Matthew didn't believe her. "I think there's more to it, Mom."

Pete and Logan entered the kitchen. "Anything we can do to help?" Logan said.

"Where you guys been?"

Matthew noticed the smudges on their faces and jeans. He guessed they'd both slipped their boots off on the back porch since they stood in stocking feet. Logan seemed to bond with the guy that he himself couldn't get along with.

Logan pushed his hat back on his head. "I was showing the grounds to Pete. We found the old Chandler cemetery."

Nora stirred melted butter into the potatoes. "I'd heard that some of the Chandlers are buried on this property."

The knife Matthew held a moment earlier chopping tomatoes clattered to the tabletop. "Don't anyone start about the family legacy and why I should keep this house. I'm sick of it!"

Logan held up both hands in surrender. "We didn't say a word." He winked at Nora.

"So I hear that the real estate agent and her mother are coming to dinner." Matthew sighed.

"Sweet." Logan's eyebrows rose. "What about Amelia's friend, Keri?"

"We have plenty of food," Nora said. "Invite her if you want."

Logan pumped his fist in the air. "Yes!" He was already punching in her cell number before he left the room.

Nora turned to Pete. "Could you please bring plates, goblets and silverware from the china cabinet in the dining room. I want to wash them and set the table with the Chandler best tonight."

"Sure, honey." Pete kissed her on the cheek.

Matthew sat at the kitchen table and stirred the salad vegetables together in the bowl. Right about now he wouldn't mind escaping to the BlueBird. Even if it meant putting up with Wanda.

Logan lit the candelabra in the middle of the dining room table. The glow of the candles danced on the tray ceiling and cast a softness over the room's dark interior.

"Beautiful room in the candlelight," Nora remarked.

"Yeah, you can't see all the deterioration." Matthew smirked. He was seated in the head chair, leg propped on a cushioned stool that Logan had brought earlier from the parlor.

Nora looked at him over the top of her glasses. "I wish you'd give this place a chance."

He hated that prodding look from her. "Not you too? I've had more lectures about keeping this house than I care to remember."

"I just don't want you to make a mistake."

"Too bad I'm the last Chandler heir."

"What about John?" Logan asked. He was filling the goblets from a crystal pitcher of water.

"My father gave up his rights when he moved his business to the UK years ago." Matthew took a sip of the water Logan sat in front of him. He needed coffee. "At least that's my understanding."

Nora nodded. "John had a falling out with his father, Austin, after we were married. One day he came home and told me he was washing his hands of the Chandler family. He even wanted to change our last name. Thankfully, I talked him out of that."

Matthew leaned against the back of the chair and crossed his arms. How ridiculous. What had his father been thinking?

"After we divorced, John moved overseas. I haven't seen him in years."

Matthew was happy for his mom that she'd been able to forgive John after the pain he'd put her through. But he was not interested in going there himself. Reconciliation with a father who hadn't contacted him in twenty five years was the furthest thing from his mind.

The doorbell interrupted his thoughts.

"Must be our guests. I'll get it."

Logan disappeared through the arched doorway into the hall. Matthew smiled to himself. Logan was obviously smitten with the red head.

Logan returned a few minutes later with Amelia, Keri and a woman who looked to be in her early sixties with a sad smile. She must be Ruth.

"We're happy you could join us tonight." Nora pointed to the three prepared place settings. "Please have a seat."

Ruth was shorter than Matthew had imagined. She was a nice looking woman with short brown hair, and her daughter looked nothing like her. Matthew noticed that Ruth and Keri were smiling as they'd entered the room. But not Miss Real Estate Agent. By the look on her face, she obviously wasn't happy to be here. He nodded curtly toward her and received the same response back.

Funny, he never thought of her by her first name.

Pete entered the dining room, cheeks flushed, and stumbled over a chair. He caught himself and plopped next to Nora without a word.

Couldn't the guy stay sober one night? Matthew sniffed the

air again. Yep, definitely whiskey. Pete must have been out on the back porch with his flask.

Matthew watched his mother proudly set the serving platters on the table with the delicious food she'd prepared, face glowing. Ok, well maybe he'd try to lay aside his differences with "Amelia" tonight. His mom had gone to a lot of work and with Pete already drunk, he didn't want to cause any further scenes. He and Amelia could come to a truce. Just for tonight.

"This is a wonderful dinner, Nora. Thanks so much for inviting us." Ruth chewed a bite of meat. "I haven't eaten such a tender roast in ages."

Nora looked at Matthew and laughed. "I wasn't sure how it would turn out using the old cook stove. That thing's been around for a while."

Ruth nodded in agreement and took another bite.

Pete turned to Ruth. "So I hear you're familiar with the history of this house?" His words slightly slurred. He reached for his glass of water that would have tumbled over save Nora's quick reaction.

Nora's face reddened. Matthew wanted to choke the guy. He watched the excitement of the night drain from his mother's eyes. Now she was in survival mode with a drunk husband beside her. And of course, Pete had to bring up the thorn in Matthew's side. He'd give his next paycheck if he could escape this table.

"Yes." Ruth cleared her throat. "Actually, Amelia and I lived here when she was a little girl. I was the cook and housekeeper for Austin and Evelyn Chandler for a number of years after my husband passed away."

Matthew felt like someone had hit him with a two by four. Now all of Amelia's wacky actions and comments made sense. She had a deep emotional attachment to this house.

He felt like a jerk.

CHAPTER 11

*M*atthew raised an eyebrow at Amelia, seated to his left. Probably a strategic move by his mother. "So you grew up in this house?"

Amelia smoothed her napkin, obviously trying not to make eye contact. "Yes, I did."

"That explains a lot."

Maybe Logan had been right about those sapphire blue eyes. Captivating.

"I doubt we'll ever agree about this house," Amelia said with a pleased smile. "But I'd love to show you through my eyes."

Matthew searched her face for signs of sarcasm but didn't see any, and there was none dripping from her voice. He gave her a half grin. "Tell you what. Let's call a truce. And we'll agree to disagree. I'd like to see the house you know and love."

He was surprised when she pulled a tissue from her pocket and swiped at her cheek.

"Allergies." Amelia blew her nose.

Yeah, right. Matthew repositioned his aching leg. "Don't you think it's time to get past the formal business names? Mind if I call you Amelia?"

"Not at all. Matthew."

Saturday morning Matthew answered his cell, his voice thick
with sleep. He grabbed a tissue from the bedside table and
wiped some drool from the corner of his mouth. Good thing
whoever it was couldn't see him right now.

"Good morning."

Checking the clock next to him, he couldn't believe he'd
slept until after 9 a.m. Never happened.

Amelia's voice came across the line. "Were you serious about
seeing the house from my view?"

Too perky for him this morning. "Yeah. I am. How about
tomorrow afternoon? My mom and Pete are leaving in the
morning." Thank goodness. They were both getting on his last
nerve.

"About 2 p.m. would work for me."

"Perfect. Let's start in the attic. I want to see what kind of
treasures my ancestors left for me." Could be a big haul up there.

"See you then."

Matthew disconnected. He could see the frown on Amelia's
face at the mention of selling the Chandler antiques. Well, it was
a huge step that he'd even mentioned exploring the house at all.

He lay back on the bed, hands intertwined behind his head,
and stared at the tray ceiling. The bright Colorado sunshine
filtered through the lace curtains, filling the room. A memory
flittered of a little girl he'd played with up in the attic so many
years ago. Could it have been Amelia?

Matthew woke the next afternoon from an hour nap in the
sunroom and started for Evan's study when he heard a knock.

Logan was out for a while and his mom and Pete had left earlier. It was a relief to be on his own.

"Coming," he called out.

The tapping sound of the crutches echoed on the hard wood floor as he moved down the hallway. When he opened the door, Amelia stood on the porch, smoothing the wrinkles from her peach colored tunic top.

"Lovely afternoon, isn't it?"

She stepped into the vestibule dressed in leggings and boots, obviously ready to dodge the layers of cobwebs and dirt upstairs.

A little fancy for exploring an attic. Matthew looked down at his own NY t-shirt and sweats, one leg cut away to accommodate the cast. No big deal, that was her call. He led the way to the bottom of the steps.

"How long since you've been to the top floor?" he said.

"Years. I doubt anyone else has either. As Austin and Evelyn aged, they couldn't manage the climb."

He wasn't sure if he could either.

He motioned up the steep staircase. "You first. I'm a little slower."

Amelia looked at his casted leg and then up the fourteen stairs. "You sure you're up for this?"

"Yeah. I'm good."

Even if he wasn't, he wasn't about to say so. He could see the doubt in her eyes.

Amelia walked up the first set of steps. Matthew took a step and stopped to watch her. Had to admit, she had a nice figure. But he didn't want to get distracted. He focused on the step in front of him and then the next.

Amelia waited for him on the second floor landing. Bright light streamed through the stained glass window, creating a pattern on the worn hardwood.

Matthew took one step at a time, pausing before the next

one. He could see her covering her mouth, her eyes twinkling. She was laughing at him.

Out of breath, Matthew joined her, trying to breathe normally. "The altitude . . ."

"Gets to a lot of people." Amelia gave him an amused look.

"Emma sure loved stained glass, didn't she?" He pointed to the window above them.

"Austin told me once that Evan looked at those windows as a sign of prestige. So he spared no expense installing as many Tiffany windows as Emma wanted. Each window has a unique pattern of roses, and no two windows in this house are the same."

Matthew started up the next set of steps. Only five. This would be a piece of cake. He pointed to a rotting board with his left crutch. "Careful. Looks like this step is in bad shape."

"Here, let me help you."

He pulled away. "Since that repairman's estimate was so outrageous, maybe Logan would have time to look at this staircase before he leaves."

Amelia looked at him, brows knit together.

"Logan started out as a carpenter, like his Dad. But then he realized he loved numbers more and switched to the financial world. Too bad he's not staying longer. He could help get the house ready to sell."

Amelia nodded.

Mathew noticed the grimace on her face. He seemed to do that to her.

He climbed the last two steps and stopped on the third floor landing. Water spots marked the wood floors.

"Looks like some damage up here too." He pointed to the water stains on the ceiling. "I'll need to have the roof checked soon."

Amelia stepped onto the landing beside Matthew. "If you

want another estimate, I can text you some names and phone numbers."

Matthew's stomach clenched. The house was proving to be a money pit.

Amelia stood at the palladium window that looked over the property and in the distance toward the mountains. "Look at the beautiful view."

"Should be a good selling feature." Matthew pointed to a set of steps at the far corner of the landing. "Must be the staircase that comes up from the kitchen."

Amelia nodded and pulled a tissue from her pocket to blow her nose. "Allergies are kicking up again."

Matthew moved toward a closed door and turned the knob. A musty odor escaped the room when he stepped inside, Amelia close behind. The large area was filled from wall to wall, covered with cobwebs and thick dust. Dingy white draping covered undistinguishable objects in one corner.

"This will be a job."

Matthew balanced on one crutch and reached for the chain hanging from the ceiling. A dim bulb spread sparse light. He waved his hand in front of his face. The smell was overwhelming.

"I'm guessing this room's been closed up for years."

Amelia cringed. "I hope we don't find any mice."

"Who knows what we'll find up here." Matthew peered at her. "Are you sure you're up for it?"

Amelia squared her shoulders. "Yep, I've wanted to do this for a long time. Let's get started."

"How about this corner first?"

Matthew left a trail of dusty footprints on the weathered hardwood floor. He pulled a dustcover off a tall object. A five drawer tallboy chest.

"This is in good condition. Probably can get a fair price for it."

"Or place it in one of the bedrooms to be enjoyed by family," Amelia offered.

Matthew shrugged and pulled a cover from a painting of a small town settled at the foot of a mountain. Probably Chandler Springs.

"Not my style. This can go to the auction too."

Amelia winced. She scribbled a note on the legal pad she'd brought along. "How about this cedar chest? Back in the day, we called it a hope chest."

"Really? Why?"

"Not sure. I guess young girls started collecting their dowry, 'hoping' to get married."

Matthew grinned. "Sure glad I'm a guy. Couldn't imagine...."

A stale odor mingled with the smell of moth balls escaped when he lifted the chest lid. Sheets of yellowed tissue paper filled the top of the trunk. Matthew handed them one by one to Amelia. She stacked them carefully on a nearby chair.

Next he pulled out a box. He opened the lid and held up a garment. White silk, it looked like, unfurled to the floor. Huh, a wedding gown. There was enough lace on it to clothe three brides.

"Beautiful. I think Emma wore this when she married Evan." Amelia touched the lace-gathered throat. "Too bad it's not been better preserved. Someone in the family may want to wear it someday."

Matthew shot her a look. "Not sure who that would be." He frowned and started to toss the gown aside. "Probably not in good enough shape to sell."

Amelia held out her hand. "Would you mind if I held onto it? I have a friend in town who restores vintage clothing. I'd love to see what she could do with it." Amelia smoothed the dress against her and then scratched a note on the legal pad. "By the lace neckline, the mutton sleeves, the high waist, I would guess the 1890's. That would fit the timeframe of Evan and Emma's marriage."

Matthew continued digging in the cedar chest. "Sure ... you can have it. I'll never have any use for it." Definitely not. He held up a bag filled with yellowed lace. "You can have this too."

Amelia opened the bag. She shook it out carefully and smiled at it, as if it were alive. "The matching veil," she said.

You could have fooled him. It looked like a ball of wrinkled rags.

Matthew dug to the bottom of the chest. "I think that's about it." His hand touched something hard and square. "Oh wait. What's this?"

He pulled out a small box. The top was decorated with baby angels holding pink lambs. He lifted the lid. A folded dress for an infant. He read the attached note out loud.

"Our dear daughter, Emily Victoria. Born September 28, 1905. Went to be with Jesus on October 17, 1905." Matthew looked at Amelia. "This attic is full of surprises."

He couldn't help but notice Amelia swiping at a tear. Allergies again? He wasn't buying it this time.

"How sad. I didn't realize Evan and Emma lost a baby. And strange Austin never mentioned her." She made a note. "I will have to do more research."

Why she would want to know was beyond him. It was his family, and he didn't even want to know.

Matthew handed her the box. "Do you want to take this with you?"

"Yes, I'd love to." She laid it by her growing pile of treasures. "Let's see what else we can find."

Matthew hobbled to the other corner of the room and lifted a drape. A life size rocking horse stared back at him.

Amelia touched the real horse hair mane. "I rode this horse when I was a kid. I'd sneak up here and rock and rock and pretend my dad was still alive. One day Austin found me.

Without scolding, he told me there were cookies and milk waiting for me in the kitchen. After that, the attic door was locked."

"For your own protection?"

"Never found out for sure. Probably my mom's choice. I couldn't be breaking any valuable Chandler antiques." Amelia pointed to a stack of boxes and containers in the opposite corner of the room. A dusty angel sat perched on top of the boxes. "Too bad it's been uncovered for so long. I wonder if it can be salvaged."

She tiptoed over, apparently watching for mice. Matthew followed her.

"I remember some of the beautiful Victorian Christmas decorations Austin and Evelyn used every year. The house was enchanting during the holiday season."

"Mmmhmmm."

Matthew barely noticed her comment as he inspected the note on the back of a painting leaning against the same wall.

"This could be valuable. I wonder if there's an art dealer in town."

He looked over at Amelia. The look on her face said it all, which was 'why are you such an unfeeling cad?'

"Sorry, I gotta go. I just remembered an appointment."

She turned and left the room, dust flying.

Matthew heard the sound of her boots on the stairs and then the front door slam.

Well that ended well.

Not.

He looked around the full room. They'd have to try for another day. He pulled the light string and started for the door in the dim light when a memory slammed him in the face.

He was ten years old, huddled in a dirty corner of this very room. Tears streamed down his face. His knees were pulled to his chest. The loneliness threatened to suck the air out of him.

His dad didn't want him.

He'd buried the memory so long ago. For a moment, a feeling of sadness and abandonment washed over him. In his usual way, he shook it off. He closed the door behind him. Those memories weren't going with him today.

Amelia stood in the yard and stared at the house. Lost in the memories, she didn't know how long she'd been standing there. Obviously her pep talks to herself about letting this house go weren't working.

Matthew Chandler's uncaring attitude wound her up like piano wire. Could he have been more of a jerk?

She punched her fists into the pockets of her parka. Yeah, she was angry – and not just at him. She felt like an idiot for letting him get to her.

She started toward her car and then remembered his casted leg. What if he fell? She hesitated. No, he didn't deserve that, no matter how he'd treated her.

She stomped up the sidewalk and onto the front porch. Thank goodness she hadn't locked the front door behind her earlier.

"Hello?"

Amelia looked up the steep stairs. Matthew stood on the second floor landing, a smirk on his face.

"I thought I should come back and check on you."

Matthew looked down at her. "Really? Why?"

"Just to make sure you got back down the stairs okay."

Matthew shrugged. "Oh yeah, why shouldn't I? No big deal."

Amelia walked half way up the staircase as he started coming down. "Here, let me help you."

"Not necess...."

Matthew set his good foot on the next step, but his heel

slipped on the slick wood. The crutches threatened to fly out of his hand.

Amelia grabbed his arm to balance him. Her eyes narrowed. "Why are men so obstinate?"

"Beats me. That's just the way we're wired." He grinned at her and bumbled down the next step. "I got it. Thanks. Short meeting, huh?"

"No meeting. I just had to get out of there."

"Oh. I see."

But did he really see? She doubted it. He had no idea what she was going through. Better to distance herself from him. And from the memories of this house.

CHAPTER 12

The whiff of fresh baked banana muffins plastered a smile on Amelia's face as she stepped into the kitchen, Harley close at her heels. "Smells wonderful, Mom."

"Good morning. Just pulled a dozen from the oven. Want a sample?"

"I'm running late. I'll take one for the road."

Ruth laid a muffin on a napkin and handed it to her.

Amelia balanced the delicious smelling treat in one hand and slung her purse over her shoulder. "Time got away from me this morning. Could you let Harley out?"

Ruth set the other muffins on a rack to cool. "Sure. Going to Denver today?"

"Yeah, big meeting. Riding with some of the other agents so I can catch up on paperwork during the commute."

Amelia picked up her business bag and threw the long strap over her free shoulder. Who needed a workout at the gym after carrying this stuff around all day?

"You're just too busy."

Amelia ignored her mother's comment, pinched a bite of the

banana muffin and popped it in her mouth. "Mmmm... seriously, Mom. You need to sell these."

The fine lines crinkled around Ruth's eyes. "Already have a couple of orders for the week."

"You know, selling your baked goods would be a great little business for you. Keep you out of trouble and give you a little cash." Amelia kissed her on the cheek and headed toward the front door. "Oh, and I have a showing at the Chandler's tomorrow afternoon."

Ruth peered at her daughter over the top of her glasses. "I'm sure you'll enjoy seeing Matthew."

Amelia's face puckered like a third grader being teased on the school yard. She put up her hand. "Oh, stop, Mom. That man makes me want to chew glass."

"Interesting that every time I mention his name, you blush."

"Yeah, yeah. Whatever. Gotta go. Love you."

"Love you too, honey. Have a good day."

Amelia patted Harley on the head and stepped into the bright sunshine. Not bad for a February day. There wasn't a cloud in the sky. She said a quick prayer the weather would hold today for the commute to Denver. She'd rather not get stranded in an un-forecasted snowstorm somewhere along the way.

She stepped into her car and drove three blocks to her office. Her mother's words played in her head about Matthew. No way. She hadn't gotten his comments in the attic out of her head or his obvious resistance to her help on the stairs. Besides, they had nothing in common. He was a client and nothing more. And she intended to keep it that way.

Matthew settled into Evan's study, staring at his computer. Sweet. Three e-mails from Stacy with news about prospective clients. He and Logan would be busy in the coming months. Just the way he liked it. And he was keeping positive thoughts about nailing the Grant account.

Matthew drained the last drop from his coffee mug. Not like his New York brew but he'd learned to tolerate it until he could get back home. Another cup sounded good. He'd better get used to waiting on himself since Logan was leaving tomorrow. He swung his casted leg to the floor and hobbled out of the study into the long hallway toward the kitchen.

Halfway down the hall, Matthew stopped at the arched dining room doorway. The huge oval table with twelve matching chairs, china hutch and sideboard filled the room. From the look of things, not much had changed since Evan and Emma's day. He could imagine the Sunday dinners they'd enjoyed here with their children. Much different than his child-hood memories of popping a frozen meal in the microwave and then eating on a tray in front of the TV after his mother came home exhausted from a long day at work.

He had to admit the dinner party here the other night wasn't half bad. Could he make memories of his own in this house? Probably. But that wasn't on his radar at the moment.

Shaking away the thoughts, Matthew focused on the day's agenda. After he finished with work e-mails and a phone conference, he hoped Logan would help him clean the house for the showing later. Amelia had mentioned the couple were looking a second time and seemed very interested. He had to admit she knew her stuff and he trusted her instincts. He could only hope for a contract on the house soon.

The next day Amelia stopped at home for a late lunch and then headed to Rose Haven to meet her clients at 4 p.m. Thoughts of sabotaging the appointment ran through her mind. Tell them the roof leaked. Tell them the electrical wiring was so ancient, the house could burn to the ground. Tell them the place was haunted. She laughed out loud. Yeah, right.

A silver Escalade sat in the circular drive when she pulled up. Wonderful. Her clients were on time. And wealthy, judging from their car. She half expected a contract before the day was over.

She parked behind their vehicle and stepped out of her SUV. The middle-aged couple sat in the porch wicker rockers, deep in discussion, like they already owned the place.

"Hello." Amelia pulled the lock box key from her purse. She hoped Matthew had thought to clean up a bit. He could be rather messy. She unlocked the door and allowed Mr. and Mrs. Murray to go in first.

"Nice to see you again. It's a lovely day." Mrs. Murray brushed away some stray hairs falling from her blonde updo. "I just love this house," she commented to her husband as she stepped inside the vestibule.

Mr. Murray winked at Amelia. "That's all I've heard since our showing last week." He removed his black fedora. "Do you mind?" He motioned to the coat rack in the corner and pulled off his overcoat before she could reply.

"Not at all. Make yourself at home."

Amelia continued down the hall. Feeling comfortable here was a good sign. If the house had to sell, she wouldn't mind it being owned by this nice couple.

Amelia ushered the Murrays into the study. She was startled to see Matthew sitting at Evan's desk, leg propped up on a chair. "Oh, so you are here."

"Yep, don't mind me. You can shut the door if you want." Matthew never took his eyes off the computer screen.

Amelia followed the couple back into the hallway and pulled the pocket doors closed. That man drove her crazy. "Take a look around. And let me know if you have any questions."

"We will. Thank you." Mrs. Murray handed paint samples to her husband that she'd pulled out of her purse.

Amelia stepped into the parlor to give them privacy. She couldn't help but overhear Mr. Murray saying, "You know, Barbara, this place could use some brightening up. What if we had all the wood on the staircase painted white?"

"Oh, I love the idea. And this purple would be a lovely color for this wall."

Amelia felt sick. No, please don't change the interior of this house. She took a deep sigh and reminded herself for the hundredth time those decisions were out of her hands.

Thirty minutes later, Matthew could hear voices in the hallway. Great. He hoped lots of discussion would mean a full price offer. He shifted his aching leg. He couldn't wait for his doctor appointment tomorrow and totally expected to be released to fly home next week.

Looking at the wall of floor-to-ceiling bookcases behind Evan's desk, he pulled a large binder off the shelf to prop up his foot. A small leather book wedged behind the notebook caught his eye.

He pulled it out and flipped to the first page. Smooth, neat penmanship identified the journal as Evan Chandler's. Matthew studied it for a moment. He opened the top desk drawer and threw the book into the back. Maybe he'd read it some other time. Or give it to Amelia since she loved the Chandlers so much.

Matthew sank into the desk chair he was going to be occupying for ANOTHER three weeks - according to his doctor. He stabbed his fingers at the computer keys. He'd gone to the appointment that morning ready to say good-bye to the doctor, the cast and this suffocating town. And what had he gotten? He scowled at the screen, more at the echo of his doctor's words than at anything he was seeing there.

"We're not there yet, Matthew. If you try to travel with this leg you'll be taking a risk with that clot. Let's revisit this in say, three weeks."

If Matthew could have stomped out of there, he would have. But he couldn't stomp. Couldn't kick. And couldn't go back to New York where he belonged.

Logan popped his head through the study door. "Can I get you anything?"

Matthew frowned. "Yeah, a plane ticket to New York."

"That stinks. Can't believe your doctor wouldn't release you yet."

Matthew raked his hands through his hair. "The walls are closing in, Logan. I have to get out of this house."

He stood for a moment, trying to gain his balance on the walking cast. At least one good thing had happened today.

Logan picked up the dirty coffee mug and glass from the desk. "Seriously, Matt. I should stay another week."

"Nah, we need you back in the office. Like yesterday." Matthew grabbed the knee scooter parked next to the desk. He'd balked about it at first but had to admit it was way better than crutches. He hoped to never see those torturous things again.

"Don't forget to elevate your leg tonight." Logan stepped into the hallway, carrying the tray of dishes to the kitchen.

"Yes, Mother. And I already took my medicine." Matthew followed him on the scooter down the hall.

"Good boy." Logan filled the sink with hot water and soap. "I'm going to miss bossing you around."

"Right back at ya." Matthew poured a mug of coffee and

maneuvered with one hand to the table. "How was your date last night with Keri?"

"Not really a date." Logan poured his own cup and sat down at the table. "We're just friends."

"Yeah, yeah. I've heard that before." Matthew drained his drink. He'd better stop for the night. It was getting late. "Can't believe I have a blood clot. I thought that was for old people."

Logan shrugged. "Can happen to anyone. You gotta take care of yourself. I worry a little about you alone in this big ole' house."

"My mom wants to come for another visit this weekend." Matthew stood. "I think she was happy I'm not going back to New York yet."

"What about Pete?" Logan stacked the dirty dishes from the table into the sink of bubbles and started washing them. "I know you'll miss seeing him."

"Yeah, right." Matthew balanced his knee on the scooter and picked up the towel to dry. "He's going to a family reunion, but Mom didn't want to go. Said she'd rather visit me."

"Smart lady." Logan finished the last glass and pulled the sink stopper. "What is it with you and Pete? I've never quite understood all that."

Matthew stopped drying the coffee mug in his hand and looked at his friend. "For starters, he's too loud and obnoxious. And a know-it-all. He rubs me the wrong way. I prefer to ignore him."

"He does treat your mom well." Logan opened the silverware drawer.

"Yeah, but is it an act around us? What about when they're alone?" Matthew set the last clean coffee mug on the shelf. "I don't trust him. Especially when he's had a few."

"True." Logan grabbed the broom from the pantry and started sweeping the floor. "Maybe you should talk to her while you're alone this weekend."

"Yeah, maybe." Matthew wheeled over to a kitchen chair and plopped into it. "Would you look at us? We're like a couple of housewives in here. What the heck happened to my life?"

"Don't worry... I won't tell the guys at work."

"Thanks. And I won't tell them about the funny maid's uniform you fancy." Matthew threw his friend a fake grin. Without thinking, he started arranging the sugar dish and salt and pepper shakers in the middle of the table. Yep, he was losing it. Time to change the subject. "Hey, guess what I found today."

"A million dollars stashed in the back of Evan's desk?" Logan grinned.

"I wish. I'll show you." Matthew tried to stand but didn't have the strength in his bum leg. He fell back against the chair.

"Maybe you should consider that bone stimulator thing the doctor mentioned," Logan said.

"Yeah. Anything to get this leg back in shape so I can get home." Matthew held onto the table and pulled up to a standing position. His leg balanced on the scooter, he took off through the kitchen, down the hall and headed toward the study.

Logan followed him. "This will get easier."

"Yeah, I have to believe that to keep my sanity."

"Speaking of going insane, you haven't mentioned Eva lately. She still texting you?"

"Mysteriously that stopped a few days ago. Maybe she has her sights on some other poor sap. You'll have to get the scoop when you get back to work."

"Sure." Logan moved a stack of folders so he could perch on the edge of the desk.

Matthew settled into Evan's chair and dug into the back of the desk drawer. He pulled out the leather journal.

"Apparently it was written by the one and only Evan Chandler."

Logan whistled. "Great find, Matt." He picked it up. "Do you mind?"

Matthew shrugged. "Help yourself."

Logan turned to the first page. "Wouldn't it have been cool to see this house when it was first built? Can you imagine how beautiful it was?"

Matthew shrugged again. "Yeah, sure."

Logan gritted his teeth. "We see eye to eye on a lot of things in life, but this house isn't one of them."

"Amelia and I had the very same discussion the other day. It's just one point we'll have to agree to disagree on."

There was no way he'd ever love this house the way Amelia did.

CHAPTER 13

The next morning Matthew sat in Evan's study, his casted leg propped on a pillow. The clock on the edge of the mahogany desk taunted him. He shifted his weight to ease the throbbing. It seemed like torture to wait another hour before taking a pain pill. Couldn't those little clock hands move faster? He hated how such a small, inanimate object ran his life these days.

The screen lit on his cell phone. Good. He needed a distraction. He picked up his phone. A text from Eva. She needed to talk right now. Yeah, good luck with that. He wasn't in the mood for her nonsense. He hadn't heard from her for days. Why now?

He focused on his computer screen and ignored the text.

A few minutes later, the phone screen lit up again. *You'll want to talk to me. This is about the Grant account.*

"Logan," Matthew yelled. "Can you come here for a second?"

Logan poked his head in the doorway, dressed in jeans and a Garth Brooks t-shirt, hair still damp from his morning shower. He held up his coffee cup. "Can I get you some?"

"In a minute." Matthew held out his phone for Logan to read.

"Seriously?" Logan frowned. "We pitched that proposal after she left Canon. How does she know about it?"

"No idea." Matthew tapped his pen on the desk. "I have a bad feeling about this."

Logan set his mug on the edge of the desk. "I get heartburn anytime Eva's name is mentioned."

Matthew nodded as he punched numbers into the phone keypad. Eva answered on the first ring.

"Hello, Matthew. I knew you'd want to talk to me." Her high-pitched voice grated on his nerves like a drill hammer.

"Logan is here with me." Matthew pushed the speaker button on his phone.

"Great. I can tell you both my good news. How's Colorado treating you boys?" Eva sounded like she was talking through a tin can.

Matthew could feel the sarcasm drip through the phone. He exchanged glances with Logan. He'd like to step on her manicured toes with his casted foot right about now.

"Going great."

Matthew tried to curb his own sarcasm. No point being adversarial until he knew what she was up to. And clearly she was up to something. "What's this about the Grant deal?"

"Just wanted to let you know that I just landed my first account with Liberty Financial." Eva paused like she was counting to ten for dramatic effect. It took all the strength Matthew had not to hang up on her. Until she said, "It's with Charles Grant."

"What. What?" Matthew and Logan said at the same time.

Matthew felt his body go rigid, his head throbbing worse than his leg.

"We've developed quite a rapport. I had no doubt that I could pull it off." Another maddening pause, punctuated by a shrill laugh. "But it was so easy, it's almost embarrassing."

Matthew looked at Logan's red face. His happy-go-lucky

friend was livid. He could imagine the look on his own. This was unbelievable. Matthew cleared his throat and took control of his voice.

"Eva, you do know we've worked on that account for months."

"Sorry it was so tough for you both. Only took me a week. I knew it'd be a piece of cake when my boss introduced me to Mr. Grant at a company party."

Matthew wanted to hit something. Probably a good thing she wasn't standing in front of him. "Logan and I have some work to do. We're signing off." He hit the disconnect button before she could reply and dropped his phone on the desk.

Logan sank into the couch. "I'm speechless."

"No way. We did not just have that conversation." He'd give anything right now to hop on a plane to New York and confront her in person. His throbbing leg reminded him that wasn't happening. Man, how he hated being immobile.

"Yeah, I wish it was all a bad dream," Logan said. "But we both know Eva too well. She'll stop at nothing to get what she wants. But how could this have happened?"

"This is the worst time ever for me to be out of the office." Matthew looked at his casted leg. Probably a good thing he couldn't get up very easily. He'd be throwing things.

How ironic. The woman he'd recommended for employment at Canon Financial was now his nemesis.

Matthew sat in the sunporch listening to voice mail messages. He punched in Amelia's now familiar number. He should just put it on speed dial. She must have called while he was napping.

She answered on the first ring.

"Hey, I got your message." Matthew glanced at the clock. Had he been asleep that long?

"Thanks for returning my call. I have some news on the house."

"Great, did we get an offer?"

"Yes, you did." Silence.

Matthew could hear some hesitancy in her voice. "Okay, that's good news, right?"

"It came in $50,000 below your asking price."

"No way." Matthew rolled his eyes. Would someone really believe that he'd accept a low ball offer?

"I tried to persuade them the house was worth every penny of the listing price. But all they could see were dollar signs for repairs and upgrades."

"Yeah, tell me about it." He remembered his first walk-through.

"So, do you want to counteroffer?"

"Nope. I'm set on my asking price."

"Okay. Well, these buyers were firm too. I imagine they will walk away."

"That's fine. I'm not in a big hurry to sell." Matthew sat up a little straighter. Were the pain pills messing with his mind?

"Oh, so your plans have changed then?" Amelia's voice sounded hopeful.

"You could say that. My doc hasn't released me yet to travel. I'll be here for a few more weeks."

"Did Logan go back to New York?"

"Yep. He left this morning. I already miss the big clod." It got lonely around there. But he wasn't about to tell her that.

"Well, let me know if you need anything. Will you be around later today? I can bring the paperwork by for you to sign to reject the offer."

"Yep, I'll be here."

"I'll come by on my way home. About 5:30."

"See you then."

Matthew disconnected the call. Well, that was a first. Maybe there was hope they could have a civil conversation.

Amelia parked in the circular drive and locked her car. Matthew had actually remembered to turn the porch light on. Awesome. She could get up the porch steps without killing herself. When she knocked on the door, he opened it almost immediately.

"Thought I'd bring you some dinner." Amelia handed him a foil wrapped container. "Keri just made this roast and potatoes today."

"Smells great. Thanks. My mom left me some frozen stuff to nuke. This will be so much better." Matthew put the container in the basket on the front of his scooter. "Come on in."

Amelia smiled to herself and looked at the smaller cast on his leg propped on the knee scooter. "How's it feel to have that clunky cast off? Looks like you're getting around better."

"Yep, this was a great little invention." Matthew wheeled down the hallway. "Let's go in the dining room where you can spread out your paperwork."

Amelia stifled a giggle as she followed him down the hall. He looked like an over-sized kid on a scooter. There were only a few sheets for him to sign but she didn't object. She loved being in any room in this house.

Matthew stopped at the dining room and flipped on the light. He set the foil-wrapped container on the table.

Amelia dropped her purse in a chair and pulled the paperwork out of the business bag. "I just need your signature here." She pointed to the yellow arrow attached to the paper. "And your initials here and then here."

Matthew looked over the contract. "Was this the couple from a few days ago? Who wanted to paint the staircase and hallway?"

Amelia nodded. "Yes. They really loved the house. Especially her. Except they wanted to change everything about it. I told them you'd probably be offended by their low offer."

Matthew appeared amused. "Not offended. But not accepting it either." He scribbled his signature and then initialed and pushed the papers across the table toward her.

Amelia straightened the documents and filed them in her business bag. She would call the Murrays later with the bad news. Well, bad news for them. Actually, good news for her. So far, the house was still owned by a Chandler. She pushed her chair back from the table.

"I don't want to keep you from your dinner."

"Thanks again for bringing it. That really was thoughtful of you."

Amelia followed Matthew out of the room and into the hallway.

"Hey, would you like to stay and eat?" he said. "I imagine Keri sent plenty."

Amelia hesitated. "Okay. If you're sure." Maybe the guy wasn't a complete jerk. And besides, she always hated to leave this house.

"Yep. I'd love the company. And I can show you what I found today." Matthew paused. "My great-grandfather Evan's journal."

Amelia's heart raced. She'd heard stories about Evan's journal but long given up hope of finding it.

"Really? Can I see it?"

"Sure." Matthew led her to the study and picked up a leather bound book from the desk. "Here you go."

"What a treasure." Amelia ran her hand over the cracked cover and lifted it to her nose. Ah...she loved the smell. She could dive into it, like a bowl of chocolate. But she resisted. She wanted Matthew to know his family stories. She sensed that he needed to know.

"Where did you find it?"

"Hidden in the bookcase behind other books."

"Austin told me he'd searched for it for years." What stories this book must hold.

"Well, I guess it was meant for me to find."

"Yes, I think it was."

Could this be the great discovery that would lead Matthew to his family roots and keep him in Chandler Springs?

She could only hope.

CHAPTER 14

$\mathcal{M}$atthew crossed the behemoth boot onto his opposite knee and silently cursed it. The same way he was cursing the e-mail that stared back at him from the screen of his laptop. It was from Logan, who was not the one he wanted to swear at. It was that spiteful woman, Eva. How had she persuaded Charles Grant to sign with Liberty Financial?

He uncrossed the boot and let his foot drop to the floor. Bad idea. He winced. It seemed like the thing was never going to heal, and he had to get back to New York. Because Eva - bless her devious heart - was Grant's new consultant.

Matthew's phone chimed. It was Amelia. Good, just the distraction he needed before his blood pressure went through the roof.

"Good morning."

"Hi there. I've scheduled a showing for 1:30 today. Will that work okay in your schedule?"

"Yep. Will you be showing the house?"

"Actually, it's another realtor in my office."

Matthew twirled the pen on the desk. "Oh." He wouldn't mind Amelia getting the sales commission.

"If you can arrange it, clients are always more comfortable if the owner is not present for the showing."

"Since I'm a little more mobile, I've been thinking about looking around this property. Care to give me a tour?"

He bet she would know every each inch of Chandler land.

"Sure. I'll be over around one p.m."

"See you then."

Matthew disconnected the call. The bright sunshine streaming through the window of the study was calling his name. He had to ... needed to ... get out of this house and who better to spend time with? He made some notes on the pad in front of him about an upcoming deal he and Logan were working on. The blonde haired, blue eyed real estate lady came to mind again. He reminded himself that this was strictly business. He was leaving in a few weeks and would never see her again.

When Amelia pulled into the circular drive that afternoon, Matthew stood on the porch waiting for her. Was it his imagination? Or was her head cocked, and was there a slight smile at the corners of her mouth when she stepped from the car?

"There's a Gator in the barn. It'll make the tour easier for you over the rough terrain."

The moment was over. Matthew grimaced at the thought of not being in charge. He'd let her help him this one time. He gave her a curt nod of agreement and started down the porch steps, one at a time, the boot cast slowing him down. He'd like to throw the thing in the nearest lake.

Matthew climbed onto the Gator when Amelia pulled up. He could tell from her body language that she wanted to help. Better to back off, Lady.

Amelia shot around the side of the house into the brittle vegetation. Matthew held onto the roll bar and wondered if he should have grabbed a helmet. But he liked that she was a fearless driver, for a girl.

"What do you think of the appointment today?" he said. "Serious lookers?"

"Some people are hard to read. It's an older couple, and they seemed very interested in the listing. We'll know more after the showing."

Amelia eased the Gator next to the black iron fence that surrounded the small cemetery.

When she stopped, Matthew steadied himself on his good leg. He wasn't taking a chance of humiliating himself by falling in front of her. "So this is where my ancestors are buried."

A rusty lock hung on the gate, unclasped. After a bit of pushing and pulling, Matthew pushed the squeaky hinges open. He looked at Amelia through the fence and raised his eyebrows.

Amelia pulled a bunch of Columbines from the ground. "I've found that my life is just too busy and I have to take time to stop and smell the flowers." She lifted the blooms to her nose and inhaled their fragrance. "Beautiful."

Mental note. Remember that she likes flowers. He hobbled to the largest headstone. Engraved in the granite was: *Evan Charles Chandler, loving husband, father, Founder and Mayor of Chandler Springs, Colorado. Born 1870. Died 1955.*

Matthew pulled his ball cap off and held it in his hand. Amelia stood quietly beside him. The man he'd heard so much about. And now he'd inherited his house. The urge to fight tears surprised him. It had to be the pain meds. He never reacted this way to people he knew, much less to people he'd never met who were long dead and gone.

Matthew moved to the next headstone and read out loud. *"Emma Jane Thompson Chandler. Loving wife, mother and friend to all. Born 1875; died 1954."*

Amelia leaned toward Matthew. "From what I hear, she was a remarkable woman."

Matthew nodded his understanding and walked to a smaller

marker that simply read: *Emily Victoria Chandler. Born September 28, 1905. Went to be with Jesus on October 17, 1905.*

"Amelia ... here it is." Matthew pointed to the headstone. "The Chandler baby that died."

"So strange that she's not mentioned in the family genealogy." Amelia pulled a pen and paper from her shirt pocket. "I want to do some research. Her birth and death were before the state kept files, but it's worth a try."

Matthew nodded solemnly. "You'd think there would be some kind of record."

Amelia's eyes welled up. "I really wish Austin was here. I'd loved to sit and talk with him."

"I'd love to see the old man again too. The questions I could ask him..."

Matthew's sentence faded as he walked toward a marble statue in the far corner of the fenced area. He motioned to Amelia. A baseball and bat were engraved on one side, a cross and a lamb on the other.

"In loving memory of our son, Luke Charles Chandler," he read. *"Born in 1901. Disappeared in 1908 at 7 years old. God please keep him in your tender care."*

Matthew could hear Amelia sniffing beside him, and she finally spoke. "So sad. From all the family accounts I've read, he was never found."

Overcome by his own thoughts, Matthew didn't trust his voice. He twisted the ball cap in his hands. What was happening to him?

"In case, you're wondering," Amelia said, "Austin and Evelyn are buried in the Chandler Springs cemetery, as are many of the other family members."

"Wonder why they aren't all buried here?" Did he really care? And would he be responsible for moving the bodies when the property sold?

Amelia sighed. "Laws changed over the years about burials

on private property. Too bad all the Chandlers can't rest together in peace, though."

Amelia pointed to the outline of a small building in a far tree grove. "Let's go see."

"Sure. What is it?"

Matthew allowed Amelia to exit the fenced plot and then latched the gate. They climbed on the Gator and took a bouncy ride over rough, overgrown ground. The pair arrived at a small rectangular building with a steeple on top.

Amelia chuckled. "I guess I have been here before."

"I had the feeling you knew." Matthew looked at her with what he knew was a sly grin. He couldn't help himself.

"Austin told me that toward the end of Evan's life, he built this chapel for Emma and the family. Keri and I loved to play in here when we were kids. We'd arrange our favorite dolls in the pews and then take turns standing behind the pulpit, preaching a sermon to them." Amelia's smile was dreamy, as if she was wrapped in the memory.

Matthew pushed open the wooden door, removed his hat and stepped inside, the boot cast echoing on the wooden floor. An altar and three rows of wooden benches filled the small room, separated by a narrow aisle.

"Strange the door wasn't locked."

Amelia stepped in and touched the delicate lace cloth covering the altar table. "I don't remember it ever being locked. I've heard that Evan wanted it accessible at all times."

"For such an old building, this is well-kept."

Matthew inspected the small stained glass window depicting a cross above the altar. The colored light spread through the tiny nave. Dollar figures ran through his head. He wished he'd known about this place. It should have been added to the MLS listing.

Great, he was back to his old self. It was spooky how this place had played tricks on his mind.

Amelia blew the dust from the cover of the Bible lying on the altar table. "I remember Austin and Evelyn coming here. Even in their later years, they made it out here on the Gator."

"Did Evan and Emma actually hold services here?"

"I don't think so. I'd have to ask my mom, but I think this was more of a memorial to the family and used for special family gatherings."

"Look." Matthew pointed to a small memorial in the corner. The angel statue matched the one in the graveyard. "Another memorial to their baby daughter."

Amelia turned and stepped beside him. She pulled a tissue from her pocket. "It's so sweet the way they loved their children."

Determined not to get too sentimental, Matthew turned to the opposite corner. "And here's a memorial to their son."

Amelia dabbed her eyes. "Evan and Emma must have grieved for him the rest of their lives." She touched the cross painted in a stained glass window by the pews. "This is a beautiful place. I'm glad we came in."

"Thanks for the tour. " Matthew started out the door and limped back to the Gator, his head spinning. This was the family he didn't want any part of.

And yet...

Matthew sat at Evan's desk, trying to connect to the WiFi. Working remotely had its challenges. He rebooted his computer and the hot spot again, hoping for an internet signal. Finally he closed the laptop lid. Work would have to wait. He hadn't slept well last night thinking about Evan and Emma's tragic loss of two children. Get a grip, man. This house had to be messing with his mind.

Now he was talking to himself. He needed more coffee. He

picked up the empty mug and headed for the kitchen. He wouldn't be here much longer. This would all be over soon. He poured himself a cup and sat down at the kitchen table. Too bad Logan wasn't here.

Matthew's phone rang. Amelia. "Hi," he said, more eagerly than he'd intended to. "What's up?"

"I have news on the house." Her voice quivered.

"You sound upset. Is it bad news?"

"Since you want so badly to sell, I guess it's good news for you. You've received a full price offer. You have 72 hours to respond." Her voice sounded more robotic than human.

"That's awesome!" Matthew hesitated. "Amelia, I know how much this house means to you. But I just can't keep it. I have no use for it."

"Yeah, I know. Oh, I have another call coming in. I'll talk to you later."

Matthew could feel the abruptness in her voice as she hung up. He stared at his phone. Did he actually feel sorry for her? This was his house to do as he pleased. Was this sweet blonde worming her way into his heart?

Eager to shake those thoughts out of his head, Matthew caught sight of the journal he'd left on the desk the night he'd tried to give it to her. He ran his hand over the old leather cover. For the first time, he felt a strange connection with Evan Chandler. Maybe he did want to know...

He opened to a yellowed page.

It's difficult to write these words. We are in a living hell. Luke has been missing for two days and we've searched everywhere. It about kills me to see the tired, drawn look on Emma's face. The other children don't know how to act without their brother.

Sheriff Taylor suspects a disgruntled worker from the mine. I'm so angry at the thought of someone taking my son. For God's sake. He's only seven years old. If they have a grievance, they can approach me and talk man to man. Don't hurt my innocent child.

God, I've believed in you most of my life. You've blessed me with Emma, the children, this beautiful home. But how can you take my son? I'm so angry. Why didn't you protect him?

Matthew pulled the covers closed with his finger as a page marker. These were the words of his great-grandfather. The man who seemed to have had everything. Family, money, success. Yet life dealt him a cruel hand through his young son's disappearance. Matthew reopened the pages and continued reading.

I've noticed that Emma barely lets the other children out of her sight. I'm terrified that something will happen to one of them and she is too. I got so angry the other day when Ruby went out for a ride on her pony without telling us. I'll never forget the look of surprise on her face when I raised my voice to scold her and then grabbed her into a hug. Hearing her say "I'm sorry, Daddy" were the sweetest words.

Lord, please bring Luke home. We love and miss him so much. Please God, I beg you to answer our prayers.

Amazing that Evan could still pray. Would he be able to pray in such a desperate situation?

He closed the journal. Luke. The son memorialized in the cemetery and the family chapel. He closed his eyes. He couldn't imagine the tragedy of a father losing a son. But in his case, his own father had voluntarily walked away.

He pushed the thoughts away. He couldn't deal with them right now. He picked up his cell and punched in Amelia's number.

"Hello, Matthew." He could feel the chill through the phone line.

"Just wanted to let you know I'm reading an interesting entry in Evan's journal about their son, Luke."

"Oh really?"

"Want to come for dinner tonight and read it?"

"Sorry, I have a showing tonight. Maybe some other time."

Was she ever going to forgive him for selling the house? "Ok. Sounds like the family was pretty devastated when he disappeared."

"I'm sorry. What an awful thing for the Chandlers to face. Thanks for letting me know. I'd like to hear any updates."

The iceberg had warmed some. The Chandlers seemed to always affect Amelia that way. But Matthew sensed this wasn't the time to mention the house.

"I will," he said. "Talk soon." He disconnected the call.

CHAPTER 15

*M*atthew wasn't giving up on Amelia. Selling the
house didn't mean he couldn't be friends with
her. At least in his eyes. There was something about the kind,
thoughtful real estate lady. When they'd eaten together the
other night, he couldn't help but notice her delicious smile. And
her captivating sapphire colored eyes.

Under his convincing charm, she'd finally agreed to let him
bring dinner to her house that night. He'd prefer to eat alone
with her, but she'd mentioned needing to help her mother.

Matthew parked in front of Amelia's house promptly at 5:00
p.m. Pete and Nora had rented a car for him and brought it up
on their last visit. It felt good to be independent again after
being cooped up in that house for way too long. Carrying two
pizza boxes in one hand, he balanced a bag of salad fixings in
the other. He was getting the hang of walking in a boot and left
the scooter at home.

Amelia opened the front door when he rang the bell.

"Someone here order pizza?"

"Totally. You're just in time." Amelia held the screen door
open for him to enter.

Harley bounded toward him, tail wagging a hundred miles an hour.

"Hi there, boy. I have something for you." Matthew stepped into the kitchen and set the pizza boxes and grocery bags on the small square of counter space available.

"Smells wonderful in here."

Matthew pulled a chew toy from the bag. Harley snatched it from his hand and ran to the living room.

"You'll be his friend forever." Ruth opened the oven and pulled out a pan of golden brown cookies. The delicious aroma of melting chocolate and brown sugar filled the kitchen.

"Thanks for coming over," Amelia said. "Mom got an order from a lady at church so we started baking early."

The counters of the small kitchen were covered with canisters of sugar, flour, a mixer, cookie sheets and a rolling pin.

"Point me to a cutting board and knife and I'll get started. Oh, and a salad bowl." Matthew sat down at the kitchen table, centered in the middle of the room.

"Sure thing." Amelia handed him the requested items and turned back to the counter to stir another batch of cookies.

Matthew picked up the knife and started on the cucumber. Way out of his normal but he was enjoying this. He watched Harley saunter back into the kitchen and plop under the table with a piece of the bone hanging from his mouth. Anyone who dared try to take it away from him would risk losing a finger. Or two.

Matthew pushed freshly chopped tomato on top of the greens. "All done."

Amelia wiped her hands on her apron. "Fabulous, I'm famished. I could eat both pizzas by myself."

Not a chance. Matthew watched her pull the apron over her head. Her form fitting blouse and jeans complimented her trim figure. She sure didn't get a shape like that eating two pizzas.

"Let's eat." Ruth slid into the chair beside Matthew. "Do you mind if I say grace?"

"Not at all." Matthew removed his hat and bowed his head. He hadn't prayed before a meal in years. Good memories of his childhood days. Before his dad left. He took the hands offered by Amelia and Ruth.

"Father, thank you for this lovely day. We are so grateful for Your provision. Bless Amelia and please bless Matthew. We ask that you bless this food, in Jesus' Precious Name. Amen."

"Amen," Amelia said and let go of Matthew's hand.

Matthew didn't want to let go of her warm one. He'd like to hold it a while longer, though that would make it hard to eat. And Amelia wasn't having it.

Amelia opened the pizza boxes with enthusiasm. "Dig in."

"Mmmm. This is good," Ruth said through a bite and wiped her mouth with a napkin. "I haven't had pizza in a month of Sundays."

"Haven't heard that saying in a long time." Matthew bit into a slice of pepperoni and caught the string of extra cheese in his mouth.

"Not from your generation. But hang around me long enough and you'll hear a few of them."

Ruth had a kindness about her that Matthew didn't see in many people in his New York world.

"If you don't have something positive to say, don't say anything at all." Amelia grinned at her mother. "Can't tell you how many times I heard that during my teenage years."

Ruth patted her daughter's hand. "It must have sunk in." She looked over at Matthew. "Her daddy was that way. He grew up poor but made a good life for us."

"I definitely miss his positive nature," Amelia said.

"He'd be so proud of you." Ruth blinked rapidly as she picked up her glass of ice tea.

"Thanks Mom." Amelia squeezed Ruth's other hand.

Matthew reached for another piece of pizza. It was almost like Amelia's dad was sitting at the table with them. The hormones flowing through the room at the moment were suffocating him. The slice was gone in three bites.

He stood and stacked plates on one arm and salad bowls in the other. "Let me clear the table so you two can continue with your baking."

"Thanks." Amelia pulled a bowl of batter from the fridge. "This should be ready, Mom." She set it on the counter in front of Ruth.

"I have to thank you both for helping tonight. This has made my fun hobby even funner."

"Funner, Mom? Is that even a word?" Amelia laughed.

"It is in my world."

Matthew watched, fascinated, at Ruth's quick movements as she greased two baking pans with shortening and shook in a tablespoon of flour in each, poured in the banana bread batter and smoothed it with a spatula. Nothing to it.

"Have you ever thought of starting a business?" he said.

"Actually, I've gotten a few orders from ladies at church. But I'm too old to get started this late in life." Ruth slid two loaf pans into the hot oven.

Matthew and Amelia protested at the same time: "No, you are not!"

Ruth sat down across from Matthew. "Okay, you two. If I agreed – and that's a big if – what would it take to get started?"

"I have lots of time on my hands. I could check out the Colorado business laws for you." Matthew bit into a warm macadamia nut cookie from the plate in the middle of the table. "Mmmm.... You wouldn't have any trouble selling these." He finished the cookie on the second bite and reached for another. "I can help you write up a business plan, apply for a license." He counted the steps off on his fingers. "Then we could get a website created so you could start marketing your product."

"Whoa." Ruth held up both hands. "I lost you after step one."

Matthew sat back in his chair. "Okay. Just think about it. Maybe start with the advertising."

Ruth nodded. "Okay. Sounds doable."

"You need a catchy business name." Matthew pulled his smartphone from his shirt pocket and scrolled to the Notes app.

Ruth slid back into the chair next to Matthew. "What do you think of Ruth's Mountaintop Bakery?"

"Not bad. Or even something generic like Ruth's Baked Treats." Matthew reached for another cookie. He was going to have to stop. He'd already noticed the buttons on his shirts getting a little tight with the recent inactivity.

"How about Ruth's Sweet Delights? That's how my tongue reacts when I bite into one of these." Amelia scooped batter onto the cookie sheets.

"I like it." Ruth sipped thoughtfully at her ice tea and nodded. "Let's give it a go."

"Awesome. I'll print business cards and flyers to distribute around town." Matthew typed a list on his phone. "Call me tomorrow and I'll get the specifics from you."

It seemed strange not to have Stacy here to help him do business. He felt like his right arm was missing.

"With my help, you are going to be the most successful baking entrepreneur in Chandler Springs." He crammed another cookie in his mouth.

The following evening Matthew sat in Evan's study contemplating the journal when his cell buzzed. He answered on the first ring. "Hey Logan." Matthew took a sip of his hot coffee. "I was just thinking how I missed you refilling my coffee cup."

"Yep, I bet. How you doing rambling around in that big ole' place alone?"

"Good news. Received a full price offer on the house yesterday." Matthew pulled the paperwork from the folder Amelia had dropped off earlier. "Looks like a cash deal. Couldn't ask for anything better."

"Sweet. So you're accepting it?"

"Yep, I'll be responding by 5:00 p.m. tomorrow."

"How's Amelia taking the news?"

"Not a happy camper, as you can imagine. But it shouldn't come as a shock to her. She's known my plans from the beginning."

"Yeah. True. I can't help thinking about how much she loves that house."

"That's the way life goes sometimes. She'll get over it." Matthew twirled the pen on his desk. He hoped she would anyway. And that she would forgive him for selling it.

"You'll never believe who visited me today."

"From the tone of your voice, probably Eva."

"Bingo. She said she was stopping by to pick up the last of the files from her old office. I have my doubts."

"What did she have to say?" Matthew sat back in the leather chair and rubbed his forehead. This couldn't be good.

"After she planted herself on the corner of my desk, she started gushing about landing the account with Charles Grant. I could barely stand to listen to her." Logan cleared his throat. "Then she asked if you were back in New York yet."

Matthew snickered. "She'll be the last to know."

"I highly doubt it. The woman makes it her business to know everything." Logan paused. "Oh, and she had the nerve to mention celebrating her new account with us when you return."

"Not happening on my watch. No way."

Matthew felt physically sick. That woman was a piece of work.

Logan chuckled. "I couldn't wait for her to leave so I could fumigate my office."

"I don't blame you." Matthew ran his fingers through his hair. "We've got to come up with a plan, Logan. You know this isn't right."

"I'm getting to the best part, Matt. Not five minutes after Eva sashays out of my office, Stacy calls me."

"Stacy can't stand Eva."

"She wanted to make sure we know she's not a gossip."

"Stacy? She'd be the last person I'd label as one."

"Yep, that's what I told her. But she had information she thought we should know. A few of our consultants were at a big meeting yesterday and talked with some staff from Liberty Financial where Eva works now."

"I wonder what they think of her."

"Well here's the kicker, buddy. The scuttlebutt is that Eva's assuming Grant will sign with her. But he hasn't made it official yet."

"Seriously?" Matthew sat straight up in the chair, almost spilling his coffee. "She made it sound like it was a done deal."

"Apparently she's telling everyone Charles Grant is her new client. What planet is that woman living on?"

"I'd sure like to send her there on a one-way ticket." Matthew leaned back in his chair. "Any way you can verify this?"

"Stacy e-mailed me a contact list. I'll make some calls tomorrow."

"You know what this means, my friend? We still have a chance at getting the account." Matthew wanted to shout. And dance. And have a drink to celebrate. What a week. Opportunities to land the Grant account. And a full price cash offer on the house.

But the one person on his mind would not consider this a celebration.

CHAPTER 16

"*B*ut Keri, I just don't know how to handle this."
Amelia's frustration bubbled over into tears.

"Matthew Chandler may be a big shot in his world," Keri said, "but it's not the end of your world."

Amelia took a deep breathe and closed her eyes. "Yeah, I know. It's all so confusing. When he first came here, I could barely stand him. But now...." Amelia's voice trailed off momentarily. "The other day, when we went to the cemetery, he was dressed in jeans and a ball cap, he looked so different than his first day at Rose Haven. And kind of cute the way his bangs fell below the cap brim. I'd never noticed before."

"Uh oh," Keri said. "I know where this is going."

Amelia took another deep breath. "What baffles me is how he can let go of Rose Haven so easily. What is he thinking?" She balanced her cell phone under her chin and rubbed Harley's soft fur. His head in her lap, he seemed to sense her jumbled emotions.

"You have to remember Matthew doesn't have the sentimental ties to the house like you and your Mom. Have you talked to her? What does she think?"

"I haven't told her yet about the full price offer. But I know she'll be upset. She understands how much Austin and Evelyn wanted their house to stay in the Chandler family."

"I'm sorry, Amelia. I really am. You've done everything in your power to persuade him to keep it. It's a shame, really. Maybe he'll have a midnight revelation and reject the contract." Keri giggled.

Amelia did not. "I'll try to stay positive."

"It's not just the house though, is it? How do you really feel about him?"

Amelia stopped stroking Harley's head. "I don't know. I can't deny I'm attracted to him. But I don't think he's really my type."

She paused. Was it time to speak the truth she'd known for a while? Keri had been her best friend for a long time, and she trusted her with her life. "After losing Brian, I'm afraid to love again." There, she'd finally said it.

"I'm sorry, friend. The thing about God is, He's not gonna take away your ability to love. I just don't believe we only get one shot at it, do you?"

"Honestly, I'm not sure. But I'm not ready to jump into a relationship. Especially since Matthew's leaving soon." Amelia looked at her watch. "I have a showing in thirty minutes. Talk to you soon. Love you."

"Love you too. I'll be praying for you."

Amelia put her phone down. Maybe Keri was right. "Well, Harley, what do you think? Should we give Matthew a chance?"

Matthew wandered the long hallway of the house, so deep in thought he barely noticed the clunky boot on his foot. Wasn't he getting what he'd wanted? The house and its contents would be sold. He'd been so eager to get back to New York and wash his hands of this place. Why did he feel this twist in his gut, then?

Maybe he'd eaten something bad. He'd have to stop by the pharmacy when he was out later for some antacids.

He walked into the study and immediately felt like someone was watching him from behind. He turned around and found himself staring into the eyes of Evan Chandler who stared back at him from a picture, probably taken when he was mayor from the look of it. Weird. He'd been in this room 100 times since his arrival. Why did the picture stand out now?

He walked closer to the wall and studied the man's face. Receding hair line, thick mustache and twinkling blue eyes.

Matthew sat down at the desk. He'd cut way back on pain meds. What was going on? The memory of the cemetery visit with Amelia flashed through his mind. What would happen to the graves when a new family took over this property? Would they care about the people buried there? Did he care? Or was he only thinking of the cost if the bodies had to be moved?

He needed a break. Hot coffee and fresh air sounded good. He stood from the desk without pain. Excellent. His leg was getting stronger. Hopefully this boot would come off soon.

The old wood floors in the hallway creaked as he loped past the front parlor, thinking about Evan and Emma and their life here with their children. They were his family. No matter what his own father had done, or not done.

He stepped into the kitchen, thinking about Emma at the old stove, stirring a pot of soup for Evan and the children. He poured a cup of coffee and carried it back down the long hallway. Okay, if he kept the house, how could he balance it all? His work, his life was in New York. He walked through the vestibule to the front door. He grabbed a jacket from the coat rack, opened the screen door and stepped out on the veranda.

Lowering himself into a white wicker rocker, he sipped coffee and watched the sun lower behind the mountains, leaving a splash of blue and pink hues across the sky. Evan's journaled words he'd read that morning came back to him. This was the very setting he and Emma had enjoyed together so many years ago.

An unrecognizable rush of emotion splashed through Matthew. He'd never felt this way about anyone before, much less relatives long gone.

Rocking and thinking, he sipped hot coffee. He touched his neck and realized the constant tension and stress of his job were almost nonexistent here. And the beautiful real estate agent. Yeah. He could get used to having her around.

Matthew pulled his cell phone from the OtterBox and punched in Amelia's number. When he heard her sweet voice, he left a message.

"Hi Amelia. I'm enjoying a magnificent Colorado sunset on the veranda and wondered if you'd like to join me? If you're free, come over."

She would probably think he was nuts. But who knew? Maybe he was.

Amelia stepped into the kitchen. Harley trotted after her. Always her faithful shadow.

"Hi Mom."

"Well hi there." Ruth pulled a tray of cookies from the oven and wiped her hands on her apron.

"Sure smells good in here."

"I'm making cookies and a cake for the church bake sale." Ruth grinned, flour smeared on her cheek. "Want a sample?"

Amelia could never resist her mother's yummy treats. "Sure." She pulled a glass from the cabinet and poured cold milk from the refrigerator.

Ruth handed her two cookies on a napkin. "How's the real estate business these days?"

"Finalizing the Carpenters' sale. Should be a nice commission. I can really use it right now. We've had a slow start this year." Amelia bit into the warm chocolate chip cookie. "Mmmm. Heaven on a napkin." She sat down at the kitchen table.

"What about Austin and Evelyn's house? Any interest?"

"Matthew received a full price offer yesterday." Amelia lifted the glass to her lips. Should she be honest with her mom?

"Oh, I see." Ruth dropped into a kitchen chair across from her. "Will he accept it?"

"He hasn't signed the papers yet, but yes, I think he will. He has until 5:00 p.m. tomorrow." Amelia bit her lower lip to stop the tears.

"I'm sorry, Amelia." Ruth placed a hand over hers. "I know how much the house means to you."

"Yeah, Mom, it does. But I have to live with Matthew's decision. Unfortunately, there's not a thing I can do about it."

"Sure wish I had money. I'd buy it for you, honey."

"Thanks, Mom. I know you would. How do you feel about the sale?"

Ruth touched her hand. "So many wonderful memories in that house. It's certainly a shame it won't stay in the family. Didn't you tell me that Matthew's the last Chandler heir?"

"Yes, he is."

"Hmmmm...And you will miss Mr. Chandler...Matthew when he goes back to New York, won't you?"

"What do you mean, Mom?" Amelia took another gulp of milk. She wasn't ready to talk about her feelings yet. They were still too confusing.

"Don't try to avoid my question, Amelia Jane." Ruth narrowed her eyes. "I'm your mother. I know these things."

"I have to say I'm attracted to him. But as I was telling Keri earlier, he's not my type." Amelia put the last bite of cookie in her mouth.

"And what is your type? I know you've grieved over Brian.

But honey, he's been gone two years. You're still a young woman. Don't you ever think about marriage and children?"

"Sometimes. But it's hard to replace Brian's face with anyone else's. My wedding dress still hangs in the back of my closet." As the lump in her throat rose she had to struggle to swallow the cookie. She grabbed a tissue.

"I know how hard it is, honey."

Amelia felt a slight stab of guilt. "You're talking about when Daddy died. I didn't mean to stir that up --"

Ruth put up her hand. "You're not stirring up anything that I don't already think about every single day. Which is why I can say your heart will heal. It'll take time, but it will happen."

Was it actually possible she'd never put it together that her mom had suffered exactly the same feelings she had? Amelia looked miserably at the tissue, which was now in shreds.

"How?" she said. "How did you heal?"

"It was lots of things. Mostly Austin and Evelyn's help. Giving me a job. Giving us a place to live."

Another parallel: the attachment to the house. Amelia abandoned that tissue and pulled out another one.

"Feel what you feel," Ruth said. "You know that I'm praying for you."

All Amelia could do was nod.

Amelia listened to the voice mail message. Hearing his voice gave her a jolt she wasn't expecting. It felt risky, but this wasn't love, right? He was asking her over to hang out. What could be the harm? Especially since he wasn't going to be around much longer.

Hoping he'd still be on the porch, she pulled on her coat and scarf and snapped on Harley's leash. "Come on, boy. Let's go for a walk."

Harley would be her protector if things got out of hand. The thought of Harley attacking Matthew made Amelia giggle.

Approaching the house, Amelia could see Matthew sitting on the veranda, gazing toward the horizon. Harley let out a howl of welcome.

Matthew looked up and waved. "A wonderful night for a walk."

The street lamps began flickering on. "Sorry I missed the sunset." Amelia let go of the leash. Harley bounded up the steps and jumped up on Matthew.

"Down, boy. It's good to see you, too." He grinned at Amelia. "And your owner." Matthew pointed to the vacant rocker as Amelia stepped up on the porch. "Have a seat."

Her foot tangled in Harley's leash and she fell forward toward Matthew's lap.

"Whoa, watch out there." Matthew grabbed her arm and pushed her back on both feet.

"Sorry, so clumsy of me." But she kind of liked his musky smell. "What did you want to talk to me about?"

Matthew looked off past the porch, into the rose garden beside the house. "I've been doing some soul searching about my family. And about this house."

"Really?"

Amelia felt hope rising, but she squashed it down. He couldn't be reconsidering, right? This was Matthew Chandler, after all.

"I know, call me crazy. Selling this house is all I've talked about since I arrived. But seeing the family belongings in the attic. And then the cemetery..." Matthew looked away, toward the mountains. "And Evan's journal."

"My, my, Mr. Chandler. I never realized you were so sentimental."

Amelia stroked Harley's fur. This was a huge step for her client. Her friend. Her ... couldn't go there yet.

"I had a flashback when we were in the attic that day," he said.

And that was all.

Amelia sat silent. She wished he could confide in her. Was that door opening? She studied his profile. Nah, this was the guy who probably never confided in anyone except maybe Logan, and even then, she couldn't picture them discussing their feelings.

Finally she spoke. "I hope it was a good memory."

"Not really. It happened so long ago, the memory's jumbled and I'm not sure what was reality and what I imagined." He looked at his cell phone, as if for a distraction. "It's not important."

Amelia felt the door close .... no, slam shut on the subject. "So, did you invite me here to tell me you're not signing the contract?"

She studied his face. The normally overconfident man had a look of confusion.

"I don't know. Still weighing my options. I'll let you know by 4:59 p.m. tomorrow."

"Not to put too fine a point on it," she said.

She tried to keep the hope out of her voice as she settled into the rocker and watched the fading horizon with him.

CHAPTER 17

"*L*ogan. Call me when you have a chance."

Matthew disconnected from voicemail. His stomach rumbled again. He popped another antacid, trying to calm the flip-flops. He'd distracted himself for the last hour by Googling the laws for establishing a business in Colorado. He'd designed a promotional flyer and business card he thought Ruth might like. But he still couldn't keep his mind off of Amelia . . . and this decision. He was getting nowhere, so he decided to call Logan. The cell phone vibrated, and Logan's name appeared on the screen.

"Thanks for calling me back."

"Hey, how's it going?"

Logan's voice immediately calmed Matthew's nerves. "You have a few minutes to talk through some stuff with me?"

"Sure. What's up?"

"I signed the papers to sell the house."

"That's great, Matt. You'll be home in no time." Logan paused. "But you don't sound happy. Isn't that what you wanted?"

"I thought I'd be ecstatic. Then I couldn't sleep last night. My stomach feels like it's tied up in knots."

Logan chuckled. "Something you ate? You aren't doing your own cooking, are you?"

"Probably not food related. I think it's about the sale."

"Really? Since you've signed the contract, isn't it a done deal?"

"No idea. I'd have to talk with Amelia about that."

"Okay. So let's brainstorm here for a minute. Let's just say that you're able to break the contract, what then?"

"I don't know, Logan. I can't explain how I feel right now. It's weird really." Matthew paused. "This isn't like me."

"You've got that right, buddy. I'm talking to Mr. Businessman who makes good, solid decisions and gets things done." Logan gave a soft laugh. "I have the feeling Amelia plays into this decision."

"Yeah, she does."

"So you want to live in Colorado?"

"I don't know, man." Matthew popped another tablet in his mouth. "Still weighing my options."

Matthew woke with a start. He swung the heavy cast over the side of the bed and hobbled to the window, the first light of sun peeking over the mountains.

In his dream a woman was strolling through the rose garden, open parasol protecting her fair skin from the Colorado sun. A man wearing a bowler hat stopped to gaze into the woman's eyes, a deep love flowing between them. Children ran and laughed, rolling in the grass and calling for their parents to come watch them play. The Victorian house shone in the fading sunlight. Looking up at the windows, happiness shone from every pane.

The scene then changed to a young woman standing in a dreary tenement room. A crying baby on her hip, she tried her best to satisfy him with a spoonful of applesauce. Worry and fear etched her face, making her look far older than her twenty years.

Matthew shook his head to clear the cobwebs. He had been dreaming, hadn't he? The thing just seemed so real.

Did he really want to sell this house? Now he wasn't so sure. He'd have to talk to Amelia later about options to break the contract. There had to be some, right? At this point, he'd pay the prospective buyers off, if he had to. There was too much history, too much of the Chandler family legacy here to let this house go.

And Amelia. Sweet Amelia always seeped into every thought.

That afternoon Matthew sipped coffee in the study. He picked up Evan's journal and flipped to the last page. Maybe he'd find a clue about what had happened to little Luke. On the back inside cover he noticed the edges had been pried away and then resealed. Using his pocket knife, he pried the backing off and pulled the cover away. A skeleton key attached to a string lay inside a small well, designed to be hidden in the back cover.

Surprised, Matthew pulled it out of the hiding place. From the looks of the key, it had been there a very long time. He turned it over and inspected the back for markings. Nothing. What did it open? And the bigger question was why was it hidden in Evan's journal?

Maybe Amelia could shed some light on the mystery.

The next morning Matthew answered the knock on the front door. Amelia stood on the porch bundled in a parka and fluffy scarf. The cold wind tossed her blonde hair.

"Hi there. I stopped by to pick up the sample flyer and business cards for my mom."

"Come on in." A gust of wind caught the front door. "Wow, the weather sure changed overnight."

Amelia stepped into the vestibule. "Yep, that's Colorado weather for you. Can be 60 degrees one day and a blizzard the next."

Matthew led her to Evan's study. He handed her a folder and a business card. "Let me know if Ruth wants any edits."

"Thanks, I will." Amelia nodded her thanks. "I appreciate you doing this. I'm not sure she would have ventured out without our nudge. And your help."

"Not a problem." He pulled the key out of his pocket. "Oh, by the way, any idea what this might open?"

Amelia accepted the key and turned it over."Where did you find it?"

"Very strange. It was hidden in the back of Evan's journal."

"No kidding. Why would he do...." Amelia stopped mid-sentence. "Matthew. This may be the key to the bedroom upstairs. It's been missing for years."

Amelia's heart raced as she climbed the stairs to the second floor, Matthew beside her. For as long as she could remember, she'd imagined what the locked bedroom contained. As a child she'd envisioned stacks of money and even gold treasure that she could gift her mother with to buy their own home. Then she wouldn't hear her mother crying on the phone about the house they'd lost to foreclosure when her father died. Her other daydreams had included a candy store and a room full of children's toys and books and beautiful dresses.

Matthew brought her back to reality. His boot cast caught on a step, causing him to stumble.

"Can I help?" She put her hand on his arm to steady him. As usual, he pulled away.

"Nope. I'm good." He grabbed the bannister and continued his labored climb.

Okay, fine. Just see if she tried to help again. Why were men so stubborn? Amelia climbed the stairs past him and waited on the landing. Thank goodness he couldn't read her mind.

Amelia followed Matthew down the long hallway and stopped at the door in front of them. He pulled the key from his pocket and inserted it. With some effort, the rusty lock finally clicked, and he turned the doorknob. Now finally... after so many years. Matthew had found the key. But why was it hidden in Evan's journal? Did he put it there? Or someone else?

Amelia followed Matthew into the room. Musty, stale air hit her in the face. She protected her nose and mouth with her hand. Much like the attic, years of dust and cobwebs coated the contents of the room. A single bed covered with a handmade quilt was set up under the window. Tattered cotton curtains barely clung to the curtain rod, looking like they'd fall down any minute.

Toys, stuffed animals, toy soldiers and a baseball glove and ball lined shelves on the opposite wall. In the opposite corner, a wooden rocking chair. Next to it, a pipe and Bible on a small table. Strange things to find in a little boy's room.

Matthew picked up the pipe. "This must have been Evan's." He laid it back on the table and thumbed through the Bible. "Wonder why Evan's belongings are in here?"

"No clue. If Austin ever mentioned anything about this room, I was too young to remember."

"Looks like it was occupied by one of the Chandler boys. Wonder why it was closed up?" Matthew picked up a small Bible from the shelf and opened it to the first page. "This belonged to Luke Chandler."

Amelia was immediately beside him. "This must have been his room."

Matthew nodded. "Could Evan have locked it up after Luke disappeared?"

"Seems likely, doesn't it?" With a grimace, Amelia wrapped

her arms around herself. "So sad. I can't imagine the family's pain."

"Yeah me too." Matthew picked up Evan's Bible. "I'm taking this downstairs to look through."

Amelia covered her mouth to conceal a smile. His great-grandfather may have more influence on Matthew than he ever imagined. "Let me know if you find anything interesting in there."

"I will." Matthew stuck the Bible under his arm and headed for the door. "Almost feels like this room has been lost in time."

Later that evening Matthew sat in Evan's chair in the study and opened the Bible. The first page read "To Evan Chandler, love from Emma and your children. Christmas 1909." Matthew flipped to a marked passage "Psalms 91 "He that dwelleth in the secret place of the Most High, shall abide under the shadow of the Almighty." The passage was underlined in blue ink and a smeared note in the column read "My hope comes from God."

Hmmm....Evan must have had some kind of faith. How could a guy keep believing in God when two of his children had died so young?

Matthew noticed the edge of a newspaper clipping and pulled it from the pages of the Bible. The headline on the yellow, crinkly page read "Chandler boy still missing."

Matthew's stomach clenched as he read the first two lines .

"The seven-year-old son of Chandler Springs mayor Evan Chandler has been missing for over a year. Luke Chandler is now presumed dead."

Matthew laid the clipping aside to show Amelia. This whole thing about Luke was starting to get to him.

The only thing to do was what he always did: get more information.

$\mathcal{M}$atthew arrived at the cafe ahead of Amelia. He hated to admit it to himself but he was like a sixteen year old at the moment. Having her agree to meet with him was right up there with Kelly Clark back in 11th grade saying she'd go to prom as his date. He sat down at a table by the window and studied the menu, though it hadn't changed since the last time he was here. And probably hadn't since the place opened.

Wanda sauntered to the table. "So you're still in town."

Matthew raised his head to see the red hair was now blonde and spiked in more directions than he could have imagined the strands would go. "I'll be around for a few more weeks." He lifted his booted foot.

"Great. Gives us more time to talk you into staying." She winked at him and motioned toward the couple entering the cafe. "Or she will."

A stocky man Matthew had never seen before held the door open for Amelia. Matthew shrugged at Wanda's comment. Better to play it cool. She had a big mouth, and he'd rather the whole town not know his business.

Wanda peered down at him. "One black coffee and one hot tea?"

"You got it." Wanda knew them too well.

Amelia pulled off her long coat and the man hung it on the coat rack inside the door. She walked over to the table, dressed in a pink skirt and matching silk blouse, blonde hair flowing past her shoulders. The man followed her. Reminded Matthew of a lost puppy dog.

"Good morning." Matthew stood. The still unnamed person pulled out Amelia's chair before he had a chance.

"Thanks." Amelia smoothed her skirt and perched on the seat. The man stood silent, watching her. "Oh. Where are my manners?" she said. "Matthew, this is Darrin Wilson."

Darrin stuck out his hand. "I've heard a lot about you."

Uh oh. Had the old geezers at the counter been spreading gossip about him? Or was it Wanda? "Only good things I hope." Matthew returned the firm handshake. The guy must work out.

"Of course." Darrin kissed Amelia's cheek. "Glad I bumped into you this morning. Text me and we'll have coffee." He turned to leave and nearly knocked the drinks off Wanda's tray as she approached the table.

"Hey there, sugar."

Matthew watched Wanda wink at the guy as he headed for the door. He must be the town stud. He expected stuff like this in New York but in this sleepy little town? He realized Amelia was staring at him.

"Friend of yours?" Nice save. Maybe the guy was Amelia's boyfriend. They seemed. What was the word? Intimate.

"Darrin? Oh, I've known him for years." Amelia flipped her hair over her shoulder. "We dated in high school."

Well, that was a long time ago. And now? Matthew wanted to ask but stopped himself.

"And before I forget, thank you for the beautiful bouquet of flowers."

"No problem." Should he just tell her the truth? That he was falling for her. The words stuck in his throat. Instead he heard himself saying, "A well-deserved gift for an excellent realtor."

"Hardest listing of my life." Amelia blinked hard. "But you already know that."

"Yeah, I do." Matthew looked away. He had to give her kudos. As much as she hated the idea of selling Rose Haven, she was a professional and did her job well.

Amelia pulled a large manila envelope from her business bag. "Let's order first and then I'll show you my treasures."

When Wanda reappeared, Matthew ordered the full breakfast plate for himself and oatmeal with wheat toast for Amelia.

"Excuse me a minute." Amelia slung her purse over her shoulder and headed for the restroom.

Matthew picked up his cell phone to check the latest stock market prices, but his eyes followed the blonde leaving the table. Normally buried in the headlines of the New York Times, he wasn't used to such good-looking company this early in the morning. He realized she was the first woman whose wardrobe he'd made positive note of. The mountain casual look fit her so well. A nice change from the women in New York who looked like they were prancing down a designer runway.

Amelia returned to the table as Wanda delivered their steaming food. "Have you heard from Logan since he returned to New York?"

Strange question. "I've talked to him a few times." He turned off his cell and stuck it in his pocket.

Amelia leaned forward. "Has he mentioned Keri?"

"No," Matthew mumbled through a bite of eggs. "Why?"

"Just curious. She told me they've been texting or Skyping almost every day since Logan went home." Amelia blew on the hot tea and then took a sip.

"Nope. He hasn't said a word to me." He'd have to call Logan later and give him heck. He took a bite of crisp cooked bacon from the stack on his plate. Wanda must have thought he looked starved today.

"I know they really hit it off when he was here." Amelia smeared plum jelly on the last bite of wheat toast and scraped the bottom of the oatmeal bowl.

"Long distance romances can be a challenge." Was he preaching to himself?

"Absolutely. But I've heard some success stories." Amelia wiped her mouth with her napkin.

Time to change the subject. "So what do you have to show me?"

Matthew motioned toward the manila envelope on the table. He chewed the last bite of bacon and laid the napkin in the middle of the empty plate.

"On second thought, let's go to the public library. I can spread this stuff out on one of their long tables."

Amelia picked up her business bag and purse while Matthew stuck his credit card in the payment holder and handed it to Wanda when she walked by.

Amelia reached for her wallet. "I can pay my portion."

"Too late," Matthew said. "This one's on me."

"Thank you. I will treat next time."

Matthew smiled at the suggestion. Not on her life.

Wanda appeared with his card and receipt. "Thanks for coming by." She held one hand to the side of her mouth like she was going to whisper to Amelia. But the whole place could hear her. "Figure out a way to keep him here."

"That would be a miracle."

Amelia pulled her coat off the rack and slipped it on. Matthew held the door for her as they exited the cafe.

Amelia pulled her sunglasses in place over her eyes. "The library isn't far. We can walk. That is if you don't mind." She looked down at his booted foot.

"Sure, I'm getting pretty good at walking in this thing."

Matthew kept her pace. He looked at her gloved hand. He'd love to hold it. But how would she react?

"How's your leg?" she said.

"Feeling better every day. Can't wait to start beating Logan again at racquetball."

"Seriously? Can you play that soon?"

"Doc says the blood clot dissolved and that bone stimulator thing made my leg stronger." Matthew made a fist pump in the air. "Made my day."

"That's great news. Glad to hear it."

"Yeah, me too. I didn't think it was ever going to heal."

In the next block, Amelia pointed out the Chandler Springs Park. "Let's cut through here to the library."

"Nice park." Matthew stopped at a wrought iron bench and lowered himself on the seat. "We're not in any hurry." He hated to admit it, but the high altitude still got to him. He took slow, deep breaths hoping Amelia wouldn't notice.

Amelia sat next to him. "I just love this place. Hearing the birds singing makes my heart happy."

"Never thought of it that way. In New York City the birds are just noisy and messy." Matthew wrinkled his nose at the thought. He'd lived in the city too long.

"We have several birdhouses in our backyard. Mom and I can sit on the back porch for hours and watch them." Amelia paused. "With my cup of tea, of course."

"No doubt." Matthew grabbed the arm rest of the bench to raise himself up. Sick of feeling like an invalid, he hoped Amelia took note that he was getting around much better. When she stood, he still wanted to hold her hand. Maybe next time.

Two blocks later they reached the entrance to the Chandler Library. The massive two-story granite building, with a grand two column entrance, covered the city block.

Matthew snorted. "My family's name is all over this town."

"The Chandlers made a lasting impact on this community, you know." Amelia flashed a smile.

The smile that Matthew loved. He pulled open the massive oak door and allowed her to enter. "Evan really knew how to build 'em."

Amelia nodded in agreement. "Let's find a private table."

Winding through the extensive collection of books, they made their way to the back of the library. Amelia pointed at the stained glass on the far wall. "Austin told me the windows were imported from Italy. Evan insisted on using only the finest materials in his buildings."

Matthew studied the carved oak ceiling beams. "This building's in great shape for its age."

"It's a historical landmark, along with the courthouse and the Chandlers' home."

"My great-grandfather was a smart businessman." Who knew -- maybe his business instincts had passed through the family genes.

"Yep, he certainly was. This looks like a good spot." Amelia placed her business bag on a table and pulled out several manila envelopes, a binder and a small laptop.

"You've done some serious research on the Chandlers. I'm impressed." Matthew slid into the chair next to her. The soft scent of her perfume mixed with her hair products made him want to sit closer.

"Wait until you see everything I have to show you. Then you can be impressed."

Amelia smiled and then seemed to wipe it away. Huh.

Matthew sat back and watched as she flipped through papers and pictures.

She pulled a stack of black-and-white photographs from a manila envelope. "Here's a family picture taken about 1907 in front of the house."

Matthew studied the vintage picture. Evan and Emma in

wicker rockers on the front porch, appeared surprisingly content. The oldest boy, the spitting image of his daddy, looked like he wanted to push his younger brother off the edge any minute. A young girl, dressed in a pinafore and matching bonnet, stood next to Evan. Emma lovingly gazed at the infant sleeping in her arms.

"Four children," Matthew said. "Bet that kept their house lively."

"Several more children were born in later years, including your grandfather, Austin. He told me stories of strangers that showed up at the Chandler House asking for help. He said his mother could never turn anyone away."

So different than Matthew's own childhood.

Amelia continued. "During the holidays, Evan and the older boys decorated the outside of the house and invited the whole town to a Christmas party. Evan delighted in giving every child who attended a gift. Emma and the girls baked for weeks and served cookies and punch. The Chandlers created a lasting legacy with the local community."

"Quite a family."

"And I've heard the naming of the house was rather an important event." Amelia picked up the picture again. "See the sign hanging by the front door? It reads 'Welcome to Rose Haven'. Emma chose that name."

"Seriously?" Matthew wanted to laugh. He couldn't imagine naming a house. But the look on Amelia's face stopped him. She was intense about this stuff. He covered the smile with his hand. What a girly name. How had Emma talked Evan into that one? He would have chosen Stoneridge Manor or Stagwood Estates.

"A few folks in town refer to it as the Chandler House but most do call it Rose Haven."

Huh. On the pros and cons list he was keeping mentally, another reason not to keep the monstrosity.

Amelia laid another picture on the table. "This was taken just before Evan passed away." She turned it over. "It's dated 1955. He had just turned 85. He looks well for his age, don't you think?"

No doubt the same man as the picture in the study back at the house. Only older. "Yeah, he does. How long did he live?"

Amelia opened the binder to Evan's biography page. "He died a few months later."

"Well it's nice to know long life runs in my family."

"Let me tell you about the Chandler family and the history of the house."

She flipped to another tab in the binder.

"Evan and his brother, Nathaniel traveled from Kansas to Colorado in 1888. They staked a gold claim not far from here but struggled for several years." Amelia stopped for a sip from her water bottle.

"Was that during the Gold Rush days?" One of his favorite times in history.

"Yep. The story goes that they got caught up in the excitement of seeking their fortune. Evan decided he couldn't live without his childhood sweetheart, Emma Thompson, so he returned to Kansas to marry her in 1895."

"Wonder what happened to his brother, Nathaniel?" Matthew slid a chair next to his and elevated his foot.

"I've never found it in writing, but Austin told me his Uncle Nathaniel was killed in a mining accident."

"Huh. Too bad." Matthew cleared his throat. Another tragedy that must have affected Evan's life.

"Mines were so primitive back then. Many workers lost their lives in accidents." Amelia brushed a loose hair out of her face.

Matthew leaned on one arm and watched her. He was getting into this story. Oh wait, this was his family history.

"After Evan and Emma were married, they returned to Chandler Springs. They built a small four-room log cabin and their first son, Will, was born in 1899 in that very cabin. The same year Evan and Nathaniel discovered a rich vein in the mountain that sits behind Rose Haven. Evan named it Thompson Mountain in honor of Emma's family in Kansas. Evan and Nathaniel formed the Chandler Gold Mine." Amelia stopped to take another long drink of water.

This might be a good time to bring up what he'd found out. "That reminds me," Matthew said. "I got the accessor's report back."

"Oh? I'd almost forgotten about that."

"Yeah, there's a good chance there's still a significant gold vein in that old mine." He had to bite his lip to avoid the observation that he could still be sitting on a gold mine, even if he sold the house. Too cheesy.

"Wouldn't that be something? We didn't think to list the mine with the house. So you still own it."

"That would be way cool." Owning a gold mine. Never in his wildest dreams...But he had the uncanny sense that further conversation wouldn't go over big with Amelia. Better drop it for now.

Matthew pointed to the papers spread in front of Amelia. "Tell me more about my family."

She smiled at him, like she was impressed. "In 1900 Evan and Nathaniel established Chandler Springs. Evan and Emma built a two-story clapboard house on the current property, and in 1901 Luke joined the family. Amelia was born in 1903." Amelia paused. "Kinda cool that we share the same name."

Matthew's eyes met hers when she looked up. She quickly turned them back down to the documents.

"The baby girl we found out about while exploring the attic was named Emily Victoria. She was born in 1905 and died a few weeks later. Why she's not listed in this genealogy is still a mystery."

"Yes, it is."

"It may have been very traumatic for Emma and she never

spoke about the birth and death to the children. So Austin wouldn't have known about it."

"Maybe. Who really knows?"

"I'd like to find out. Their third daughter, Suzanne, was born in 1907, the twins Rose and Ruby in 1910 and your grandfather, Austin in 1915."

"The seemingly perfect family did have their losses, though."

"Tragedy struck during a spring thunderstorm in 1901, when a lightning bolt hit the roof. The family escaped but the house burned to the ground."

"Wow, that's a stroke of bad luck. I can't imagine the family losing everything."

"They decided to live in the small log cabin that still stands on the back edge of the Chandler property. You can imagine how crowded it was with all the small children."

No, actually he couldn't imagine that many people living in such a small space. But he nodded anyway.

Amelia flipped to another tab in her binder. "Evan had plans drawn up to build a new house, not far from the site of the one destroyed in the fire. It was a grand Victorian, and Evan kept most of the details from Emma to surprise her. In 1902 the Chandler family moved into their dream home. And that's the place that you now own."

"For a short time, anyway."

Amelia ignored him and flipped the page. "In the summer of 1910, The Healing Refuge Inn was built."

Now that was a new one on him. "What exactly was The Healing Refuge Inn?"

"Emma wanted a place to help people. A wing of private rooms and a common area kitchen were built just south of Rose Haven. The layout was similar to a boarding house and could accommodate up to five families and three individuals at a time. Austin told me Evan didn't really like the idea much. But Emma had her heart set, so Evan finally gave in to her."

"Obviously that building is gone. What happened to it?"

"Sadly, the clapboard structure caught fire in 1954. It was torn down and never rebuilt. But here's a picture of your great-grandfather, Evan, hanging out the shingle on opening day." Amelia pushed the picture toward Matthew.

Matthew studied the black-and-white vintage photograph. Evan stood on the top rung of a wooden ladder. In one hand he held a hammer, and in the other a sign "The Healing Refuge Inn".

When Matthew looked up, Amelia sat with arms folded. She seemed satisfied that she'd conveyed the family history to the last Chandler heir.

"Impressive history lesson." Matthew motioned to the binders and pictures spread on the table. "How did you end up with all this?"

"Austin and Evelyn were quite the genealogists. Austin offered it to several family members, but no one wanted it. He couldn't stand the thought of his family history being tossed in the land fill when he was gone, so he entrusted it to me."

"He made a wise choice."

"Austin was the kindest, gentlest man I've ever met. He always had a new joke or just came up with funny things to say." Amelia's voice grew husky. "I guess in a way he was the father I longed for after losing my own."

Matthew could totally relate.

Amelia continued. "He and Miss Evelyn would have a plate of fresh baked snicker doodle cookies and a cold glass of milk waiting for me when I got home from school. We'd sit in the wicker porch rockers and talk until Mom reminded me I had to get my homework done. I loved being with them. Their home was a place of safety for me and Mom during some turbulent years." Amelia tilted her head. "What are you thinking?"

"I'm happy you have good memories. But that's not my story.

The house has been a source of pain that's nagged me since my childhood."

Amelia bit her lip. "I'm sorry, Matthew. I truly am."

"I want those old wounds to heal. But I don't know how to make that happen. Going back to my life in New York is all I know right now."

Matthew looked away. What had just happened here?

It was like the words had tumbled out on their own.

$\mathcal{A}$ melia convinced Matthew to go with her to Georgetown the next day to grocery shop. Something about better prices. Not that money mattered much to him. Sure, he'd go along if it meant spending more time with her.

They parked and walked into King Soopers. Amelia grabbed a cart and set up her purse, shopping list, calculator and coupons in the child's seat. Matthew followed her up and down each aisle, his hands stuffed in his pockets. This was her turf, and he felt like a square peg in a round hole. He couldn't remember the last time he'd been in a grocery store.

Amelia stopped in the natural foods aisle in front of the nut butters. Matthew looked over the prices. What the heck? One little jar cost that much? He decided to keep quiet when she pulled the $9 jar off the shelf and put in the shopping cart. He hoped she had a coupon.

In the produce aisle, Matthew watched her inspect the avocados. She picked one up and squeezed it. It must not have met her qualifications. She put it back and picked up another. After watching her for a few minutes, he realized she was testing for ripeness. He'd have no idea how to pick a good one.

His always came sliced or mashed when he ordered them at his favorite restaurants.

Amelia put a jar of probiotic yogurt in the cart. "I think I'm about done."

She ate some very strange things. What happened to good old peanut butter and jelly? Matthew followed her to the registers at the front of the store. Amelia handed the cashier her coupons. The clerk scanned them and announced the total. "Your total is $104.72."

Amelia swiped her debit card while Matthew helped the bagger load the bags back into their cart. It had been years since he'd done that for his mom. Outside the store, groceries loaded in the trunk, he opened the driver's door for Amelia and then opened his own and slid into the passenger seat.

"Thanks for coming with me." Amelia looked at her receipt. "Woo Hoo. I saved 37% today using coupons. That makes me happy."

"That's great." Honestly, he'd never have gone to all the trouble. But he liked seeing her reaction.

Out of the corner of his eye, Matthew noticed a young boy standing on the sidewalk in front of the store. Dirty, ragged clothes hung from his thin body. He held a sign that read "My daddy can't work and my family is hungry." The flicker of the dream he'd had several days earlier went through Matthew's mind.

Amelia started the engine to pull away.

"Hold on a second. I'll be right back." Matthew opened his door and was out of the car before she could respond. He approached the woman standing next to the building holding a crying baby.

Matthew motioned toward the ragged boy. "This your son?"

"Y ... yes, sir."

Her hesitancy made Matthew wonder if she thought he was the store manager and would run them off.

"I'd like to help."

The woman's eyes widened. "Thank you, sir. My husband was hurt at work and will be laid up for a while." She motioned to several other children playing on the sidewalk. "The kids are hungry."

Matthew tried to smile to reassure her. "What's your name?"

"Abby Reed. We live right outside Georgetown."

"I'll be right back."

Matthew re-entered the store. This was the craziest thing he'd ever done, but he thought of Emma at the back door of Rose Haven handing out food. Minutes later he walked back outside and handed the woman a King Soopers gift card.

"I hope this will help."

Abby looked at the amount. "$200?" Her eyes filled with tears. "I don't know how to thank you."

"Pay it forward. Someday when you're back on your feet, help someone else. That's all the thanks I need."

Matthew slid into his seat. It was an amazing feeling to help someone else. That was a switch. He never thought about the struggling people in New York.

"That's the nicest thing I've ever seen you do," Amelia said.

Matthew shrugged nonchalantly as she pulled out of the parking lot. "They needed help."

"Most people wouldn't give them a second thought. Or assume they were running a scam."

Matthew shook his head. "Even if she wasn't honest with me, I still did the right thing. Past that, it's between her and God."

Where had that thought come from? Was reading Evan's Bible every day having an effect on him? He looked over at Amelia.

Her eyes widened. "I think the Chandler legacy is rubbing off on you."

She merged on to the highway and headed toward Chandler Springs.

"Maybe it is. Wouldn't that be something?"

Matthew carried the last grocery bag from the trunk into Amelia's kitchen. He hated the thought of going home to an empty house.

"Come watch the sunset with me."

He held his breath. How did he get this needy?

"How could I refuse an offer like that?" Amelia pulled several bags of flour and sugar from the grocery bag and stacked it in the pantry. "Let me grab my warmer coat."

Well, this was awkward. It seemed too weird to follow her to her bedroom. "I'll wait in the car."

Thirty minutes later Amelia sat on his front porch bundled in her parka and fluffy scarf, watching the pink and orange clouds swirl as the sun set over the mountains.

Matthew squeezed her wrist. "We seem to enjoy each other's company."

She blinked rapidly.

Oh, wow. She's not going to cry, is she?

Finally she spoke, her voice soft. "Not at first. But yes, I do like spending time with you."

"Yeah, our first few meetings were pretty intense, weren't they?" Matthew was surprised at the gentle tone of his voice.

Amelia clasped her gloved fingers together. "Honestly, I never expected you to be anything but my real estate client."

"That's in my DNA. When I have an agenda, I'm all about it." Matthew lifted his chin. "Speaking of the house, after your Chandler family history lesson yesterday, it's like this place is talking to me." He swept his hand toward the windows behind him.

"Seriously?" Amelia looked at him with raised eyebrows. "What's it saying?"

"That I should keep it." Matthew clenched his jaw. "But like I mentioned the other day, too many childhood ghosts still living here. There's not room for all of us."

Amelia sat back and moved with the motion of the rocker. "This may sound cliché, but don't let those memories run your life."

"Yeah. It's totally different when I'm in New York. Never think about this place. Or the past."

Not as much as he did now, anyway. Okay, enough of that. He hadn't invited her over to talk about his hang-ups. The rocker rungs clicked on the wooden porch surface for several minutes as they rocked like two old people.

Finally he broke the silence. "I ...

But Amelia spoke at the same time. "Sorry," she said.

"You go first."

She cleared her throat. "I understand where you're coming from about getting rid of old demons."

"Oh?" Matthew touched the top of her gloved hand.

She looked at him, eyes brimming.

Uh oh. This couldn't be good. He squeezed her hand. He didn't know what to do with tears.

"Two years ago my fiancé, who was my best friend, died in a motorcycle accident. It happened just weeks before our wedding."

"Amelia, I'm so sorry." Matthew fumbled for words. What did you say to something like that? He landed on, "I had no idea."

"My heart still hurts. I truly loved Brian." Amelia pulled a tissue from her pocket and dabbed her eyes.

"And I'm sure he loved you."

Matthew wanted to hug her. But this wasn't the right time.

"So we all have memories."

Amelia shivered and shrunk lower into the chair.

"It's getting chilly out here. Let's go inside." Matthew stood and waited for her to do the same. He put his hand in the small of her back as they walked toward the front door.

"How about a cup of tea? I'm good at boiling water."

Amelia hugged herself. "I'm really cold. A hot drink sounds lovely."

She followed him into the house and down the long hall into the kitchen.

Matthew felt sad for her. He'd never lost anyone that was so important in his life. Oh wait, his father. Well, after so many years, those feelings had died.

Amelia sat quietly at the table while he filled the tea kettle and then made a pot of coffee. He was still groping around for words that didn't sound lame. Seriously, he wanted to do more than just say the right thing. He wanted to make it better ... somehow. Good grief, where was his vocabulary?

When the tea kettle whistled, he pulled a flowered mug out of the cabinet. He carried the steaming water and a container of tea bags to the table.

"Thanks." Amelia dunked a tea bag.

Matthew heard the buzzer sound on the coffee pot. He limped over to the counter, his foot throbbing. He'd walked too much today. He poured a cup of coffee and drank half of it before he limped back over to the table.

"Is your foot bothering you?" Amelia said.

"A little. I've been on it quite a bit today."

Before she could respond, his cell phone buzzed. His mom's number showed on the screen. "I better take this. It's my mom and she hardly ever calls this late." He set his coffee cup on the table. "Be right back."

"Sure. Take your time." Amelia sipped her tea.

Matthew stepped into the hallway. "Hi Mom."

"Matthew. I'm glad I caught you. Hope I'm not calling too late."

"Nope. Amelia's here and we're having coffee." Matthew

stared down the long hallway to the front door. The conversation about ghosts came back to him. He shook his head. No such thing.

"How is she?"

"Huh? Sorry, Mom. What did you just say?" He shook his head again to clear it.

Nora laughed. "I asked how Amelia is."

"She's okay. Figuring out a way to forgive me."

"For what?"

"I accepted a full price offer on the house a few days ago."

Nora sighed. "Oh, Matthew. You can't let that house go."

"That's what the house is telling me." Matthew rolled his eyes. "I'm sure that makes no sense to you. I can't explain it myself."

"I'll be praying that you make the right decision." Nora paused, and he heard her take a deep breath. "I called to talk to you about your dad."

Silence.

"Matthew?"

"What about him?"

He fought the urge to disconnect the call. He couldn't hang up on his Mom, but there wasn't anything about John Chandler he wanted to hear.

"You know John still lives in the U.K."

"Yeah, I'd heard that." Hurry up and let's get this over with.

"Well, over the last year he's been e-mailing me and we've had a couple of phone conversations. We've made our peace, Matthew."

"That's great, Mom. But what does that have to do with me?"

His foot was starting to throb. Maybe he should go sit in the office. He took a few steps down the hall.

Nora took a deep sigh. "He wants to talk to you."

Matthew stopped. "Not interested."

"Matthew, I know this is hard. Your dad made many mistakes."

"Yeah, he did. And the biggest one was deserting us."

He leaned against the wall. He could feel the veins in his temples pounding. The mention of his father always seemed to bring on this reaction.

"He realizes that now."

"It's about time. Only took twenty-five years."

He'd like to hit a wall. The thought of Amelia sitting in the kitchen stopped him.

"Your dad is a stubborn, prideful man."

"I guess it runs in the family."

"Please don't let bitterness toward your dad ruin your life. It's like a poison that eats from the inside out. I've forgiven him. You can too."

"Yeah. Whatever, Mom."

As far as he was concerned, this conversation was over. Before he could say so, Nora continued.

"John is coming back to the U.S. for a risky medical procedure. He wants to see you."

"No way."

"Would you at least think about it? He'll be at the University Hospital in Denver."

To satisfy her, he heard himself say, "I'll think about it. But I'm not promising anything."

"Thanks, honey. I'll talk to you soon. Love you."

"Love you too, Mom."

Matthew hung up and stepped back into the kitchen. Amelia was standing at the back window, tea cup in hand.

"Something interesting out there?"

"Watching the stars twinkle over Thompson Mountain. And thinking this was the same view Evan and Emma had so long ago."

Matthew nodded, but his mind wasn't on his great-grand-parents. "That was a hard conversation..."

Amelia turned and looked at him with kindness in her eyes. "Sorry. Care to talk about it?"

His first thought was to downplay it. But he blurted out, "My dad wants to see me."

"Oh?" Amelia set her tea cup down and focused on his face. "How long has it been?"

"I haven't seen him since I was ten. That's when he decided he had better things to do and walked out on me and my mom."

Amelia slid her small frame into a kitchen chair. "Any idea why he wants to see you now?"

Matthew picked up the mug he'd left on the table and gulped the last of his coffee. Good thing he made a full pot. It could be a long night. He walked across the kitchen and poured a fresh cup.

"Apparently he's having some serious health issues. He's coming back to the U.S. for a risky heart procedure at University Hospital in Denver."

"I've heard there are some excellent doctors there." Amelia stood and set her empty cup in the sink. "Will you go visit him?"

"At this point, I'd rather drive nails into my body." Matthew sighed. "I told my mom I'd think about it. But I highly doubt it."

Amelia looked into his eyes. "Could this be some of the old ghosts that are haunting you?"

"Could be." Matthew crossed his arms.

"I just wish they'd magically disappear."

CHAPTER 20

*A*fter Amelia left, Matthew knew he wouldn't sleep so he went upstairs and opened the door to Luke's room. He no longer locked it, but somehow it didn't seem right to leave the door standing open. He stepped in and took in the surroundings.

The edge of a gold picture frame on the bookshelf reflected the light flooding through the tattered curtains. He hadn't noticed it before. Curious, he walked over and picked it up.

A younger version of the picture in his study, the man was obviously Evan. A young boy stood beside him wearing a baseball jersey, bat slung over his shoulder. Matthew backed up a few steps to the rocking chair and plopped down. This had to be Luke.

Questions flooded his mind. He couldn't imagine how his great-grandparents had coped not knowing what happened to their son. What had Evan written about the tragedy?

Matthew opened the journal to the spot he'd marked the day before and continued reading the masculine scrawl.

. . .

"Last week at a town meeting, a drunk pulled a gun. Yelled that he wasn't happy with the way I'm running the town and wanted to get rid of the 'problem'. Thank goodness the Sheriff was there and disarmed the man without incident. Danger has become part of my job. Campaigning for the upcoming election starts soon. Emma has mentioned more than once the possibility of not running for re-election. I wish she would leave it in God's hands. I'm happy and want to continue serving as mayor of this fine town. I suppose I do enjoy the prestige more than she ever has. Emma's such a kind, gentle woman. She asked me the other day if my job was getting to be too much....says she can see the stress written all over my face. Even one of the children asked her if I was sick. Do I need to slow down? And spend more time with Emma and the children? And what about God? My relationship with Him is not as close as it used to be. "

Matthew closed the book, using his index finger to mark the spot. His stomach grumbled. He'd been here a while but wasn't ready to leave yet. Somehow he felt closer to Evan in this room than any other place in the house. Had he gotten his business sense from his great-grandfather? Possibly. And this was the place to learn more about him. He flipped to the first page.

"The workmen installed the new stain glass window yesterday at the top of the grand staircase. When you stand at the bottom of the stairs, the light glimmers through the radiant colors of glass. Emma will love it. I'm hoping this beautiful home will replace the feelings of loss and despair from the night our clapboard home burned to the ground. The sound of the lightning bolt hitting the roof and the smell of smoke still plays through my mind."

Matthew closed the journal. The pride of ownership was

evident through Evan's words. He and Emma loved this place. The house he now owned. Maybe it wasn't just an old creaky monstrosity like he'd first believed. Could he see himself living here? And what about Amelia's love for the house and her memories of growing up here? Too bad she couldn't afford it.

His cell phone vibrated. Logan.

"Hey, Logan."

"Got a minute? Just wanted to run an idea by you."

"Sure. What's up?" Matthew laid the journal on the side table and sat back in the rocker.

"I've been talking with Keri." Logan paused. "I invited her out here for a visit. She's never been to New York and wants to see the big city."

"Whew, man. This sounds serious."

"It's like.... I don't know. We've just clicked."

Matthew could hear the excitement in his friend's voice. He felt a slow grin spreading across his face. "I'll give you the advice you've given me. Take your time. Don't make any rash decisions."

"I hear ya." Logan chuckled. "But my advice to you was about dating Eva. That's a whole different ballgame."

"Tell me about it. I hope that blunder doesn't come back to haunt me."

"Me too, man, me too. Back to Keri. You'll be coming home soon. What if she flew out here with you? And you could ask Amelia to come too."

"I see how you slipped that in there, buddy." Matthew stood and walked out of Luke's room, closing the door after him. "I don't know that Amelia would come. We seem to have a love/hate relationship at the moment."

"Why's that?"

"At times we get along great." Matthew stood looking down the long hallway. "But then this house seems to get in the way."

"Ah, the house."

"Yep, this house. I don't think we'll ever see eye to eye on the subject. But I'd love for her to see our world in New York. I'll talk to her."

"Let me know. And I have news on the Grant account."

"Cool. I hope it's good."

"According to several reliable sources, Eva has not, I repeat has not, signed with Charles Grant."

Matthew let out a deep breath. "You've got to be kidding. So she flat out lied to us."

"Yep, sounds that way."

A slow chuckle started in Matthew's throat and turned into a full-blown laugh.

"Did I miss the joke here?" Logan said.

"We'll deal with her later. But this is such a huge relief. We need to be on our A game now and land that account."

"Already on it," Logan said. "Any idea when you'll be back? We could schedule a Skype conference call with Grant, but I'd really prefer a face to face meeting when you return."

"Big doctor appointment next Tuesday. If he finally gets this thing off my foot, I'll be home soon. This has been the longest six weeks of my life."

"Call me after the appointment and I'll get Stacy to set up the meeting."

"You got it." Matthew thought for a moment. "Any way to keep this meeting a secret? I think it'd be in our best interest for Eva not to catch wind of our plans."

"Good idea. Stacy has a good relationship with Grant's assistant. I'll ask her to keep things tight."

"Great. Talk to you on Tuesday."

Matthew disconnected the call and took the stairs one at time, holding onto the railing for his balance, the journal in the other hand. Had Evan ever dealt with a deceptive employee?

How would he have handled it?

Matthew turned over in bed that night and punched the pillow. Again. Darn, the antacids were downstairs. He sure could use one right now. And why couldn't he find the off button to stop the thoughts that were repeating in his mind?

Could he and Logan keep Eva from finding out about their meeting with Grant? He sure wasn't going to take a chance on her really stealing it from them. Every time he drifted off to sleep, he heard her pouty voice and jerked awake. And the bulky cast on his foot sure wasn't helping any.

Darkness filled his bedroom. Finally he got up, pulled on his robe and slippers and walked down the long hall to Luke's room, where he pushed the door open and sat down in Evan's rocker. In the past days, he'd found solace in this room. But tonight was different. He had too much running through his head.

Amelia came to mind. She wasn't like any other woman he'd ever met. He'd never considered a serious relationship. Until now.

And the house. Should he let the sales contract stand? Or try to stop it?

Plus ... did he want to see his father again after so many years? Could he forgive him, like his mother had?

Not to mention ... could he and Logan finally nail the Grant account?

He sat and rocked until the first peeks of light shone through the tattered curtain. Then he needed coffee. He took the back stairs, one at a time, down to the kitchen. While the coffee brewed, he sat down at the table and opened his laptop, where he'd left it the night before.

He opened his e-mail to shoot off a message to Eva and let her know exactly what he and Logan thought of her deception. Anger rose from a place deep inside that he hadn't visited in a long time. He popped an antacid in his mouth and sat back to chew the tablet.

A verse came to him that he'd read the day before. About peace. He opened Evan's Bible to the bookmarked page in 2 Thessalonians and read it again. *Now may the Lord of peace himself give you peace at all times in every way.* Did God really give peace?

The anger began to fade. Along with the pain in his gut. He turned back to the e-mail and hit the delete button.

He'd deal with Eva another time.

On Tuesday morning, Matthew closed the front door and took one step at a time off the porch. Amelia waited in her SUV, ready to take him to his doctor appointment.

"Morning," he said when he opened the car door and climbed in.

"Hey there," she greeted him. "I brought you some coffee for the trip to Denver."

"Thanks." Matthew pulled the mug from the holder and took a sip. "Mmmm. So I finally won you over to my side."

"Not on your life. I'll be a tea lovin' girl forever." She flashed him a smile. "Mom and I had breakfast at the Blue Bird earlier. The coffee is a gift to you from Wanda. She knows how much you love the stuff."

"Good ole Wanda." Matthew took another sip of the black steaming drink. "What color was her hair today?"

Amelia laughed. "It's brown again. Who knows about next week, though."

Amelia exited Chandler Springs and merged on to I-70.

"Yep. Never a dull moment with that woman."

Matthew watched traffic fly by them. He wasn't super happy about Amelia taking him to this appointment. Just one more instance of feeling like a wimp. After today that would all change. He hoped.

"I talked to Logan a few days ago," he said. "He had an idea that I wanted to talk to you about."

"Okay." Amelia gave him a sideways glance and then focused back on the traffic in front of her.

"Logan invited Keri to visit him in New York. He was thinking she could travel with me when I leave soon."

"Those two really have the hots for each other."

"Yeah, that's what I hear. Anyway, Logan suggested that you come too."

Matthew watched her from the corner of his eye. Amelia kept her eyes on the road. No reply.

"Is that a good or bad reaction? Can't really tell."

"It's an 'I'm not sure' reaction, Matthew." Amelia gripped the wheel. "Sometimes it takes me time to process."

"Fair enough. Take all the time you need."

Matthew sat back in the seat. Other women would jump at the chance to spend time with him. But Amelia wasn't like any other woman he'd ever known. And that was a huge part of his attraction to her. He watched the snow-covered mountain peaks flying by his side of the car. He had to admit this was a beautiful part of the country. And it was growing on him.

"Lots to consider," Amelia finally said. "Any idea when you might go?"

"Really depends on what happens today. Get the cast off and I will probably leave in the next week to ten days."

"That's pretty short notice. Let me think about it. And talk it over with Keri."

"Sure."

Matthew hoped Keri could convince her. Since he had obviously failed.

∾

Later that day when they returned to Chandler Springs,Amelia dropped Matthew off at his house. He'd invited her for dinner but she declined because of a house showing that evening. Was this getting to be a thing with her? He hoped not.

Matthew unlocked the front door and thought about dancing down the long hallway. Freedom! The heavy, ugly cast was finally gone. He probably had the biggest smile ever when the doctor told him earlier that day that his foot had healed.

He sat down in Evan's office and punched in Logan's number.

"Hey buddy," he said when Logan answered. "Good news."

"You got it off, Matt?"

"Yep. That thing is long gone. Forever."

"Best news I've had all day. When are you coming home?"

"Looking at schedules right now and figuring out what I still need to wrap up here. I'll keep you posted."

"Did you invite Amelia to come? Keri is super excited but I asked her not to say anything yet."

"Yeah, I invited her earlier. She's thinking about it."

"Okay...I'm surprised she didn't jump at the chance. To me it's a no brainer. Take a vacation and visit the Big Apple." Logan paused. "She works too hard and needs to get away."

"Totally agree," Matthew said. "I wanted to try to convince her. But somehow that didn't feel right." He twirled the pen on the desk. "I'm not getting my hopes up. I don't think she likes me that much and this trip might feel like torture to her."

"I'll have Keri talk to her. She'll convince her."

"Keri can try. But Amelia knows her own mind and doesn't budge once she's made it up."

"I have the feeling it'll work out, Matt. Just wait and see."

"See you soon, buddy. Can't wait to get home."

There was no place like home. And a huge bonus if Amelia agreed to go with him.

CHAPTER 21

"*A*melia, please call me."

Matthew hit the text button and started toward Evan's study. He'd never be tempted to back down on a business deal. So why was this relationship so hard? He'd just entered Evan's office when his phone vibrated, and her number showed on the screen.

"Hi Amelia. Thanks for calling me back so quickly." He could feel his grin from lobe to lobe.

"Good morning. What's up?"

"I'd like to talk to you. Can we meet at the BlueBird in an hour?"

Matthew picked up his empty coffee cup and started back down the hall. Sweet. No more carrying around a ton of bricks. His right foot felt light as the old floorboards creaked under him.

"I have an appointment at noon. But I'm free until then."

"Works for me. Thanks."

Was he hearing some hesitancy in her voice? It was time to find out exactly where he stood with her.

Amelia entered the cafe, dressed in leggings, boots and a multi-colored cardigan trimmed in lace. She spotted Matthew at their usual table. He stood to pull out her chair.

"I've ordered your tea." He motioned to the steaming cup, teabag steeping.

"Thank you." Amelia sat down and let him position her chair.

Matthew slid into his seat. "I spent most of last night in Luke's room thinking."

"And ... ?"

"I'm going back to New York at the end of next week." He sat his coffee cup on the table. "I'd really like you to go with me." His hand went over hers.

"I've been thinking too," Amelia said. Her phone buzzed in her purse on the floor.

Pulling her hand back, she looked at him apologetically and reached down for it.

"Sorry. Tiffany is texting about a meeting this afternoon."

Matthew gave her a stoic nod.

Amelia poked a few buttons and laid the phone, screen side down, on the table. "Where were we?" She brushed a stray hair from her face. "Oh yeah. New York."

"You need a break from all that." He motioned toward her cell.

"Yeah, I do. It would be nice to get away." She picked it up again and scrolled to her calendar.

"There's one glitch. I have a big meeting during the time we'd be gone ..."

Matthew broke eye contact with her.

Amelia lifted her eyebrows. Was she imagining his reaction? This was really a big deal for him. "I've asked one of the other agents to cover for me. Shouldn't be a problem."

"Logan is pumped Keri's going." Matthew cleared his throat.

Amelia studied his sturdy facial features. Was it her imagination? Or was Mr. Smooth Businessman, trying hard to control his feelings?

"Keri basically talked me into going. Said we couldn't miss our golden opportunity to see the Big Apple."

Amelia watched Matthew rub the back of his neck and let out a big sigh. What was up with him today? She'd never seen him this way.

"I'll book the tickets this afternoon," he said finally. "Logan's sister is an airline attendant and lives in my building. Her apartment is set up as an Air B&B when she's on overseas flights. He'll check to see if the dates could work for you and Keri to stay there."

"Good arrangement." Amelia was surprised how happy she felt right now. She'd walked in here not knowing what her answer would be.

"Come over tonight for dinner. We'll make plans." Matthew left Wanda a twenty on the table. The uncertainty had passed and he was back to himself.

"Sounds lovely."

∼

Amelia knocked on the Rose Haven door at 6 p.m.

"Welcome." Matthew opened the door wide enough for her to enter.

"Smells wonderful. Have you been cooking all afternoon?" Amelia stepped into the vestibule. She took her coat off and hung it on the coat tree in the corner.

Matthew shot her an amused grin. "Nope. Have to give kudos to Keri. That girl is an amazing chef."

He led Amelia down the hall to the dining room. Glowing candles and a flower center piece filled the center of the table.

Amelia lowered herself into the chair that Matthew pulled

out for her. "I feel like a special guest. Even the best china and crystal goblets."

"Aren't you glad I didn't sell it all?" Matthew looked at her with a playful smile and sliced the roasted chicken with a carving knife.

"I think Evan and Emma would be honored we're using their stuff." Amelia filled her plate with chicken, mashed potatoes and green beans. "Ah. Keri out did herself," she said through a bite of potatoes smothered in gravy. "This is amazing."

"She's a great cook. How long have you known her?" From the large bites of food he was downing, Matthew seemed to be enjoying the meal himself.

"We go way back to elementary school. She used to protect me from the playground bullies. We've been great friends all these years." Amelia wiped her mouth with the linen napkin.

"Save room for dessert. She also brought a dozen of her famous German Chocolate cupcakes." Matthew chewed the last bite of his meat.

Amelia leaned back in her chair and glanced around the room. A wonderful meal, in a wonderful house with a wonderful man. Oh brother, where did that thought come from? Matthew's voice interrupted her.

"So when can you get away to go to New York?"

"Next Friday will work." Amelia reached for a cupcake from the open box on the table and took a bite. "Ummm.... Heavenly." She handed one to Matthew.

He peeled back the paper and stuffed half of it in his mouth. "Agreed." He finished it in two bites and reached for another. "Have you ever been to New York?"

"Actually, I haven't. The farthest east I've been is Pennsylvania." Amelia stood to clear the table.

"Well, it's definitely different than here. A much faster paced life. And you might find people aren't quite as friendly."

"I think I can survive." Amelia picked up both empty plates.

"Here. Let's use this. I found it in the butler's pantry."
Matthew stood up and walked to the corner of the room. He
pushed a four-wheeled cart toward her. "We can take it all in
one load."

Amelia filled the cart with dishes, glasses and silverware. As
Matthew pushed it down the hall, she blew out the candles.
Wouldn't it be fun to entertain here with Matthew? She slapped
the thought away and joined him in the kitchen.

Matthew piled the dishes in the sink. "I can wash those
later."

"There's not much to do. I don't mind helping." Amelia
opened the lower cabinet to look for dish soap and turned on
the hot water before he could protest.

"Okay, then. You wash and I'll dry."

"Deal." Amelia wiped the first plate with a soapy dishcloth.
She rinsed and placed it in the dish drainer. "You do know how
to dry dishes, don't you?"

"Of course. My mom still insists I help her when I visit."

Amelia laughed. "You have a great Mom."

"Yeah, I do actually. She was determined to teach me to at
least boil water and sew on a button before I left for college."

In a playful mood, Amelia flicked a handful of suds toward
Matthew. The bubbles landed on his cheek.

"Hey. Now you're in for it." He aimed the dishtowel and
snapped at her leg, missing on purpose. Matthew laid down the
towel. "I'd much rather do this."

He pulled her into his arms and found her warm lips before
she could protest.

Matthew's cell on the counter buzzed. With a startled look,
Amelia stepped back. She couldn't help glancing at the screen.
Who was Eva? And why was Matthew's face so flushed?

Matthew grabbed his cell and hit the off button. He didn't
say anything.

"If you need to return the call, I'll give you privacy." Amelia took another step back. She was almost surprised how disappointed she felt about the interruption.

"Nope. It can wait until later." Matthew dried the last of the silverware and lifted the stack of clean plates into the cabinet. "Want to watch the sunset from the veranda?"

"Sure. If you'll make me some hot tea."

"Like I told you, boiling water is one of my specialties." With the tea kettle boiling and coffee brewing, the two stood awkwardly for a moment.

Would he try to kiss her again? Amelia couldn't decide how she felt and was relieved when the tea kettle whistled. Pouring his coffee into a ceramic mug, Matthew waited while Amelia added a tea bag and boiling water to her cup. They both stopped at the hallway tree and wrapped up in winter coats, gloves and scarves before opening the door and stepping out on the veranda.

"Are we crazy, or what? It's pretty chilly out here tonight." Amelia pulled the parka hood over her head.

Matthew settled into a wicker rocker. "But it's such a clear night. And we're just in time to watch the sun set over the mountains." He pointed to the thin wispy clouds turning brilliant shades of orange and red in the distance.

Amelia sat down in the chair beside him. "I never tire of this view."

The two rocked in silence, sipping hot drinks as the sun sank behind the mountain. Matthew stretched his long legs in front of him. "So nice to have that thing off my leg." He looked over at Amelia. "When I first arrived here the silence drove me crazy."

"I couldn't imagine it any other way." Amelia pushed her chair gently back and forth, the rockers creaking on the porch surface.

"Never thought I'd admit it, but it's growing on me." Matthew drained his coffee cup. "Looking forward to getting back to New York, though."

"Oh, by the way, what kind of clothes should I take?"

"Mainly casual. And definitely bring your boots. Pack something dressy and we'll catch a Broadway Show." Matthew looked at her with a slow smile that built.

"I'd love that." Amelia felt her pulse increase. Was she finally getting excited about the trip? Or about him?

"I'll have Logan pre-purchase tickets. Any show in particular you'd like to see?"

"You choose. I'd be happy to see any of them." To be honest, she didn't follow the latest shows on Broadway. She'd trust him on this one.

"I'll check the listings tomorrow."

"Perfect." Amelia stood. "It's a little chilly out here for me." She picked up her teacup. "I should go. I have an early meeting tomorrow."

Matthew stood and walked with her to the porch steps. He leaned toward her like he was going to kiss her again. She pushed the teacup toward him. "Thanks for the meal and ..."

She almost barreled down the steps, a heaviness in her stomach. When she reached the car door, she looked back at Matthew, standing on the porch, still holding her cup. The confused look on his face almost made her feel sorry for him.

But seriously, who was Eva?

CHAPTER 22

*T*he porch light was on when Amelia arrived home.
Barking loud enough to wake the neighbors, Harley
bounded toward her as she opened the front door. One lone
light shone in the corner of the living room meaning her mom
had already gone to bed.

Amelia put her finger to her lips. "Shhh.... Harley." He
jumped up on her parka, almost knocking her over. "Down,
boy." She patted his head. "I'm happy to see you too," she
whispered.

He followed her down the hallway to her room, her ever
faithful companion.

Amelia turned on the light and sat down in her corner over-
stuffed chair. She'd always thought of it as her "thinking" spot.
A safe place to contemplate and pray over huge decisions, like
the risk she'd taken to buy the real estate company. And a place
to grieve when first Evelyn and then Austin Chandler had
passed away. And later Brian. Yep, she'd spent many hours in
this chair.

Right now her mind raced with the happenings of the past
few hours. She picked up her phone to text Keri. She was

surprised to see it was after 11 p.m. Maybe it was better to sort out her feelings first.

Why had she reacted when Matthew seemed like he wanted to kiss her again on the porch? The first one had been a total surprise but she hadn't objected. She'd actually gotten caught up in the moment. Until they were interrupted by his phone.

Had it been her imagination, or did he act strange when he found out who was calling? He'd never mentioned an Eva that she could remember. Was she feeling a little jealous? She shifted in her chair.

Matthew Chandler. What a complicated relationship it had been so far. Starting with a strong dislike for each other, to being his real estate agent, and then on to a casual friendship. Now they'd had their first kiss. Almost.

His handsome face came to mind. Her insides no longer twisted when she thought of him. She really did like Matthew. A new relationship had been so scary for so long. It seemed the men she loved in the past had died. Her daddy, Brian. Could she stand the thought of losing Matthew? She decided to put the question aside for now. The peaceful answer floated through her head as her eyelids grew heavy.

The next day at work, Tiffany reminded Amelia about an important quarterly meeting with real estate executives in Denver. When she clicked on her calendar, her heart sank. It was scheduled for the same day she'd planned to fly to New York with Matthew and Keri. Maybe this was a sign she wasn't supposed to go after all. Since leaving Matthew's last night, she couldn't shake the sad feeling of leaving him standing on the porch. She picked up her cell and punched auto dial.

"Hey, you got a minute?" Amelia balanced her phone under her chin while she shuffled through paperwork.

"Hi there," Keri said. "Yeah, waiting on a roast to finish. What's up?" Keri said.

Amelia sighed. "Just realized I have a super important meeting the day we're leaving for New York.".

"Can you change it?"

"I wish. These quarterly meetings are set up by the bigwigs in Denver. I'm a little peon in their eyes and just expected to attend."

"Oh." Amelia could hear the disappointment in Keri's voice. "Maybe Matthew would agree to leave a day later."

"I hate to ask him. He was kind enough to purchase our tickets. Can you imagine the fee to change flights for all three of us?"

"True. Anyone else in your office that could go in your place?"

Amelia thought for a moment. "Yeah. That might work. Dan would probably agree. He likes to rub elbows with the big guys."

"Ok. Well let me know. I'm really praying that you can work it out."

"Me too. Talk later."

Amelia started to mention the kiss with Matthew but thought better of it. Keri would know soon enough. She checked her calendar again. No mistake. It was the same morning as the flight to New York. She shot off an e-mail to Dan, praying that he'd be willing to attend in her place. She really did want to make this trip.

Amelia exited the real estate building at 5:45 pm and headed for her car. She rubbed her neck to release some of the tension. It had been a long day. Warm pajamas and a good movie were calling her name. And a hot cup of tea.

At Main Street she surprised herself when she took a left

rather than a right and headed toward Rose Haven. She hadn't heard from Matthew all day. She parked in the circular drive and climbed the steps to the front door. She knocked several times. Probably should have called or texted first. As she turned to leave, Matthew opened the door.

"Hey."

She loved the way he looked in baggy jeans and a wrinkled t-shirt with his bangs hanging over his forehead. Definitely not his normal business attire.

Matthew clenched his jaw. "Didn't know if I'd see you again."

"Me either. Last night was...well, confusing."

He stood and looked at her, his face like stone.

"I came by to apologize." Amelia rubbed the back of her neck again. It was really hurting. "I'm sorry, I shouldn't have left so abruptly last night."

"And why did you?"

Darkness had fallen, and a cold breeze whipped through the porch. "Would you mind if I come in? So we can talk?"

Matthew opened the door wider, his face still impassive. "Come on in."

Amelia stepped inside. The house was always cool but at least she was out of the wind. She motioned to the coat rack. "Mind if I hang up my coat?"

"Suit yourself." Matthew watched her hang up the coat and scarf.

Amelia could feel the chill and it wasn't just the cold house. She watched his facial features. What was it she'd heard? The eyes were the way to the soul?

"I've really offended you."

Matthew looked at her. His eyes at the moment were steel grey. "Just trying to figure out where you're coming from. One minute we get along great, the next minute you're shoving a teacup at me and running to your car."

Amelia suddenly wanted to kiss him. Kiss away the hurt and anger he obviously felt at the moment.

"I did a lot of thinking last night. After losing Brian, I had built up the idea in my mind that I couldn't face another relationship. So I've been alone all these years."

Amelia followed Matthew into Evan's study. "But last night something shifted. I can't explain it exactly. But I've decided fear isn't going to run my life."

Matthew's face softened. "What's different this time?"

Amelia laid her hand on his chest. "I have a peace when I'm with you that I haven't had in a long, long while."

Matthew pulled her into his arms. She wasn't afraid this time.

Matthew and Amelia exited the taxi onto the busy New York City street. He watched her crane her neck to see the top of the twelve story building in front of them.

"Here we are." He paid the driver, grabbed their overnight bags and started toward the door.

"Wait."

Two steps ahead, Matthew turned around to watch Amelia. He set the bags on the sidewalk.

She twirled in circles on the sidewalk, her arms flying. "I just want to take it all in."

Matthew watched with a lazy smile, slow and relaxed.

"This is better than I ever expected. I just want to stand here and look at the skyscrapers and the street jammed with cars and the people scurrying to their next destination." Amelia stopped to catch her breath.

"Slow down there." Matthew grabbed her arm when she started to tilt. "You'll have plenty of time."

Amelia picked up her purse and started toward the

revolving door as a bell man stepped out to pick up the luggage the taxi driver had unloaded from the trunk and set on the sidewalk.

The doorman tipped his hat at Matthew. "Nice to see you, Mr. Chandler."

"Thanks, Everett. Seems like I've been away forever."

Matthew led Amelia toward the elevators.

She stared at the glittering gold and seemed impressed. "Beautiful lobby."

With a nod of satisfaction, Matthew pushed the elevator button. "It's a great place to live."

When the doors opened, Matthew stepped inside after her, his hand on her back. He pressed the button for the 7th floor.

Amelia glanced at the mirrored elevator wall.

"You look beautiful, by the way."

"Thank you." She fluffed her hair. "I owe Dan at the office big time for covering that meeting for me."

"Yeah, how will you repay him?" In his office, Matthew knew they received cash awards and bonuses.

Amelia smiled at him. "Oh, probably a large coffee."

Her sapphire eyes melted his heart. "Aren't you the big spender?"

"Yep, that's me."

The elevator dinged. "Here we are."

They stepped into a long hallway and turned to the left. Matthew stopped in front of 728 and inserted his keycard. The door opened into a hall lined with modern art. At the end, a large open room showcased the New York skyline through the picture window.

"Beautiful." Amelia walked to the glass. "Almost takes my breath away."

"Yeah, that's how I felt when I first saw this place. But then my schedule got so crazy busy. Now I hardly ever open the curtains." He pointed to the street below. An ambulance sped by, a taxi maneuvered through traffic. People scurried like ants, hurrying to their next destination.

"I love it! I'd never get tired of this." Amelia sat her travel bag on the floor and watched the people.

"Logan's sister, Heather, lives on the tenth floor. I'll take you up in a few to meet up with Keri."

"Those two were so cute at the airport. I think Keri has it bad for him." Amelia giggled.

Matthew winked at her. "And I think he feels the same for her." He sat his business bag and backpack on the floor "Actually, I'm happy for them. Logan is a good guy."

Amelia nodded. "It'll be fun to see what happens."

Matthew flipped on the light in the kitchen as Amelia followed. "The maid service cleaned in here yesterday." He pulled two bottles of water from the refrigerator and handed one to her. "Let me know if you need anything. Our luggage should arrive soon."

"I'd love to look out the window until then. Then I'll go upstairs to rest for a bit." Amelia took a gulp of the water and twisted the cap back on.

"Take all the time you need. We can order in tonight or go out. Your choice."

"Let's go out. I want to see more of this fabulous city." Amelia settled into the chair in front of the window.

"Italian okay? I'll call for reservations at my favorite restaurant. Guaranteed the best place in town."

And he would make sure they had the most secluded table in the place. This night would be perfect.

"Sounds delicious."

"Can you be ready by six?" Matthew was thinking about a run while Amelia people watched. Or at least a little jog.

"Absolutely."

Matthew spent the afternoon in his home office getting things squared away before he went to work the next day. As good as it was to be back, he couldn't keep his mind off Amelia. Normally he never thought about anything but the next account. Go figure.

At 5:45 Matthew knocked on the door where Amelia was staying. Keri answered the door.

"Hi Matthew. She's almost ready."

At that moment, Amelia stepped from the bathroom dressed in a suede jacket, pencil skirt and knee high boots.

He loved the way she dressed. "You look great."

"You don't look so bad yourself." Amelia slipped her purse over her shoulder. "See you later," she said to Keri.

Moments later, Matthew and Amelia exited the lobby. "The restaurant is just a few blocks away. Do you mind walking?"

"It's such a lovely evening. Let's enjoy it." Amelia took his arm and fell into sync with his steps.

Two cars and a taxi blared horns on the busy street. "Quite different than my sleepy little mountain town," Amelia commented.

"Yep, I've lived here so long, I hardly notice any more." Matthew shrugged. "I hope you like Italian food."

"One of my favorites. Oh, by the way, I called Mom earlier. She and Harley are doing fine."

"I'm glad that puts your mind at ease."

"It does. I'm not away from Mom much, and I worry about her. She's a trooper, but she lives with chronic pain."

"Really? You've never mentioned that about Ruth."

"Some days the arthritis is so bad she can't get out of bed. And then that causes bouts with depression." Amelia looked away.

"Really sorry to hear that. Are there any treatments to help her?"

"She's following a strict diet now and goes to a Chronic Pain

Clinic every week. That's why I'm so excited about her new business. It gives her something to look forward to and gets her mind off her health." Amelia exhaled. "I'm praying that God will heal her."

Matthew stopped and looked at her. "Do you believe that?"

"What, that God can heal her?

"Yes."

"Actually, I do. Does that surprise you?

"I'm not sure how I feel about God. We haven't been on speaking terms for many years."

They started walking again.

"I'm sorry ... but I would give Him another chance."

"Why?"

"We all have our disappointments in life when things don't work out like we think they should. But God is still in control. And He still works in our lives."

Time to change the subject. "Ahh ... here we are."

Matthew pulled the restaurant door open for Amelia. The fragrant aroma of baking bread assaulted his nostrils.

"Good evening, Mr. Chandler." The maitre d' led them to a table in a private corner. He pulled out the chair for Amelia.

"Thank you, Tony." Matthew sat down and opened the drink menu. "Would you like a drink?"

"You know that I'm really more of a teetotaler," Amelia said with a sweet smile. "But this is a special occasion. I'll make an exception tonight."

"And I'll skip my normal mixed drink and join you." Matthew ordered a bottle of white wine.

Amelia opened her menu. "This is a wonderful place."

"It's the first Italian restaurant I visited when I moved here. Never had a reason to try any others."

The waiter arrived with two glasses and a wine bottle chilling in a gold bucket. Matthew stared at the menu but the conversation about God had thrown him off a bit. He shook his head and focused his eyes on the selections.

"I highly recommend the triple plate. Their lasagna is the best in town. And the eggplant parmesan and veal meatballs with linguine are quite good too."

He looked up and caught a strange look on Amelia's face. Of course, she'd never order a meal that would serve three people. "Tell you what. I'll order that, and we'll share."

Amelia let out a sigh of relief. "Great. And I will have a salad."

"Glad that's settled." Matthew opened the wine bottle and poured two glasses. He set one in front of Amelia. "To the future."

She tapped his glass but her smile had faded a bit. Maybe he shouldn't have said that.

"What's on the agenda for tomorrow?"

"I have a meeting in the morning. You can lounge and enjoy yourself. I have the feeling my living room curtains will be wide open, with you planted in front of them."

"You got that right!" Amelia took a sip of her wine.

"My meeting should end by noon, and I'll pick you up for lunch. Then we'll see some sights, have a nice dinner."

Amelia clasped her hands to her chest. "Sounds like a perfect day."

On the walk back to the condo, Matthew grabbed Amelia's hand. It was warm, just like her warm heart. He hoped the awkward moments of the evening had passed. The God conversation played in his mind again. He'd just let it go for now.

"I'll walk you up to Heather's apartment."

Matthew allowed her to enter the building first.

"It's really been a lovely day, Matthew."

"I'm happy that you agreed to come."

They stepped into the elevator. Their conversation seemed a bit formal. Being with her was what mattered to him right now.

On the tenth floor, Matthew inserted the key card and the

door clicked open. Voices from the other room drifted into the hallway.

When Matthew and Amelia entered the living room, Logan and Keri were cuddled on the couch watching a movie.

Logan hit the mute button on the TV control. "Hey, you're back. How was dinner?"

"Wonderful." Matthew and Amelia said at the same time. And then laughed together.

Keri motioned to the empty Chinese food cartons spread on the coffee table. "We decided it was take-out night."

"Looks like you're enjoying yourselves." Matthew made a thumbs-up to Logan. "We don't want to interrupt."

"I'm wiped out," Amelia said. "This girl is going to bed."

Matthew leaned down and kissed her warm lips. "Get rested up for tomorrow."

"Mmm....I can't wait."

"Night all." Amelia headed for the bedroom.

"Good night." He'd better leave now before he changed his mind. He let himself out.

"See you tomorrow." Logan called and the movie started again.

Matthew exited the apartment. Logan and Keri seemed so comfortable together.

Would Amelia ever be that at ease with him?

The next morning Amelia filled the tub with warm water and watched the bubbles multiply. She couldn't remember the last time she'd enjoyed a relaxing bubble bath. She looked over at the Navy blue beaded silk dress hanging on the back of the door. She hoped Matthew would like it. Was she dressing for him? That hadn't happened for a long time, not since losing

Brian. Matthew Chandler was certainly making an impression on her.

She lit two candles Heather had left for her and Keri and laid back in the tub. Relaxed by the warm water, she nodded off for a few minutes. She finished her bath, styled her hair and applied a light coat of make-up. She chose a tunic top and leggings to go with the boots Matthew had requested that she bring. When she stepped out into the hallway, she could hear Keri humming in the kitchen.

Ah... she'd never heard Keri do that before. Keri and Logan didn't seem to have obstacles in their relationship. And Keri seemed so sure about him. Amelia wished she could be that sure about Matthew. What was it that was still niggling at her?

"Smells wonderful in here. Looks like you're in your element."

Two empty bowls, slices of buttered toast and jelly were on the table.

"The bacon is almost done." Keri turned to the stove and lifted the lid to turn the meat.

"You rock. How have I survived without you?"

Keri grinned. "I'm always here for you."

Amelia sat down at the table. "Hey, has Logan ever mentioned someone named Eva to you?"

Keri set a bowl of steaming oatmeal in front of Amelia. "I don't think so." She started to turn back toward the stove. "Oh wait. He did mention someone by that name."

"Any idea who she is?" Amelia took a sip of her hot tea.

"If I remember right, she's a colleague of Matthew and Logan's."

"Oh." Who was this woman?

And why did Matthew seem so secretive about her?

CHAPTER 23

On Matthew's first day back to work, he found himself whistling as he stepped into the atrium of Canon Financial. The space had taken on a new look. Fresh paint and decor. New furniture. He hadn't been gone that long. Had he?

"Chandler, welcome back." Harry, one of his older colleagues slapped him on the back. "How's the leg?"

"Much better. Thanks."

Good ole Harry. One of the wise mentors who'd taught him a lot about the financial world. What had it been? Ten years ago?

Matthew pushed through the glass doors into the office hallway and stopped at Stacy's desk.

"Mr. Chandler." Stacy stood up to welcome him. "So good to see you."

"It's great to be back," Matthew replied with a triumphant grin. "Were you able to arrange the meeting this morning with Eva Pearce?"

Stacy nodded. "Yes. She'll be here at 10 am."

"Thanks." Matthew knew there was no love lost when it came to Eva. Stacy was professional enough not to say anything.

But he could see it in her eyes. He started toward his office, but he turned and looked back at his assistant. "Good job on keeping things going while I was away."

"You're very welcome."

Matthew made a mental note. Stacy deserved a bonus. A very nice one. He unlocked his office and stepped in. Nothing had changed in here. Same view, same furniture. He'd waited for this day for so long. Why did he feel different here?

Stacy appeared in the doorway with a mug of coffee. "Thought you might need this first thing." She sat the steaming black drink on his desk.

Matthew took a sip. "Really appreciate you, Stacy."

"Always happy to help." She turned to leave.

"You kept the place going." Matthew took another sip. "And kept Logan out of trouble."

Stacy laughed. "That was a big job. We're all very relieved that you're back. It just wasn't the same around here without you."

"Thanks." Matthew wished he could turn off the strange feelings rolling through his head at the moment. Wasn't this what he'd wanted? To return to work at Canon?

Stacy stepped out of his office and closed the door behind her.

Waiting for his laptop to boot, Matthew sipped his coffee and swiveled to look out on the Hudson River. A tugboat chugged by. Sailboats floated lazily on the calm water. Sometimes his life here felt like that tugboat, always trying to be the best, always striving for the next new deal. He'd prided himself in having the best performance in the company. But the sailboat. Ahh, floating, enjoying life. No pressure. No stress.

Wait, was that how he felt in Chandler Springs?

A knock on the door interrupted Matthew's thoughts. "Come in."

Logan stuck his head in. "Hey Matt. It's about time you came back to work."

"Yep. It's really good to be back." Matthew repositioned toward his friend.

Logan slid into a chair next to the desk. "Have you talked to Eva since you returned?"

"Nope. This will be our first conversation."

"Should be interesting. With her you never know."

"I don't have to ask how your evening went with Keri." Matthew peered at him over the top of his coffee mug.

"Not sure if I've ever believed in a soul mate. But I think I've found mine." Logan's cell phone pinged. "Hey, she's texting me to say good morning."

"You deserve happiness with her, man."

"There's just something about her. We really connect."

Matthew gave his friend a satisfied nod. What was it about those two women from Colorado? He couldn't wait to meet his blonde date for lunch. But for now, he had to keep his mind on business.

Eva opened the office door and entered without knocking. Dressed in a black slinky dress, stiletto heels and more makeup than a Broadway actress, she made her grand entrance.

Matthew's mind went back to Amelia. He was starting to love her – what did she call it? – Boho/mountain look.

"So you're finally home." Eva closed the door behind her, looking directly at Matthew, ignoring Logan.

Matthew pointed to the empty chair. "Have a seat."

Eva swung her way across the room and sat down across from the two men. She glanced at Matthew's mug of coffee. "Tell Stacy I'll take mine with cream and sugar."

"Later Eva." Matthew had little tolerance for her at the moment. "Right now we're here to talk about the Grant account." He focused on her face.

Eva flashed a sly grin. "I knew you'd be happy to hear that Charles Grant is my new client."

"That's not the way we're hearing it." Matthew felt the irritation rising up his neck. "Want to tell us the truth?"

Eva batted her eyelashes at him. "Not sure what you're talking about, Matthew."

Her flirty movements, the ones he'd never noticed before, almost made him laugh out loud. Logan had nailed it. This woman was a piece of work.

"We know for a fact that Charles Grant has not signed with Liberty Financial. Or with you."

"Where did you hear...."

Matthew held up his hand. "Stop, Eva. Stop the games. Stop the lies."

Eva's face turned to a pout. "But..."

"Nope. We're not going there either. This meeting is over." He stood and started toward the office door to let her out.

Eva looked down and pretended to brush the wrinkles out of the front of her dress. When she stood up, her face had twisted.

"This is not over. You will be sorry," she hissed and stomped past Matthew. The office door would have slammed if he hadn't grabbed it.

Matthew looked at Logan. "Wow. What a diva performance."

"You got that right." Logan flopped on the couch. "Tell me again how you let that lady worm her way into your life?"

Matthew ran his hands through his hair. "I was attracted to her, okay? She always wanted to have the best and be the best. I was fascinated that we had the same goals in life."

"Until she went over the deep end." Logan stood and moved toward the door. "It'll be interesting to see how this all plays out."

"This is the end. Period." Matthew took a deep breath.

He'd make sure of it.

Matthew entered his building elevator and punched the button for the 10th floor. He almost had to restrain himself from skipping down the hall. The Eva meeting behind him, all he could think about was spending time with Amelia. He couldn't believe his good fortune in finding a woman like her. And all because of an old house in Colorado.

Matthew took Amelia to his favorite old world deli where he picked up the picnic basket he'd ordered earlier. As much as Amelia begged to know where the taxi was taking them, he refused until they arrived at Central Park. Matthew paid the driver as Amelia exited the cab. He grabbed her hand, picnic basket in his other.

They walked through the grass, hand in hand, looking for a place to eat. A couple with two small children were gathering trash and folding their blanket. Perfect timing. Matthew and Amelia grabbed the open spot.

Matthew unwrapped bruschetta, sliced cheese, crusty bread and a container of grapes. He spread a cloth on the ground and then pulled out a bottle of wine and two glasses.

"Hope you don't mind the light lunch. Dinner will make up for it. I promise."

"Not at all." Amelia looked around. "The flowers alone create the perfect ambience."

"Just wait."

Finishing the bread and cheese, Matthew popped a grape in his mouth and pulled the last one from the stem. He rolled it against Amelia's lips.

"Yum, one of my favorites. Thank you for such a tasty lunch."

"And now we are off."

Matthew stood and reloaded the picnic basket with empty food containers. A perfect lunch. With the woman he was starting to love.

Matthew reached for Amelia's hand to balance her as she stepped up into the white carriage. Her heart pounded as she settled next to him. When he extended his arm over her shoulders, she didn't protest but leaned into him.

The driver nudged the horses forward, and the carriage rolled into a slow pace. Matthew pointed out buildings and landmarks, laughing and recounting funny stories about his New York experiences with Logan. The time they'd gotten locked in the top of the Empire State Building. And the day he and Logan went to the Statute of Liberty dressed in business suits and a bunch of women from Alabama thought they were tour guides and wouldn't stop asking them questions. She had tears rolling down her cheeks. She'd never laughed so much with him.

The carriage rolled to a stop and Matthew jumped out first. He put his arms around her waist and lifted her out. She felt like her feet hadn't touched the ground since arriving in New York City.

"Want to know what's next?" Matthew said with a teasing sparkle in his eyes.

"Yes, I'd love to know."

"It's a surprise. Not going to tell you."

Amelia made a face and stuck her tongue out at him. Could this be the same uptight businessman who had ticked her off the moment she'd met him?

"We're just a few blocks from my condo. Do you mind walking? I'd like to stop there for a few minutes."

"Not at all. I'd enjoy the walk."

They set off down the street, holding hands and talking like they'd known each other forever. Amelia felt the walls around her heart melting.

Later that day Amelia snuggled into the lounge chair, positioned in front of open curtains in Matthew's apartment. The New York skyline shimmered in the bright sunlight. She'd told Matthew she planned to take full advantage of this magnificent view since he'd been called in for a last-minute meeting at the office. Lost in the activity outside the picture window, Amelia jumped at the knock on the door. Matthew would have used his key card. She tiptoed to the door to look through the peephole. A dark-haired woman stood in the hallway. She looked innocent enough.

Amelia opened the door. "Yes?"

"Is Matthew home?" The woman, dressed in a tailored suit and matching spike heels, pushed her way in. She slung her Gucci bag over her shoulder.

Startled, Amelia replied, "No, he's at his office."

The woman frowned, her penciled eyebrows drawn together. "And who are you?"

Amelia hardened her eyes. "I'm a friend of Matthew's." She was being sized up and that didn't sit well coming from someone she'd never met.

Finally the woman stuck out her perfectly manicured hand adorned with a diamond ring. "Eva Pearce. Matthew and I are very good friends."

Amelia caught the emphasis on "very good". So this was Eva. Well, well.

"As I said, he's not here. I'd be happy to give him a message for you."

"I'd like to wait for him, if you don't mind." Eva started down the hall like she owned the place. "Mind if I get a bottle of water from the fridge?" She was already at the doorway to the kitchen.

"Help yourself."

Obviously the woman had been here before. Amelia felt a twist in her gut that said: *Matthew, I hope you can explain this.*

Eva pulled a water from the refrigerator and unscrewed the cap. She took a long drink and followed Amelia into the living room.

Well, if this wasn't awkward. Amelia picked up her cell and texted Matthew.

Eva perched on the arm of the couch, staring at her. "So you're here visiting?"

"Yes, I am," Amelia said with forced control.

Eva sipped her water. "What do you do for a living?"

Being questioned by Matthew's alleged girlfriend was the last thing she wanted to be doing, but she said, "I own a real estate company."

"Oh, you must be the chick from Colorado that's selling that old house Matthew inherited."

Amelia cringed. She'd never been called a 'chick' before. What had Matthew told this woman about her?

"Yes, that's right."

"I'm so happy that Matthew's back. I've been lonely without him."

Amelia faked a smile. "Is that right?"

"Has he ever mentioned me?"

"Sorry, I don't think so." Amelia wanted nothing more than to get away from this person.

"Really? That's surprising considering how close we've become."

Amelia's stomach dropped. Was that why Eva had texted him the other night? When he'd acted so strange. She didn't know what to say. Right now she just wanted to wipe the smug look off this woman's face.

"He should be here any minute."

"Mind if I use the restroom?" Eva stood and started down the hall before Amelia could reply.

"Sure." She started to direct her but realized Eva knew the way. Yep, she'd been here before.

Amelia picked up her cell phone when it pinged. Matthew was on his way home. What a relief. Her mind racing with questions about this strange woman, she heard the key card click and the front door open. She stepped into the hallway and saw Matthew coming in the front door.

Eva exited the bathroom at the same time. She ran down the hall to meet him and tried to pull him into a hug. "I'm so happy you're back."

Matthew pulled away from her. "Eva." Anger filled his face. He nodded toward Amelia. "I guess you've met."

Amelia grimaced. "Yes, we have."

"I just wanted to stop by to make sure we're on for tonight." Eva blinked rapidly.

Either the woman had something in her eye or she was batting her eyelashes at Matthew. Who did that? Amelia watched from a distance.

"And to see how your leg is doing." Eva stepped closer.

Matthew took two more steps back from her. "As I told you this morning, my leg is great." He frowned. "And we don't have any plans tonight."

"Didn't Logan tell you? There's a party at Woody's. A gathering of old friends from the office. I thought it would be nice if we go together."

"I have other plans."

Amelia watched the fallen look on Eva's face. The woman actually believed that he would take her.

Eva stepped toward him again. "You've been gone so long. I was hoping we could catch up."

Matthew put both hands out in front of him. "Good bye, Eva."

He grabbed her arm and led her down the hallway. Amelia

cringed at her loud protests. Matthew opened the front door, pushed her out and shut it.

Amelia headed for the living room lounger, head spinning. She felt like crying.

"Hey, sorry about that." Matthew walked in the room and stood beside the chair.

Confused, Amelia stayed silent.

"What did she tell you?"

"That you are very good friends." She wished she could turn off the tape of Eva's arrogant words that played over and over in her head.

"Amelia, look at me." Matthew touched her cheek. "Eva and I dated but it was never serious. At least not on my part."

"I'm not sure what to believe." He did throw her out. But still...

Matthew stepped in front of the window and looked down at her. "I'm telling you the truth. She means nothing to me."

Amelia stood. "I'm sorry Matthew. Right now I just can't do this. I'm going upstairs."

She let herself out.

CHAPTER 24

$\mathcal{M}$atthew heard the click of the front door. He raked his fingers through his hair. Eva had some nerve showing up here. But he wasn't about to let that woman ruin this new relationship. He'd give Amelia some time to cool off a bit. And he'd make it up to her.

But he didn't see Amelia until later the next day. Her text told him she and Keri were going to do some sightseeing on their own. Her silence after that told him she was still mulling over that whole scene with Eva. The longer he mulled it over, the more sure he was that she'd have her bags packed when he went to pick her up that night for the Broadway show. By the time he tried to use the key card to enter Heather's apartment, his hands were so sweaty he dropped the darn thing on the carpet twice.

"Nervous much?" Logan said.

Matthew clenched his teeth and put his arm out to stop Logan from entering. "We better announce we're here. Wouldn't want to surprise them."

Logan shot his friend a full grin. "Smart idea."

Matthew knocked on the door frame of the open front door. "Amelia."

Amelia appeared around the corner in a Navy blue beaded dress. She flung her arms in a dramatic fashion. "What do you think?"

Matthew whistled. "Wow. You look amazing."

She glided down the hall toward him. "You don't clean up bad yourself." She turned to Logan. "Keri will be out in a minute."

"I'll wait in the living room." Logan disappeared through the doorway.

Amelia turned to Matthew. "I'd like to talk later. About what happened yesterday."

"Of course." He laid his hand on her arm. Was it his imagination or did she stiffen when he touched her?

Amelia eyes glimmered. "But first, I want to experience the Big Apple."

Amelia wanted to pinch herself. She was really sitting in a theater box at a Broadway play. Matthew reached over and laid his hand on top of hers. Eva's face shot through her mind. She wanted to pull away from him. She took a deep breath and tried to relax.

Matthew seemed to be enjoying himself. He'd told her earlier that a friend from college was playing the main character in this production. Did Matthew only date beautiful women? The actress was drop dead gorgeous, even without the stage makeup. She considered herself attractive but never beautiful.

During intermission Amelia and Keri excused themselves for the powder room. "Can you believe that we're really here?" Amelia said.

Keri sighed. "This has been an unbelievable trip. I don't want it to end."

"It's not going to be easy to leave, is it?"

Amelia knew her friend so well. She started to say something about Eva but changed her mind. She'd never seen Keri with such a glow. Logan was good for her. Could she ever be as sure about her feelings for Matthew as Keri seemed to be about Logan?

Keri stood close to the mirror to check her make up. "I dread saying goodbye to him."

"I'm sorry. Distance can be hard on a relationship." Amelia stuck her hands under the running water in the sink and then dried them. "Chandler Springs won't be the same without Matthew around, that's for sure."

"Do you think there's any future for you two?"

Amelia's feelings were so jumbled, an answer could take hours. She looked at her watch. "We better get back. The second act is about to start."

Laughing, the two couples exited the elevator and headed for Heather's apartment. Logan pulled out the key card to open the front door.

"This has been the most fantastic night." Keri entered first, Amelia behind her. "Oh, did you check the pictures on your phone yet? I want to make sure we got some good ones."

Amelia kicked off her high heels and pulled her cell from her small beaded bag. "Yep, I'll send them to you." She scrolled through, choosing the best and texted them to Keri.

"Don't get too comfortable, ladies," Logan said. "We have one more surprise for you." Amelia saw him make a thumbs up behind his back at Matthew. "And you might want to grab something warm for this one."

What were these two up to? Amelia opened the hall closet and pulled two folded shawls from the top shelf. She was glad she'd thought to bring them.

"Where are we going?" Keri asked.

"You'll see." Logan led her to the front door.

Amelia slipped her shoes back on and followed Matthew back to the elevator. She was surprised when Matthew pushed the up button. She couldn't imagine where they were going. She didn't know anyone on the upper floors. She hoped this would be a good time to be alone so they could talk.

When the doors opened, Amelia and Keri stepped out first. The outdoor terrace on top of the building had been transformed to a glittering dance floor. A perfect night, the stars shone above them. A table in one corner was spread with food and bottles of champagne chilling in gold buckets.

"Oh my." Amelia couldn't find the words. She heard Keri, standing next to her, suck in her breath. "You boys have outdone yourselves tonight."

"Only the best for our ladies." Logan bowed and kissed Keri's hand. "Would you like to dance?"

"I'd love to."

Soft music played from hidden speakers. Amelia watched her friends as they made their way to a corner on the opposite side of the terrace. It almost seemed like they were floating. She realized Matthew was beside her.

"Would you like to dance?" he whispered.

Amelia hesitated. They needed to talk first. She had to get things straight in her mind before she could move forward with him. She hated the way she'd felt stiff with him earlier. They'd had such fun together yesterday. Before that woman had ruined it.

She pointed to covered chairs under a palm tree that twinkled with white lights. "Could we go to the corner over there and talk first?"

Wordlessly, Matthew guided her to the secluded spot, his face full of concern.

Amelia smoothed her dress and sat down. "Matthew." She'd barely gotten the words out when the roof access door flew open.

Eva Pearce, dressed in a black sequined cocktail dress with a neckline that almost went to her waist, staggered across the roof in teetering black heels.

"Matthew," she yelled. "I've been looking all over town for you."

Obviously she'd had a few too many.

Matthew cringed. "Eva, this is a private party."

Eva gaped at Amelia. "Your little girlfriend here won't mind if I join you. Will you, sugar?"

Yes, she did mind. Very much. Amelia opened her mouth to respond but thought better of it. She'd let Matthew handle this.

"Eva, I'm not asking you to leave. I'm telling you."

Matthew grabbed her by the arm and started toward the exit door.

"Well, I'm not leaving until you and Logan tell me that you're not pursuing the account with Charles Grant."

"Why in the world would we tell you that?"

"Because it's my account, that's why. And you stole it from me."

Matthew's eyes smoldered at her. Amelia had never seen that kind of anger in him. "Eva, I think you have a screw loose."

Eva turned on him, her own eyes matching Matthew's spark for spark. As Amelia watched in disbelief, the woman balled up her hands into fists and hammered them into Matthew's chest. "Don't you ever..."

Logan stepped between them and grabbed Eva's wrists. Amelia scurried to stand beside Keri, who flung an arm around her shoulders.

"That's enough, Eva," Logan said, teeth clenched. "Security is on their way up. I'd advise you to leave now."

Eva's twisted face gave Amelia the shivers. "You will be sorry, Matthew Chandler," she hissed. "You will all be sorry."

She staggered to the exit, grabbing a table on the way to regain her balance. As she reached it, two uniformed security officers opened the terrace door. When Eva saw them, she flounced past them. "Good evening, gentleman."

"Everything okay up here?" the tallest officer asked.

"Yep, we're fine." Matthew gave him a thumbs up. "Thanks for coming up so quickly."

"We had a report of a disturbance," the shorter officer said, reading a message on his phone.

"The problem just left." Matthew motioned to the hallway. Eva was holding onto the wall, trying to get to the elevator. "She's intoxicated. She'll go sleep it off."

Why wasn't he mentioning the fact that Eva went after him with her fists?

"Anything else we can do for you?"

When Matthew replied no, the two men left the rooftop and shut the door behind them.

"You okay, Matt?" Logan straightened Matthew's bowtie. "I've never seen Eva so violent."

"Yeah, I'm good." He turned to Amelia. "Let's pick up where we left off."

She slipped her hand in his. "That woman is cray cray." No doubt in her mind who to believe now. "Can we start over? I'm sorry I ever doubted you."

Matthew held his hand out to her. "Will you dance with me now?"

Amelia moved close to him. His left hand fell naturally into the small of her back. It felt so right. She laid her head against him. This was nice. She lost track of time as they glided over the terra cotta terrace.

When the song ended, Matthew found her lips. A lingering kiss, it was soothing to her soul. She felt the earlier misgivings melt away. She hugged him.

"What a night. I'm about ready for some food," Matthew said. He led her to the table she'd spotted earlier.

Amelia's idea of a snack was cheese with crackers and fruit. The table was covered with fresh baked bread, cheese, bowls of cantaloupe, watermelon and grapes and wedges of cheesecake topped with whip cream.

"Mmm."

She filled a plate and sat at the nearest table. Matthew joined her with a glass of bubbling champagne in each hand. She pulled off a chunk of bread and buttered it while she watched him fill his plate. She studied him while he ate. He was a handsome man, with a strong jawline and piercing eyes that changed with his moods. Why had she never noticed this before?

"Too bad you and Keri only have one more day here. I'm going to miss you." Matthew took a sip of his drink.

"I have the feeling that we'll be back." Amelia forced a smile. But in truth she felt like crying. She didn't want to leave.

"I hope so." Matthew laid his hand over hers. "I've been doing a lot of thinking. Is there any way to get out of the contract on Rose Haven?"

Amelia stopped in mid-bite, put her fork down. Was he teasing? She didn't see it in his eyes. She tried to steady her voice as she lined up her thoughts before she spoke. Her emotions were running wild.

"As your realtor, I've never had this happen before."

Matthew nodded. "Me neither."

"Some of the agents in Denver might know. I'll check when I get home. There must be a way."

Matthew chuckled. "I could pay off the buyers."

"Yeah, right. I'm sure you would try." Amelia smiled at his

confidence. Wasn't that why she'd been so put off by him at first? "Let me see what I can do."

"Thanks. And for the time being, could you keep this under wraps? I don't mind if your Mom and Keri know. But no one else."

"Of course." Amelia couldn't finish the food on her plate, wondering what this meant, his wanting to keep the house. "That was scrumptious." She looked around for Logan and Keri. "Did they leave?"

"Yep, wanted to give us some privacy."

"Ah, that was nice of them." Amelia stood. "It's been a wonderful evening." She paused. "Even with Eva's antics."

"That woman is something else." Matthew took Amelia in his arms. "But I'm so glad that I've found you."

Matthew walked Amelia back to Heather's apartment. Even with the Eva fiasco, it had been an amazing day. He dreaded putting Amelia back on the plane to Colorado.

"See you tomorrow." Matthew pulled her close to him. "I better go." He kissed her warm lips. "I really better go."

He backed up to the door, pulling her with him. At the door, he leaned down and kissed her again. He could feel the stiffness from earlier drain from her. He could get used to this. "See you tomorrow." He closed the apartment door and headed for the elevator.

When Matthew entered his own apartment, it felt so empty. He walked to his bedroom, pulling off his coat and bow tie. He'd been so busy since arriving home, he hadn't thought of Evan's journal. He'd spend a few minutes before bedtime reading the thoughts of his great-grandfather.

Matthew looked on the nightstand where he thought he'd left the book when he'd unpacked. Nope, not there. He looked around the room and then switched the light on in the living room. Maybe Amelia had decided to read it. Not there either. Where could it be? The thing didn't just walk away. Exhausted, he finally decided to go to bed.

He'd find it tomorrow.

CHAPTER 25

*T*he next morning Amelia and Keri left the apartment early to check out some of the city's boutiques. At the Vintage Shoppe, Amelia decided to splurge on a purple suede fringed jacket. It was way out of her price range, but Keri convinced her she needed it. And she agreed that Matthew would love it.

Laughing about the pushy sales lady who enunciated each word as if she were talking to someone half deaf, the girls exited the store. "You just have to have this little number my dear," Keri said, imitating the nasal accent. "It will go perfect with that jacket."

"Yeah, right. Could you imagine me wearing that skimpy thing to a sales meeting?" Amelia rolled her eyes. "I. Don't. Think. So."

The packed sidewalk bustled with people. Amelia took a few steps into the sunshine and stopped.

"Look who's standing on the corner," she whispered. "I think that's Eva."

A woman dressed in a fur coat, hair piled high, stood on the corner, staring at them.

"Does she really think she's incognito with those sunglasses?" Keri started toward her. "I'll tell her exactly what we think of her."

"No." Amelia grabbed Keri's arm. "Don't make a scene. I'm not stooping to her level."

Keri stopped. "Yeah, you're right. But she makes me mad."

"She definitely has problems." Amelia switched her boutique bag to the other hand. "Let's go the other direction and ignore her."

The two set off the opposite way down the street.

"Matthew's not going to be happy when he hears about this," Keri said.

"No, he won't. But he'll talk to her." Amelia paused. "I hope."

"Yeah, a lot of good that does. You saw how she turned on him last night."

"That was unbelievable. The woman has some real problems." As much as Amelia hated leaving New York the next day, she would be relieved to leave Eva behind.

Amelia and Keri window shopped several more city blocks until their feet ached. Amelia couldn't shake the feeling they were still being followed. But she refused to let Eva spoil her morning with her best friend.

Matthew and Logan arrived at the apartment soon after the girls.

"Matthew," Amelia said. "Would you mind if we go to your apartment? I need my window fix."

He liked the way she referred to it as "her" window.

"Of course." They exited Heather's apartment, and he held the elevator door open for her. "Would you mind helping me look for Evan's journal?"

Amelia raised an eyebrow. "Absolutely. You positive it got packed?"

"I remember laying it on the nightstand our first night here."

When the elevator reached the 7th floor, Matthew held the open door and allowed Amelia to step off. He followed her down the hall. He felt a pang when he realized again that she was leaving tomorrow. Even the elevator would feel empty without her.

"Weird about the journal. Has your cleaning service been in there?"

"Nope, not since we've arrived."

Matthew opened the door to his apartment. He and Amelia looked everywhere they could think of. Including under the bed. No journal.

"I'll check the house when I return home. Maybe you dropped it."

"That would be great. Thanks." For a book he'd never cared much about, he missed reading Evan's thoughts.

Matthew handed Amelia a bottle of water from the fridge. He had been avoiding the subject of Eva and was almost relieved that Amelia hadn't mentioned her. But they needed to talk before she went home. Amelia kicked off her shoes and plopped cross-legged in her favorite chair in his living room.

He sat down in the stuffed chair next to her. "So, can we talk about Eva?"

"I'm not sure there's anything else to say." Amelia sighed. "She proved last night that she's looney tunes."

"I want to clear the air with you." Matthew loved looking into her sapphire eyes.

"Okay." Amelia uncapped her water and took a sip. "I'm listening."

"Eva and I attended the same college but didn't know each other well. Her daddy is a State Senator in Connecticut." Matthew uncapped his bottle and took a gulp. "I worked in his campaign office as an intern after graduation and he helped me get the job at Canon Financial."

He watched Amelia's face. Surprisingly she showed no emotion so he continued.

"Senator Pearce asked me about a year ago to help Eva get a job. So I had a conversation with the bigwigs and the HR people at Canon and she was eventually hired." He took another sip and wiped his mouth with the back of his hand. "Somehow Eva got the idea that she owed me and then took a physical attraction to me. I have big time regrets now that she talked me into going away for a ski weekend in Connecticut."

Matthew stopped. He'd rather forget this part of the story, but Amelia needed to know the truth.

"I had too much to drink, things went farther than I'd planned and we slept together. Now she's got the idea that we are a couple. You've seen for yourself how she responds when I tell her that I'm not interested."

Matthew needed a stiff drink after all that. For now the water in his hand would have to do. He drained the rest of it in a few gulps.

"I can't prove that she was following us, but Keri and I saw her this morning when we were out shopping." Amelia pressed her lips together.

"Oh, man. I have a bad feeling about this." If she ever tried to hurt Amelia ... Matthew crushed his water bottle in his hand. "If you were staying here any longer, I'd be tempted to get a restraining order against her."

"What about for yourself?"

"Nah, I don't think she'd ever hurt me." Matthew rolled his eyes. "She's in love with me, remember?"

"Please be careful. I don't trust that woman." Amelia sipped her water and stared out the window.

"Enough about Eva." Matthew moved from his chair to stand next to hers. "Let's talk about us."

Amelia unfolded her legs and made room in the oversized chair to invite him to sit with her.

He did. "I really like you."

"After a very rocky start, you're growing on me." Amelia gave him a wide-eyed look that dissolved into laughter.

"I was so determined that I was selling that house. . ." Matthew laughed with her. "So what's next for us?"

"I don't know, Matthew. We live almost 2000 miles apart. How would that work?"

Matthew put his arm around her. "I can always hop on the red eye any time to come see you."

"Yes, but ...

Matthew covered her mouth with his finger. "And we will Skype and text and talk every day. Much like Logan and Keri do now."

"I'm okay with all that for a short time." She snuggled against his arm. "But I'm a touchy, feely person. I want to have dinner with you and play frisbee with you and Harley and watch the beautiful Colorado sunsets from your porch." She paused for a moment. "And debate about what color Wanda's hair will be next."

He let out an uproarious laugh. "I know. Me too." He pulled her closer and kissed her. He'd never felt like this for anyone before.

They sat talking and looking out over the city until the sun began to set. Matthew couldn't wrap his mind around her leaving the next morning.

Matthew and Logan drove back to the office after dropping the girls off at the airport. Amelia and Keri had offered to take a taxi but were quickly told that wasn't going to happen.

Matthew looked over at Logan as they entered Canon

Financial. "Already too quiet without them." He unlocked his office door.

"Yep. It's going to be a long month before I fly out to Colorado to see Keri." Logan followed him into the office.

"When you decide on a date, let me know. I might go with you." Matthew sat down at the desk and opened his laptop. "Guess it depends on what happens with the house."

Logan perched on the edge of the leather couch.

"Maybe this is a good time to talk." Matthew looked up from his computer. "What would you think about a new business venture?"

Logan cocked his head. "I'm listening."

"With our track record here, I think we could open a Canon office in Denver." Matthew watched his business partner. "And be successful."

Logan looked at him. And laughed.

"What's so funny?"

"I've been thinking about the same thing. Couldn't sleep last night for turning the numbers over and over." Logan took a long, deep breath. "We'd have to be on our A game to convince the bigwigs. I don't live on what-if's and I know that's not your MO either."

Matthew nodded. "And what about the Grant account? We have that big meeting with him next week."

"If we can land it, that could be our ticket to a new office in Colorado. Show the big boss how we roll. Then how can he say no to us?" Logan let out a satisfied sigh. "Those two girls from Colorado sure have roped our hearts."

Yes. No. Maybe? Matthew swallowed, not ready to go there yet. Not totally, anyway. "I'll start on a business plan. You make sure we're ready for the Grant meeting."

"I'm on it." Logan made a fist pump in the air. "It's been a long time since anything here got me this jazzed."

"Yeah, honestly? Me too."

Matthew sat back and wondered what the blonde real estate agent was doing right now.

The next morning Matthew and Logan had just sat down for breakfast at a shop down the street from Canon. Logan was recounting his Skype session with Keri from the night before when Matthew's cell buzzed.

"Hi Mom."

"Matthew. I'm glad I caught you before you started your day."

"I'm having breakfast with Logan."

"How is he?"

"Mean as ever." Matthew shot Logan a grin across the table. "He's great, Mom. I haven't talked to you since I returned to New York."

"We would have come up to say good-bye if we'd known you were leaving."

"Yeah, I know. Seemed like everything happened fast. I got my clearance to fly and couldn't wait to get back here. But I'll probably be back in Colorado sometime soon."

"Oh?" Nora sounded surprised.

"Logan and I are talking about the possibility of opening a Canon branch office in Denver."

"Really?" Nora's voice was hopeful. "I'd love it if you lived closer. I assume that means you'll keep the house in Chandler Springs?"

"Amelia's doing some research to find out if I can break the sales contract." Matthew took a deep, calm breath. He had faith in her.

"That would be wonderful." Matthew could hear the joy in his mother's voice.

"Amelia's a miracle worker. I really think she'll find a way."

"I'll be praying for that." Nora stopped.

Matthew started to tell her about the past few days with Amelia. Before he could start she said, "I called to talk to you about your dad."

Not this again. "What about him?" How could his mood tank so fast?

"You're a grown man. I can't make you do anything. But ..."

"Just say it, Mom." He pushed away the plate of food he'd been enjoying up until now. He hated when people danced around the subject.

"John will arrive in Denver soon, and his surgery is scheduled for the end of the month. If you're back in Colorado by then, it wouldn't be far to travel."

To satisfy her, Matthew heard himself respond, "Yeah, I will think about it."

"Thank you. I'll talk to you soon. Love you."

"Love you too, Mom. Bye."

Matthew disconnected his phone. "My dad wants to see me." He could feel a tightness in his chest. "I haven't seen him in like 25 years."

"Sorry, man." Logan sipped his coffee. "Why now?"

Matthew shrugged. "Apparently he's having some serious health issues. He's returning to the US for a risky heart procedure in Denver."

"Health problems will do that to you." Logan forked the last bite of his omelet.

"Do what?" Matthew drained his coffee cup.

"Put life in perspective." Logan grabbed the ticket when the server laid it on the table. "This one's on me."

"Thanks," Matthew said. "Mom says he's even apologized to her."

"Well, that's progress." Logan drained his coffee cup and nodded when the server appeared to refill it. "Are you going to see him?" He stirred liquid creamer into the steaming mug.

"I don't know. I told her I'd think about it."

"Your mother can be very convincing."

"Don't I know it."

Was she ever going to let this die? He doubted it. But he'd find a way out of seeing the man who had abandoned him so long ago.

CHAPTER 26

*A*melia and Keri pulled into the driveway later that day. The sun was peeking through the clouds after the brief rain shower they'd driven through on 1-70. The mountains were a stark contrast to the high rise buildings and crowded streets of New York City.

"It's so good to be home," Amelia said, opening the car door. The red rose bush by the front door was getting its first bud. She'd planted it some years before for her mother but always felt welcomed just seeing it.

Ruth opened the front door and Harley bounded out, almost knocking Amelia down.

She pushed her furry friend's front paws to the ground. "Hi there, boy."

Ruth watched them from the porch. "I think someone missed you."

Amelia rubbed Harley's head. "I missed you too, Buddy."

As she struggled to haul her suitcase and carry-on bag from the trunk with Harley pawing at her calves, she turned to Keri. "Different life here, isn't it? No bellboy."

Keri scowled. "And no Logan."

"Can't believe how much I miss those two already."

Keri followed Amelia onto the front porch. "Yep. Me too."

The sweet aroma of vanilla mixed with brown sugar lingered in the living room when they stepped into the house.

"Goodness, it smells wonderful in here." Amelia walked into the kitchen and picked up a cookie from the plate on the table.

Ruth followed them into the room. "Welcome home." She kissed Amelia on the cheek. "I've missed you both." She greeted Keri with a similar kiss. "Enjoy some freshly baked cookies and milk."

"I remember this from our school days." Keri sat down at the table and bit into a warm chocolate chip cookie, followed by a chug of cold milk. "Ah...just what I needed after such a long trip." She wiped her milk mustache with the sleeve of her shirt.

Amelia's face crinkled in laughter. "I'll have tea with my cookies."

She filled the tea kettle and turned on the burner. There was something soothing to her about pouring hot tea from a whistling kettle. And heaven knew she needed soothing. She couldn't believe she was missing Matthew this much.

Ruth pulled a pan of browned cookies from the oven. "So tell me about the trip."

"It was wonderful. I never thought I'd fall in love with such a big city." Amelia bit into one of the sweet treats. "Mmm... these are heavenly."

"We had a great time, couldn't have asked for better weather," Keri added.

"And how did it go with your gentlemen friends?"

Amelia and Keri looked at each other and burst out laughing. "Mom, you are so old fashioned," Amelia answered with a smirk.

"Well, you know what I mean."

"You'll be happy to know that they were perfect gentlemen. They showed us around town, took us to a Broadway show."

Amelia poured the boiling water into her teacup. "They even arranged a midnight dance on a rooftop terrace."

Sweet memories she'd savor for a long time. A perfect trip except . . . She decided not to mention Eva to her mom.

Ruth wiped her hands on her apron. "Sounds very romantic."

Amelia nudged her friend. "I think Keri is in love."

"I don't know if I'd go that far. But I enjoy being with him." Keri beamed and looked at the time on her cell phone. "Well, I better scoot. Prepping for a big catered dinner tomorrow night." She stood up and grabbed another cookie. "I'll take one for the road."

Ruth pulled a zip lock bag from a drawer. "Of course, take as many as you want."

"Thanks. But I'll just take this one." Keri held up the cookie she'd wrapped in a napkin.

Amelia hugged her best friend. "Keri, I can't thank you enough for talking me into going with you."

"Let's do it again." Keri pulled on her coat and headed to the door.

"Deal," Amelia mumbled through a mouthful of cookie. "I'll walk you out." She stepped out on the porch, out of her mother's hearing.

"It's going to be lonely without them," she said.

"Tell me about it. I can't believe I miss Logan so much already." Keri pulled her keys from her purse. "We are Skyping tonight after I get some of the prep finished."

"That'll put a smile on your face."

"Most definitely." Keri stepped off the porch and headed for her car.

"Talk to you tomorrow."

Amelia turned and chased Harley up on the front porch. She'd love to take him on a walk to Rose Haven to sit on the porch and watch the sunset. But Matthew wasn't there, and the house sat empty. An overwhelming ache of sadness filled her.

∼

Matthew sat at his office desk, scrolling through a list of financial advisors located in the Denver area. He scribbled a note on the legal pad in front of him. Logan would be interested in knowing how few firms were listed. That would be a great point to add to their proposal.

Matthew opened his e-mail for the day. Sweet. Stacy had sent a calendar appointment to finalize a big account he and Logan had been working on while he was in Colorado. Not quite the size of the Grant account but he loved seeing their hard work come together.

Matthew's cell phone vibrated. Amelia's name appeared on the screen.

"Good morning," he answered.

"Hi Matthew. I received your message."

He tilted back in his chair and felt a smile spreading across his face.

"Any news on breaking the contract?" He knew he was expecting her to pull off a miracle, but a guy could hope.

"Sadly, no. I'm sorry." He could hear the disappointment in her voice. "I've talked to several seasoned agents and they've all given me the same response. They don't believe it's possible."

"Not the answer I wanted." Matthew tapped his pen on the desk. "I'm not ready to give up, though."

"Me either. I'll keep digging. There must be a way."

"Short of ...." Matthew stopped. He better not say out loud what he was thinking.

"Yeah, let's not do anything illegal." Amelia paused. "Thanks again for a delightful time in New York."

"You're a great tourist." Matthew chuckled. "And believe me, it was my pleasure."

"Have you found Evan's journal?"

"Nope. No idea what happened to it."

"I went by the house and looked. Nothing." Amelia sighed. "I hope it shows up soon."

"Yeah, me too." Matthew sat back in his desk chair. "Hey, how about a Skype session tonight? Logan says it's the next best thing to being together."

"I'd love to. Could we connect before 7 p.m. my time? I promised Mom I would help her with a large baking order. Her business really picked up while I was gone."

"Nice. Customers will be lined up at her front door."

"I hope so. It would really help her financially. And she seems so happy."

Matthew looked at the legal pad he'd scribbled on earlier. "Before I let you go, I have a business question."

"Okay, shoot."

"I've been doing some research and wondered about the real estate market in Golden." Matthew heard Amelia suck in her breath. "Seems like a good location for us to pitch to Canon for a new office."

"Seriously?"

"I'm preparing a business proposal now. It'll take some time but if the big bosses agree...."

"That would be awesome. I'll put out a few feelers."

"Thanks. Looking forward to Skyping with you later." Matthew could imagine the smile on Amelia's face. He wondered if it matched his own.

Matthew heard a knock on his office door as he hung up the phone. "Come in." He expected Stacy or Logan. His heart dropped when Eva waltzed in.

"Morning." She closed the door with her foot and kept her eyes on him.

"Hello Eva." Matthew's voice sounded monotone with no hint of a welcome. What was she holding behind her back? "Coming by to apologize?"

Eva looked at him with innocent eyes. "For what?"

He didn't feel like playing her games today. "What can I do for you?"

"I have something for you." Why did she make it sound like she was giving him a gift? She held out the old leather book.

"The journal! How did you get this?"

Good thing there was a desk between them. With his emotions over the top right now, he might not be responsible for his actions. He took a breath and steadied his tone.

Eva looked at him. "From your condo."

What was this woman's problem? "Why did you take it?"

Eva's look was smug. "I borrowed it."

"Eva, borrowing is when you have permission. You did not have my permission and that is stealing." Matthew took another deep breath. Stay calm.

"Well, I'm returning it now."

This woman had no accountability filter. "So why did you take it?" Matthew asked again.

"I just wanted to read your thoughts."

He could imagine the look on her face when she realized the journal entries weren't his. He decided to play along. "And what did you think?" he asked.

"Some boring stories from an old man who lived a long time ago."

"Amelia and I searched everywhere for this journal before she left."

Eva's complacent features took a sudden turn. Her eyes looked wild. "Don't mention that person" – she spat out the word "in my presence." Her face turned a deep red.

"I can. And I will. You're in my office, and it's time for you to leave."

Matthew stood to show her the door. He hoped it would hit her back side on the way out.

"You're not dating that chick, are you?" Eva grabbed his shirt by the collar as he approached her. "Remember the fun we had together?"

Matthew pushed away from her. "Eva, this is your final warning. Leave now or I promise you I will call Security."

Eva turned toward the door. "You don't have to get in such a huff. You were a lot of fun until that woman came to town."

Matthew shut the office door after she flounced out. For the millionth time he asked himself how he'd ever gotten involved with her.

Now Sweet Amelia ... was another story.

CHAPTER 27

*M*atthew couldn't stay away much longer. Two nights in a row he'd dreamed about the hint of Amelia's fragrance touching his nose while gazing into her beautiful sapphire eyes. He needed to see her. Not just on Skype but in person. He opened his laptop to check his calendar. Sweet. He still had a couple weeks of vacation left for the year. He picked up his cell phone to call Logan.

"What would you think about a trip to Colorado next week?" He continued before Logan could answer. "We can wrap up a few things here in the office this week and then head west."

"As usual, we're on the same page." Logan laughed. "I was just searching flights for Denver." Matthew heard Logan's keyboard clicking as he typed. "There's a flight next Monday morning."

"Perfect. Book a seat for me and I'll pay you back."

"You got it."

Matthew's mind wandered to Amelia. He tried to imagine what the blonde real estate agent might be doing at the moment.

"Matt, you still there?"

Oh yeah, he hadn't finished his phone conversation with Logan.

"Did you get my e-mail?"

"Yeah, I did."

"And?" Why was he so antsy for an answer? It was crazy how much he wanted to do this.

"The proposal to open a Denver office is sounding better every day. But you know me, Matt. I don't jump in too quick. Never have."

"Yep. I respect that about you." Take deep breaths. "Let's just start with this. Amelia has lined up a few properties to show us in the Denver area. You game?"

"Worth a look, I guess." Was there hesitancy in Logan's tone? "You've given me a lot to think about."

"My gut instinct tells me this could be a successful office. And you're one of the best in the business."

Matthew could hear Logan tapping on his desk. Funny that they had some of the same quirks.

"Right back at ya, buddy."

"Finding property while we're out there would be a sweet step in the right direction."

Matthew wrapped up the call. He hung up thinking he'd never wanted a deal so badly in his life.

The next morning Matthew dialed his mother's number. She'd called the night before while he and Logan were playing racquetball. "Hi Mom. I got your voice mail."

"Good morning, Matthew." Nora sounded out of breath.

Despite his frustration with her at times, he worried about her. "You okay, Mom?"

"Pete and I just got back from a walk. The hills and high altitude here don't always mix well for me."

"Should I call you back?"

"No, I'll sit down and sip some water while we talk. I'll be fine."

Matthew heard the ice dispenser and then water running.

"Ok. If you're sure."

"Yes. I really wanted to talk to you. Any chance you'll be coming out here soon?" Nora took a deep sigh, still trying to catch her breath.

"Yep, coming back out next Monday for a few weeks." And it couldn't come soon enough.

"John's arriving next week. Will you go see your dad before his surgery? He wants to talk to you."

Matthew rubbed his forehead. "I'm still not sure, Mom."

"It would mean so much to him. How about if we go together?"

Matthew hated it when he felt like she was begging. He'd do anything for his mother. Except this ...

"Maybe. Can I let you know?"

"Yes. Please seriously consider it. With his health issues, you may not have many more chances to speak with him."

Everything within him was screaming 'no'.

"I might bring Amelia."

"That would be lovely. Your dad will like her. Let me know what time works best for you. Bye. Love you."

"Love you too, Mom."

Matthew hung up. There had to be a way to avoid this.

Matthew couldn't get the conversation with his mother out of his head. He didn't feel comfortable talking to Amelia about it - not yet. The day before leaving for Colorado, he opted to run it past Logan and asked his best friend to join him for a drink after work.

As soon as they were settled at Woody's with tall mugs of cold beer, Matthew said, "I'm still not crazy about the idea of seeing John."

Logan took a swig of his drink. "I think you should go. Bring this painful experience to an end. Do it for yourself. And for Amelia."

Matthew peered at his friend. "Amelia? What's she got to do with it?"

"Emotional wounds affect other relationships. Make peace with your dad now and have a good life with Amelia ... if that's what you want."

Matthew hesitated. "When did you get so smart?"

Logan shot him a goofy smile. "Seriously though, that's why our world has gotten so wacky. Too many people stuck in their pain."

"Somehow I see Eva in that cycle."

"Yeah, me too. I don't know much about her personal life but she's got some deep stuff going on."

"Isn't that the truth." Matthew stood. "Well, I'll see you bright and early."

"Yep, I'll be over at 6:30."

"You got it. I wouldn't miss this trip for anything."

Matthew laid a twenty on the table and followed his friend out of the crowded bar.

Matthew and Logan arrived at Denver International Airport on Monday as the sun was lowering over the mountains.

"Happy to finally be here." Matthew stared out the huge glass windows facing west and whistled. "I can see why Amelia loves this place so much."

Snow covered peaks filled the western horizon. The urge to ski didn't buzz his brain this time. He knew he'd be back on the slopes someday but definitely not this trip. He stopped and pulled on a blue and orange hat from his backpack. It fit perfectly.

"I see you've been brainwashed." Logan touched the brim of his own cap.

"A gift from Amelia. She's a huge Broncos fan and thinks I should be too."

"Next thing I know you'll be tailgating at Mile High Stadium and acting like the rest of those crazies."

"You never know. Amelia has a way of talking me into things I never thought I'd do." Matthew slung his backpack over his shoulder and grabbed the handle of the carry on bag.

Logan picked up his bag and followed Matthew through the crowded airport terminal. "There they are." He pointed to the girls sitting in chairs on the front row of the waiting area. Keri stood up and flew into his arms.

More reserved in a public area, Amelia walked to Matthew and gave him a hug. "I love the hat."

Matthew leaned down and kissed her. "I had the feeling you would. So great to see you."

"I hope you don't mind. Keri and I wanted to take you to a nice restaurant in Idaho Springs on the way home."

"Fine by me."

"It won't be nearly as fancy as your favorite places in New York."

"Right now I'll be happy with food. Traveling all day makes me grumpy." His stomach growled. "Are you sure I don't need to rent a car while I'm here?"

"Between Mom, Keri and me, we can keep you and Logan covered for rides." Amelia handed him the keys to her SUV. "Wanna drive now?"

"Sure, if you're my navigator."

Matthew took the keys and pulled out the handle of his suitcase. Amelia grabbed his hand as they walked toward the car,

Logan and Keri not far behind. It felt great to be in the driver's seat again.

Thirty minutes later Matthew eased the SUV onto I-70. Soft music played from the front speakers. "Nice music. What station is this?"

"Christian radio. Totally my favorite after a long day. Somehow it just soothes my soul."

Matthew looked over at her. She definitely soothed his soul. "I've missed you." It was hard to keep his eyes on the road.

"Yeah, I've missed you too."

"I have a favor to ask. And if you'd rather not, that's totally fine." Matthew slowed for traffic ahead of them.

"Okay. What is it?"

"My mom has been hounding me to go see John this week." Matthew gripped the steering wheel.

"How do you feel about that?"

"Honestly, I hate the idea. But..." Matthew tried to push the emotions back down, way down where he'd kept them for so many years.

"I'll go with you. I can be your moral support."

"I was hoping you would say that." Matthew turned into the restaurant parking lot where Amelia's GPS had guided them.

"Absolutely. It would be my pleasure." Amelia pulled down the mirror visor. "And can I just say that I'm proud of you for making this decision."

"Still fighting with myself about it."

Amelia laid her hand on his arm. "It can't be easy. But sometimes the right thing is not the easiest thing."

"Don't I know it."

He would just think about being with Amelia and not about facing his father for the first time in years.

∽

After dinner, wine and dancing, Amelia sat in the back seat with Keri on the trip to Chandler Springs.

Logan turned and looked at them. "You two doing okay back there?"

"Yes, thanks. I was telling Keri about a big biker dude that came in the office and made an appointment to look at houses tomorrow."

Matthew stared at her in the rearview mirror, one eye brow raised. "Need any assistance?"

Amelia smiled at his concern. "I'll let you know. He seems innocent enough."

"Well, I wouldn't take any chances. Take another agent with you. Or better yet, call me." He'd never felt this protective about anyone before.

"Thanks ... you will make a fine bodyguard." Amelia continued her conversation with Keri.

Two days later Matthew and Amelia headed to Denver. Where had this overpowering dread to face his intimidating father come from? He hadn't felt it so strongly since he was a boy.

Amelia pressed her eyes closed as they drove through the Eisenhower Tunnel. "Dark places have always twisted my stomach."

"Really? Any idea why?"

Matthew watched her grab the door handle. He could see the fear on her face.

"I'm not sure." Amelia's seatbelt kept her in place but her back went stiff. "Okay, maybe something that happened in my childhood."

Matthew wanted to find out more but decided not to press. Bright sunlight filled the SUV as they drove out of the tunnel. "What station was it that you listen to?"

Amelia hit the preset button. Light praise music filled the car. She relaxed, eyes closed. "Much better."

"It is nice."

He'd felt tense too, standing in front of the closet earlier debating on what to wear. Finally, he decided to be himself and choose a polo shirt and pressed trousers. His dad hadn't seen him in years. Why would it make any difference how he was dressed today?

"Maybe you'll be surprised. People do change, you know."

Matthew shrugged. "I wish it was that simple. The old man never had time for me. Kids at school talked about playing softball with their dads. I had no idea what that was like." Matthew gripped the steering wheel. "When John was home, he wasn't really there. Not for me, anyway."

"I'm sorry. That really stinks."

"Yeah, tell me about it. No clue what it's like to have a father."

"Maybe this is your chance?"

Matthew wanted to believe her. But . . . "Oh, by the way. Did I tell you where we're going today?"

"No, actually you haven't."

"You sure are trusting, Miss Richardson." Matthew looked at her with a sly grin.

"I don't think I need to be concerned."

"We're going to the Brown Palace in downtown Denver."

"Really?" Amelia's eyes lit up. "Oh my goodness. That's one of my very favorite places."

"My dad only chooses the best."

Matthew was happy to see the tension in her face from earlier had faded.

"Hey, you just called him your dad ... instead of John."

"Yeah, I did."

Matthew turned into the parking lot. When they walked into the hotel lobby, Nora waved and stood from a plush chair to greet them.

"Good morning." She gave Matthew a kiss on the cheek when he hugged her. "It's good to see you again, Amelia."

"You too, Mrs. Bennett."

"Please, that name makes me sound like my elderly mother-in-law. Call me Nora."

Amelia smiled, nodding her agreement.

Matthew felt like his insides were rumbling. Why was he so nervous? "Have you seen John yet?"

"Why don't you two go to the restaurant and I'll go get him."

Matthew held out his arm for Amelia, and they followed the signs. He thought about the powerful clients he'd dealt with at Canon. He squared his shoulders. John Chandler was not going to intimidate him.

He pulled out the chair for Amelia and summoned a waiter. Ten minutes later, Matthew was ordering coffee and muffins when his father shuffled toward him. A cane in one hand, his other arm was intertwined through Nora's. This was not the powerful man Matthew remembered.

Matthew stood. "John." He kept his voice monotone.

John hobbled to the seat across from his son. "Matthew." He took off his hat and laid it on the empty chair beside him. "Thank you for coming."

Matthew nodded his greeting. This was so awkward. What should he say? That his mother made him come? The thought brought a little curve to his mouth.

"Here, sit next to Matthew." Nora pulled out the chair for John.

The air felt thick. No one spoke. Finally Matthew said, "We've ordered coffee and muffins. Would either of you like anything else?" He looked at Amelia. "And of course, hot tea for Amelia."

"I'd love some hot tea." John laid his cane on the floor and scooted his chair to the table. "You look good, Matthew."

"Thanks." How could his father know whether he looked good or not? He hadn't seen him in years.

Amelia sat quietly, sipping the tea the server had just delivered. Matthew glanced at her. She looked beautiful with the red rose teacup raised to her lips. His one calming factor of this whole horrible morning.

Nora finally broke the silence. "Matthew's a big shot on Wall Street."

Oh Mom, please don't go there. Matthew sipped his hot coffee and didn't say anything.

"Is that right?" John asked. "The apple doesn't fall far from the tree."

Uh no, I'm nothing like you. But my great-grandfather . . . He was surprised at his own thought.

John looked around the table. "Can we have dinner tonight?"

"Sorry, I wish I could. I have to get home for a dinner party tonight," Nora said.

Amelia looked at Matthew. "I think that would be lovely."

Of course, she did. She wasn't going to let him off the hook so easily.

"Are you sure you're up to it?" Matthew pointed his question toward John.

"I need a few good meals before I have to deal with hospital food." He made a face. "I'll go back to my room now and rest." John stopped to catch his breath. "Meet me back here in the dining room at 5:30."

"We'll be here," Amelia said.

Matthew and Amelia both nodded their goodbye.

Nora stood to help John from the table. "Thank you," she mouthed to Matthew as they walked away.

Matthew sighed a deep breath of relief as he watched his mother and father leave the restaurant. "Glad that's over. Took all I had to stay at the table."

Amelia finished the last bite of muffin and wiped her mouth. "It's sad that his life has taken such a turn."

"I wish you would have let me respond to the dinner invitation." Matthew scowled at her. "I really don't want to stay."

"Oh, sorry. I guess I got caught up in the moment." Amelia's face turned pink. She swallowed hard.

Matthew sat silent, lost in his thoughts. He drained his coffee cup. Could this day get any worse? He didn't want Amelia to be upset with him. She was his ally.

"We have some time to kill. Want to take a tour of the hotel?

"Oh, yeah. I'd love it!" Amelia's smile lit up the room. Matthew was amazed at how she could roll with the moment.

That evening Matthew sat in the Brown Palace restaurant scrolling through the stock prices on his phone while Amelia was in the ladies' room. When he looked up, his dad was standing in front of the table.

"John."

"Hi there, son. I made it." John plopped into the chair.

"We could have helped you." Matthew turned off his phone and stuck it in his pocket.

"No need. I'm not dead yet." John waved his hand. "Your mother was a little overprotective this morning. Made me feel like an invalid."

Matthew agreed. He loved his mother but hated when she hovered over him.

"Where's your girl?"

"Amelia? Oh, she'll be here in a few minutes." Matthew picked up the menu.

"She seems really nice. Is it serious?"

Strange questions from a man he barely knew. "Could be."

"Evading the old man's questions?" John leaned on his

elbows and stared at Matthew. Which annoyed him just like it had when he was a boy.

"I do like her, yes. We enjoy spending time together. And she loves Rose Haven. She was devastated when I signed the sales contract."

"I can understand that. I hear she's Ruth's girl?" John's bushy eyebrows raised as he waited for Matthew's reply.

"Yep, she lived in the house when her mom worked for Austin and Evelyn." Strange that he always thought of them by their first names instead of Grandma and Grandpa.

"Are you keeping the house?" John's eyes seem to glare into Matthew's soul.

"I don't think so. Too many ghosts. I honestly want to be rid of them for good."

Why couldn't he just tell his dad the truth? That he'd found Evan's journal and was growing closer to the Chandler family. And that he was trying to find a way to keep the house. It was too much.

He pulled his cell from his pocket. "Sorry, just got a call that I need to take ..." Matthew left his father sitting at the table.

Amelia met Matthew in the hall as she was exiting the restroom. He grabbed her arm and guided her to the front door of the hotel, his face burning.

Amelia scrunched her face in confusion. "What happened?"

"I just can't do this. Talking to him brings up too many bad memories." Matthew held the door for her as they stepped outside.

"So you walked out on him?" Amelia whispered.

"Yeah, I did."

"I'm sorry." Amelia hugged his arm. "I was hoping ....." Her voice trailed off.

"Yeah, you and my mom. I knew it wouldn't work. Too much water under the bridge." He unlocked the car and opened her door.

"True, but it doesn't have to end that way. " Amelia slid into the passenger seat.

"I only wish it were that easy."

Witnessing Amelia's delight during the hotel tour had been the highlight, but otherwise this day had been a disaster. He walked around to the driver side and slid under the wheel.

"Let's talk about something else."

CHAPTER 28

*T*he silence on the drive back to Chandler Springs was driving Amelia nuts. She wanted to ask Matthew what had happened with his dad. His stony gaze at the road told her to do otherwise. It was better to give him his space. He'd talk when he was ready.

She switched on her favorite station. Soft music filled the car as they moved up the mountain pass toward home. She said a silent prayer that Matthew would find the answers he'd been searching for. And that his relationship with his dad would be restored.

Should she voice her opinion? Matthew wasn't happy with her for agreeing to the dinner in the first place.

"I liked your dad," she finally said.

"He was on his best behavior today." Matthew scrunched his face. "But I have too many bad memories of his broken promises."

"Did you have a chance to talk?" She didn't mention that she'd stalled her return to the table to give them privacy.

"Talk about awkward."

"He probably felt the same way. What do you say to your only son after being disconnected for so many years?"

"That he was an arrogant jerk?" Matthew drummed his fingers on the steering wheel.

This wasn't going well. Time to move on. "Thanks again for taking the hotel tour with me. I hope you weren't too bored."

Matthew's face relaxed. "It was pretty cool. Some of the architecture was similar to my house."

"Yep, built in the same time period." Did he realize he'd actually said "my house"?

Matthew looked at the clock on the dashboard. "It's almost 9:30. I guess we could have gotten a hotel room." He looked over at her with a grin. The muscles in his face had relaxed.

Amelia let out a sigh of relief. Matthew was back to his old self. "Yep, and we'd be the talk of the Chandler Springs gossips by next week." Amelia shook her head. "No thanks."

"Let me rephrase that. We could have gotten two rooms."

"The drive doesn't bother me." Amelia hummed along with the music.

"Actually, this commute is a breeze compared to New York traffic. And I have a lovely companion keeping me awake."

"Thank you." Amelia's cell phone lit up. "It's my mom, wondering if we're doing okay." Amelia tapped in a reply and hit send. "I'm still trying to get used to the idea of her texting."

"I hope mine doesn't try." Matthew filled the car with a booming laugh. "I talked to Logan earlier. He and Keri were going out tonight."

Amelia was thrilled for Keri. She deserved the best and Logan seemed to be the one. "They are getting pretty serious."

"Like us?" Matthew asked.

"I think I'm finally getting there."

Had she said that out loud? But it felt good.

Matthew exited into Chandler Springs and pulled into

Amelia's driveway. He turned the car off and walked around to open her door. When she stepped out, she nestled into him and stood on her tiptoes. His lips were warm and soft. Yes. She knew in her heart that she was ready for a relationship with this man.

Saturday morning Matthew punched his pillow and rolled on his left side. He couldn't believe he'd been awake since dawn. And why had he promised to go to church with Amelia? The thought made his insides turn somersaults.

He looked at the alarm clock again. 5:45 a.m. As hard as he tried, sleep eluded him. He decided to get up and do something productive. Coffee first.

A fresh brew in hand, Matthew padded down the hall to Luke's room. Evan's rocker had become one of his favorite spots in the house. When he set the mug on the end table, his hand knocked the Bible to the floor.

Logan appeared in the doorway. "You're up early. I heard a crash in here."

"Yeah, I knocked Evan's Bible off the table."

Matthew leaned over to pick it up. A passage on the open page was highlighted. Matthew hesitated. He hadn't thought about this kind of stuff since he was a kid in Sunday School. Couldn't hurt. Maybe it would put him in the mood to go to church with Amelia.

"This verse is highlighted. Matthew 6:15 – '*But if ye forgive not men their trespasses, neither will your Father forgive your trespasses.*' And there's a handwritten note in the margin. Looks like Evan's script. '*If I want God to forgive me, I must forgive others.*'"

Matthew used his index finger for a book mark. Did he want God's forgiveness?

"So what do you think?" Logan sat down in the chair across from him.

"That my great-grand father was a smart man. And a great man of faith." Matthew had always felt a relationship with the Lord was a personal decision and hadn't ever discussed the subject, even with his best friend.

"I believe he's right, Matt."

Matthew's expression drew a laugh from Logan.

"Don't look so surprised. I believe in God. And I pray."

"Learn something new about you every day." Matthew inserted a bookmark in the Bible page. "Let's go have some breakfast." He would think about all this later.

Matthew stood next to Amelia during the worship service. Leaning over he whispered, "Do you know any of these songs?"

"Most of them," she whispered back. "And I hear some of them on the radio."

"I never thought of listening to this kind of music until it was playing in your car the other day."

"I like filling my mind with the good things of God."

Matthew nodded slowly. Amelia's sweet personality definitely reflected that.

The music ended, and the pastor invited the congregation to be seated.

Here came the boring part. He hoped Amelia would poke him if he started snoring. He was a little surprised when the pastor stepped on stage in a polo shirt and jeans. Church had sure changed since he was a kid.

The pastor read a scripture reference for the congregation to follow.

"What did he just say?" Matthew leaned over and whispered too loudly in Amelia's ear.

The woman in front of them turned around and glared at him.

"Pastor Brad asked us to turn to Matthew 6:15," Amelia said softly.

"Really? That's the verse I just read in Evan's Bible." Matthew flashed a fake smile when the lady turned around again. Look lady, give me a break. This is an important moment. Maybe this service wouldn't be such a snore fest after all.

"Come on Mom. Tell me what he's got planned."

Amelia sat at the kitchen table the next morning sipping hot tea while bacon sizzled on the stove.

"Nope, he swore me to secrecy. But you will love it." Ruth flipped the pancakes, Harley standing on guard next to her, waiting to catch a dropping crumb.

"And how did Matthew know my birthdate anyway?"

"I guess a little birdie told him."

"Uh huh."

Amelia buttered the hot pancakes that Ruth set in front of her. Her mom could never keep a secret. She'd get the info out of her somehow.

"Logan and Keri have really gotten close."

"That's wonderful. They seem right for each other."

Ruth flipped a pancake into Harley's bowl and set it in front of him. He devoured it in two bites, sniffing for more.

"I hope it works out. Keri's never really had anyone special in her life. And that's hard to believe considering how awesome she is."

Ruth nodded. She slid into a chair and took a bite of bacon. "Could there be a double wedding in the future?"

Amelia grimaced. "I highly doubt that. I don't think Matthew Chandler is that type."

The thought of marrying Matthew gave her a giddy feeling

inside. But she wasn't going to admit that to her mom. Not yet anyway.

Alone in the big house, Matthew walked from room to room and thought about Evan and Emma. From what he'd read in the journal, they'd stuck together through some pretty serious stuff. Losing two children was enough to drive any couple apart.

Matthew looked at the family portrait on the fireplace mantle. But Evan and Emma still had that thing that had always eluded him. Even with his hefty stock portfolio and the business track record, that thing was always just out of reach. That thing called happy.

He climbed the stairs and walked to the end of the long hallway. Luke's room still fascinated him. When he opened the door, the musty smell lingered. He really should have his cleaning service try to wash the ragged curtain and bedspread. Or he could get Amelia to help him pick out new ones.

But he couldn't bring himself to change anything in Luke's room. It was like a preserved time capsule. He sat down in Evan's chair. He put his head in his hands and thought about the underlined scripture and comment in Evan's Bible. And then Amelia's pastor had mentioned the same scripture. Coincidence? He was starting to think maybe it wasn't.

He'd longed for a relationship with his father since he was a kid. But the missed birthdays – the compliments he never gave - the silence after Father's Day presents he'd agonized over for weeks had made him tough. And the more he pushed down the feelings, the more strength he had to just not think about the man. After so many years could he really forgive him?

Since his arrival here in Colorado, he laughed more. He wandered around an old house instead of freaking out about the latest stock prices. He could get used to hanging out at the diner, chewing the fat with Wanda and sitting on the porch watching sunsets. With Amelia.

Was there a future for him and Amelia? Could he really forgive John, his dad? So many questions. Would he ever find the answers? He picked up the journal, lying next to Evan's Bible. Fitting place for it.

I lost my sweet Emma yesterday. We both knew it was time but I'm dying inside as I say goodbye to the woman I've loved most of my life. After 60 years of marriage and 8 children, I'm lost without her. Today the house is lively with our children and grandchildren visiting but they just can't fill the hole in my heart. I'm so thankful they all made it here before Emma took her last breath. It was touching to hear their final goodbyes to their mama and grandma.

I don't expect it to be long before I join her, but sure will miss her every day until then. Thank you Lord for a wonderful life and the privilege of loving a woman who loved life, loved You and loved her family. Thank you for our children, grandchildren and future great-grandchildren. Emma is with baby Emily and little Luke now. I can picture the joy on her face as she rocks the baby in her arms and bounces our little son on her knee.

Matthew closed the journal. A wet mark appeared on the cover. Good grief, was he crying? He couldn't remember the last time he'd done that. He'd never dreamed he'd grow so close to his great-grandparents. And wished for the hundredth time that he'd had the privilege of knowing them.

Matthew missed his relaxing times on the screened sun porch. He had work to do, but he stretched out on the lounger and scrolled through stock prices on his phone. The bulky cast that had haunted him a few months ago was now a distant memory.

His phone buzzed, and Amelia's name appeared on the screen. "Hey. How are you?"

"I'm wonderful. Especially because I have good news for you about the house."

Matthew sat up, the stock market forgotten.

"I've confirmed that the contract can be broken if a member of the family protests the sale."

"Best news I've had in a long time." Matthew made a fist pump in the air.

Amelia continued. "Your dad, John Chandler, would have to sign."

Matthew's gut twisted. "No other options, huh?"

Amelia sighed. "Afraid not."

"No way. I'm not going to deal with him again." How could he trust his father for anything? Besides, Matthew had just ditched him at the restaurant.

"Are you still there?" Amelia asked.

"Yep, I'm here. My mom visits him. She would take the document for me."

"Matthew..." He could hear the disappointment in her voice.

"Yeah, I know." The verse about forgiveness came to his mind. He wished it would magically help, but he didn't hold out much hope.

"I'll go with you." Amelia paused. "For moral support."

"Thanks for your help. Let me know when the contract is ready."

Matthew disconnected the call. He would go but there was a good chance he'd end up walking out.

Just like last time.

CHAPTER 29

*T*he screen door banged when Matthew stepped out on the back porch and jogged down the steps. The dry grass crunched under his feet on the path toward the cemetery. He'd intentionally not invited anyone else to come along. Unlatching the gate, he slipped into the sacred space and pulled off his ball cap.

Evan's granite headstone glistened in the bright sunshine. Amazing how the man who had lived so long ago had come alive to him through his journaled words. He was starting to wonder if he'd gotten his own business drive from his great-grandfather. They were so similar. Evan could be gruff and business-like but Matthew noticed his softer side too. Especially with Emma and with their children. Could he be heading this direction with Amelia? And would he ever be as good a partner in a relationship as Evan clearly was?

There was only one area where they seemed to have come from different gene pools, and that was this faith thing. Evan had had a strong belief in God. Where did his own relationship stand with God? Matthew didn't really know. Well, yeah he did.

He'd told Amelia that he and God hadn't been on speaking terms for a long time.

The minutes ticked by. He moved to Emma's headstone. Through Evan's point of view, Matthew had come to respect and admire his great-grandmother. She was a strong woman who loved her husband, her children and also had a deep faith in God.

A chickadee said its name, and a squirrel skittered up the oak tree that sheltered the gravestones. As Matthew stood a few more minutes in the quiet place, he realized in one respect, that issue of faith, he had become just like his father. And that couldn't be. It just couldn't be, or he was lost. He pulled his hat back on and walked toward the house.

He'd made his decision.

Matthew had just stepped from the shower when his phone buzzed. He wrapped a towel around his waist and sat on the bed.

"I'm so glad you want to go to church with me again tomorrow, Matthew," Amelia said when he answered.

"I'm game if you can keep that little old lady from staring at me, like she did last week."

Amelia laughed. "I'll try."

Matthew tucked the phone under his chin and pulled on his pants. "What time are you coming by?"

"About 10:45ish."

"Sounds good. Is Ruth going with us?"

"No, she goes early to put out her baked goods for the coffee and fellowship time. She has a contract with the church now to deliver muffins and scones every week. She's elated."

"That's super. I'm so happy her little business is taking off."

"Yeah, me too. She's wanted to do this forever. And it's

finally happening." Amelia was quiet for a moment. "Speaking of my mom...I'm a little worried about her."

"Really, what's going on?" Matthew tucked the phone under his chin again and pulled on his shirt.

"I'm not sure."

Matthew leaned against the dresser. He used to get annoyed when woman talked about their problems. Funny how things were different with Amelia.

"She's been preoccupied and a little snappy, which isn't like her."

"Have you asked her if anything is wrong?"

"No. I guess I should talk to her."

"Yeah. That would be a good idea. Maybe something you can help with."

"Maybe."

"So what are you doing this sunny Saturday morning?"

"Showing a house this afternoon. Walking Harley later. That's about it. I live a pretty simple life."

"Never thought I'd want to give up my fast pace but this one is looking pretty good right now." Matthew sat on the bed to tie his boots.

"What about you? What's on your agenda today?"

"Logan and I are getting started on some repairs on Evan and Emma's old cabin. Such nice weather, we thought we'd tackle the roof today."

"Wow, that is a huge job. I'm impressed." Sweet. He could hear a smile in Amelia's voice.

"The lumberyard delivered the materials yesterday. Logan's worked construction with his dad so it shouldn't be a problem. I'll be his gopher."

"Let us bring you dinner." Amelia chuckled. "And just in case you're wondering, I'm not cooking."

"Oh good." Matthew let out a loud laugh. "Everything that

Keri makes is awesome. Logan and I will be starving after working all day."

"We'll come over about 5:30 to prep."

"See you then." Matthew hoped he and Logan didn't do anything stupid. Like fall off the roof. He couldn't wait to see Amelia.

Amelia knocked on the door at 5:25 p.m. Matthew answered, still in stained work clothes and boots, dirt smeared on his cheeks and forehead from sweating. Logan stood behind him, looking like his twin.

"Hey, I've never seen you so dirty."

"Yeah, Logan really made me work hard today." Matthew pushed his baseball cap to the back of this head.

"We brought supper." Keri held up the insulated food bag.

"You two go clean up while we get it ready." Amelia stepped into the vestibule, and Keri followed her to the kitchen.

"Have you talked to my mom lately?" Amelia asked as she loaded plates and glasses on the four wheeled cart.

Keri looked up from the bag of food. "Not in the last few days."

"Something's up with her." Amelia filled a glass with ice. "Even Shirley from church mentioned that she's not been herself."

"In what way?"

"Shirley couldn't put her finger on it but she says Mom's been really preoccupied."

Amelia pushed the full cart toward the kitchen door. Before Keri could reply, Matthew stepped into the kitchen.

"You clean up well." Amelia touched the collar of Matthew's clean shirt. He pulled her into him and kissed her.

"Ummm... I was waiting for that clean shower smell kiss."

Amelia stepped back. "It's a beautiful night. Let's eat at the table outside."

"Great idea." Matthew pushed the cart loaded with plates, silverware, glasses and napkins out of the kitchen and down the long hall.

Amelia and Keri followed, each carrying two covered dishes, leaving a trail of decadent smell that Logan followed when he appeared in the hallway. He ran ahead and held the door open for Matthew and then for the girls.

Keri spread the tablecloth while Amelia went back in the house for a vase. Matthew and Logan walked to the rose garden with shears, bantering about who would choose the best rose blooms. They chose three open flowers and appeared back on the porch as Amelia stepped out the front door with a vase of water.

"You've outdone yourself, Keri." Matthew sniffed at the food she had loaded on his plate. Logan nodded, his mouth already full.

"Thanks. You two worked hard today and needed a good meal."

"Save room for dessert. We have apple pie." Amelia ate small bites and watched the guys shovel in the food and then help themselves to seconds. They certainly had worked up an appetite.

Matthew sat back with a satisfied look on his face. "Logan, should we tell them our good news?"

"Yep. And we'll have my favorite dessert to celebrate."

"Drum roll, please." Matthew had such an adrenaline rush, he felt like he could run a marathon.

Logan beat on the table, huge grin on his face.

"We found out today that we got the Grant account!" Matthew beamed from ear to ear. He pushed Logan a knuckle bump across the table.

Amelia let out a little squeal. "Took him long enough to

realize that you two are the best."

"That is so awesome. You two really deserve it." Keri finished the last bite on her plate and stood. "I'm really happy for you." She started stacking dirty dishes. "When did you find out?"

"Stacy called this morning. We have a videoconference with Grant next week to seal the deal."

"I'm so happy for you." Amelia said. "You both deserve this account."

Matthew fist bumped Logan across the table. "Longest wait of our lives."

"Can I get you more food?" Keri asked.

"I'm saving room for that pie." Logan smiled up at her.

"Coming right up." Keri started toward the front door.

"Let me go get the cart." Amelia took the last sip of her tea and stood.

"No, I'll get it for you." Matthew was up and to the door before she could protest.

Amelia heard a familiar bark and saw Harley dragging her mom down the sidewalk. She stood to greet them. "Hi Mom. You're just in time for dessert."

Ruth stepped up on the veranda, her hair in a mess. "Thanks honey. Harley's been pacing ever since you left. I think he needs to see you."

"Come here, boy." Amelia crouched with her hands on her knees. Her mom seemed really frazzled. Was she sick?

Ruth let go of the leash and the gigantic teddy bear bounded toward Amelia, almost knocking her over.

"I love you too, Harley." Amelia playfully pushed him away from her face as his slurpy tongue reached out for her. She glanced at Ruth's tight lipped grimace. She'd just have to ask her later what was going on.

"Well, we have company." Matthew pushed the cart out the front door. "Hi, Ruth."

"Hey, Matthew."

Harley ran for his friend.

Matthew bent to pet him. "Hi Harley. Bet I could find some leftovers for you."

"Have you eaten, Mom?" Amelia asked. The knot in her stomach tightened when she noticed the tension in her mother's drawn face. What was going on?

"Yes, I had dinner earlier." Ruth answered with a shortness in her voice.

"We have a fabulous apple pie waiting for us." Logan's broad smile was contagious.

"Maybe I'll just have some coffee." Ruth started toward the front door. "Matthew, could you help me make it, please?"

"Sure. Let me finish this up and I'll be right there."

Logan stood to help.

"No, I think Matthew and I can handle it." Ruth went through the door, Matthew following, pushing the cart of dishes.

"Wonder what that was all about?" Keri said.

"With my mom, you never know. She's probably cooking up something with him." Amelia laughed at her own pun. "Cooking up something. Yep, that's my mom."

In the kitchen alone, Ruth helped Matthew unload the dirty dishes from the cart. "I wanted to speak to you in private."

Matthew raised an eyebrow. "Ok, shoot."

Amelia had said earlier she was concerned about her mom. Maybe this was it? His mind went straight to the possibility that Ruth didn't want him seeing her. Good grief, where did that come from?

"I'm worried about Amelia." Ruth wouldn't look at him. But she began piling dirty plates in hot, soapy water.

"Really, why? She seems fine to me." Matthew grabbed a

towel to dry. Ruth was acting like somebody else's mother, and it was making his palms sweat.

"A woman showed up at my door a few days ago. Said she wanted to surprise her boyfriend with some cookies and that he didn't know she was in town." Ruth shot him a sideways glance. "She told me her name was Eva Pearce."

Matthew nearly dropped the plate he was drying. He set it on the table and leaned against the counter, trying to keep his face from betraying the anger already burning just beneath his skin. "Go on."

"She was very friendly. Took an interest in the pictures in my living room, and you know me – she got me talking about Rose Haven and the gold mine and Amelia. And then I was flabbergasted when she told me she was in a serious relationship with you."

Matthew choked on nothing. Ruth looked at him with none of the usual sparkle on her face. The lines around her eyes were tight, her mouth hard. "If that's true, then you better not hurt my daughter. She's been through too much already."

Matthew extended his arm toward her shoulder. "Ruth, that woman –"

The kitchen door swung open, and Amelia poked her head in. "This seems like a serious discussion." She raised one eyebrow.

"Oh, I was just asking Matthew a question about my bakery business." Ruth stepped away from him and slid a knife into the apple pie. "And he was kind enough to give me some good advice."

Amelia shrugged and picked up three dessert plates. "Join us outside when you're done." She left the kitchen.

"Will do."

Matthew waited until her footsteps faded before he turned back to Ruth. He had to tell her something, but it wasn't going to be about Eva's wacky visits while he and Amelia were in New York.

"Eva Pearce is a woman I used to date." Matthew couldn't believe she'd have the nerve to show up here. "Her daddy is a state senator and I saw him at a New York event several years ago. He invited me to their home at Thanksgiving and I reconnected with Eva. I thought she was beautiful and smart and fun to be with." Matthew shrugged. "And I had to admit, I liked the idea of being connected to her prestigious family.

"Is she dangerous?" Ruth said, slicing pie with more force than she needed to. "She seemed too interested in us."

"I don't think so." Matthew pulled the sink stopper and watched the bubbles drain down the sink. "She's just obsessed with me and can't seem to get it that I'm not interested in a long term relationship with her."

The bubbles popped like the questions in his mind. Did Ruth believe him? This visit was over the top, even for Eva.

Ruth brushed her hair back with the hand not holding the knife. "Harley didn't like her at all. He very rarely growls or bares his teeth. I had to call him down a few times while she was there."

"Harley's a good judge of character."

"So you can understand my concern."

"I wouldn't worry about it, Ruth. Eva is probably back in New York by now." Matthew filled the tea kettle with water. "Let me make you a cup of tea." He started the flame under the kettle. "And if it makes you feel better, please know that you can call me any time. Logan and I can be at your house in a matter of minutes."

"Be where? For what?" Amelia appeared in the kitchen door again.

"Just a little secret between me and your mom." Matthew tried to grin.

Amelia stuck out her lower lip. "Hey, no fair. You're not supposed to have secrets."

"It is when a certain lovely lady's birthday is coming."

"Oh ..." Amelia closed her mouth. A smile spread across her face.

"Come here." Matthew held his arms out and pulled her into a hug. He watched Ruth at the sink, finishing the dishes but trying to hide a smile. "I'm going to Denver on Thursday to see John. And get the contract signed. Want to go with me?"

"Of course. I'll check my schedule and let you know later."

"Let's do something fun while we're there. Be thinking of where you'd like to go." He'd already decided this would be a much better trip. And being with Amelia would ensure that.

The next morning Matthew woke thinking about Ruth and their conversation from the night before. What in the world was Eva doing in Chandler Springs? It made no sense. He walked downstairs to start breakfast. While the coffee brewed, he punched in Eva's number and cleared his throat.

"Well, I can't believe you're actually calling me."

Matthew cringed at her tone.

"Hello to you, too, Eva. I hear you were in Chandler Springs."

"As a matter of fact, I was." Her voice sounded cool and confident.

"Strange for you to show up here."

"Do you always have to make such a big deal out of every-thing?" Eva let out a dramatic sigh. "If you must know, I was attending an International Convention with Liberty Financial in Denver. We had some free time, and I decided to find out what was so great about that mountain town that you seem to love so much."

Why did he not believe a word she was saying? "And you're back in New York now?"

"Well, of course. Where else would I be?" Eva spat out the words. "You've made yourself perfectly clear when it comes to us."

Us? What a joke. Matthew couldn't count many times in his life that he'd been speechless. But this was one of them.

Before he could respond, Eva continued, "I've given up trying to reason with you, Matthew. I'm more of a woman of action, and you clearly don't want that." He could hardly hear her for the background noise. "I'm in a crowded restaurant. I think this conversation is over." The line went dead.

Matthew stared at the screen on his cell. Had Eva just hung up on him? Not that he really cared. He sat down at the kitchen table. That was one of the strangest conversations he'd ever had. But maybe, just maybe it was his last with that bizarre woman.

He could only hope.

CHAPTER 30

*M*atthew and Amelia drove to the University Hospital on Thursday afternoon. Since his visit to the Chandler Cemetery a few days earlier, Matthew knew keeping the house was the right thing to do. He'd put the past with his father aside for today and look at this as another business deal. Something he'd done hundreds of times during his career. His goal was getting John's signature.

Matthew and Amelia stepped inside the hospital room. The pale, frail man lying in the bed looked nothing like the father he remembered from a few days ago. Matthew removed his hat.

John opened his eyes. A weak smile formed on his lips. "Son, you came."

"Amelia is with me." Matthew motioned toward the window.

"Hi, Mr. Chandler." Amelia gave a slight wave and lowered herself into a chair.

"She's a good one, Matthew. You need to keep her."

Matthew lowered his voice. "I'm working on it."

"I've had lots of time to think the last few days. I just want to tell you . . . " John coughed, tears running from his eyes.

Matthew grabbed the water cup on the bedside table. "Here." He helped John sit straight up and put the straw to his lips.

John took a long drink and wiped his mouth. "Seems to happen more and more these days."

Matthew watched him. The proud, arrogant father he remembered had become a helpless, frail old man.

John squeezed his eyes shut. "I wish I could change the past. But, sadly, that's not possible."

"I'll be honest. You haven't been my favorite person for a long time." Matthew looked away. There was more to say, but the words wouldn't come.

A week ago, Matthew would have turned and walked out the door. But today felt different. Was it really possible to forgive this man? He had to admit that he saw sincerity in his father's eyes. The pain of the past was fading. But ... On to business.

"Amelia has the paperwork to break the sales contract on Rose Haven. Are you up to signing it for us?"

Amelia stepped to the bed, papers in hand.

"On one condition." John looked straight into Matthew eyes.

Oh, man here it comes. Matthew knew it had been too good to be true. He took two steps back from the bed. "And that is?"

John started to speak but another coughing spur took his breath. He fumbled for the water straw and gulped, tears in his eyes from the hacking.

"Promise me, son," John said in an unsteady tone, "that you will be a better man than I have been."

Before Matthew could respond, he heard Amelia whisper, "He already is."

Matthew stood a little taller.

"To hear that from your lady friend is double assurance. I'm really pleased you're keeping the house. And I'm ready to sign." John reached out a hand connected to wires and accepted the pen from Amelia. "Is this a sure-fire way to break that contract, little lady?"

Amelia gave him a warm smile. "Our real estate lawyers assure me it will."

"I trust you to do the right thing."

John looked over the document and then scribbled his name. He handed the papers to Amelia and lay back on the pillow.

"So many bad choices that I wish now I could change. I had a falling out with Austin, my dad, over moving my business to the UK. He felt the revenue should stay in the United States. I'm sorry to say that I never reconciled with him." John stared at the ceiling. "My mom, Evelyn, called me numerous times, begging me to make peace with him. I wasn't about to apologize. I just knew he was wrong and was being a pigheaded old man. I built my successful company despite his objections." John paused. "But now as I'm lying in this bed, not knowing my fate, it all seems so trivial. I'd give anything to sit and talk with my dad one more time."

As Matthew opened his mouth to respond, a nurse entered the room. "Time for your meds, Mr. Chandler."

John frowned at Amelia. "They pester me day and night in this place."

"Time for us to go anyway. Thanks for signing the contract." Matthew stood and replaced his cap. "I hope the surgery goes well. Mom said to tell you she will be up later to visit."

Amelia touched John's hand. "Bye, Mr. Chandler. I'll be praying for your operation to be successful."

John patted her hand. "Thank you kindly."

Matthew and Amelia left the room. Walking down the cold, sterile hall, he let out a sigh of relief. Mission accomplished. And he'd learned something he never knew about his father and grandfather's relationship.

But in a way he wished he didn't know. Now he had to ponder the question: did he want the same thing to happen with him and John?

Matthew accepted Ruth's offer for dinner when he and Amelia returned to Chandler Springs later that afternoon. While she helped her mother in the kitchen, he played with Harley in the front yard. His cell phone vibrated.

"Hi, Matthew," Nora said when he answered. "I haven't heard from you in a few days,"

"How's it going?" Matthew tucked the phone against his shoulder and threw the frisbee for Harley.

"Doing okay. How's life in the big town of Chandler Springs? I assume you are still there?"

"Yep, still here." A smile covered Matthew's face when Harley grabbed the frisbee mid-air.

"I'm really glad to hear that, son. You sound happier than you have in a long time."

"You know, Mom. I really am." He sat down on Amelia's porch glider and watched Harley run across the yard to greet the mailman. "I never thought I'd say it. This place has been good for me."

"I've been praying you'd realize that for yourself."

"There's still issues to work out. But I'm getting there." Matthew smiled at Amelia when she stepped out on the porch and handed him a glass of ice tea. "I found Evan's Bible." The screen door slammed when she walked back in the house.

"Really?" Nora sounded surprised.

"I've been reading it. He made some interesting notes in the margins. It's starting to make sense."

"That's wonderful, Matthew." Her voice was light and pleasant.

"I can't wrap my brain around it, but somehow I'm connecting with Evan and Emma." Matthew gulped the tea. "When I saw John at the hospital, he told me about his falling out with Austin years ago."

Nora sighed. "And did he tell you that they never reconciled?"

"Yeah, he did. And that he regrets it now." Matthew could almost hear his mother telling him not to make the same mistake. "He signed the paperwork, and Amelia will be doing her part this week. Looks like the house is still mine."

"I'm really glad to hear that, son." Matthew could hear mumbled voices in the background. "Pete needs me. I'll talk to you later."

"Bye, Mom." Matthew disconnected and sat down on the porch swing. After all that he'd learned in the past week, it was time to do some deep soul searching about his relationship with his father.

The next morning Matthew sat in Evan's rocker with a cup of fresh coffee. It had become his morning routine to come to Luke's room with a steaming mug and read from Evan's journal.

Emma and I talk often about the legacy we want to leave for our children. What is important in life? They live in a fine house, have plenty of food and clothes. Toys are never scarce. They understand these are material possessions. We've also taught them spiritual things. They know who God is and love Him in their own little ways. They've seen our family help others in need. Emma and I desperately want to leave a family legacy. For our children and their children and their grandchildren. How do we do that, Lord? We pray this house will be a blessing to many Chandlers in the future and they will sense Your love and peace in this house.

Matthew closed the journal. It was sobering to think that when his father was gone, he'd be the last Chandler. Unless he married and had a son. The thought of marrying Amelia and having a little boy brought a smile to his face. And what about his own father? Did Matthew want to come to the end of his life with the same regrets that John now had?

Matthew's thoughts were interrupted by a light tap on the bedroom door. "Come on in."

Logan stuck his head in. "Hey, just wondered if you want to explore the cabin tomorrow."

"Sure. Let's do it." He could use a distraction from the thoughts about his father.

The next morning Logan sat in the kitchen drinking steaming coffee from a ceramic mug. The rain at dawn had stopped, and the sun peeked through the clouds.

Matthew stood at the wood burning stove flipping pancakes in a cast iron skillet. "Good thing my Mom taught me to cook."

Logan shot him a grin."Glad we won't starve."

"Well, there's always the BlueBird Cafe. Maybe we'll go there tomorrow. See what Wanda's up to."

"That lady is a trip. I bet she's got a story."

"Yeah, we'll have to ask her sometime."

Matthew set a plate of pancakes on the table next to the bacon whose aroma filled the kitchen.

Logan reached for the butter and syrup. "You ever been inside the old cabin?"

"Nope. I guess we'll find out how good our roof repair job was since we've had all this rain."

Logan forked a bite of pancake and reached for the plate of bacon.

"How was your date yesterday with Keri?" Matthew chewed his pancake and washed it down with coffee.

"Awesome, as usual. I never knew the rides at Elitches could be so much fun." Logan finished his pancakes. And the bacon left on the plate.

Matthew took the last swig of his coffee and stacked the dirty dishes in the sink. "I'll wash these later. Let's go explore."

"Right behind you." Logan grabbed his ball cap from the coat rack and followed Matthew out the back door.

Logan cupped his hands over his eyes. "It's amazing how blue the sky is here."

"Have you noticed the low humidity? Another reason to love Colorado."

Matthew walked to the edge of the lawn, Logan in step beside him. In the distance, past the cemetery, they could see the roofline and chimney of a structure at the foot of Thompson Mountain. Matthew pulled his i-phone from his pocket and stopped to snap a picture.

"Amelia will want to see this."

Within five minutes Logan stepped on the cabin porch, careful of the rotting wood. One hinge hung loose from the doorframe.

"Your family left some cool landmarks."

Matthew pushed the door open. Logan followed him in. A massive rock fireplace filled the far wall. A blackened pot hung over the fire pit.

"Hard to imagine that Emma cooked the family meals here." Matthew said.

Beyond the cobwebs and dirt, dishes and pans lined a corner shelf. A stained rug lay in front of the fireplace, full of burn marks from hot embers. Through the doorway to the bedroom, Matthew could see the footboard of a bed and the rails of a chair. "I'd love to restore this place."

"Right up my alley. Then when it's finished, you can rent it to me."

"You're catching the Colorado fever."

Matthew grinned at his friend. This could be their best adventure yet.

The corners of Logan's mouth tilted into a smile. "I just might be."

Matthew pointed to the wood floor at the foot of the old iron bedstead. "Do those boards look different to you?"

Logan bent down and ran his hand over the wood. "Yeah, the grain runs the opposite direction. Maybe they've been replaced over the years?"

"This family seems to hide things in the strangest places. Let's take a look."

Before Logan could reply, Matthew was on his knees. He pulled out his pocketknife and pried up one end of the board. He lifted it away and stared into the space below.

"Can't see anything... too dark."

"Here. Let me give you some light."

Logan turned on the flashlight on his cell phone and pointed it toward the hole.

"I see something." Matthew stuck his hand in and pulled out a small metal box. "Well, well. What have we here?"

Matthew fiddled with the rusty hinge on the front of the box. It finally gave way, and he opened the lid. A musty odor filled the room. He pulled a folded paper from the top. Parts of it disintegrated in his hands. "Too bad that wasn't better preserved."

Underneath, more crumbled papers filled the box. Matthew held one up to the light to read the faded print. "Looks like receipts and papers from Evan's mining company. Wonder why this box is under the cabin floor?"

"Who knows? Hiding the contents from someone? Someone hid it here and forgot about it?" Logan tilted his head to one side. "Leaving treasures for future generations to find?"

From the bottom of the box, Matthew lifted a leather pouch.

He untied the string and dumped the contents in his hand. Three nuggets of gold glimmered in the sunlight.

He stuck his hand into the bag and pulled out a piece of parchment. The markings were faded but legible.

Matthew whistled. "Unbelievable, Logan. This is the map to Evan's mine."

"So cool."

"Think it's a coincidence that I hired a mining crew last week to start on the vein the accessor found?"

Logan shook his head. "Nope. This was all meant to be."

"I'm starting to think so too." Matthew replaced the floorboard. "Let's take the box with us. Maybe some of these papers can be restored. And find out the value of these nuggets." He kicked the board back in place. "Amelia will be so jealous that she wasn't with us today."

Matthew and Logan stepped out of the cabin, onto the porch. Matthew replaced the contents of the metal box while Logan closed the door.

He pointed to the meadow in front of them and the snow covered mountain peaks in the distance. "So this is the view my great-grandparents had every day."

"No comparison to our home in New York."

"Isn't that the truth? It's all making sense now."

The pieces were falling into place. If Canon Financial would approve the Denver office, they'd have it made. At this point he honestly didn't care if he ever set foot in New York City again.

The next morning Matthew texted Logan. Seemed funny to text someone in the same house. But it was a big place. Stacy had called earlier, apologizing several times for interrupting their vacation. But Mr. Kennedy had requested a video conference with them at 10 a.m. Matthew assured Stacy she'd done the

right thing. He and Logan were more than willing to be available for the CEO of Canon.

Logan walked into Evan's study as Matthew connected to
the link Stacy had given him. Walter Kennedy appeared on the
screen, grey hair perfectly combed. His steel blue eyes had a way
of commanding conversations. Matthew adjusted the volume.
Logan sat down in the chair next to him so they'd both be
visible on the screen.

"Good morning. Thanks for joining me at such short notice."

"We're happy to hear from you, sir." Matthew knew this was
the time to pull out all the stops. He'd even dressed in a polo
shirt and pressed trousers, clothes he hadn't worn in several
weeks. Nice that his feet weren't visible and Kennedy couldn't
see his flip flops under the desk.

"I've studied your proposal on the Denver office and
consulted with our board and with our attorneys." He cleared
his throat. "You boys have presented a compelling plan, and I
want you to know that I've seriously considered it."

Matthew tried not to grin too big. This was it. The last piece
of the puzzle was falling into place.

"But I'm sorry to say that we've decided to decline."

Matthew looked over at Logan and wondered if their reac-
tions mirrored each other. "We're sorry that you feel that way,
sir." If it sounded so good, why were they saying no? "Can you
tell us what made you come to that decision?"

"I like you boys. Always have. And I commend you for the
great job you've done helping establish this firm to be one of the
best in the state." He took a sip of water from the glass on his
desk. "But you also know that decisions like this come down to
the bottom line. The board felt that opening a new office could
spread us too thin in our fickle economy."

"We appreciate you letting us know." Matthew controlled his
voice and reminded himself to stay in the business mode. Even
though he wanted to scream right now.

"Have a nice finish to your holiday. See you when you return to work." The video cut off and Walter Kennedy was gone.

"Well, we have our answer." Matthew disconnected from the link and closed his laptop lid. "Just not the one we wanted."

"What now, Matt?" Logan frowned. "I really thought we had it in the bag."

"My investments can't be liquidated for several years so that's a no go. I'd thought at one time that the proceeds from the sale of this place would give us a good start. Now I'm planning to keep the house."

The mine might be profitable but who knew how long that process could take? He could ask his father for a loan. But that definitely wasn't happening.

"With our business instincts, I have no doubt, Logan, that we'll figure something out." After all, they were the power team.

"I hope you're right, buddy. I hope you're right."

CHAPTER 31

*M*atthew chuckled out loud at the text from Ruth.
He answered back that he would love to come
for a birthday dinner. And he was planning his own surprise
celebration with Amelia for the day after her birthday. He'd
convinced Ruth that Eva had been lying. She'd hugged him and
told him that she believed him. All was well.

Logan walked into the kitchen in wrinkled pajama bottoms,
scruffy beard and bedhead.

"You're a mess, man. Must have had a great time with Keri
last night."

Logan snorted. "Yep, we went to Elitches again. Most fun
I've had in years."

"Sit. You need coffee." Matthew poured a cup and set it in
front of Logan. "Amelia is thrilled about you and Keri."

"I'm pretty happy about it myself." Logan took a sip of the
steaming liquid. "Ah, your strong coffee always perks me right
up." He made a face.

"Glad I could help." Matthew poured a cup and sat down at
the table. "Amelia went to the hospital with me yesterday to see
John."

"How did that go?"

"Better than I ever thought." Matthew felt a relief he hadn't sensed in a long time. "My dad actually apologized, Logan. Can you believe it?"

"Wow, no kidding. And how did you respond?"

"I didn't say much. He did most of the talking." Matthew finished his coffee. "But for the first time, probably ever Logan, I could tell he was sincere."

"Proud of you, Matt. You did the right thing going to see him." Logan drained his cup.

"Wasn't on my top ten list of things to do, that's for sure. But having Amelia with me seems to make things easier with John. Somehow she connects with him." Matthew set the coffee cups in the sink. "Oh, by the way, Ruth texted earlier." Matthew smiled. "She's having a birthday dinner for Amelia tomorrow night. You're invited."

"Is Keri coming?"

"Of course." Matthew slapped his friend on the back.

"Yep, I'll be there."

Matthew had decided it would be a perfect time to talk with Amelia when they were alone after the party. It was time to tell her how he felt about her.

That afternoon Amelia locked the real estate office door and headed toward her car. Her cell phone buzzed. She set down her business bag and purse to answer it.

"Hey, Matthew."

"Hi. I couldn't wait to tell you what Logan and I found at the cabin yesterday."

Amelia scrunched up her nose. "Was it something dead?"

"Nope. We found the map of Evan's mine." He waited for her response.

"Seriously? How did you know it was in the cabin?"

"Lucky guess, really. I had a dream a few nights ago about Evan. We were standing at the back of the cabin, facing Thompson Mountain. As we talked, we walked around to the front porch and went inside. Then I woke up."

"Wow."

"Pretty bizarre, huh? I never would have thought to look in there. Logan noticed the floorboard pattern in the bedroom was different. We pulled it up and found a small metal box."

"That's where the map was hidden?"

"Yep, and some other things. Let's have dinner tonight and I'll show you."

"Sounds great. Why don't you and Logan come over? Mom is making a roast and there's always plenty."

"See you in about an hour?"

"Perfect." Amelia picked up her briefcase and bag and unlocked her car door. "And by the way. I have news on the house contract." She slid into the driver seat.

"Ok. Shoot."

"Not good, I'm afraid. Even after a long conversation with them, the buyers aren't budging."

Matthew sighed. "What about the contract that John signed?"

"They told me very plainly that they don't care about any contract and will see us in court, if necessary."

"Oh, man. I was hoping it wouldn't come to that. Where do you think we stand?"

"No idea. Our attorneys are pretty confident the contract John signed would break the sale. I'm not sure they anticipated any pushback from the buyers."

"Well, I'm not giving up. It's my house."

Amelia wanted to give him a high five. Even though that was more of a guy thing. She loved to hear him call it his house. "We'll do everything we can. Just be prepared if we have to go to court."

"I'm ready for a fight." Matthew would do anything to keep Rose Haven.

After supper Matthew poured the contents of the pouch on the kitchen table. Amelia and Ruth's eyes widened when they saw the nuggets.

"When I worked for Austin and Evelyn, they mentioned a mining map. Austin said he and his siblings searched for it for years, without success." Ruth turned the buzzing timer off and pulled a chocolate cake from the oven.

"Beautiful." Amelia stared, captivated by the glimmering gold. "I wonder who hid these?"

"Another Chandler mystery we'll have to solve someday." Matthew stuffed the treasure back in the pouch. "I'm really glad Logan and I searched the cabin."

Logan pointed to the leather bag. "What are you going to do with all this?"

Matthew sat back in his chair. "I don't know yet."

"Have you studied the map?" Ruth asked as she beat butter and cocoa together and pulled a frosting knife from the drawer.

"It's pretty primitive. I'll definitely need help figuring out the markings."

Amelia sipped her hot tea. "There's a land agent in town. I'll call him tomorrow."

"That would be great, Amelia. Thanks."

Ruth turned from her work at the counter. "What about the tunnel?"

Matthew and Logan looked at each other. "What tunnel?"

"Oh, I'm surprised my adventurous daughter hasn't told you about it." Ruth winked at Amelia.

Amelia let out a little laugh. "Oh the tunnel. No, I hadn't told them."

"Ok, so what are we talking about?" Matthew was lost in the mother-daughter conversation going on.

"When I worked in the house, Austin told Amelia they were going on an adventure. She'd always been afraid of the dark and this little trip nearly sent her over the edge."

"Oh Mom. It wasn't that bad."

"You had nightmares for weeks afterward."

Amelia picked up the story. "Austin told me his father had built a tunnel from the house to the mine in Thompson Mountain. Back in those days, there was still a threat of Indian attacks. It was the escape for the family if they were ever in danger."

"Interesting," said Logan. "I'd like to explore this tunnel tomorrow."

"Yeah, me too." Matthew nodded his thanks to Ruth when she set a slice of chocolate cake in front of him and then Logan.

"Too bad I have appointments." Amelia shuddered. "But you two can go on another Rose Haven adventure." She took a bite of the cake Ruth sat in front of her.

"No way am I going back in that tunnel. Ever."

The next morning Matthew and Logan sat at their favorite table in the BlueBird Cafe. Wanda had just started taking their order when Amelia walked in the door.

"Well, there she is," Wanda announced loud enough for the room to hear. "If he's here ..." She motioned to Matthew. "I didn't think you'd be too far behind." Today her hair was in a ponytail with purple streaks.

Amelia's face turned pink. "Quite a welcome."

Matthew and Logan stood as Amelia sat down in the vacant chair. "Good morning." She kissed Matthew and allowed him to push in her chair.

"Now that everyone is settled, what can I get you?" Wanda pulled her pad and pen from her apron pocket and wrote down the three orders. "Be back with drinks."

"What are you guys up to today?" Amelia said.

Matthew and Logan looked at each other. "We're exploring the tunnel this morning. How about you?"

"Thank you." Amelia set her purse on the floor when Wanda arrived with a teacup and steaming pot of hot water. "Showing a house in Idaho Springs. Then another big conference in Denver." Amelia rolled her eyes. "I'll have to figure out how to stay awake." She poured the hot water into the cup and dunked the tea bag. "I remembered some more about the tunnel."

"Feel like telling us about it?" Matthew asked.

"I must have been about ten years old or so. I was hiding from my mom. She had punished me, and I told her she was mean and that I was running away to find my daddy." Amelia's voice broke. She pulled a tissue from her purse.

"Austin had taken me down to the tunnel the day before. So I packed a little bag and wrote my mom a note. I found a flashlight and tiptoed down the basement steps. The cellar was pretty creepy, but I kept going. I can be stubborn." Amelia sipped her tea. "The tunnel door was partly open from the day before, and I slipped through."

Amelia thanked Wanda when she delivered her food. Taking a bite of oatmeal, she continued. "It was so dark. I kept my little flashlight pointed on the dirt floor. I pulled my bandana headband down over my nose and mouth to keep from breathing the musty smell. To this day, I don't know how I kept going. I guess in my little girl imagination, I'd thought it would be like heaven and my daddy would be waiting for me at the end of the tunnel."

Matthew and Logan looked at each other. Matthew finally asked. "What did you do next?"

"It seemed like I'd been lost forever. I got really tired and started crying. I just wanted to be back in my warm room again.

I sat down on the dirt path and curled into a little ball. When I think now about all the bugs and mice down there ..." Amelia shivered.

"Wow, you had a lot of guts back then." Matthew stopped buttering his toast and looked at her.

"Yep, I guess I did. My mom found the note and told Austin and Evelyn where I had gone. Austin came looking for me. I was never so glad to see anyone in my whole life!"

"Did you ever make it to the gold mine?" Logan bit into a piece of bacon.

"Nope. I didn't make it that far. Austin found me, covered me in a blanket and carried me back into the basement. My mom was waiting there, crying. I felt so bad." Amelia picked up her spoon to finish her oatmeal. "Oh, and I had nightmares for weeks after that, just like she told you last night. I couldn't go to sleep by myself in a dark room for a long time."

"Maybe we should take you into the tunnel sometime to help you get over the fear," Matthew said.

"No thanks. Once was enough." Amelia finished the last bite of toast. "I better get going." She drained the last drops of tea from the cup.

"Just one more thing, if you have a minute." Matthew pulled his credit card from his pocket for the bill Wanda had laid on the table.

Amelia nodded. "Sure."

"We just found out that the CEO at Canon Financial declined our plan about the Denver office."

"Oh, I'm so sorry." Amelia tried to hide her disappointment. She couldn't imagine how the guys felt. "Did he say why?"

"Basically blamed it on the economy. Didn't want to stretch the company too thin. Yada Yada Yada. Not sure I believed him, actually."

"I was really hoping to find you a nice office out here."

"Yep, we were too." Matthew frowned. "That door may have closed for the moment but we're not ready to give up."

After Amelia left for the real estate office, Matthew and Logan arrived back at Rose Haven. In Evan's study, Matthew sat in the leather chair and Logan on the couch. Matthew picked up Evan's journal. "I wanted to read something to you that Evan wrote about the tunnel."

Logan leaned forward. "Sure."

Our family had quite a shock today. After our Luke's disappearance more than a year ago, we finally know what happened. According to Sheriff Taylor, it was a disgruntled mine worker I fired for drinking on the job. He had a wife and children and blamed me for his loss of income. In a saloon in Idaho Springs, he cooked up a plan to kidnap one of our children for ransom. Somehow he slipped into our home and grabbed Luke, then escaped through the tunnel into the mine. Tragically he didn't know or forgot about the ledge close to the mine's entrance. He and Luke both fell off it and were killed. A ransom note in the man's pocket confirmed his plan. We are heartbroken but also happy to know our son is with Jesus. We are planning a small funeral next week.

Logan stared at Matthew. "Wow."

"I couldn't believe it when I read that last night. Makes me want to explore the tunnel even more."

"Are we looking for anything in particular?"

"Not really. But you never know what we may find." Matthew finished his coffee and set the two cups in the sink to wash later. "Let's take some energy bars and water," he said. "We may be gone for a while."

Dressed in a flannel shirt, jeans and boots, Logan stuffed supplies and extra batteries into a back pack. "Anything else?" He picked up two mag lights from the table.

"You have a good charge on your cell phone?"

Logan flipped the Ottercase open and checked the charge level. "Yep. 100%. Not that it will make any difference if we don't have service underground."

"True. At least Amelia knows where we're going. If we're not around when she returns from her meeting in Denver, she'll come looking for us."

Matthew opened the basement door and flipped on the light switch. Dim light shadowed the steep, narrow stairs. He took the mag light Logan handed him.

"Have you ever been down here?" Logan asked.

"Nope. This is the first time. Never really had a reason to." Matthew started down the steps, hanging on to the rail. He looked back at Logan. "Careful. There could be rotting wood on some of these risers."

At the bottom, they both blew out a sigh of relief.

"Where now?" Logan shone the mag light on the far wall. Rows of canned goods and jars lined the space. "We sure won't have to worry about starving."

"Wonder how long some of this has been down here?" Matthew started toward a door on the opposite wall. "I think this may be it."

The steel door was barred from the inside. Matthew handed Logan his flashlight and removed the wooden slat from the braces.

"Wonder how Amelia ever got this open when she was running away." Matthew laughed at the thought.

"Maybe it was already open."

"Yeah, now that I think about it, I think she said Austin had left it open. A ten year old girl wouldn't be strong enough to remove that slat by herself."

Logan held the two flashlights while Matthew tried the door. The knob squeaked as it turned, and it finally swung open. The smell of musty earth filled Matthew's nostrils as he stepped onto the dirt floor.

"We should prop this door open." Logan looked around. He grabbed the wooden slat and wedged it between the door and the casing.

Matthew stood on the other side. "Good idea. Not sure how we would open the door from this side." He paused and let his eyes adjust to the darkness of the tunnel. "Well, here we go."

After twenty minutes, Matthew and Logan reached another steel door. Matthew's heart sank. It might be a dead end. The knob was stuck. Made sense since it hadn't been used in years.

Not one to give up easily, he tried again. A little more rotation this time.

"Here, hold my light." Matthew handed his mag light to Logan. "The door opens in. Maybe if we both push on it."

Matthew and Logan put their shoulders against the door and pushed. The door hinges screeched and gave way. The two nearly fell into each other as the door opened.

"Sorry, Amelia. The client specifically requested you." Her office manager, Tiffany, looked at the appointment again. "He was insistent about seeing the house on Locust Street at 3 pm tomorrow. Said to let you know he's already seen the inside pictures online and he's putting a contract on it. And emphasized it will be a cash deal."

Amelia pulled up the MLS listing. The house on Locust was a 100 year old Victorian, much like Rose Haven. The sale would bring a good commission. If the buyer was that interested, she could show the house quickly and still arrive home in time for her birthday dinner.

"Okay. Please confirm the appointment. And if he cancels or reschedules, please let me know right away. I have a very important dinner tomorrow might."

"Will do."

This was the first birthday she'd been excited about since losing Brian. Nothing would stop her from enjoying her party.

CHAPTER 32

*A*melia arrived at the Locust Street house early to turn on the lights. She liked her clients to have a homey feeling of the place when they stepped through the front door.

She laid her purse and business bag on the built-in seat at the front window. Within a few minutes a white Mercedes pulled into the driveway. Awesome. They were on time and then she could get to her party.

A short, stocky man exited the car. She could only see the shadow of a passenger because of the tinted windows. And whoever it was didn't get out.

Amelia opened the front door. Memories of meeting Matthew the first time at Rose Haven flooded her mind. She smiled warmly and put out her hand.

"Hello, I'm Amelia Richardson."

The man's handshake was light, almost wimpy. "Name's Rick Johnson. I'm interested in buying this house." His voice sounded like his handshake. Almost too high pitched for a man.

"Certainly. Let me show you around. Isn't your wife coming in?"

"Nah, That's not my ..." The man stopped. "She's not feeling well. Decided to stay in the car. We looked at the inside pictures online. She trusts my judgement."

"Right." Something didn't feel right about this couple but she'd met some strange people before. She put a smile on her face. "Let's start on this level."

Amelia began telling the client that the house was built in 1900 but had recently been remodeled. It didn't have the charm of Rose Haven but she wanted a sale and wasn't about to tell him that. As they walked to the back of the house, she could tell the man wasn't paying attention. She thought she heard the front door open and then close. She dismissed it as the squeaks and creaks of the old building.

The man followed her from room to room, but still seemed distracted. "Do you need to check on your friend in the car?" Amelia asked.

"Probably a good idea. I'll be back in a minute." Rick stepped into the hallway.

Amelia stood at the front window, watching the children playing in the yard across the street. She turned when she heard the floor creak behind her. Something pressed against her face and nose. She struggled to breathe. Then the world went black.

Matthew arrived at Amelia's house at 5:00 p.m. Her car wasn't in the driveway. He hoped she wouldn't miss her own party. When he pulled up to the curb, Ruth opened the door and Harley bounded out to greet him.

He patted the giant teddy bear on the head. "Hi there, boy."

Ruth met Matthew on the porch, biting her lip. "Have you heard from Amelia?"

"Not since earlier today. Maybe the showing this afternoon ran longer than she'd planned." Matthew pulled his phone from his pocket. "No text from her."

"I'll try to call her." Ruth tapped the cell phone in her hand, put it to her ear and then hung up. "Just got her voice mail."

Matthew stepped into the house. "What can I do to help? She should be here soon."

"I'm pretty much ready." Ruth walked to the picture window and looked out again. "Logan and Keri just pulled up."

Harley greeted the couple as they walked in the door. "Where's the guest of honor?" Keri set a cake on the kitchen table.

"She should be here soon." Was Matthew reassuring them or himself?

Keri checked her phone. "Texted with her this morning. She talked about how excited she was to celebrate her birthday with all of us. And especially you, Matthew."

Matthew felt a grin cover his face. "She better hurry. Or she'll miss her own party."

An hour later Matthew felt like he'd checked his phone and thrown the frisbee for Harley a hundred times. He hated watching Ruth pace. They all knew this wasn't like the reliable, considerate Amelia they all knew. She always let someone know if she would be late. Waiting around was driving him nuts. He had to do something.

"Where was the house showing?" Matthew asked.

"The big Victorian on Locust Street," Keri said. "She was excited about the listing because it's similar to your house, Matthew. But not as grand, of course." Keri checked her phone again. She looked up at them and shook her head.

"Wanna take a ride, Logan? I think we should at least drive by there."

"Yeah, sure."

"Take my car." Keri handed Matthew her keys. "And please call us just as soon as you find her." She walked over to the window Ruth had been staring out of.

Matthew and Logan rode the quiet streets of Chandler Springs. "Watch for her car, Logan."

"Yep, you got it."

"Not much happening in this town on a Saturday night." Matthew turned by the real estate office. Amelia's parking spot was empty so they kept driving. Think positive thoughts, Matthew kept telling himself. But it was hard with the punctual Amelia.

"Turn left here." Logan looked again at his GPS. "It should be the big house up on the hill."

Bingo. Amelia's SUV was the only car in the driveway. Matthew's gut twisted. He had a very bad feeling about this. "I don't like this, man."

Matthew pulled into the driveway and had barely turned the car off before he hopped out and was on the porch, Logan right behind him. The huge front door pushed open easily. He stepped in and called her name. Silence.

He walked farther down the hallway and called again. His voice echoed in the empty house. He went to the stairs. "Amelia, are you here?" he called. "I'm going upstairs."

Matthew took the steps two at a time and walked up and down the hallway looking into each room, the floors creaking with each footfall.

Satisfied that she wasn't up there, he returned to the first floor. His mind was spinning with the same question over and over: where was she?

Logan called from the parlor. "Matt, look at this."

Matthew ran into the room.

Logan pointed to the window seat. "Her purse and business bag. Do you think she's still here?"

"The house is empty. I'm calling the police." Matthew pulled out his cell phone and dialed 911, his heart in his stomach. The spinning continued. Where. was. she?

Matthew and Logan stayed at the house, as instructed by the dispatcher, to wait for an officer to arrive.

Matthew had just talked to Ruth. It was one of the hardest calls he'd ever had to make, telling her that Amelia was missing. He was so glad Keri was with her.

"The police are here," Logan said from the window.

He met two uniformed officers at the front door. This was surreal.

Matthew felt helpless as the two asked question after question. He didn't know what color clothes she'd worn that day. And he wasn't sure what time she'd arrived at the house for the showing. A thought crossed his mind. Husbands and boyfriends were often singled out as suspects. He hoped the police weren't thinking...

After what seemed an eternity, the questions were finally finished. A detective would come by the house later to dust for fingerprints. And they'd be taking Amelia's purse and business bag with them to the police station for evidence.

Matthew and Logan were on the way back to Ruth's when Matthew realized the house probably had a basement. He hadn't thought to check there. "Maybe we should go back, Logan. I didn't even think about checking the basement." He felt a cold chill shiver through his body.

Logan sat grim faced in the passenger seat. "The police will thoroughly search the house, Matt. They have your number. They'll call you."

Matthew hit the steering wheel with his hand. "I hate this. We have to find her."

"We will, buddy. We will."

Matthew was almost to Ruth's when his cell buzzed. He didn't recognize the number.

Logan looked at him. "You gonna answer that?"

"Yeah, I guess I better." He pulled the car to the side of the road. "Hello?"

"How much is she worth to you?"

"Excuse me? Who is this?" Matthew pushed the speaker button on his phone.

"Your girlfriend. I know where she is." The voice sounded male but rather high pitched and nervous.

Matthew's jaw tightened. "If you hurt her...

"Drop $100,000 cash at Chandler Park by the statute by midnight and you'll see her again."

Matthew wanted to yell but kept his voice calm. "I can't get that kind of money so quickly on a Saturday night."

"Sure you can, buddy, if you want to see your sweet Amelia again."

The line went dead.

Matthew looked at Logan. "This has to be some kind of sick joke. Someone is just out for money. No one would want to hurt Amelia. Everyone in town loves her."

Matthew raced back to Ruth's house, a plan forming in his mind. He'd always been a man of action.

And wherever Amelia was right now, she needed him.

CHAPTER 33

*A*melia opened her eyes. Pain ripped through her head when she tried to raise it. Where was she?

The damp ground beneath her had soaked through her cotton skirt and blouse. She shivered. That movement made her shoulders ache.

The knots of nylon rope pulled at her wrists and ankles. Fear rose up in her throat. She tried to scream but gagged on the cloth in her mouth.

Where was she? Who did this to her? And why? She tried to remember but the questions made her head pound harder.

She blinked a few times before her eyes adjusted to the dark. Her heart raced. The walls of the long abandoned tunnel were closing in on her. She was ten years old again and lost in this place. Now she was trapped in her worst nightmare. Her stomach churned.

Please Lord, no. I don't know if I can survive this again.

Matthew and Logan drove the short distance from Locust

Street back to Ruth's house. Driving like a madman wasn't Matthew's style, but tonight all he cared about was finding Amelia. He careened around corners practically on two tires.

When they pulled up to the curb, Ruth stepped out on the porch, Harley bounding out the door after her. "Did you find her?" Ruth's voice was shrill and her brow wrinkled.

Matthew had always been good at controlling his emotions. But the look of terror on Ruth's face nearly sent him over the edge.

"Not yet." He stepped up on the porch and petted Harley's head. "But don't worry. We will."

He gave Ruth a side hug and held the screen door open as she stepped into the living room.

Keri stood in the kitchen doorway. "I made coffee." Her face pale, she hugged Logan when he walked into the room.

Matthew shook his head. "No thanks." He touched his stomach. "Not sure I can handle it right now." He slid into a kitchen chair.

Ruth bit her lip. "Where can she be?"

Matthew hated this helpless feeling. So out of his norm. "The police are looking for her, but I think we need to come up with our own plan." He looked up at Ruth, standing by the counter. "Can I use this?" He pointed to a pen and paper on the table.

Ruth nodded and sat down in the chair beside him. She folded her hands tightly in her lap. Matthew could hear her praying under her breath.

"Ok... " Matthew scribbled on the pad. Writing a business proposal was a cinch compared to this. "We know she made it to the showing. Her purse and business bag were in the house."

"And her car was in the driveway," Logan added.

"Right. So we don't think she left the house on her own."

"That makes my stomach turn." Keri put her hand over her mouth.

Logan pushed his chair closer and put his arm around her.

Ruth turned white. "Oh, dear Lord."

"Sorry, ladies. This isn't easy." Matthew reached over and covered Ruth's cold, clammy hand. "But the four of us brainstorming could be faster than what the police have to go on."

"I think I'm going to be sick."

Ruth jumped from the table and almost ran down the hall to the bathroom. Matthew stood and followed to make sure she was okay. He stopped at the living room door.

A single lamp in the room shone dimly on the wall of pictures. He took a few steps closer. His heart beat faster...Amelia on the porch of Rose Haven with Austin and Evelyn. The photo had captured her captivating blue eyes and beautiful smile. In that frozen solid moment, he realized how much he loved this woman. The thought of living without her. No. He wasn't going there. He was going to find her. Or die trying. A passion surged in him that he'd never felt before.

Ruth came out of the bathroom and stood next to him.

"You okay?" Matthew felt her shaking when he pulled her into another side hug.

"Yeah," Ruth mumbled. She stared at the pictures on the wall. "Oh my."

"What?" Matthew hoped she wasn't going to be sick again.

"You don't suppose that woman would hurt Amelia, do you?"

"What woman, Ruth?"

"That Eva person that visited me. And I told her about the tunnel."

Eva's phone conversation ran through his mind. She just wanted to know what he saw in that place. But it wasn't true. She'd come to case it out – see how she could get to Matthew where it hurt. He plastered his hand on his forehead. He should have known.

"Logan," Matthew yelled. "Come on. We're going to my house."

Amelia could feel the edges of the rope with her fingers. She worked at them but every movement to free herself scraped more skin from her wrists. She stopped when the pain became intense. But she had to keep trying. She thought of Matthew. She had to get out of this place. Exhaustion took over and she closed her eyes.

When she woke again, the ropes seemed a little looser. She could do this. She worked at the knot until her hands slipped out.

She yanked the cloth from her mouth and took a deep breath. And another. The dank, musty smell of the tunnel filled her nostrils. But it was more air than she'd had in a while.

How long had she been down here? Her head felt like she'd been riding a merry-go-round a hundred times in a row. She put it between her knees and took slow, deep breaths. She pulled at the knot at her ankles. Her shoulders and wrists ached. She shivered. It was so cold down here. The rope on her ankles finally gave way.

Her shoes were missing. Didn't matter. She'd walk out of here barefoot if she had to. A dim light shone at one end of the tunnel. She'd just follow that glow. She tried to stand, but her legs didn't hold, and she fell into a heap.

Sobs clawed at her throat. Would she ever get out of here? What about mice and insects? Oh, dear Lord. And snakes. She couldn't go there and keep her sanity.

Matthew, please find me. He would be looking for her. No doubt about that. Please God. Help him figure out where I am. Until then she would just close her eyes. And when she woke up this nightmare would be over.

∼

Matthew and Logan jumped in Keri's car, tires screeching as he pulled away from the curb in front of Ruth's house.

"So help me, God. If Eva has hurt her..."

Matthew couldn't finish his sentence. Eva might do a lot of crazy things, but would she actually physically injure someone? Please God.

Wow, was he praying now? Somehow he knew that Amelia would be.

He stopped in front of his house and cut the engine. Taking the porch steps two at a time, he was inside. He ran down the hall to the kitchen. So focused on finding her, he was at the basement door before he realized Logan was beside him, talking on his cell.

Logan disconnected the call. "The police are on their way. I told them how to get to the tunnel." He handed Matthew a mag light. "And I grabbed a blanket."

"Good thinking. Thanks, man."

Matthew threw open the basement door. Tonight there was no worry about the stairs. At the bottom, he pulled the steel framed door open and stepped into the tunnel, Logan right behind him, their bright lights shining on the floor ahead.

"Amelia!" Matthew shouted, his voice echoing. "Amelia, are you down here?"

He walked farther into the damp tunnel. It felt different this time. Not exciting like when he and Logan had explored. But dark and hollow. He wanted nothing more than to find Amelia, but he almost hoped she wasn't in here. He knew what it would do to her.

"She's not here, Logan. Maybe my gut feeling was wrong."

"Matt . . . What's that on the ground?" Logan shone a light to the right of the path. "It's a women's shoe."

Matthew picked it up. "She is here. I remember seeing her wear these." An excitement surged through him. "But where is she?"

"Remember when we were down here before? There's another section."

Matthew sprinted ahead to the next door. Logan caught up and helped open the heavy steel door. Logan shone the light down the long dark path.

"Matt, look." Logan grabbed his arm. "There's something on the ground ahead."

Amelia was on her side, pulled into a fetal position.

Matthew ran to her, his heart racing. They'd found her. Thank God, they'd found her. Please let her be okay.

He crouched to the ground. "Amelia." He rolled her on her back.

Her face was dirty and bruised. He leaned close. Thank God she was breathing. He brushed the hair from her face. How he wanted to kiss her.

"Amelia." His voice was soft.

She opened her eyes. "Matthew," she barely whispered. "I knew you'd come."

"Of course. I'd never leave you alone. Are you hurt?" He took the blanket from Logan and wrapped her in it.

"I. don't. know. My head ..."

"Let's get you upstairs."

In one swoop, she was in his arms. He walked slowly back to the door, Logan shining the light on the uneven path in front of them.

As they entered through the doorway into the basement, two police officers were coming down the stairs.

"Thank God you found her." Darrin Wilson stepped forward and looked at Matthew. "We are searching for the suspects."

Amelia looked at Matthew and gave him a weak smile. "Thank you." She mouthed. Then she closed her eyes again.

"It could take time to get an ambulance up here tonight. It'll be faster to take her to the hospital in Idaho Springs in our car." Darrin led the way back up the steps.

"Logan, could you please go get Ruth and Keri and take them to the ER there?" Matthew took one step at a time, holding tightly to his precious cargo. Now that he'd found her, he didn't ever want to let her go.

"Sure thing." Logan bounded up the steps.

In the kitchen, Matthew set Amelia in a chair. She opened her eyes.

"Matthew."

"How are you feeling?"

He crouched down to eye level with her. All he wanted to do was kiss her. The bruises on her beautiful face made the passion surge up his backbone. He bit it back so she wouldn't see.

"Like I've been hit by a mack truck." She squinted at him. "It's so bright in here." She licked her lips. "I'm really thirsty."

Matthew uncapped a bottle of water from the refrigerator and held it to her lips while she drank.

"It's a good sign that she's talking to us." The second officer's cell phone buzzed. "We'll need to question her when she's up to it." He stepped out of the room.

"My wrists and ankles really hurt," Amelia mumbled.

Darrin sat in the chair next to her. "They'll clean and bandage them at the hospital. Are you hurt anywhere else?"

"My head is spinning."

"Dehydration and exposure." Darrin directed his comment to Matthew.

Matthew nodded. "Should we give her some food?"

"No, let's get her to the hospital first."

The second officer walked back into the room, serious faced and business like. "Carson and Harris found an abandoned Mercedes by the BlueBird an hour ago while on patrol. There was a woman's shoe in the back seat."

Matthew lifted the blanket from Amelia's feet. Her shoes were missing. "Do you remember anything?"

She tried to shake her head. "Ohhhh, that hurts."

"Let's get her to the hospital. We'll ask questions later." Darrin closed the notebook he'd been writing in. "You need help getting her to the car?"

"I got her. Thanks."

Matthew picked Amelia up. It felt so good to hold her close to him. He wished they had a change of clothes for her, but the blanket would keep her warm until they got to the ER. He followed the officers to their car.

And he thanked God again that she was safe.

CHAPTER 34

*T*he ride down I-70 in the back seat of a police car, with flashing lights and siren, was an experience Matthew hoped never to relive. It was the one downfall of living in a small mountain town with no hospital. But he'd do it again any time for Amelia.

Matthew met Logan, Ruth and Keri in the ER waiting room when they arrived. Ruth ran to him, her face drawn. She looked exhausted. "How is she?"

"Doing better. Getting some fluids for the dehydration. The doctor talked like she'd be released in a few hours."

Ruth hugged him. "Thank God you and Logan found her."

"Yes, thank God." Not a phrase that Matthew used often. But he really meant it today.

"I'd like to see her." A slight smile curved Ruth's mouth. The first one Matthew had seen since this whole nightmare had started.

"I'll take you to her." Matthew spoke to a nurse at the desk and then led Ruth through the double doors to a curtained area.

"I'm okay, Mom. Really." Amelia lay back on the pillow, both wrists bandaged. She just wanted to close her eyes and sleep. But from the strained look on her mother's face, she needed reassuring first.

Ruth kissed her daughter's forehead. "I was so worried."

"I'm so thankful Matthew and Logan found me." Her head was clearing after having food and fluids. And she was finally warm from the blankets the nurses had piled on her. "It's coming back to me now. I was showing the house on Locust Street to Rick Johnson." She squeezed her eyes closed, trying to remember. "He seemed very nervous. Actually didn't have an interest in the house at all." Amelia shifted in the bed. "And I don't know if this was real or I was dreaming. Eva was in my face, yelling that I'd received exactly what I deserved. And that Matthew would never be mine."

She shuddered and watched Matthew and her mother exchange glances. NO idea what that was about.

Matthew leaned over the bed, his chin trembling. "I'm so sorry." He kissed the top of her head.

Amelia put one wrist-covered bandage around his neck and pulled him closer. The memory of Matthew's kisses had kept her going while trapped in the tunnel. She couldn't think about Eva. She didn't even want to go there. Right now she was safe. And warm again.

Matthew looked into her eyes and smiled. "You missed your birthday party."

"I hope there's some food left. I'm starving."

Amelia released her arm from his neck, and he stood straight. She reached for the cup on her tray and took a long sip of ice water. This was the strangest, scariest, best birthday ever. And she was happy to be celebrating another year of life.

If she could just get past the fear that was starting to settle deep down in her soul.

Matthew drove Amelia home from the hospital later that afternoon. She seemed quieter than usual, but he wasn't really surprised. He couldn't imagine the thoughts running through that pretty head right now. He turned on her favorite radio station and watched her relax in the passenger seat with her eyes closed. The mountain pass from Denver was becoming familiar to him, and he enjoyed the scenery in silence as they headed to Chandler Springs.

Amelia was quiet until they pulled in her driveway. She sat up and unbuckled her seat belt. Matthew turned off the engine and stepped out to help her out of the car. She accepted his hand, hers cold and clammy, which was not at all her normal. He pulled her close to him. There was so much he wanted to say. But this didn't feel like the right time.

Ruth opened the front door, and Harley bounded out to them, wagging his tail a hundred miles an hour.

"Hi boy. I missed you." Amelia knelt to pet her furry friend.

When Amelia stepped in the house, pink and purple crepe paper and balloons hung from the living room ceiling. A Happy Birthday banner stretched across the wall. A huge smile spread across her face. "It's so good to be home."

Matthew stood inside the front door, trying to give her space.

"The first thing I want to do is take a shower." Amelia ran her fingers through her tangled hair. "I can't thank you enough." She met him at the door and stood on her tiptoes when he leaned down to kiss her. "You probably don't want to get too close right now."

Actually, he'd love to take her in his arms and kiss her like he'd never done before. When she was ready. "You always look lovely."

"Yeah, right." Amelia wrinkled her nose. "You know how to flatter a girl."

Ruth stood at the kitchen door wiping her hands on her gingham apron. "Come for dinner about 6:30 tonight. We'll have a late birthday celebration."

"Sounds great." Matthew pushed open the screen door. When Amelia disappeared down the hall to her room, he said to Ruth, "Oh, by the way, my birthday surprise has changed to next weekend. That will give her some time to rest and recover."

"I hope she'll be okay. I'm worried about how she'll process everything this time." Ruth looked at Matthew. "And thank you. You saved her life, you know."

"I'm just so happy that Logan and I found her. I don't even want to think about how it could have turned out."

Matthew stepped back into the living room when Ruth put her arms out for a hug. He had no problem hugging her back. She was one of the sweetest ladies he'd ever met. In more ways than one.

"Can I bring anything tonight?"

"I think we're good. Keri and I were able to save the food from last night." Matthew saw Ruth shiver. A night none of them would ever forget. "But it's all good now. See you later."

Matthew got in Amelia's SUV. It felt weird to drive it home, but she'd insisted. The events of the last twenty-four hours played over and over in his mind. He couldn't imagine if it had turned out differently. It was time to let Amelia know how he felt about her.

And to find Eva Pearce.

The birthday dinner that evening went off without a hitch. Matthew watched Amelia fill her plate a second time. He loved seeing her enjoy her food. She was so full of life. Logan and Keri celebrated with birthday cake and ice cream and then excused themselves to see a movie in town.

"I'll take care of the cleanup." Ruth scooted Matthew and Amelia out of the kitchen. "It's a beautiful evening. Go enjoy the sunset."

Matthew and Amelia looked at each other and laughed. He held the door for her as she stepped out onto the front porch. The sun was casting orange and purple hues over the mountains. Colorado sunsets were the best. Matthew sat down beside Amelia on the glider, Harley at her feet.

"We haven't had much time to talk in private," Matthew said softly.

"No, it's been a whirlwind for sure."

"Oh God, Amelia. I was so scared that I'd lost you." He put his arm around her and pulled her close.

"I was never so happy in my life to see you. And Logan." Amelia snuggled against him and curled her legs under her.

"While I was here, trying to decide where to look for you, something happened to me. I've never felt like that about anyone before." He tipped her head with his free hand and kissed her warm lips. "Amelia, I ..."

Matthew stopped. Headlights flashed over them as a vehicle pulled into the driveway. Officer Darrin Wilson exited the Chandler Springs police car. "Hello, folks. Hope I'm not interrupting."

Darrin petted Harley who had walked out to meet him, tail wagging. It seemed that Darrin and Harley knew each other.

As a matter of fact, he was interrupting. Matthew couldn't believe the guy's bad timing. Darrin pulled a notebook from his shirt pocket and walked up on the porch.

Amelia pointed to the chair next to them. "Have a seat."

Darrin stared at her for too long as far as Matthew was concerned. "You're looking much better."

"Thanks. I feel great."

Matthew watched the interaction between the two. Amelia's face turned a bright red, and he wondered why she felt so uncomfortable.

"I was really worried about you. And so happy when you were found."

Darrin looked like he wanted to take her in his arms any minute. Matthew wanted to wipe the smug look off the guy's face.

"Ummmm... If this is a private conversation, maybe I should get going." Matthew couldn't believe the jealous feelings running through his head. He moved his arm from around Amelia and stood up.

Darrin waved his hand. "Oh no. Please stay. I actually have some questions for you, too." He looked at his notes.

Good, get your eyes off my girl. Matthew hid a smile that tried to take over his face. His girl. Yep, he liked that. It felt right.

"Matthew.... Darrin just asked you a question."

"Oh... Sorry. Could you repeat that?" He had to get his mind back in the conversation.

Darrin read from his list. "We're hearing the name Eva Pearce. Any ideas where she could be?"

"None. Haven't seen her in several weeks." Matthew sat back down. "And that was in New York."

"Are you sure you didn't speak to her when she showed up here and talked to Ruth?"

Matthew didn't like the officer's tone. What was he insinuating? "No, I did not. I just told you that." Why did he feel so defensive? This guy was getting on his nerves.

Darrin held up his hand. "Just doing my job."

Amelia looked at Matthew. "Eva was here?" He hated the hurt look on her face, like she'd been betrayed.

"Yeah, she was."

"Why didn't anyone tell me?" Amelia jumped from the glider, hands on hips, and stared at him.

Matthew sighed. "Ruth and I thought it was better that you didn't know."

"Well, you didn't do a very good job of protecting me, did you?" Amelia whirled and ran in the house, banging the screen door.

Matthew glared at Darrin. "If there's no other questions."

Darrin closed his notebook. "How long are you in town?"

"Another week."

"I have this contact for you." He read off Matthew's cell number.

"Yep, that's it."

"I may be calling with more questions. Especially about Eva Pearce."

Matthew nodded. "Have you alerted the airlines?"

"Of course." Darrin stiffened. "I know how to do my job."

"Well, if that's all, I'm going to check on Amelia."

Matthew stood and walked to the front door. He watched Darrin walk down the porch steps to his car and leave. He felt bad that Amelia had found out about Eva's visit this way. When he stepped into the house, Ruth was in the kitchen alone.

"How's she doing?" This was unchartered territory for him. He didn't know how to handle women's emotions.

"Not well. I got her to take a half of a sleeping pill. I hope she's resting now."

"I'm sorry." He sat down at the kitchen table. He didn't know what else to say.

Ruth poured a mug of coffee and placed in front of him.

"That was a rough conversation with Officer Wilson from the very beginning. What was with that guy and the way he looked at Amelia?"

"She's known him for years. Kind of thought at one point

that maybe they'd get together. But then Brian came along."
Ruth poured her own cup and sat down at the table.

"Oh." Matthew didn't know if he should feel relieved. Or not.
The muscles in his jaw tightened.

"I overheard a little of the conversation with Darrin." Ruth
bit her lip. "So they suspect Eva?"

Matthew tried to control his response. He wanted to scream
right now, he was so angry. But he didn't need to rant in front of
Ruth. She'd already been through so much.

"Sounds that way. They will catch her. She's not as smart as
she thinks." He finished his coffee. "Please tell Amelia to call or
text me when she's up to it."

"Will do."

Ruth walked him to the front door.

"And be sure to lock your doors." Matthew checked the
doorframe. "Good. You have a deadbolt."

"Haven't used it in years. But I will start tonight." Ruth
looked tired. "And Harley is a good watch dog."

"Call me anytime, day or night. Logan and I can be here in
just a few minutes."

"I will, Matthew. Thank you."

Matthew stepped out on the porch and heard Ruth push the
deadbolt closed. Eva was not going to hurt Amelia again.

Ever.

Amelia tossed and turned. The sleeping pill hadn't done a thing
for her. And her room was too dark. She turned the light on and
dug in a dresser drawer for a night light. The soft glow helped.

But then the questions started, leading her down a dark
tunnel of a different kind.

Why hadn't her mom and Matthew told her that Eva was in
town?

And where was Eva now?

Would she try to hurt her again?

She finally fell into a fitful, dreamless sleep.

The next morning Amelia thought about going to the office, even for a few hours, but Ruth reminded her that the doctor had said to rest for a few days.

"I feel fine," she said.

"Give yourself some time. The work will always be there." Ruth pulled fresh baked scones from the oven. "Matthew said to call or text him today."

"Yeah, I will later." Amelia was still processing the fact that he hadn't told her about Eva's visit to her mom.

Ruth lifted a scone onto a plate and set it in front of her. "I heard you crying in your sleep last night."

"Was I? I don't remember."

"I almost came to your room but then you quieted. I didn't want to wake you."

Amelia looked at her left wrist. "This still hurts too. It woke me up a few times during the night."

"Did the doctor give you some pain meds?"

"Yeah, but you know how I am. I won't take them unless I'm dying." Amelia bit into the warm chocolate chip scone. "Mmmm... this is my medicine."

"You might consider at least half a pill tonight. You need to rest." Ruth turned the whistling tea kettle off and poured boiling water into a tea cup.

"Thanks, Mom." Amelia dipped the tea bag and let it steep.

"Darrin Wilson is very concerned about you."

"We've had a great connection all these years." Amelia popped another bite of scone in her mouth. "But I don't think

Matthew understood. He kept looking at Darrin in such a funny way."

"What do you mean?"

"I don't know. Like he thought Darrin was coming on to me or something." Amelia sipped her tea.

"I'd always hoped you and Darrin would get together. Then Brian came along."

"I guess it just wasn't meant to be, Mom."

"And Matthew?"

"I don't know. He's mentioned more than once that he's not the type to be in a serious relationship." Amelia savored the last bite of her warm scone. "Who knows?" She'd seen some serious changes in Matthew lately.

But how well did she really know him?

At the insistence of her mother, Amelia worked from home the rest of the week. Matthew called or texted multiple times. "Just checking to see if you are okay." And "How are you?"

It gave her a warm feeling that he cared so much. But thoughts still nagged her. Why hadn't he told her that Eva was in town?

She felt fine during the day when she was busy. She talked with Darrin several times, going over and over the same details. When she had arrived at the house on Locust Street. A description of Rick Johnson and how he acted. The person waiting in the car that she couldn't see well enough to identify. Waking up in the tunnel.

The repeated questions had become exhausting. But if there was one new clue that could break the investigation, she'd grit her teeth and oblige. She had confidence in Darrin and in the whole Chandler Springs police force.

But nights were a different story. Amelia hated the fear that twisted in her stomach when darkness fell. The terror of feeling trapped filled her dreams. She just wanted to get better. But how? She didn't mention her struggles to anyone, especially her mother, who had been hovering over her constantly. And Matthew was just about as bad. At times she enjoyed the attention.

But most of the time, she just needed her space from all of them.

CHAPTER 35

*M*atthew opened his laptop and scanned the e-mail from the hotel in Estes Park. Sweet ... they'd finally confirmed his reservations. He didn't mind paying extra to reschedule from the previous weekend. Amelia needed to get away.

Since the news had come out in the paper, people in town had been kind to her. Almost too kind. Even Wanda at the Cafe had toned it down around her. Matthew wondered how that made Amelia feel. He could only guess because she certainly wasn't talking to him about any of it. Which made him feel uneasy. But at least she had agreed to go to Estes with him.

Matthew picked Amelia up at eight on Saturday morning and planned to arrive in Estes Park before noon. He lifted her suitcase into the back of the SUV.

"How long do you think we're staying?" He grabbed at his lower back and made her laugh.

"Just brought the essentials." She flashed her gorgeous smile at him. He loved it when she did that.

Leaving Chandler Springs, Matthew entered I-70 East into light early Saturday morning traffic. He'd assured Ruth that he'd guard her daughter with his life and would text often to calm Ruth's nerves. They got along so well, and he wouldn't do anything to break that trust.

"Have you ever been to Estes Park?" Matthew asked Amelia.

"When I was a little girl, my dad took us there. I don't remember much about the trip except from pictures." Amelia took several gulps from her water bottle. "Oh, and I attended a realtors' convention there a few years ago." She stiffened in the seat.

"You okay?"

Her face looked white against her blonde hair.

"Yeah. It's passing." Amelia leaned against the headrest. "Still having panic attacks."

"Do you need anything? Should I stop?"

Amelia squeezed her eyes closed. "Maybe fresh air would help."

Matthew pulled off at the next exit. The facades of the shops and gas station reminded him of an old mining town. He parked in front of the general store, got out and opened Amelia's door.

"Thanks." Amelia stepped out and pulled her sunglasses over her eyes. "Sorry to hold up our trip."

"Don't be silly. We have all day. How you doing now?"

"Better." Amelia took a deep breath and blew it out slowly.

"Let's sit on this bench." Matthew guided her with his hand on her back.

Amelia looked away from him. "This is really hard."

"I'm sorry. I'm still trying to wrap my mind around how this happened."

"I don't know how to deal with it all. No one has ever wanted to hurt me." She still couldn't look at him.

"And no one will ever hurt you again as long as I'm around." Matthew took her hand. "I still feel like I'm responsible for this."

"Of course not. It wasn't your fault." Amelia took another deep breath.

"Indirectly it was. Eva never would have known you if it hadn't been for me."

Amelia looked at the scrapes on her bruised wrists. "She's a sick woman."

"Yep. I wish I'd realized that before she hurt you." Matthew reached over and kissed one wrist and then the other. "They're starting to heal."

"Yes." Amelia leaned over and kissed him. "I'm feeling better."

She stood, and they walked to the car. Matthew opened the door for her.

"Maybe you should talk to someone. Like a therapist?"

"I have an appointment next week."

"Should have known. You're always on top of things."

Matthew started the car and got back on the Interstate. Her wrists were healing, but was she?

Matthew and Amelia arrived in Estes Park just before noon. She couldn't ask him to stop every time she felt a little panic. She sipped her water and tried to relax. She was determined not to ruin their plans.

"There it is." Matthew pointed at the Stanley Hotel sitting on the hill like the dignified ancestor of the town. He pulled into a parking spot. "It was built by Freeman Oscar Stanley and opened in 1909."

"You've been doing your homework." Amelia was impressed.

"The internet is a fabulous thing."

He lifted the rear hatch of the SUV and hoisted his backpack out. Then he pulled out her suitcase.

Amelia slung her purse over her shoulder and grabbed her water bottle out of the cup holder."We could use the valet service."

"Nah, I'm fine. Does me good to get some exercise." Matthew

pulled out the suitcase handle and dragged it behind him into the hotel.

Amelia studied the historical pictures on the lobby walls while Matthew checked in at the front desk. The architecture, the fashions, the simpler life of the time period had always fascinated her.

"All set. And I signed us up for a hotel tour this afternoon."

"Ooh, I'd love that." Amelia hugged him.

"I knew you would." Matthew pulled the suitcase toward the elevator and held the door open for her. "We're on the second floor." He punched the number 2 button.

Amelia stared at him.

"Separate rooms, of course. You're in 207 and I'm in 214."

"I appreciate that. Thank you."

Matthew stepped out when the elevator opened, and Amelia followed him down the hall. "Here's your room." He put the keycard into the slot. The door clicked open.

Amelia stepped inside. "Beautiful." Matthew had gone all out reserving the room with deluxe king bed and jacuzzi tub in the corner. A vase of roses on a lace doily sat in the middle of an end table. Amelia stood on her tiptoes and kissed him. "You outdid yourself."

"Anything for you." Matthew pulled her suitcase to the closet. "I'll put my stuff in my room and give you some time to settle in. Then we'll have lunch."

"Perfect."

Amelia shut the door as he left and made sure it was locked and the deadbolt fastened. She lay down on the bed. Could she tell him the truth? Not if it ruined the weekend he had planned. Maybe the panic would go away if she could lie down for a little while.

And get Eva's voice out of her head. She hated this.

Please God ... Please help me.

An hour later Matthew texted Amelia to meet him in the hallway. When she stepped out of her room, he couldn't help noticing the dark circles under her eyes. She had changed to a flowered skirt, white lace blouse and sandals. She looked nice, but he could tell she wasn't herself. He wanted to ask but decided not to.

The warm, cloudless blue sky was just right for an outdoor lunch at a downtown cafe. Matthew and Amelia made the short drive and found a parking spot within walking distance. The restaurant was crowded with tourists, but they lucked out and were seated at the last table on the outdoor porch. Sipping cold drinks, they discussed everything from Harley, to the first time they met and laughed about how they'd disliked each other.

But the kidnapping was never mentioned. Matthew wanted to talk about it. He thought it might help. But somehow they danced around the subject, and he didn't want to push. So instead they talked about how good the bison burgers tasted.

Amelia wiped her mouth and laid the napkin in her plate still half filled with burger and French fries. "I'll be back in a minute."

While she was in the restroom, Matthew texted Ruth. "All is well. Having a great time." He smiled at Ruth's almost immediate reply. "Thank you. Take good care of my girl."

He didn't mention Amelia's moments of distraction. And that she wasn't eating much. Ruth just needed to know that she was safe.

When they arrived back at the hotel, the tour was just starting. Matthew loved seeing Amelia's eyes light up as they walked through the halls of the historical place, reading the plaques and examining the memorabilia. He thought, he hoped anyway, she was doing better. But as the tour guide took them to the darkest end of the basement corridor, she grabbed his arm.

"Oh no, not again."

"Are you okay?" He put his arm out to steady her as she stumbled against him.

She gasped. "I just need air."

He helped her up the steps to the main floor and out into the flower garden.

Amelia sat down on a wrought iron bench, facing the roses. She closed her eyes and took slow, deep breaths. In and out. In and out. After a few minutes the color came back into her face.

Matthew held her hand and watched her. His heart was breaking. This was his fault.

She opened her beautiful eyes and looked at him. "Let's walk through the garden."

"Amelia," Matthew said in a soft tone.

"It's okay, Matthew. You don't have to say anything." She looked out over the roses. But not at him.

"I hate seeing what this has done to you." His voice caught in his throat.

"I'm feeling better. Let's enjoy ourselves."

Matthew nodded. But inside he felt anything but joyful.

Matthew decided shopping would be good therapy and talked Amelia into walking through a few downtown shops that afternoon. He noticed her admiring a sapphire necklace in a jewelry store window.

"Be right back," he said.

Matthew returned a few minutes later and handed her a wrapped package.

Her face turned pink. "You didn't have to do that."

"No, I didn't have to. But I wanted to. Open it."

Amelia pulled the ribbon and wrap off. The sapphire necklace lay nestled in a jewelry case. Matthew fastened it around her neck. And then kissed her.

"My belated birthday gift to you."

His heart was full of love for this woman. There was so much he wanted to give her.

"Perfect for this outfit." Amelia touched the sparkling gems hanging around her neck. "Thank you. Mind if we go back to the hotel for a bit? I'd like to rest."

"Sure." Matthew took her hand. He loved the warmth of her skin.

He stopped twice to let Amelia rest on the short walk back to the hotel.

"We natives are always telling the tourists that it's the altitude," she said. "But my goodness, I should be used to it. I live in the mountains, for goodness sake."

"Not a problem."

Amelia sat on a couch in the lobby while Matthew waited for the elevator. He held it open for her when it arrived.

"I'm not sure how much time I need." Amelia pulled her keycard from her bag and opened the door. "Can I text you?"

"Of course." He kissed her on the cheek.

"Thank you. You've been really patient with me today."

"Please let me know if you need anything."

"I will. Thanks." Amelia closed the door.

Matthew walked down the hall to his room. He hated feeling so helpless. He'd give anything to help Amelia heal.

And to find Eva Pearce.

Matthew had decided to make dinner reservations at the hotel restaurant. While Amelia slept, he showered and changed into pressed slacks, a polo and light weight suit coat. He knocked on Amelia's door when she texted that she was ready.

"How was your rest?"

"Feeling better." Amelia's embroidered royal blue tunic dress matched her new necklace.

"Super. Now we can party all night."

Amelia laughed out loud. "I've never done that. I'm a 'be at home in bed by 10 pm' girl. Always have been."

"Guess I'll have to change that."

"Fat chance." She grabbed her lace shawl and hobo bag.

It was nice to hear her laugh and joke. He hoped the old Amelia was coming back. Matthew asked for directions at the front desk and led Amelia to the restaurant's outdoor covered patio. Their table had a perfect view of the famous cascade waterfalls just outside the hotel grounds. A waiter came by for their drink order. Matthew felt the small box in his inner coat pocket. This seemed like a romantic place to ask her. And to get her mind off the attack.

When the waiter returned with their wine, he waited for their food selections. Amelia stared at the menu for a long time. She seemed to be having trouble deciding.

"Should I order for both of us?" Matthew whispered.

Amelia nodded. "Yes, thanks."

She looked relieved not to have to make a choice. The waiter wrote down Matthew's order and disappeared into the kitchen.

"I was supposed to return to New York next week," Matthew said, toying with the salt shaker. "But Darrin Wilson called yesterday and said they want me in town for a while longer."

Amelia sipped her wine. "Will that work out okay with your job at Canon Financial?"

"Yeah, I can work from the house. Logan is returning to New York, and we'll tag team like we did before."

It seemed like a million years ago that he'd broken his leg and thought he was stuck in Colorado forever. Now he never wanted to leave.

The waiter returned with their meals. The steaks were

cooked to perfection. Matthew forked a bite of garlic mashed potatoes, but his thoughts were on the box in his pocket. He wondered if Amelia could hear his heart pounding. It felt like it would jump from his chest any moment. Maybe he should wait until after dessert.

Their conversation continued. They talked about how Logan and Keri would miss each other when Logan went back to New York. Matthew told Amelia that his mom had texted that afternoon and his dad's surgery had gone well. Amelia told him Ruth's gourmet bakery business had really taken off and how happy she was for her mother.

They were still dancing around what they needed to discuss most.

When the waiter returned for their dessert order, Amelia touched her stomach. "None for me. Thanks. But the meal was wonderful."

"I'll split a cream brûlée with you." Matthew gave the waiter the order before Amelia could respond.

"When he returns, do you want another drink?"

Amelia shook her head. "One glass of wine is plenty for me."

Matthew thought about his former life. By now he'd have downed a half dozen drinks and just be getting started. The thought hadn't even crossed his mind tonight.

When the dessert arrived with two spoons, Matthew persuaded her to have a few bites. Then he finished it off.

"Mmm... so good." Amelia licked her lips." But I will need to get back to the gym next week."

The restaurant was packed by now and the noise level off the charts.

"Let's take a drive," Matthew said. "We still have some daylight. And it's so beautiful here."

"I'd love to."

Amelia picked up her purse and followed Matthew to the door. He put his arm around her waist as they walked to the car.

She seemed so much more relaxed. This was a perfect time to ask her.

Matthew pulled off the highway at a scenic overlook. "Amelia. Before we get out, I'd like to ask you something."

Amelia's stomach flipped. Was it the meal she'd just eaten?

Matthew reached in his pocket and pulled out a ring case. He popped it open. "I love you, Amelia Richardson. Will you marry me?"

Amelia gasped. She'd never thought Matthew was the marrying kind. The antique diamond and blue sapphire ring shimmered in the last sun rays of the day. She could imagine how beautiful it would look on her finger.

"Oh, Matthew." She squeezed her eyes closed to stop the tears. She wanted to say yes. But Eva's face popped in her mind, and the panic feeling rose stronger and harder than ever.

Matthew waited. "Does that mean yes?"

Amelia took deep breaths and grabbed for her water bottle. She couldn't speak.

"Are you okay?"

Amelia stiffened in the seat. "Let's get out. I need air." She waited for Matthew to come around and open her door and help her out of the car. She stood at the overlook sign and stared off at the snow-capped mountains in the distance.

Matthew stood beside her holding one hand and rubbing her back with the other. "It's okay. You are safe. Just breathe."

After a few moments Amelia took a deep breath. "I want to say yes. I honestly do. But I'm not sure if I can right now."

Matthew swallowed hard. "Is it still Brian?"

"No. I think I'm finally past all that." Amelia clasped her hands. It hurt her heart to see his fallen face. "This past week has just been really confusing for me."

"I'm sorry you feel that way." Matthew snapped the ring case closed and helped her back to the car.

"Please. I'm not saying no. I just need a little time before I can say yes."

They rode back to the hotel in silence. How could she explain to him feelings that she couldn't even figure out herself?

CHAPTER 36

On Sunday morning, Amelia convinced Matthew to visit a small mountain church just outside Estes Park. Matthew didn't know any of the songs but listened to Amelia's soft soprano voice sing along with the congregation. The pastor spoke on love and forgiveness.

Matthew was into the sermon, thinking about his own father, when he looked over at the sweet lady next to him. She was digging in her purse for a tissue and wiping her eyes. He reached for her warm hand. Her left ring finger should be showing off the ring he'd bought for her.

After the service, Matthew and Amelia returned to the hotel to check out. While she packed, Matthew texted Ruth. He was glad he hadn't mentioned the engagement ring to her. He knew Amelia loved him. Again, he just needed to give her time. He hoped and prayed that talking with a professional would help her process her feelings.

In the hotel restaurant, Matthew purchased a picnic lunch and they set off for a drive through Rocky Mountain National Park. Matthew had never seen such majestic snow-capped mountains and nearly ran off the road a few times. They would definitely be returning here. They decided to stop at the Aluvian Fan picnic area to eat.

"This looks like a good spot." Matthew found a parking place and pulled the lunch from the back seat.

Amelia grabbed two bottles of water and put on a sunhat and glasses. She snapped a picture of the mountains with her cell phone and then turned to him. "How did you like the service today?"

"Actually wasn't too bad. At first I thought the pastor's voice would put me to sleep. But once he got started, I was engaged."

"I was really moved." She bit into her sandwich. "But how do I forgive someone who has hurt me so bad?"

Matthew gulped from his water bottle. He wished he had the answers that could magically take away her pain.

"I guess that was a rhetorical question. Somehow I feel my healing from that awful experience is connected with forgiveness. Just haven't figured it all out yet."

"I'm with you there." Matthew bit into a red apple and wiped the juice off his cheek with the back of his hand. "I've been thinking a lot about my dad lately. And if forgiving him brings me peace, I'm all in." He took another bite. "Relationships are hard."

Amelia looked at him. "I agree. And I'm thinking about your proposal, Matthew. I want you to know that. I'm not just blowing you off."

"I have to be honest. It wasn't easy to hear you say no."

Amelia bit her lip. "I'm sorry."

"But I'm serious. I want to give you the time you need." Matthew gathered the trash and walked Amelia to the car. How many complicated relationships had he bailed on?

Not this time.

∼

Monday morning Matthew and Logan sat once again at their favorite table at the BlueBird.

"Bummer that our vacation is almost over." Logan stirred creamer in the coffee Wanda set in front of him. "I could get used to living here."

"Yeah, I needed to talk to you about that. The police have asked me not to leave town yet." Matthew's eyes were on the menu. But his mind was on Amelia.

Logan pushed his cap back on his forehead. "Lucky you. Honestly, I don't even want to go back to New York. In fact ..."

Wanda stopped at their table. "What can I get for you boys this morning?"

Matthew had to do a double take. He hadn't noticed earlier but Wanda's hair was all one color. And no gum. Maybe she was turning over a new leaf. "I'll have two eggs over easy, bacon and pancakes."

"Give me the same." Logan's phone pinged. "My good morning text from Keri."

"Awe... How sweet." Matthew made a face.

Wanda looked at Matthew. "How's your girlfriend doing?"

So the locals thought of Amelia as his girlfriend. Not that he minded. "She's doing well. Thanks."

"Sorry to hear about that awful woman who tried to hurt her."

Matthew nodded. If Wanda knew, then everyone in town had probably heard by now.

"So the pyscho woman was an ex-girlfriend of yours, huh?" Wanda's voice boomed across the cafe.

Matthew cringed. "Not exactly. Just an acquaintance." He wished she'd hold it down.

Wanda took the hint and scooted to the kitchen to turn in their orders.

Logan looked at his friend over the top of his coffee mug.

"That's one thing about living in a small town, Matt. Everyone knows your business."

"Yeah, tell me about it."

Logan sat back in his chair. "As I started to say earlier, I've decided to take you up on your offer. When I go back to New York, I'm giving my notice at Canon."

"Wow, man." Matthew gave him a high five. "That's fantastic news."

"Is opening an independent office in Denver with you still on the table?"

"Heck, yeah. Nothing I'd rather do." Matthew nodded his thanks at Wanda when she put plates of hot food in front of him and Logan. "My one regret would be giving up the Grant account." He took a bite of the eggs. "We worked our butts off for that one."

"My brain has been working overtime. Let me do some checking when I get back in the office." Logan bit into his buttered toast. "Maybe there's a way we can take it with us."

"Seriously? That would be awesome. Let me know what I can do." Matthew gulped his coffee. It tasted good this morning. Wanda needed to give him a refill. "And never forget. We are the dynamic duo. Nothing can stop us."

"You got that right." Logan finished his breakfast. "I've got some funding ideas. We'll start on a shoe string budget but we'll make it work, Matt." His text pinged again.

Matthew looked at his own phone which was shut off. He thought he'd turned it on earlier. When he hit the power button, a text popped up from Amelia. He texted back. His heart raced at her answer.

"Amelia needs me, Logan. Gotta go." He threw a twenty on the table and ran out the door.

∾

Amelia had arrived early at her office that Monday morning. She hummed a worship tune as she unlocked the front door. Her heart was full from the wonderful weekend with Matthew. There was no doubt that she loved him. So why couldn't she say yes when he proposed?

She opened her laptop to check her calendar. Four showings and three closings for the week. Good, keep her mind busy.

Tiffany had left the bundled morning paper on her conference table. Amelia pulled it out of the bag.

Eva's picture filled half of the front page.

Amelia's vision blurred. She couldn't see the print to read the article. And didn't want to. She grabbed her phone and texted Matthew.

"Call me." She hit send.

Now she sipped the hot tea Tiffany had brought her earlier. Stay calm. Take deep breaths. She inhaled and exhaled. Her cell buzzed and she expected Matthew. It was Darrin Wilson.

"Good morning. Hope this is a good time." Darrin always sounded too cheerful, especially this early in the morning.

"I just saw the paper." Amelia tried not to cry. She felt safe with Darrin on the case.

"Oh, that's what I was calling about. I want you to know that we have a good lead on Eva."

Amelia choked on the words that came to mind. Instead, she started praying the hardest she had ever prayed in her life that the woman would be caught.

"Amelia, are you there?"

"Yeah, I'm here."

"And the good news is that we arrested a . . . just a minute. Let me check on the name. Here it is. Justin Smith. He's been identified as Eva Pearce's half brother. And he's admitted to using the name Rick Johnson to lure you to the house showing."

"Oh my." Amelia felt a weight on her chest that wouldn't let her breath.

"We'll need you to identify him."

Amelia let out a deep exhale. She had to be strong. "When?"

"We'll have a line up at 1:00 p.m. today. Can you be there?"

"Yes." She had to do this. Matthew would help her. And God.

"Keep the faith, Amelia. We're going to catch Eva Pearce."

Call waiting beeped in. She looked at her screen. It was Matthew. "Thanks for letting me know, Darrin. I really mean that. I've got another call coming in."

He disconnected.

Amelia tried to answer Matthew's call with a calm tone. But inside she was shaking.

"I got your message," he said in a husky voice. "What's up?"

Where should she start? "Have you seen today's paper?"

"No, why?"

"Eva's picture is plastered on the front page. With a full article of painful details. I couldn't finish it." Amelia couldn't hold back the tears any longer. She tried to muffle her sobs.

"I'm sorry." Matthew's words were soft, and they wrapped around her like his warm hands. "I'm coming over. Give me about ten minutes."

She could hear him telling Logan that he had to go.

Amelia disconnected the call without replying. She just wanted him to hold her. And tell her it would be okay.

While she waited for him, Amelia slipped into the restroom and tried to reapply her make up. Three coats of concealer still didn't cover the dark circles under her eyes. But at least the mascara smears were gone from her cheeks. When she looked in the mirror, she felt like she was looking at someone else.

"Amelia." Tiffany knocked on the door. "Matthew is here."

Amelia straightened her blouse and smiled at herself in the mirror. She tried to put on a happy face. She stepped from the bathroom and saw Matthew waiting for her in the reception area. He walked down the hall toward her. She wanted her heart to leap when she saw him. She'd felt some healing after their weekend together. But now she felt dead inside again.

"Hi." Matthew gave her a side hug. "You doing okay?"

"Yeah, I'm all right." She led him down the hall. "Let's talk in my office."

Matthew followed her, and she almost fell into his arms when he closed the door. He held her close, the heat of his chest against her cheek.

"What can I do?"

"Just hold me."

Matthew sat down on the couch, and Amelia snuggled against him. He stroked her hair and held her.

After a few minutes, she sat up. "Thanks for coming over. I really needed you."

"Any time." And she knew he meant that.

"Another favor. Seems like I'm always imposing on you."

"Not a problem. What is it?"

"Will you go with me to the police station for a line up this afternoon? Darrin wants me to identify Rick Johnson..." Amelia stopped. "No, his real name is Justin Smith. And get this. He's Eva's half brother."

"No kidding." He grabbed her hand. "Amelia, that's good that he was arrested. I'd say that means they're closer to catching Eva."

"Yeah, Darrin told me they have a good lead on her. He thinks they'll catch her soon." Amelia blinked rapidly. "I'll feel much safer when she's in custody."

"And of course, I'll go with you today."

"I don't know what I'd do without you." Amelia pressed her palm to her heart.

∾

Matthew convinced Amelia she needed lunch before they went to the police station. He had the feeling she hadn't been eating much lately. He thought about avoiding the BlueBird but it didn't really matter. Amelia was well known everywhere in town.

Matthew held the door for her, and they walked to their usual table in the back. He could see Wanda at the counter with some of the locals. She'd better be on her best behavior with Amelia.

Amelia glanced at the plastic menu. "Please order a salad and ice tea for me. I'll be back in a minute."

Matthew watched her go toward the restroom. Her face had paled since they'd arrived.

Wanda came to their table, chewing her gum. "So you're back already. Didn't I just see you this morning?"

"Yep, had breakfast with Logan." Matthew looked at the menu. "Now lunch with Amelia."

Wanda leaned closer to him. "How's she doing?" Her face softened.

"She's a trooper, that's for sure." Matthew didn't want to say too much. He ordered for Amelia and then a hamburger and fries for himself.

Amelia returned to the table as Wanda left. "Why do I feel like everyone is staring at me?"

"Because you're so beautiful?"

"Oh you." Amelia made a face at him.

Matthew watched her fold and refold the napkin, rearrange the sugar packets - everything but look at him and talk. He was grateful when the food arrived. He watched her move the salad around on the plate with her fork. She hadn't taken more than two bites.

"Are you nervous about the line-up?"

"Yeah, kind of. If I screw up, he could go free." Amelia sipped her tea and nibbled on the straw.

"Nah, you've got this, Amelia." He could feel his teeth gritting. He was getting her through this. NO matter what it took, what it cost.

As for Eva, they better catch her before he did.

CHAPTER 37

*A*melia grabbed Matthew's hand as they entered the police station. Did it feel as cold and clammy to him as her whole body felt? She hadn't truly felt warm since being rescued from the tunnel.

Darrin met them in the lobby, dressed in jeans and a polo shirt. "Thanks for coming." He led them to a room with a glass window that faced into a larger area. "You will be in here." He pointed at the chairs. The room was cold and unfeeling.

"This is a one-way mirror. You can see them. But they can't see you." Darrin looked at Amelia, his eyes tight and worried. "You doin' okay?"

"Can Matthew stay?" If she didn't have his strength, she was going to dissolve into a puddle.

"Not normally our policy," Darrin narrowed his eyes. "But yeah, I can allow it this time."

"Thank you." She knew he was making an exception for her. And she appreciated it. Since their high school days, Darrin always had her back when the boys tried to mess with her.

"Have a seat and we'll get started in about five minutes."

Darrin went to the metal desk in the corner of the room to consult with a sergeant working on the computer.

"This feels weird. Like they can see me too." Amelia squinted at the window in front of them.

"Yeah. But they can't." Matthew squeezed her hand. "Don't worry. I'm right here."

Five men, one at a time, walked into the larger room, each holding a number. Two were short. For a man anyway. Just as she remembered Rick Johnson.

"I'm not sure," she whispered to Matthew. Her brain whirled as she tried to recreate that day.

"If they say something would you recognize the voice?" Matthew whispered back.

Amelia turned to Darrin. "Would it be okay if number two and number five say something?"

Darrin nodded and barked in a microphone to the men behind the glass. "When I call your number, step forward and give today's date." The man with the number two sign stepped forward and did as instructed in a deep, booming voice.

"No, I don't think so." Amelia squeezed her eyes closed. What was it about "Rick Johnson" that had stood out to her that day?

Darrin barked into the speaker again and called number five forward.

The man called out the date in a high-pitched voice.

Amelia nearly jumped out of her chair. "Yes. Yes, that's him." There was no doubt in her mind. Sweat broke out on her forehead and she crumbled into the seat, taking deep breaths.

Matthew put his arm around her and talked to her in a quiet voice. They sat for a few minutes, her head on his shoulder. She sat up and wiped her eyes. Then she stood and slung her bag over her shoulder.

"Are we finished?"

"Yes. And you did great." Darrin opened the door and

pointed to the signs to the lobby. "I feel confident that we will find Eva soon."

"What makes you say that?" Matthew asked.

Darrin hesitated. "I plan to lean on this guy more heavily. Sometimes a deal will make people talk."

Amelia sure hoped Darrin would pull it off. She didn't know how much more her heart could take.

Outside the police station, Matthew opened the car door for her. "To your house?"

"No. I have a closing at 4:30 and paperwork to finish before then. Tiffany normally completes it but she asked for the day off."

"Bad timing." Matthew tapped on the steering wheel.

Amelia hesitated. "I agree. But she's such a hard worker, and she's dress shopping for her best friend's wedding. How could I say no?"

"I really wish you'd cancel this meeting." Matthew pulled into Amelia's parking spot at the real estate company.

"No way. I'll be fine." Amelia got out of the car and unlocked the door. Matthew followed, rubbing the back of his neck. "Will you be here by yourself?"

"Just for a couple of hours." Amelia could see the tension in his face when he cleared his throat. "Don't worry. I'll keep the door locked until my clients arrive."

"Ok then." Matthew didn't sound convinced. "I don't mind staying."

Amelia stood on her tiptoes and kissed him. "It's not necessary. Really. But thanks for offering."

Matthew pulled her into a hug. "Want to sit on my porch tonight and watch the sunset?"

"Absolutely." Amelia smiled at him. "Can I bring Harley?"

"Yep. See you about 6:30?"

"We'll be there." Amelia kissed him again.

Matthew stood on the outside of the glass door and watched her lock it from the inside. He waved goodbye and headed down the street to catch a ride home with Logan.

Amelia turned on the lights and started down the hall to her office. She trusted Darrin with her life. He'd catch Eva now that they had her brother in custody. A dim light shone under the ladies' restroom door. Funny, she thought she'd turned them all off earlier when she'd left. As she approached the door, it opened.

Amelia gasped. She felt like she was moving in slow motion. The woman's clothes were wrinkled and dirty, like she hadn't changed in a week. Her greasy hair was matted to her head. Had a transient gotten in here somehow?

"So, we meet again."

Amelia held back a scream. She knew that voice. It was the one that haunted her dreams.

Eva.

"How did you get in here?" Amelia's voice came out in a squeak. She couldn't move.

"You're not in the position to ask questions, now are you?"

Eva reached into her jacket. When she pulled her hand out, it held something black and hard looking. It was a gun.

Amelia's first thought was to run. But by the wild look in Eva's eyes, she had no doubt that Eva would shoot her.

"Turn around." Eva pushed her toward her office, the cold barrel against Amelia's back.

Amelia walked slowly. Lord, Jesus. Please help me. The words came automatically.

When they got to her office, Eva pushed her inside. Amelia stumbled and landed on the couch. "Sit. And don't move."

Eva's eyes darted around the room. She reminded Amelia of a cornered weasel.

Amelia watched her. This woman had truly lost it. Was she going to kill her this time? Amelia dug her nails into the couch. She had to get a grip. She wasn't the one losing it here.

"My brother was dumb enough to get caught. But they're not going to find me." Eva's distorted laugh sent a cold chill down Amelia's spine. "Or you."

Amelia's heart raced. She couldn't get hysterical. She had to think. God, please . . .

"And don't get any bright ideas, miss goody two shoes. Your darling Matthew is not going to save you this time."

Eva pushed her dirty, uncombed hair out of her eyes. This was not the fashionable woman Amelia had met in New York.

"I ... I have clients that will be here soon." Amelia looked at the clock on her desk. It was 4 p.m.

"No problem. We're going for a little ride anyway." Eva motioned for Amelia to stand. "They'll just have to reschedule." Eva cackled. "With someone else."

Amelia grabbed her purse that had fallen on the floor when Eva pushed her on the couch.

Eva waved the gun. "Leave that. You won't need it."

"But I need my keys. And my driver's license." And my cell phone.

"Fine. Bring it. But nothing else."

Eva pushed her out the office door into the hallway.

Amelia stumbled and grabbed for the wall. Irritation at being pushed around started overriding her fear. Eva had done this to her once before. She wasn't going to do it again.

"Now, I'm going to give you a few instructions. We're going to walk out of here and get in your car. And you're not going to say a word. If you scream or try to run, you'll have a bullet in your back. Got it?"

Amelia nodded.

Eva jabbed the pistol in her ribs. "Give me your car key."

Amelia dug the key out of her purse and handed it to Eva. They exited the building with Eva following her to the driver's door. Amelia looked for someone on the street she could signal. It was empty. Her heart sank. Don't panic, she told herself over and over.

There was enough time to escape. Amelia touched the door handle as Eva entered the passenger door. "No tricks."

She put the key in the ignition.

"Where are we going?" Amelia's hands shook on the steering wheel.

"To your favorite place, of course." Eva's evil grin made Amelia shiver.

Amelia looked at her with a blank stare. She wasn't up to guessing games at the moment.

"The cold, dark tunnel that you love so much."

This woman was twisted. "That's the first place Matthew and the police will look for me."

"Oh no, Miss Real Estate Agent. Not at his house. I've found one that's much better."

Amelia's stomach churned. She had to think. How could she escape from this crazed woman? She was determined to see Matthew again. And her mom and Harley.

No way would her life end like this.

Matthew's cell buzzed at 5 p.m. He picked it up, thinking Amelia was calling. Darrin Wilson's name showed on the screen. Maybe he had good news that they'd caught Eva, and he and Amelia could celebrate tonight.

"Matthew. Darrin Wilson here. Is Amelia with you?"

"No, I dropped her off at her office after we left you. She should still be there. She had a closing at 4:30."

"The clients showed up and found an empty, unlocked

office." Darrin paused. "They had read the article in today's paper and were concerned about Amelia, so they called us."

Matthew's heart fell to his stomach.

"I'm at her office now. There's no sign of her. And her car is missing."

"Oh my God." Matthew folded into a kitchen chair. No. He should have listened to his gut instinct about leaving her there alone. No matter how much she had protested.

"I'll be right there." He disconnected the call. "Amelia is missing."

"Oh God." Logan grabbed his keys off the table. "Where do you need to go? I have Keri's car."

"The real estate office. The police are there now."

Matthew and Logan made the ten-minute trip in five. This felt like twisted deja vu. Three police cars, lights flashing, were parked in front of Amelia's office.

Darrin stood on the sidewalk, hands on hips, talking with another officer. He directed his attention to Matthew and Logan.

"We found a broken window in Amelia's office. Looks like someone entered that way and surprised her."

Matthew felt like he'd been punched in the gut. All he could do was nod.

An officer stood at the front door and motioned for Darrin to come inside. "Be back in a minute." Matthew started to follow him. "Sorry, this is an active investigation so it's better if you stay out here."

Logan grabbed his arm. "Matt, Ruth needs to know."

"Yeah, she does." Matthew pulled his phone out of his pocket. Before he could dial, Darrin stepped back out.

"We just found this in the ladies' restroom." Darrin's gloved hand held the note close to Matthew's face but wouldn't let him touch it. Matthew had to squint to read it.

"Matthew Chandler . . .You may think you've won but guess

again. I never lose. And I've taken your sweet Amelia to her favorite place."

"Eva." Matthew's face turned white. "She's taken Amelia back to the tunnel."

"You sure about that?" Darrin asked. He read the note again.

"I know Eva. She's being facetious when she says Amelia's favorite place. She knows exactly how much it terrifies her."

Darrin told one of the officers he was leaving for a bit. "Let's take my car. I want to leave everyone else here in case, by some small miracle, Eva brings her back."

Matthew couldn't believe he was riding in the back of Darrin's car again. But he'd do anything to find Amelia right now. She would be so scared. He had to be there to kiss and hold her and tell her that everything was okay. Like they'd done in her office earlier.

They arrived at Matthew's house and ran to the basement door. Three sets of boots stomped down the steps toward the tunnel. Logan grabbed the mag lights still sitting on the shelf by the steel door. It wasn't completely shut, and Matthew pulled it open by himself. He stepped into the musty dark tunnel calling her name. Logan and Darrin followed behind, shining the lights on the floor and walls.

They made it through the first section. Matthew's mind raced. When this was over, he was having this thing filled in. Way too much tragedy for one place.

Logan helped him open the door to the second section and he stepped through, calling Amelia's name. Nothing. They walked the dirt path all the way to the end. Amelia was not here.

Matthew wanted to scream. Eva had led him on a wild goose chase. He could hear her evil laughter in his head. And her words came back to him: She was a woman of action.

The men made their way back to the basement and up the stairs to the kitchen. Matthew stood at the sink, drinking a glass of water. He didn't want Logan and Darrin to see the tears of frustration in his eyes.

"We have an alert out for Amelia's car." Darrin spoke into his radio. He looked at Matthew. "Don't worry. We'll find her."

"Yeah, that's what you kept telling us about Eva." Matthew smirked. "And in the end, none of us protected Amelia this time."

"Look, I know this is frustrating. I care about her too. We're doing our best, okay?" Darrin crossed his arms and glared at Matthew.

"Has anyone notified Ruth?" Logan asked.

"I have an officer that can go over there now."

"No." Matthew rubbed his forehead. "Let me tell her." It was the last thing he wanted to do. But it was only right that she hear the news from him. That her daughter was missing again. And that he hadn't protected her.

Matthew, Logan and Keri sat at Ruth's house, staring at the coffee they weren't drinking, and waiting for news. It was after midnight and still no word on Amelia's whereabouts. He couldn't just sit here. He felt like something was crawling under his skin.

"I don't doubt that Eva took her to a tunnel again. But where?"

"These mountains are full of them. They could have gone anywhere." Ruth wiped her eyes. She looked like she'd aged ten years in the past few hours.

Matthew watched Logan sit close to Keri, her head on his shoulder. Would he ever do that with Amelia again? Stop it, he told himself. Think. He knew Eva the best. Where would she take Amelia? As far as he knew, Eva hadn't ever been to Colorado before now. He called Darrin's cell phone.

"Wilson here."

"It's Matthew Chandler. I think you should question Justin Smith. He and Eva may have planned this before he was arrested."

"We're already on it."

Darrin sounded irritated. Matthew didn't care.

"And what about calling Amelia's cell phone?"

"Done. Several times in fact. Goes to voice mail." Darrin's curt answers were irritating the heck out of him. He'd just do it himself.

"Call me the minute you have news. I won't be sleeping tonight."

"Will do." Darrin disconnected the call.

Matthew punched autodial on his phone. "It's ringing."

Ruth, Logan and Keri watched him.

"Well, well. If it isn't the high and mighty Matthew Chandler." The voice on the other end was cold and harsh. "You must have found my note by now."

Matthew gritted his teeth. "Enough of your games, Eva. Where is Amelia?"

"You really blew it, you know. We could have been so good together." Eva clicked her tongue at him.

"I want to talk to Amelia. Put her on the phone."

"Matthew!" Amelia's scream reached his ears before it was muffled. Dear God, she was alive. Somehow she screamed it again, like a piercing sound that echoed like she was in a cave. Or a tunnel.

"Shut up." Matthew heard Eva yell. She cursed. The screaming stopped.

"So help me, God. If you've hurt her, Eva." Matthew felt his face burn. His blood pressure was going through the roof.

The line went dead.

"Eva." Matthew shouted into the phone. "Eva."

Nothing. He threw his cell phone on the table.

"Call Darrin back," Logan said. "The police can trace the call to Amelia's phone."

Thank goodness someone was level headed right now. Matthew sure wasn't thinking straight. He dialed Darrin's number and told him about the conversation he'd just had with Eva.

"We'll check it out." Darrin sounded a little begrudging.

Matthew paced the floor. He wanted to go out and look for her. But he didn't even know where to start.

Harley walked over to him, and he rubbed the dog's ears. Harley couldn't live without Amelia. And neither could he.

Matthew sat in the kitchen, ignoring the coffee Keri put in front of him. He looked at the clock every five minutes. Seemed like the dumb thing had stopped. Logan and Keri had moved to the living room and were dozing on the couch. They'd talked Ruth into lying in her recliner to rest.

At 2:30 a.m. Matthew's cell phone rang. It was Amelia's number.

"Amelia?" Matthew shouted into the phone.

"Not quite darling." Matthew cringed. That voice grated on Matthew's raw nerves.

"Where is she, Eva?" How could he reason with her? That had never happened.

"Why couldn't you just love me?" To Matthew's surprise, Eva was crying. "I loved you so much and you treated me like dirt."

Ruth, Keri and Logan were in the kitchen by now, listening to Matthew's side of the conversation. "Eva." He softened his voice. "Please just tell me where Amelia is." He scribbled a note and passed it to Logan, asking him to call Darrin Wilson and try to get a trace on the call.

Eva's sobs filled the line. Matthew had never heard her cry like that. This was not the woman he'd known in New York.

"Eva. Tell me where you are. I will come and get you and Amelia. And we'll talk." Matthew sounded sincere. "I promise."

"You must be insane." Eva screamed into the phone. "No way." Well the old Eva was back. "This is all your fault, you know. If you'd just listened to me."

Matthew shuddered. She was just playing him. Like she always had.

"Oh no . . ." Eva shouted into the phone.

"What's going on?"

"I'm driving her stupid car. And I can't see the road. It's so dark."

Oh God.

"Is Amelia with you?" Matthew's heart beat faster. Had Eva left her somewhere?

"Amelia who?" Eva cursed again. "I don't know any one by that name."

Matthew opened his mouth to argue but realized that Eva was losing touch with reality. He'd try one more time.

"Eva, tell me where you are. I'll come get you." His voice was gentle. "And it will be like old times."

Matthew heard a squeal of tires and shattering glass.

A scream filled the air.

The line went dead.

Matthew jerked the phone from his ear and covered his face. Logan walked over and put his hand on his friend's shoulder.

"Tell us."

Matthew wiped his eyes with the tissue from the box on the table. Ruth looked like she was going to pass out. Keri hugged her.

"There was a loud crash, screaming, glass breaking." Matthew's voice broke between sobs. "Eva told me she was driving and couldn't see the road."

No one said anything for several minutes. But they were all thinking the same thing. Was Amelia in the car?

Keri sat a glass of water in front of Matthew. He gulped it

and tried to get his thoughts together. Darrin needed to know. He punched in the all too familiar number.

When Darrin answered, Matthew couldn't get the words to come out in full sentences. "Eva called me. She ran off the road. Breaking glass. Screaming."

"Any hint where she was?" Darrin's voice wasn't as calm as earlier. This was getting to him too.

"Nope. Just said she was on a dark, curvy road. Have you been able to trace Amelia's phone?"

"We're working on it." Darrin sounded exhausted. "Hang on a second."

It seemed like Darrin had him on hold for an eternity. All Matthew could see were Amelia's beautiful blue eyes and gorgeous smile.

Darrin came back on the line. "We've got a trace on her credit card. Looks like it was used at a gas station about 50 miles from here in a little town called Frasier."

"I'm going there." Matthew started to hang up.

"Hang on for a bit. It would be better to wait for sun up."

Matthew wanted to argue. Amelia needed him. Right now. His emotions were all over the place. He'd never felt like this before.

"Yeah. Okay. But call me if you hear anything else."

Matthew and Logan sat at the kitchen table and made plans to leave at 5 a.m. Keri had talked Ruth into laying on the couch in the living room.

An hour later Darrin called. "You were right about an accident. Amelia's wrecked SUV was found in a ravine outside Frasier where the credit card was used."

Matthew held his breath. No. Darrin was not going to tell him that Amelia was dead. She had to be alive.

"From the initial report, there was a deceased female inside."

"Oh God, no." Matthew fell in to a kitchen chair. He heard Keri gasp.

"Hang on a minute. New details just came in."

Matthew's stomach churned. He realized he was holding his breath.

Hurry up, man. Hurry up.

Finally Darrin said, "We just verified with the coroner that the woman in the car was a brunette."

Matthew wanted to shout. He flopped back in the chair and blew out a huge sigh of relief. All eyes in the room were on him. "Thank God, it wasn't her."

"We think the dead woman is Eva Pearce." Darrin sounded as relieved as they all were.

"So that leads us back to the question. Where is Amelia?" Their moment of celebration faded.

"We've pinpointed a general location and have called for a volunteer search party to start at sun up."

"Tell me when and where. Logan and I will be there." Matthew grabbed the pen and paper that Ruth kept on the table.

"Uh huh.... Okay, yep, okay." He scribbled down the directions. He looked up at Logan, who gave him a thumbs up. They would find Amelia alive. They had to.

His brain wouldn't accept anything else.

CHAPTER 38

$\mathcal{M}$atthew's mind sped as fast as the car he was driving. Hang on, my love. I'm coming. He took the curves faster than normal, but Logan grabbed the door handle without complaint. He clearly understood the urgency.

Logan pointed at the flashing red lights of a flatbed tow truck idling on the opposite side of the road. "Hey, look."

Matthew slowed. A blue vehicle, roof smashed down even with the doors, was strapped to the bed of the truck. What was left of it anyway. So this was where it had happened. No one could have survived that violent roll-over.

"Thank God Amelia wasn't in there," Logan said.

It was almost as if he was speaking for Matthew, who nodded. His hands shook on the steering wheel, sweat making them slide when he tried to grip it. He had to get his head back in the game.

"No kidding," he said. "No love lost for Eva . . ."

"Right," Logan said, rubbing bloodshot eyes Matthew knew matched his own. They both needed sleep. But not yet.

"We have to find her, Logan. We have to find Amelia."

Ten minutes later, Matthew and Logan pulled into the gas

station parking lot in Frasier. Darrin and five other men stood in a semi circle, poring over a map laid out on the hood of his police car.

"Ok everybody. Listen up." Darrin took a step in front of the group and read from a text on his cell phone. "A GPS ping was traced from Amelia's cell phone around 1:00 this morning. That was about the time Matthew talked to Eva and heard Amelia scream." He passed out a map to each volunteer. "These mountains are full of old mines and tunnels. We've circled the places to search first."

Darrin nodded curtly to Matthew and Logan. "I guess there isn't any point in me telling you to sit this out and let us handle it?"

"No way." Matthew kept strong eye contact. The guy wasn't about to intimidate him.

Darrin handed him a map. "The crash site and surrounding areas were searched this morning. We believe Eva was alone."

Matthew nodded and swallowed hard to remove the lump in his throat. The twisted remains of the car . . . he couldn't even go there.

"Matt, that's good, right?" Logan gripped his friend on the shoulder. "We have to have faith that we'll find her."

Darrin pointed to a pile of gear in the open trunk of his police car. "Get a hardhat, rope, gloves, mag light and two-way radio. We're all on Channel 21. You can try communicating by cell phone, but the signal is sketchy in these mountains." He looked down at his list. "If Amelia's injured, call for help. We have a life flight standing by at St Luke's in Denver. They can be here in thirty minutes if we need them."

Matthew couldn't go there either. They had to find her alive. Thank God for Logan, who had always stood by him like a brother. The friendship that he'd taken for granted. And was now his sanity through all this craziness.

The morning sun had just peeked over the mountains when

Matthew and Logan got in Keri's car and drove to the spot
marked on their map. Matthew pulled into a wide place in the
road and turned off the ignition. He pressed his forehead
against the steering wheel. Please, God. Let us find her.

Matthew looked toward his friend. Logan sat silent but his
lips were moving. Was he praying too? Awesome. They could
use every bit of it today.

"Let's do this."

They both jumped out of the car, hoisted the back packs and
slapped helmets on their heads for protection. Matthew slipped
on his gloves and wrapped the long rope around his left shoulder. "You got the two-way?"

"Yep, right here. Attached it to my belt." Logan pulled out his
cell. "I'm going to text Keri real quick."

"You got a signal?" Matthew pulled out his own phone. No
service.

"Yeah, barely. Just one bar. Hopefully she'll get it." Logan
punched in a short message and followed Matthew up the steep
path. As they climbed the red rocks, Matthew could see the cave
opening. It reminded him of a giant yawning mouth.

He felt a sudden burst of energy burning through his veins,
his adrenaline working overtime. He reached the entrance first,
Logan right behind him, breathing deeply. When they stepped
into the cave, a damp, musty odor filled Matthew's nostrils. He
could hear dripping water from somewhere deep inside. He'd
never liked horror movies, and this reminded him of one a
friend had convinced him to see in middle school. He'd had
nightmares for weeks afterwards. He squeezed his eyes closed.
This was not about him.

"Amelia," he shouted.

The sound echoed back several times.

Logan switched on the mag light. "If Eva brought her here, I
can't imagine they went too far inside."

A garbled sound came over the two-way radio. Matthew stopped. "Who is that?"

Logan sprinted back to the cave entrance for a better signal. "Matt," he yelled. "Darrin Wilson may have found her. He's just down the road from us." Logan pointed on the map in his hand.

Matthew flew past Logan and down the path to the car. Logan barely kept up with him. "Did they give her condition?"

"Not sure. Too much static. I just made out Amelia's and Darrin's names and their location."

Matthew had to admit relief when Logan headed for the driver's side. Give him a chance to catch his breath. No telling what was waiting for them up ahead.

Logan started the car and pulled out on the highway. Matthew wanted to go faster, get there. He'd never had much patience and today was totally over the top. The few miles seemed endless. Finally Logan pulled off the road where two police cars were parked side by side at a tunnel entrance.

Matthew wasn't sure how he felt about Darrin finding her. He was Amelia's rescuer, not him.

Stop it, he told himself. Don't be ridiculous. This was about Amelia.

Matthew opened the car door before Logan could turn off the ignition and ran to the opening. Oh, God. Please let her be okay. Please. He'd never prayed as he had in the hours since Amelia went missing.

A uniformed officer met Matthew and Logan at the entrance. "She's in a pretty deep crevice that's partially filled with water." He pointed to the left, where the tunnel split two ways. "Chief Wilson and Sgt. Carson are with her."

Chief Wilson? Matthew had no idea that Darrin was the Police Chief. Right now he didn't care if Darrin was President of the United States.

Matthew and Logan turned into the left tunnel and could

hear Darrin shouting. They ran to the hole where he was on his hands and knees at the rim looking down.

Matthew fell to his own knees and leaned as far over as he dared. Amelia lay face up in the water, her eyes closed. His first instinct was to jump in.

"Amelia," he yelled. No response. He looked at Darrin. "Has she talked to you?"

Darrin shook his head. "We just found her. The rest of the volunteers are on the way."

Matthew looked at the rocky sides of the deep hole. It was a risk. But he didn't care. "I'm going down there."

Darrin studied the circumference of the hole. "We have a rescue team on the way."

"How long before they get here?"

Matthew could see the pinched look on Darrin's face.

"An hour. Maybe two."

"No way. She can't wait that long."

And neither could he. Matthew slung his backpack to the ground.

Darrin held up his hand. "By protocol, I should go."

"No offense buddy, but I don't know that you can fit in that tiny space and get her back up here."

Darrin stared at him. "Yeah. You're right."

"We're wasting time." Matthew picked up the rope. "I take full responsibility."

"Wait." Darrin stood to his knees. "Carson," he yelled. "Get the equipment out of my trunk to make a harness."

Matthew watched Sgt. Carson run toward the daylight of the cave opening. His mind whirled. Hurry. I have to get down there.

Darrin pointed to a huge rock. "I'm going to set a basic rigging system that we'll attach to the base of that boulder over there. We'll lower you over the edge in a harness and you'll rappel down to her."

Matthew nodded. His legs felt like Jell-o. But he wasn't about to let anyone know that.

"We'll bring Amelia up first." Darrin grabbed the equipment that Sgt. Carson handed him. "Do you know what a bowline knot is?"

"No, tell me," Matthew said.

Darrin picked up the rope from the ground. "Tie it like this." He demonstrated for Matthew. "When you get down to her, slip it over her head and adjust around her waist. This knot won't cinch down too tightly on her."

Matthew took the rope and twisted it into the knot Darrin had shown him.

"Perfect." Darrin pulled off his gloves and handed them to Matthew. "You'll need these. They'll give you the dexterity to tie the knot and still protect your hands."

Matthew pulled his cell out of the Otter box and wallet from his back pocket and slipped them in the front pocket of the backpack he'd thrown on the ground. He took a deep breath to calm his shaking hands and pulled on the right glove and then the left. He fastened the harness around his waist and turned to Logan.

"Say a prayer for me. And for Amelia, buddy."

"Yep, on it." Logan slapped his back. "You got this, Matt." They gave each other a quick hug. "Take this to wrap her in." Logan secured a blanket over Matthew's shoulder.

"Good idea." Darrin motioned for the three volunteers who had just arrived to start lowering Matthew over the edge. "Can you balance your legs on the sides of the hole as we lower you down? Like when you're rappelling a rock wall?"

"Got it." To himself he added, Hang on, Amelia. I'm coming.

Matthew climbed over the edge and put both feet on the rocky surface. Thank goodness he'd gained the strength back in his right leg.

Darrin motioned to the team behind him maneuvering the rope. "Okay, we're giving you a little more slack."

Matthew took another step against the wall and waited for the rope to lengthen. He could see Amelia below him. She reminded him of a limp rag doll, floating in the water. Another step. And then another. He was almost there. He looked up and saw Logan at the rim, with that goofy grin, giving him a thumbs-up. One more step and he was in the cold water. It caught his breath for a second, and he took a deep gulp of air.

He was beside her. And silently began begging her to wake up. Her eyes fluttered open. The beautiful eyes he loved so much. He wanted nothing more than to hold her tight and never let go.

"Hi." The greeting squeaked out of his mouth. He was freezing. He couldn't imagine how she felt. He thought he saw her lips move but didn't hear any sound.

"We're going to get you out of here."

Amelia lay so still it was scaring him. He had to get her out of here. Now. He didn't know how much longer she could hold on. Her face was puffy, and her lips were tinged in blue. Her blonde hair floated in the water.

Matthew unfastened his harness. He lifted her out of the water and secured the bowline knot around her waist, tucking the blanket around it. He said another prayer. This had to work. It had to. She was a fighter.

Matthew paused. He leaned toward her and kissed her lips. They were so cold. He thought he saw a slight curve of her mouth. "See you in a few minutes," he whispered.

Freezing water rained down on him as she was lifted toward the top. He pushed away his own thoughts of discomfort. Every minute could mean life or death for her.

The rope stopped abruptly. He felt like his heart stopped too as Amelia fell back toward him a few feet.

"Logan?" Matthew shouted. "What's going on?"

Logan appeared at the rim. "Sorry about that. We've got it now."

Amelia started moving upward again. Matthew watched the rope harness slowly raise her up until she was at the top of the hole. He felt dizzy and realized he'd been holding his breath. He filled his lungs with air to make the climb back to the top.

Matthew could hear Darrin's and Logan's voices as they talked to Amelia. Logan threw the rope back down to him, and Matthew cinched it around his waist. He put his feet on the rocky wall and inched his way back up.

At the top, Logan grabbed his hand and pulled him onto dry ground. He could see four uniformed men carrying Amelia's blanket-wrapped figure out of the tunnel on a stretcher.

"What did they say about her condition, Logan?"

Logan shook his head and swiped at his eyes. Matthew had never seen his friend cry.

"Tell me."

"Her pulse is very weak. They're life flighting her to St. Luke's in Denver." Logan wrapped a blanket around Matthew's dripping clothes.

"When you lowered me down, remember what you said? Keep the faith." Matthew grabbed his backpack. "That's what I'm doing. Amelia is a fighter."

"Yep, you're right."

Logan picked up his equipment and followed Matthew out of the tunnel. He threw him the keys to the car. "You drive and I'll call Keri and Ruth. And navigate for you to the hospital."

Matthew dried his hair and clothes the best he could before he got in the car. They heard the blades of the helicopter as it lifted off and watched it ascend over the mountains.

Amelia was in good hands and on her way to one of the best hospitals in Denver.

Please God, get her there in time.

CHAPTER 39

*M*atthew and Logan zipped through rush hour traffic to Denver. Matthew's last glance of Amelia's paste-white face was imprinted in his mind. He gripped the steering wheel and drove in silence.

Logan reached in the back seat for water and handed him a bottle. "You know that she's getting the best care possible."

"Yeah, I do."

Matthew turned up the heater full blast. Since slipping in the ice cold water, he couldn't seem to get warm. He couldn't imagine how Amelia felt.

"Did anyone know how long she'd been trapped in there?" he said.

"Darrin guesstimated several hours. No one really knows." Logan uncapped his water and took a long drink.

"I can't thank you enough." Matthew's voice broke. He couldn't believe what he'd just done.

"You were the brave one, man."

"If you only knew." Matthew gulped his water. "Amelia has a favorite radio station. Mind if I turn it on?"

"Go for it." Logan leaned back in the seat and closed his eyes. "We all need sleep."

"I was thinking of calling my mom. She and Pete don't live far from the hospital. Maybe later we could go by there and grab a shower. And maybe get a few ZZZZ's."

"Great idea." Logan gulped the last of his water and reached for another bottle. "Keri and Ruth are on their way. Ruth's pastor and his wife are driving them."

"That's nice of them. I'm so glad Ruth has such a great support system."

Two hours into the drive, Logan looked at the GPS and directed Matthew to the hospital. He pulled into a spot in the ER parking area, and they went inside through double glass doors.

A nurse asked Matthew what his relationship was to the patient.

"Fiancé," he answered, without thinking. That was still his plan, anyway.

The engagement ring that had been in his backpack was now in his jacket pocket.

Logan waited in the family area for Ruth and Keri to arrive. Matthew walked quietly into the ER room, praying for the best but prepared for the worst.

Amelia looked tiny in the big bed, eyes closed, covered in layers of blankets, including around her head. Her face was more pink than when he last saw her. He told himself that was a good sign. He touched her hand, but he was afraid to kiss her.

"Has she been conscious?" Matthew asked the nurse, who was typing notes on the computer at the foot of the bed.

"In and out." The nurse looked up from the screen. "Would you happen to be Matthew?"

"Yes, I am."

"She's called out your name a few times." She clicked off the

computer and pushed the stand toward the door. "Talk to her.
She can hear you."

Matthew leaned over the bed. "I'm here, love. Open your
eyes."

He loved this woman so much. She was strong. And she had
so much to live for. The machines she was hooked up to beeped
and whirled. He brushed a strand of hair from her face and
studied her rounded nose and perfect lips. Her hand felt like an
iceberg. He rubbed it to get the blood flowing again and kissed
her cheek.

The door opened, and Ruth rushed in. She stood at the foot
of the bed and watched Amelia. Then hugged Matthew. "How is
she?"

"Haven't been here long but I think her color is starting to
come back."

"Thank God." Ruth walked to the other side of the bed and
held Amelia's hand. "She is so cold."

"Yeah, Darrin's guessing she was in the water for a little
while." He didn't want to freak her out with the truth. He
pointed to the heating blankets. "These will help bring her body
temperature back up."

"I talked to the doctor before I came in." Ruth's face was pale
and drawn. "It's been touch and go because her pulse was so
weak. He said he's seen patients recover and then a few that
didn't ..." Ruth choked up.

Matthew walked around the bed and put his arm around her
shoulder. "Your daughter is strong."

"Yes, she is." Ruth pulled a tissue from her pocket and wiped
her face. "I love her so much."

"Me too." Matthew kissed Amelia's hand. "And I can't live
without her."

"I hear that you were a hero."

"Logan always exaggerates. I was shaking in my boots."

"Doesn't matter." Ruth hugged him again. "This is the second time you've saved my daughter."

"Guess you heard about Eva."

Ruth nodded. "Such a tragedy."

"I never realized how messed up she was. If there was anyone at Canon Financial that seemed like they had it all together, it was Eva."

Matthew looked down at Amelia. He sucked in a breath. Her eyes were open, following him. He leaned down and whispered, "Hi" and kissed her cheek. Amelia squeezed his hand.

His love was back.

Amelia shifted her eyes to the other side of the bed toward Ruth.

Ruth took her hand. "Hi there, sweetie."

There was a knock on the door, and a young man and woman stepped in. "Hope this is a good time."

"Sure. Come on in," Ruth said. "Pastor, this is Matthew Chandler."

The man with kind eyes turned to Matthew. "Brad Williams. And this is my wife, Emily."

Matthew shook his hand. This was the pastor who had spoken about forgiveness the Sunday he'd attended church with Amelia.

"We'd like to pray for Amelia."

"Absolutely." In the past few days Matthew had seen how prayer worked. And Amelia needed it now, more than ever.

"We like to hold hands, if that's okay."

Matthew nodded and took Amelia's hand, careful not to disturb anything she was hooked up to. Her hand was warmer. Ruth walked over to him and took his other hand. Brad and Emily stood on either side of Ruth, with their arms around her.

"Father, we come in the name of Jesus and ask that you touch and heal our precious Amelia. We know that nothing is impossible with you. And we ask that she will get out of this bed and lead a normal life. In the name of your son, Jesus Christ. Amen."

Matthew felt a comfortable warmth in his face. A simple prayer. But it touched him to know that others loved Amelia like he did. And that they believed in prayer. He had a deep sense that he couldn't explain. Amelia was going to be okay.

He leaned over and whispered to Ruth. "I'm going out to the waiting area and let Keri and Logan come in."

Ruth hugged him. "I think she's going to be okay."

"Yep, me too."

Matthew kissed Ruth on the cheek and thanked the couple for coming. He stepped into the hall and sank against the wall, blowing out a sigh of relief. He felt light, as if a huge burden had been lifted from his back.

~

In the waiting room, Matthew dialed his mother's number. He'd sneak away later for a shower and a nap at her house, a few miles from the hospital.

When he went back to see Amelia, the nurses were preparing to move her to a room.

"She'll be in ICU first," the blonde nurse told him.

Matthew stood in the corner with Ruth and watched the flurry of activity. Brad, Emily, Logan and Keri had gone to the coffee shop.

Matthew watched Amelia. She followed the nurses with her eyes and seemed responsive, and her color was so much better. He told Ruth about his mother's offer.

"That's so kind of her but I think I'll stay here with Amelia."

Matthew and Ruth followed Amelia's bed to the ICU on the 7th floor where she had a wonderful view of the mountains. Ruth sat in the recliner and dozed while Matthew talked to Amelia and stroked her hair. He talked about the plans to open an independent office with Logan in Denver and live in Chandler Springs. For the first time since this nightmare began, he saw the corner of Amelia's lips turn up slightly. That smile that made his heart turn to a pile of mush. His love was back.

The middle of the afternoon, Matthew left the hospital and drove to Nora's house. Logan and Keri had decided to go back to Chandler Springs with Brad and Emily. They were exhausted and needed to take care of Harley. They promised to return the next day.

When Matthew knocked on his mom's front door, John answered. What is he doing here?

Matthew slung his backpack on his shoulder. "I didn't expect you."

"I came by to visit. Heard you were coming so I decided to stay and see you."

Matthew stepped into the house. He was tired and dirty and really didn't feel like dealing with any emotions about his dad right now.

Nora stepped from the kitchen and wiped her hands on a dish towel. "Hi son." She started to kiss him and backed away.

"Yeah, I know it's pretty bad." He pointed to his backpack. "Good thing I have a change of clothes."

"Help yourself. You know where the shower is." Nora stepped into the kitchen to turn off a buzzing timer.

John started to say something, but Matthew brushed past him toward the bathroom.

He let the hot shower run over his head and down his back. The realization hit him. He'd almost lost her. Oh God. In this private place, he could finally let out all the fears and emotions he'd been stuffing.

He scrubbed his face. It felt good to let the tears mingle with the water. He stepped out of the shower feeling clean physically and mentally. Now it was all about Amelia's recovery.

Nora had the food on the table when Matthew reached the

dining room in clean clothes and combed but wet hair. The roast and potatoes smelled so good. He was annoyed that John was still there, but he decided not to say anything.

"Let's put some in a container and you can take it to Ruth," Nora said. "She needs to eat too."

"Good idea." Matthew reached for a homemade roll and smeared it with butter.

John sat on the other side of the table eating. He hadn't said a word.

Awkward was the only word Matthew could come up with. Even after the small progress they'd made before John's surgery. if he'd known John was here, he might not have come.

Matthew reached for a second helping of meat and potatoes. "Where is Pete?"

"He went on a fishing trip with one his brothers. He'll be home tomorrow night."

"Oh." Matthew shoveled the food in. He felt like he hadn't eaten in a week. Now that he felt better, he guessed it wouldn't kill him to talk to John. "So how did your surgery go?"

John looked up at him. "Went well. I've been feeling pretty good."

"Glad to hear that." But was he? Or was that just an empty gesture?

"Going through an operation like that changes your outlook on life." John pushed his plate away. "And makes you realize how much you care about the people in your life." John stared at him.

Matthew looked away. This was getting way too uncomfortable. "Thanks Mom. I need to get back and check on Amelia."

Nora handed him a container of food. "Didn't you want to rest?"

"I'm fine. The shower gave me a shot of energy." Matthew stood up and walked to the front door. "I'll catch a few winks on the couch in Amelia's room." He kissed his mother's cheek.

"Bye, John," he mumbled and was out the door before his father could answer.

Matthew returned to the hospital as the sun dipped behind the mountains. He'd give anything right now to sit on his porch with Amelia and Harley and watch the sunset. When he walked into Amelia's room, she was watching HGTV on the screen mounted on the wall across from her bed. That was the last thing he expected to see.

"Amelia." He rushed to the side of her bed and kissed her sweet lips.

"Hey there." Her voice was hoarse.

"Oh my gosh. You look so good." He bent down and looked into her eyes. They hadn't changed. Still as beautiful as ever.

Amelia flushed. "I guess they gave me some wonder drugs in this IV." She held up the tube taped to her hand.

Matthew could still see her face when they pulled her out of the water-filled hole. "How much do you remember?" He sat on the edge of her bed.

"Not a lot. But I remember hearing your voice."

"The nurses told me to talk to you, that you could hear me." Matthew wanted to hold her close. But with all the lines and tubes, that wasn't happening.

"They were right. I thought I was going to heaven, but your voice pulled me back here."

Matthew's voice grew husky. "I'm so glad that you came back to me."

"I want to go to heaven someday. But not yet."

She looked like an angel to him.

"Did your mom tell you that the pastor and his wife were here?"

Amelia nodded. "Yeah, she did."

"We stood around this bed and prayed for you." Maybe later he'd tell her it was an experience he wouldn't trade for anything. "I was trying to keep the faith, but I knew then that you were going to be okay." He kissed her again.

"As I was waking up, you know what I was thinking?"

Matthew raised an eyebrow. Nothing bad, he hoped.

"That I was so happy I hadn't lost that beautiful engagement ring you tried to give me." Amelia touched her empty left ring finger.

"You mean this one?" Matthew pulled the case from his jacket pocket and opened it. Okay. This wasn't exactly the way he had planned it, but it would definitely work.

"Amelia, I love you, and I want to spend the rest of my life with you."

"Yes. A thousand times yes!" Amelia raised the hand taped to the IV to brush tears from her cheeks.

Matthew pulled the ring out of the case and slipped it on her left finger. "I don't know if they'll let you wear it in here."

"Just let them try to make me take it off. They'll see how strong I really am."

Matthew watched Amelia as she touched the sparkling jewels.

His girl was back. Thank God.

CHAPTER 40

*M*atthew sat up and popped the kinks from his back. He'd dozed a few hours on the couch in Amelia's room. He looked over at Ruth, stretched out in the recliner, covered with a blanket. Hopefully she'd gotten some sleep.

Matthew stood and walked to the side of the bed. Amelia was watching TV on closed caption.

"Good morning." He leaned down and kissed her. Her lips were even warmer than yesterday.

"The nurses said I'm moving to a regular room today." Amelia hit the off button on the TV control.

"That's great. How you feeling?" He ran his fingers through his hair. She'd never seen him with bed head.

"Much better." Amelia lifted her left hand. "See my beautiful ring? Some gorgeous guy gave it to me."

Matthew gave her a pretended pout. "Should I be jealous?" He kissed her hand.

"Never." Amelia motioned to her mother, still sleeping in the chair. "Could you talk her into going home today? She really needs a good night's sleep."

"I'll try. But neither of us want to leave you."

"I'm doing much better." Amelia took a sip from the water cup on her tray. "Thanks to you and Darrin .... and so many others. But Mom's exhausted. I don't want her to end up in here with me."

"Yep, we definitely don't want that. I think the pastor said he's coming by again today."

"Good. I'd love to see Brad." Amelia pulled at the pillow that had slipped to the side of the bed. "Maybe Mom will go back to Chandler Springs with him."

"Here, let me help you." Matthew fluffed up the pillow and slid it behind her head. "But I'm staying."

Amelia smiled. It made Matthew happy to see her full teeth again.

At a knock on the door Darrin Wilson popped his head in. "This a good time?"

"Come on in." Amelia sat up straighter in the bed and pulled the covers up to her chin.

Matthew gritted his teeth. He was engaged to marry this woman. Why was he still so jealous of this guy?

Darrin removed his hat. "Just wanted to see how you're doing." He walked to the side of the bed. "You look much better."

"Thanks to all of you." She looked at Matthew.

"Do you want me to take care of the details about your car?" Darrin asked.

Amelia hesitated. "Matthew, would you mind? I know Darrin is really a busy guy."

"Sure, no problem." A long, slow breath eased out of Matthew's lungs, deflating the jealousy that had been about to blow him up not fifteen seconds before.

Darrin wrote out the information and handed it to Matthew. "Here's where the car was towed. You'll need to clean it out and notify the insurance company."

"Got it." Matthew tucked the paper in his shirt pocket.

"Well, I gotta run. My sons have softball games and I promised I would be there.

Sons? Why hadn't somebody told him the man had kids? That would have saved him a whole lot of trouble. Matthew passed his hand over his mouth to wipe off the smile that suddenly popped up. It didn't really matter. He knew now - and that closed the books on the whole thing. Unless, of course, he didn't have a wife.

"Thanks for stopping by." Amelia lifted her left hand. "Oh, you're one of the first to know that Matthew and I are engaged."

"Congratulations! That's awesome." Darrin smiled at Matthew. "I really mean that."

Matthew lifted his chin. "Thanks."

"You are definitely invited. I'll get a save the date card out soon." Amelia's calm tone quieted Matthew. He hadn't felt that way in several days.

"Looking forward to it." Darrin replaced his hat. "See you later." He motioned for Matthew to step out of the room with him.

"I need to ask Amelia some questions," he said once they were in the hallway. "Do you think she's up to it?"

"How about tomorrow? I don't think she needs to think about all that yet."

"Sure. We can wait." Darrin stuck out hand. "You're getting a fine woman, I hope you know that."

"Oh yeah, she's the best." Matthew returned the handshake. "Thanks for all you've done for Amelia." Matthew tried to hide his grin. But he couldn't help it. Amelia loved him.

There was never any reason to be jealous of this guy.

Amelia couldn't catch her breath. Darkness surrounded her. A dim light shone above her. How would she ever get out of here?

She shivered in the water-soaked clothes. A scream rose to her lips but came out as a pitiful squeak.

Amelia sat straight up in bed, gasping for air. The light shining through the blinds reflected on the bare wall. She was in the hospital. And safe.

She hugged a pillow against her chest, taking deep breaths. Then she remembered. The nurses had moved her from ICU to a regular room earlier that morning. Her room was empty. Matthew and her mom had gone to the cafeteria. She heard a knock on the door, and Pastor Brad stepped in.

"It's great to see you." Amelia tried to smile and push away the memories. She was alive. That was worth celebrating.

"And I could say the same." Brad stepped in and stood by her bed.

"You just missed Mom and Matthew. They went to the cafeteria for lunch."

"That gives me a chance to talk with you." Brad looked at her, soft wrinkles gathered at the corners of his kind eyes. "How are you doing? And I don't want that pat answer that you're fine."

Amelia bit her lower lip. "You know how hard it was after the first time with Eva. My life was turned upside down for weeks afterwards." She picked at the threads on her blanket. The fear was fading. "I'm praying that I can work through this."

Brad nodded at her. "Glad to hear that."

"Several people have told me what Matthew had to do to rescue me out of the hole where I'd fallen. Somehow his courage is giving me courage." She took a sip of water. "Does that make any sense?"

"Yeah. I think it does."

"And you know me well enough to know that I wouldn't ever want anyone to die. But knowing that Eva is gone...."

"Yeah, I heard about that. Ruth told me at first that they thought it was you in the car."

"Oh my." Amelia tried to control her voice. "They've all been through so much."

"Through hard times like this, I've seen families come together stronger than ever. I pray that happens for you and your family." Brad clasped his hands in front of him.

"Thank you. That's my prayer too."

Brad gave her one more long look as if waiting for her to say something else. "We're praying for a quick recovery. I'll see you soon." Brad left the room and closed the door.

Amelia laid back on the pillow. Matthew had risked his life to go down into that awful place and pull her out - and that wasn't something her button-down business man did on a day-to-day basis. He could have killed himself too. That was courage. She swallowed hard. She'd have done it for him in a heartbeat, no question.

But she didn't feel brave right now. Not when she thought about facing God with bitterness toward Eva still smeared all over her heart. But what did it even look like to forgive? Could she let go of those destructive feelings as courageously as Matthew had held on to her?

Matthew and Ruth stepped from the elevator as Brad entered the family waiting area.

Ruth put her hand on Brad's arm. "You're so kind to come visit Amelia again."

"You know I love you and Amelia like family." Brad squeezed her hand. He turned to Matthew. "Good to see you again."

Matthew took a step forward. "I appreciate your support of Amelia and Ruth, too. Puts a new perspective on churches and pastors." Matthew paused. "And God."

Brad shook Matthew's hand. "Awesome. Glad to hear that."

"I remember a sermon you gave recently on forgiveness. I'm surprised that I'm still thinking about it."

"One of the hardest things in the world for most of us." Brad made eye contact with him. "But I'll tell you, when you can do it, it's so worth it."

"You sound like you're speaking from experience."

"As a matter of fact, I am." Brad looked at his phone calendar. "I have a little time before my next visit. Can I buy you a cup of coffee?"

"I just came from there. But I'm always up for coffee."

Matthew led the way to the elevator. This should be interesting.

In the cafeteria, Matthew and Brad found a table in a quiet corner. Matthew sipped the steaming black drink while Brad talked.

"This isn't an easy experience to talk about. But somehow I feel like it's something you need to hear." Brad lifted the Styrofoam cup to his lips and took a long drink.

"Ten years ago I had an argument with my dad. He didn't agree with some of my decisions. I thought I knew best and cut myself off from all communication with him. My mom had died when I was young and after that, Dad was alone." Brad's voice caught in his throat. He took another sip. "God was trying to work on my heart those years when we were estranged. I kept dreaming about Dad, that I should call and make things right with him. But I wasn't really listening. I was convinced that I was right, and he was wrong."

This was sounding familiar. Matthew shifted in his seat. John's face when he told him about his own differences with Austin flickered through Matthew's mind. He nodded for Brad to continue.

"The days slipped by and months became years. I got married, and life was really busy. And I buried the hurt and pain of not having my dad in my life."

Matthew grimaced. Is that what he'd done all these years? Trying to not think about his father? Instead he'd concentrated on being the best at Canon Financial, the prestige of the Manhattan penthouse, surrounding himself with beautiful women. Eva...

"A year later my dad died in a car accident." Brad's voice was strong and brought Matthew back to the moment. "I never reconciled with him. And I've always regretted it."

Matthew rubbed the back of his neck. Wow, he really thought Brad was going to tell him that they'd worked it out. "Sorry to hear that." Matthew shifted on the stool. "I was about ten when my dad divorced my mother and disappeared from my life."

Brad nodded. "That's a tough age to lose your dad."

"No doubt. I saw him recently for the first time in 25 years." Matthew stared into his coffee and then looked up.

"How did that go?" Brad asked, his voice kind, not judgmental.

"Hardest thing I've ever done." Yeah, he wasn't going to tell him he walked out. "But it's weird. Ever since I arrived in Chandler Springs it's like God has put this idea of forgiveness right in my face. Everywhere I turn."

"Yeah, He's like that."

"My dad seems different now." Matthew rubbed his forehead. "But I just don't know if I can trust him."

Brad kept steady eye contact. "I've found that forgiveness is a journey. I make the decision to forgive someone but it doesn't happen overnight. It's something I keep working at. Even when I don't feel like it."

Matthew drained his cup. "Thanks. I'm glad we got to talk."

"Me too." Brad stood and threw their empty cups in the trash. "Let me know if I can do anything else." Brad handed him a business card. "If you ever need to talk, here's my number."

Matthew got on the elevator with him. When Brad got off

on the second floor, Matthew leaned against the elevator wall before he pushed the button for the fifth floor. Brad was different than he'd first thought. Pretty down to earth for a pastor. He pulled out his phone and scrolled to his dad's number. Amazing the old guy knew how to text. He shot off a quick message.

"Let's talk."

It might take years but he was willing to try.

When Matthew entered Amelia's room, Nora was chatting with Ruth. They seemed to get along so well. Good thing since they'd soon be related.

"Hi Mom." Matthew kissed her cheek. Her perfume brought back the comfort of the roses in Emma's garden. Whoa, that was totally out of left field for him. But it was true.

Nora held onto his wrist for a moment. "Ruth's been giving me the latest report. I'm so glad Amelia is better."

Matthew walked over to the bed and touched Amelia's hand. She looked up at him with a sleepy half smile. "We're both doing great, Mom."

"Well, God was watching out for you both."

That was the truth. Matthew had never really believed in all that before. But now?

"Your dad is out in the waiting room. He really wants to see Amelia. Would you go get him?" She gave him a quick smile and went straight back to her conversation with Ruth as if it wasn't up for discussion.

"Sure, Mom." Wow, God. You aren't wasting any time with my dad, are you?

Matthew closed Amelia's door. He hesitated in the doorway of the family waiting area and spotted his father in a corner seat reading a newspaper. Somehow John seemed older, but his face wasn't as drawn today. He bounced one crossed leg as he read.

Matthew drew in a breath and released it. He could do this. "Hi Dad."

"Matthew." John lowered the newspaper, his brow wrinkled, two dimples deepened between his eyes. "Good to see you, son." He slowly pulled himself to a standing position.

"You too, Dad."

Matthew softened his tone. John seemed shorter than Matthew remembered. Should they hug? No, he wasn't ready for that yet. One step at a time.

John folded the newspaper and laid it on the side table. "I really wanted to come with your mom to see your girl today."

"Thanks. That means a lot."

Deep inside, Matthew felt a faint urge to leave. That's what he'd always done. He couldn't look his dad in the face. But at least he was talking.

Matthew walked over and sank down into a faux leather couch. It felt hard and unforgiving, something he hoped not to be. "Could we sit here a few minutes and talk?"

"Sure." John lowered himself down onto the parallel seat.

"My whole life has changed in the last 48 hours. And I thought I'd lost the woman I love." Matthew stared at the TV on the wall in front of them before he spoke.

"I heard that you are a hero."

Matthew finally looked at his father. The wrinkles around John's eyes crinkled when he smiled.

"No, not really. Somehow God gave me the courage to do what I needed to save her."

John sat silent, unmoving.

Matthew wanted to retreat back into his own safe shell. His dad hadn't changed a bit. A poster on the sterile wall announced help with addiction. He wished this forgiveness thing was as easy as going into rehab.

After minutes of awkward silence, John craned his neck and tilted his head toward Matthew.

Uh oh. Here it comes. Matthew braced himself.

"After years of fighting against it, I've finally come to a place of belief in God." John stared at his hands. "I was hesitant to tell you that."

Did his narcissistic father really say that? This day was full of surprises.

"Good for you, Dad." And he really meant it.

"I've let too many years slip by, Matthew. And I want to figure out a way to work out things between us."

"It will take time, Dad." Matthew looked into his father's tired eyes. He'd never felt sympathy for the man but today was different. "No idea what that looks like, but I'm ready to give it a shot."

"I'm sorry, son. I made some really selfish decisions through the years. And I never stopped to think how they impacted you and your mom." John laid his hand on Matthew's arm. "Coming so close to death has been a wake-up call. I really don't know how to be a father. But I'm ready to try."

Looking into his father's worn face, Matthew could almost hear the words he'd read in his great-grandfather's journal. The importance of family. Learning how to forgive. Being a man of faith and integrity.

And despite the hurts of the past, John was his father. Nothing would ever change that fact.

John let out a deep exhale. The muscles in his face relaxed a bit. "I always thought you were just like me, Matthew. You have my business sense. But I'm realizing that you're really not."

No, he wasn't like his Dad. Not at all. He'd never really put two and two together until now. But through Evan's journals he'd discovered he was more like the man who had lived at Rose Haven so long ago.

The words "cautiously optimistic" came to Matthew's mind.

He was ready to try this new relationship. And did he want the faith that his great-grandparents had? Even his father had made that choice. Was it time to give that a shot for himself?

Amelia, Matthew and Ruth arrived home in Chandler Springs late the following afternoon. The medical staff had told Amelia several times that she was a true miracle. On the way home, the discussions centered around a hot shower and comfortable bed.

When Ruth opened the front door, Harley met them, wagging his tail a hundred miles an hour.

"Hey, boy." Amelia knelt down and buried her face in his fur. She felt the sore muscles in her body relax a bit. It was true. There was no place like home. "Wow, what smells so good in here?"

Keri stepped from the kitchen. "Logan and I thought you all needed a good home cooked meal."

Amelia met her friend at the doorway and pulled her into a tight hug that lingered a bit longer than usual. Thankfulness was the word that came to mind. For a friendship that had lasted a lifetime.

"That's awesome. You are the best."

"I'm just so thankful that you came home to us." Keri kissed her cheek.

As she stepped away, she grabbed Amelia's hands. Amelia felt the diamond squeeze between Keri's palms.

"And what's this?" Keri pointed to Amelia's left ring finger.

"I finally said yes."

Amelia looked over at Matthew. She couldn't believe the love she felt for this guy right now. Was it just gratefulness for saving her life? No, a love had slowly developed over the months and she wanted to spend the rest of her life with him.

"Smart girl. You've got yourself a good guy there."

Keri motioned toward Matthew and Logan talking. Amelia followed her gaze. She loved the way Matthew held his head while he listened to his friend.

Logan pulled on padded mitts and slid a meat loaf from the oven to the table. "She's training me well." He winked at Matthew. "Good to see you, buddy."

"Back at ya, man."

Logan gave Amelia a hug. "And I've never seen you look better."

He let go, and Ruth handed him a bowl of whipped potatoes to set on the table. "We're ready to eat," she said.

"It's so good to be home." Amelia's heart was full. She was home with the family and the fur baby that she loved.

"While we're all standing, I'd like to pray before we eat." Ruth took Matthew's hand and then Logan's. Amelia felt Matthew's other hand slide into hers. She stole a glance at him as her mother thanked God for her safe return and for the food. He was nodding his head in agreement and said Amen when Ruth finished. She was beyond thrilled to realize this was the first time they had looked at each other with God in both their minds.

"Let's eat. I'm starved."

Amelia reached for a bowl. It made her heart happy that Matthew was finding his own faith in God and not just going through the motions for her.

Thirty minutes later, after much conversation and laughter, every bowl and plate sat empty. Amelia was surprised how much she had eaten. This was the first meal she'd really enjoyed since Eva's first attack.

Keri and Logan insisted that Ruth rest while they cleaned up. "And you two go enjoy." Keri scooted them out of the kitchen.

"The front porch?" Matthew and Amelia said at the same time.

Amelia laughed. "Absolutely. I think we're just in time for the sunset." She looped her arm through his and walked with him out the front door, Harley close on her heels.

"It's a little chilly tonight." Matthew wrapped an afghan around Amelia's shoulders. The warmth chased away the shivers. Was she really cold? Or remembering the trauma of the cave? She hoped to never feel that cold again.

She pushed the thoughts away. Every moment was precious to her now. She was here, on the porch swing, safe and with the man she loved. Who had proved not once, but twice, that he'd do anything to protect her.

Matthew put his arm around her. "Never thought I'd be excited about watching a sunset."

Amelia searched his face. And lost herself there. This man's bravery had convinced her that he truly loved her. "Me too."

The sun dipped below the mountains. Orange, blue and pink hues highlighted the low hanging, wispy clouds. God was sure showing off for her.

Matthew moved gently back and forth with the swing. "When you're up to it, we should start making plans."

"I had lots of time to think in the hospital." Amelia curled her legs under her. The swinging motion was always so relaxing. "What would you think about a fall wedding? It's so beautiful here when the leaves are turning."

"Sounds like a great idea." Matthew kissed the tip of her nose. "And on the Chandler property, where we first met."

Amelia wrinkled her lip. "I still can't believe I fell in love with you." She snuggled closer to him. "But right now, I just want to savor this moment."

"Because I didn't think I'd have any more."

CHAPTER 41

Two weeks later, Matthew held the door for Amelia at the BlueBird Cafe, one hand on the glass, the other in the small of her back. It was getting harder to keep his hands off of her.

She tossed a smile back over her shoulder that pretty much melted him from the core out. Hence the inability to stop touching her.

"Thank you, kind sir," she said.

Those weren't words that had typically described him, but he was starting to believe her. He followed as she wove between the filled tables to the back of the restaurant. Yep, she was going right for their favorite spot, where half the town would still be peering at them over the tops of their menus. Not that he would be aware of anything but her anyway.

"Let me get that chair for you," he said.

She slid into it and visibly tried to keep a straight face. "Okay, who are you and what have you done with my Matthew?"

"You just said I was a 'kind sir,'" he said. He eased into the opposite chair and waited for the smile. Yeah. There it was.

She looked around as if she hadn't been there at least a thousand times. "We haven't been here in a long time. Not together, anyway."

Matthew smothered one of her hands with his. Good grief, was he sweating? He was actually sweating. "You remember the first time we met here?"

Amelia rested her chin on her hand, looking at him. "Back when I thought you were a pompous, conceited fool?"

Matthew frowned. "Really? Me?"

"Oh, yeah. I almost bought Rose Haven myself. Just to be rid of you." She gave him a sly grin.

"Well, I guess I was slightly..."

"Aggravating? Rude? Stubborn?"

"Okay, Miss Richardson. And how do you feel about me now?"

Amelia's face softened. "It's amazing that I fell in love with you. Don't ask me how that happened."

"I think you just want the house. And I'm the ticket to your long time dream."

"You know that's not true." Amelia paused. "Well, not entirely."

"Hey, y'all." Wanda appeared at the table. "Haven't seen you in a while."

Amelia held up her left hand to show off her sparkling engagement ring.

Wanda shot Matthew a surprised look. "So you finally did it. I was afraid you were going to let her get away."

"Not on your life, Wanda." He was getting used to this quirky lady. Hairstyles, gum and all.

"So you're keeping the house?"

"Yep." He hoped Amelia would hear something soon about breaking the contract.

"Everyone in Chandler Springs will be relieved to know that."

And he was sure she would spread the word. Today Matthew didn't even care.

Wanda pulled her pad and pen from her apron pocket. "What can I get for you?"

Matthew looked at the menu. "I'll have two eggs over easy, three slices of crispy bacon and the short stack of pancakes." He touched his stomach. "I'm going light today."

Wanda scribbled his order. "And black coffee, of course."

"Yep, you got it."

Wanda turned to Amelia. "And for you, my lovely."

"I'll have wheat toast, lightly buttered, yogurt with granola and fruit and hot tea." She looked at Matthew. "I have a wedding dress to think about."

Matthew gave her a flirty wink. "Yep. And I can't wait to see you in it."

"Be back in a few with your drinks." Wanda left the table, bantering with other customers as she headed for the kitchen.

"Put her on the guest list," Matthew whispered as she walked away. "She's a hoot."

Amelia took out her phone to add a note. "Oh..... I got an e-mail on the way over here and didn't have a chance to read it." She pulled up her messages. "Oh, Matthew." Her eyes brimmed with tears.

"What?" His heart dropped. What had happened now?

"These are happy tears, love." Amelia read from the message. "'We are pleased to inform you that the sales contract on Rose Haven has been cancelled.'"

"Seriously?" Matthew blew out a huge sigh. "Oh, God. Thank you."

A peace descended on him that he'd never really felt before. And a new energy surged from within.

Amelia continued. "The prospective buyers aren't happy. But they didn't have a choice. The contract with John's signature did the trick."

Matthew touched her hand. "What would I do without you?" Amelia raised an eyebrow.

"You were the one who convinced me to go to my dad when I was fighting so hard against it. Never in my wildest dreams would I have thought I'd have my father to thank for anything." Matthew stared in her eyes for a long time. "You're good for me, you know."

"I could say the same for you. How many times have you rescued me now?" Amelia sipped the hot tea that Wanda had set in front of her.

Matthew looked at her over the top of his coffee cup. When he thought of Eva, it was like a pain in his shoulders that he had to shrug away. But this wasn't the time to mention her. The shimmer in Amelia's eyes told him she was healing.

"As many times as necessary," he said.

"While we're waiting for our food, I brought something to show you." Amelia pulled several pictures from her purse. "Austin gave me this photo of Evan and Emma's wedding when they married in 1897. I'd love to re-create it."

Matthew studied the image. Evan stared into the camera, straight faced, his collar squeezing his neck. How could he breathe in that thing? No wonder he wasn't smiling. Emma held his arm with one hand and a bouquet of flowers in the other. They both looked so young.

"Okay, so I'm not wearing a suit like that. The collar alone looks like it would choke me to death."

"But I think you'd be so handsome in a tux."

Matthew made a face. "Maybe. But no cummerbund." Living in this mountain town had sure changed his taste in clothing. "What about the cake?"

"My mom doesn't make tiered cakes. So we agreed it would be better to call Jeanie at the bakery next week to start exploring ideas."

Matthew nodded. "Just make sure one layer is chocolate."

"Of course." Amelia added another note to her list. "We'll have a taste test sometime soon to choose flavors."

"Yum." The promise of chocolate might actually get him through the whole receiving line experience.

"I've been thinking about Emma's dress. I'd love to get it restored, but it may be very expensive."

"I'm fine with that. Her dress is very special to you." He paused. "To both of us."

At this point, it almost felt like Evan and Emma were going to be at the wedding. They'd become that real to him.

"And I want to carry roses, just like Emma did." Amelia pointed at the picture. "I've already been discussing ideas with Danielle at the flower shop." Amelia stared at her lap.

"What?" Matthew said.

"This is a little awkward. I'm not sure about the budget."

"Amelia, look at me." Matthew gently lifted her chin. "Don't worry about that. You choose what you like. Okay?"

Amelia feigned a smile that didn't reach her eyes. "Okay." She took a sip of her tea. "It's just hard for me to remember that I don't have to worry about money."

She nodded her thanks when Wanda set plates of steaming food in front of them.

"Finances will change some since Logan and I are leaving Canon. But we've got this." Matthew leaned forward in his chair. "So don't you worry."

He decided not to tell her that he was constantly running numbers on the new office and would be relieved if his New York condo sold quickly.

"I'll try." Amelia giggled. "I just had a random thought."

"Yeah?" Matthew hoped it was far from discussing finances.

"Harley."

"What about him?" Matthew lifted his fork to his mouth. "Oh, I get it," he said through a bite of eggs. "Is this a package deal?"

"Yep, he goes where I go. I hope that's not a deal breaker." Amelia nibbled on her wheat toast.

"Of course not. I love the big mutt." Matthew poured syrup on the stack of pancakes and took a bite.

"And he loves you." Amelia poured the bowl of fruit into her yogurt and stirred it. "How do you feel about kids?"

This was new territory for him. He'd never really thought about children. "I wouldn't mind having a couple." He wiped his mouth. "But not as many as Evan and Emma."

"No kidding. I can't even imagine ..." Seeming satisfied with her breakfast creation, Amelia put a spoonful in her mouth.

"It'll take some time for Logan and me to get established here and get the bank account built up again." Matthew gulped the last of his coffee. "Even with Charles Grant as our first client." He waited.

"You're taking the Grant account with you?" Amelia almost squealed. "Oh, my gosh."

"Yep. Worked out a deal with Canon." Matthew nodded when Wanda stopped to refill his cup. "Honestly, it was a miracle. Logan and I have never heard of that happening."

It was really pretty hard to fathom how things were falling in place. He was so used to planning and engineering everything...but this. This was like Someone Else was doing the work for him.

"What about Evan's mine? What do you think will happen with it?" Amelia wiped her mouth with the napkin and folded it on the table.

"Oh yeah. It should produce some income too."

Wanda stopped with the bill. "No hurry."

Matthew paid for the meal and left a nice tip. Now that he was staying in Chandler Springs this would be one of his favorite hang outs.

∾

The next afternoon, Amelia spent extra time dressing for dinner at Matthew's. Turning multiple ways in the full-length mirror, she liked her turquoise broomstick skirt, lace blouse and boots. She hoped Matthew would too. She grabbed her shawl as she said goodbye to Ruth and Harley. His drooped ears and tail between his legs made her laugh.

"Sorry boy. I know you love Matthew, but you can't go this time."

"Have a great time," Ruth called from the kitchen. Her voice sounded lighter than it had in a while.

Amelia unlocked the car door of her rental and slid in. She hummed a favorite praise and worship song as she started the SUV and drove to Rose Haven. She could have walked but wanted to keep her hair and makeup fresh. As she drove the few blocks, she had no idea what Matthew had planned for the evening. The invitation had come in her e-mail box from Keri. She suspected Matthew had put her up to it.

He stepped out on the porch when she pulled into the circular drive and got out of her car. "You look lovely."

"Thank you." She climbed the steps and pulled him into a hug and then a kiss. She could just stand here all night.

"You clean up well."

"These old things?" Matthew barked a laugh. "I had to dig in the back of my closet to find them."

Amelia had to admit she hadn't seen him wear a collared polo shirt and pressed trousers with dress shoes in ages.

He held the front door open for her to enter. "I've been ordered to stay away from the backyard until you arrived."

"Really? By whom?" Amelia was convinced he knew what was going on.

Matthew made a face. "By Logan and Keri."

"Ahh. Something special must be happening out there tonight." Amelia stepped into the vestibule.

"If Keri made the meal, it's got to be good." Matthew rubbed his stomach. "Let's go, I'm starved."

Amelia laughed at him. "You're always hungry."

The couple walked arm in arm through the house and out the back door. Matthew shaded his eyes as the sun lowered over the mountains. "Hey, someone cut the lawn."

"It looks beautiful." Amelia wasn't looking at the grass, but at the gazebo wrapped in thousands of twinkling white lights and the purple organza draped through the freshly painted white railings.

"Wow, Keri and Logan really went all out." Matthew said with a wide grin.

Amelia balanced against his arm as they walked across the lawn and up the gazebo steps. A white linen-covered table glowed in candlelight, with a place setting for two. A decorated vase of red roses stood in the middle. Amelia's eyes filled with happy tears. So perfect.

Matthew pulled out an upholstered chair for her. "Keri thought of everything, didn't she?" He pulled a wine bottle from the chilling bucket and popped the cork. "I hope you will have a drink with me tonight."

"Oh, yes. I'd love some."

Matthew filled her wine glass. The dark liquid glimmered in the twinkling lights. "Is there a special reason for this dinner, Amelia?"

"No idea. Didn't you plan it?"

"Nope." His straight face made her wonder if he was serious. Okay...then who? Before she could come up with an answer, the smell of delicious food wafted in the air.

Matthew had raised the covered dome off the plate that brimmed with steak filet, mashed potatoes, asparagus and a roll. "Keri outdid herself."

"Mmmm." Amelia cut a piece of the meat and bit into it. "I

think Keri needs to expand her business. She's outgrown her home kitchen."

"Maybe Logan and I can help her work out a business plan." Matthew sighed at the taste of the garlic mashed potatoes. "I'll be the first to give her a rave review."

"Me too." Her stomach did a little flip. Was this the right time? But she'd promised herself not to keep anything from him.

"I had a showing last night."

Matthew wrinkled his forehead. "Oh. How did it go?" His voice sounded flat.

"I know where you're going with that, Matthew. Everything was fine. The couple were older and seemed very nice. They've asked for a second look next week."

Matthew frowned at her. "I don't like the idea of you showing a house at night by yourself."

"Yeah, you've made that very clear." Amelia stopped. Why ruin such a perfect night? She took another bite of steak. "Let's take a walk over to the chapel after dinner. I overheard Logan say he'd been doing some work there."

"He asked me a few weeks ago if he could spruce it up. Doesn't take him long." Matthew finished his last bite of food and sat back in the chair. Amelia was still eating. "I love watching you."

"Really? Some women don't like to eat in front of guys."

"Well, I'm glad you don't mind." He poured another glass of wine and clinked it against hers for a toast. "To us. Though I didn't know if we would ever get this far."

Amelia laughed. "Yep. You can say that again." She sipped her wine. She wanted to spend the rest of her life with this man. "How is your dad doing?"

"Quite well, actually. His doctor expects a full recovery."

"That's great. I'm really glad."

"Believe it or not, I am too." Matthew gulped his wine and poured another glass. "More?"

"No, thanks. I've reached my limit."

"Let's go see the chapel."

Amelia covered the empty plates. "I'm ready. Lead the way, Mr. Chandler."

Matthew touched the freshly trimmed paint on the chapel door. "Logan did an outstanding job. Most of this wood was rotting."

Amelia stepped inside, Matthew behind her. "Oh my, heavenly." The fragrance of fresh cut roses filled the small space.

"Someone has been working in here." The pattern of light from the stained glass window shone on the altar table. "Ah... Evan's Bible." He picked it up and sat down on the front pew.

Amelia sat beside him and put her head on his shoulder. "I had a dream about our wedding last night."

"Tell me."

"I was walking down the aisle of a very small church." Amelia cleared her throat. "It was this chapel."

Matthew took her hand.

"And I was wearing Emma's dress and veil."

"I'm sure you looked beautiful in it."

"So what do you think? Would you want to get married here?"

"Or we could just get married in the barn and use blocks of hay." He grinned at her.

Amelia flicked him on the arm. "No way. That sounds more like Logan and Keri's style."

"This small place won't hold many guests."

"The wedding could be family only."

"I would invite Nora, Pete, John and Logan." Matthew counted his guest list off on one hand.

"And my mom and Keri. I think that would work." Amelia paused. "And Evan and Emma in spirit."

"Definitely." Matthew looked at Evan's Bible in his lap. He'd learned about love and family from the man. And about faith. "What about all your friends and associates? You know almost everyone in town."

"We could invite them for a reception. Especially the old biddies that gossiped about me, saying I'd never get married."

"I showed them, didn't I?" He touched her cheek. "I surprised even myself when I fell in love with you."

Amelia leaned against him. She'd never tire of his warmth that radiated into her soul.

"I'm taking Emma's dress and veil to a seamstress friend on Monday. She's well known for restoring vintage clothing."

"But you know, Amelia. If she can't save it, I'll buy any dress you want."

Amelia kissed him again. "Thank you, Matthew. I'm so looking forward to being your wife."

"Can we elope tonight?" He kissed her again.

"Nope. As much as I would like to, I want a beautiful wedding."

"And you will have it, my love."

The sound of voices in the yard interrupted their conversation. Matthew walked to the Chapel door. "What the heck?"

Amelia peeked around his shoulder. People were gathering on the lawn. Rows of chairs filled the space facing the pavilion. Wanda from the BlueBird clung to Darrin Wilson's arm.

"What?" Matthew looked back at Amelia.

"Didn't you know? They're married and have a couple of kids."

Before Matthew could respond, Logan yelled, "There's the happy couple."

Matthew and Amelia stepped from the Chapel holding hands and strolled toward the party. Logan led them up the pavilion steps. The dinner plates had been cleared away and a three-tiered cake filled the table.

"Happy engagement party!" the crowd yelled in unison and then broke into applause. Balloons and streamers filled the sky.

Matthew looked at Amelia. "Did you know about this?"

"Not a clue." She shook her head. "We have some sneaky ... No some awesome friends."

Later that evening, after the guests had gone home, Matthew sat in his childhood bedroom on the second floor. Nothing had surprised him more when he'd told Logan last week that he was moving Evan's rocker to this room. The beloved Bible lay on the table beside him with several scriptures bookmarked that he'd been reading. Amazing things had happened in his heart since he'd first arrived here.

This place, this room really, was where it had all begun. In the house that he'd sworn he didn't want but now loved. Marrying the girl who irritated him to no end in the beginning. Now the house felt empty without her. But in just a few short months, Amelia would be here with him. Forever.

And his father. He could barely wrap his mind around that one. The pain he'd buried from years of abandonment and rejection were finally chipping away.

Matthew stood and gazed out the second story window onto the circular drive below. This time he didn't see the haunting memory of his father driving away. Instead his eyes were drawn to the stars twinkling over the mountains that were as bright as his future with Amelia.

"I'll make you proud, Evan," he whispered. "I'll make you proud."

ACKNOWLEDGMENTS

With Gratitude to .....

My family – Thank you, Mom, for your excellent proof-reading skills. I'm so grateful that you helped me make this book better. Carla, you've been one of my biggest cheerleaders on this writing journey. Thank you for believing in me. Gary, I really appreciate when you provide meals and take on extra household tasks that give me more time to write. I love you all!

Nancy Rue – you're an awesome coach/mentor/editor and helped me tear this story apart. Then you taught me how to put it back together and to be a better writer. Thank you for this amazing journey we made together.

Gordon Saunders – Thanks for your guidance on the publishing process. I'm grateful for your fun ideas and for your expertise.

Anna Coleman – Thank you for catching my vision for the book cover from the very beginning. Your illustration is beautiful and even better than I had envisioned.

Joy Carroll - your prayers and encouragement made such a difference on this journey. Thanks for being such a great friend!

My Book Prayer Team – your prayers were invaluable and

carried me through some very hard places as I wrote this book. Thank you!

Blakely Coffey – I'm so grateful you took the time to answer my questions. The rescue scene came to life because of your excellent details.

Yolie Brown - thank you for the beautiful author photos and the tea cup. You bless me with your photography skills!

My writing partners – Kim Mahone and Josephine Young – you've been with me since the early stages of this story. Thank you for being my cheerleaders. It's been so fun to dress up in Victorian fashions and sip tea together!

Roberta Perno - for sharing several of your zany adventures that took root in my imagination and became a part of my story.

And most of all to the Lord Jesus for giving me creative ideas, inspiration and determination. I had an idea for a story but felt overwhelmed at the thought of writing it. I'm beyond grateful for the awesome people You surrounded me with that helped bring Matthew and Amelia's story to life.

ABOUT THE AUTHOR

Margie Wood's heart is to help others find their way to forgiveness. She infuses this mantra into her fiction novels, where her characters live imperfect lives and experience truth and freedom.

Margie's publishing credits include devotionals in Gary Chapman's *Love is a Verb*, as well as Mark Littleton's *God Still Meets Needs* (both under the name Margie Christenson). She actively participates in the American Christian Fiction Writers Colorado Springs group and serves as Secretary on their board.

A long-time Colorado resident, Margie fosters a love for Victorian mansions and the Rocky Mountains. Her happy places are sipping tea in Victorian dresses and hats with good friends, and writing retreats in the serenity of the majestic mountains.